HOT SKY AT MIDNIGHT

HOT SKY AT

MIDNIGHT

Robert Silverberg

 BANTAM BOOKS New York Toronto London Sydney Auckland SPECTRA ™

Published simultaneously in the United States and Canada

Bantam Books are published by Bantam Books, a division of Bantam Doubleday
Dell Publishing Group, Inc. Its trademark, consisting of the words "Bantam
Books" and the portrayal of a rooster, is Registered in U.S. Patent and Trademark
Office and in other countries. Marca Registrada. Bantam Books, 1540 Broadway,
New York, New York 10036.

PRINTED IN THE UNITED STATES OF AMERICA

For Alice K.

*Who taught an old dog
a couple of new tricks*

▼ ▼ ▼

O Western wind, when wilt thou blow,
That the small rain down can rain?
Christ, that my love were in my arms
And I in my bed again!

—ANONYMOUS

▼ ▼ ▼

THAT'S MY MARK, Juanito told himself. That one, there. That one for sure.

He stared at the new dinkos coming off the midday shuttle from Earth. The one he meant to go for was the tall one with no eyes at all, blank from brow to bridge of nose, just the merest suggestions of shadowy pits below the smooth skin of the forehead. Not even any eyebrows, just bare brow-ridges. As if the eyes had been erased, Juanito thought. But in fact they had probably never been there in the first place. It didn't look like a retrofit gene job, more like a prenatal splice.

He knew he had to move fast. There was plenty of competition. Fifteen, twenty couriers here in the waiting room, gathering like vultures, and they were some of the best: Ricky, Lola, Kluge. Nattathaniel. Delilah. Everybody looked hungry today. Juanito couldn't afford to get shut out. He hadn't worked in six weeks, and it was time. His last job had been a fast-talking fancy-dancing Ukrainian, wanted on Commonplace and maybe two or three other habitat worlds for dealing in plutonium. Juanito had milked that one for all it was worth, but you can milk only so long. The newcomers learn the system, they melt in and become invisible, and there's no reason for them to go on paying. So then you have to find a new client.

"Okay," Juanito said, looking around challengingly. "There's mine. The weird guy. The one with half a face. Anybody else want him?"

Kluge laughed and said, "He's all yours, man."

"Yeah," Delilah said, with a little shudder. "All yours." That saddened him, her chiming in like that. It had always disappointed Juanito that Delilah didn't have his kind of imagination. "Christ," she said. "I bet he'll be plenty trouble."

"Trouble's what pays best," Juanito said. "You want to go for the easy ones, that's fine with me." He grinned at her and waved at the others. "If we're all agreed, I think I'll head downstairs now. See you later, people."

He started to move inward and downward along the shuttle-hub wall. Dazzling sunlight glinted off the docking module's silvery rim, and off the Earth shuttle's thick columnar docking shaft, wedged into the center of the module like a spear through a doughnut. On the far side of the wall the new dinkos were making their wobbly way past the glowing ten-meter-high portrait of El Supremo and on into the red fiberglass tent that was the fumigation chamber. As usual, they were having a hard time with the low gravity. Here at the hub it was one-sixteenth Earth-G, max. Probably the atmosphere bothered them too. It was clean here, with a lot of oxygen in it and no garbage. They were accustomed to the foul filthy soup that passed for air on Earth, the poison that they breathed all the time, full of strange stinking gases that rotted your lungs and turned your bones to jelly.

Juanito always wondered about the newcomers, what it was that had made them choose Valparaiso Nuevo in particular, of all the worlds in space. Everybody wanted to get away from Earth, sure. That was easy to understand. Earth was a mess. But there were plenty of other satellite worlds to run off to. You could get nice fresh air and a decent climate on any of them. Those who came to Valparaiso Nuevo had to have special reasons for making that choice. They fell into one of two main classes: those who wanted to hide, and those who wanted to seek.

The place was nothing but an enormous spacegoing safe house. You had some good reason for wanting to be left alone, you came to Valparaiso Nuevo and bought yourself a little privacy. But that implied that you had done something that would make other people not want to let you alone. And a lot of those people came to Valparaiso looking for the ones who didn't want to be found. There was always some of both going on here, a lot of hide-and-seek, some people hiding, some seeking—with El Supremo looking down benignly on it all, raking in his cut. And not just El Supremo.

Down below, the new dinkos were trying to walk jaunty, to walk mean. But that was hard to do when you were keeping your body all clenched up as though you were afraid that you might go drifting off into midair if you put your foot down too hard. Juanito loved it, the way they were crunching along, that constipated mudcrawler shuffle of theirs.

Gravity stuff didn't ever bother Juanito. He had spent all his life out here in the habitats, the satellite worlds, and he took it for granted that the pull was going to fluctuate according to your distance from the hub. You automatically made compensating adjustments, that was all.

Juanito found it hard to understand a place where the gravity would be the same everywhere all the time. He had never set foot on Earth or any of the other natural planets, didn't care to, didn't expect to. The settlements on Mars and Ganymede were strictly for scientists only, and Luna was a damn ugly place, and as for Earth, well, you had to be out of your mind to want to go to Earth, even for a visit. Just thinking about Earth, it could make you sick to your stomach.

The guard on duty at the quarantine gate was an android with a flat plastic-looking face. His name, his label, whatever it was, was something like Velcro Exxon. Juanito had seen him at this gate before. As he came up close the android glanced at him and said, "Working again so soon, Juanito?"

"Man has to eat, no?"

The android shrugged. Eating wasn't all that important to him, most likely. "Weren't you working that plutonium peddler out of Common-place?"

Juanito said, smiling, "What plutonium peddler?"

"Sure," said the android. "I hear you."

He held out his waxy-skinned hand. Even the machines had to be bribed on Valparaiso Nuevo. Juanito put a fifty-callaghano currency plaque in it. The usual fee for illicit entry to the customs tank was only thirty-five callies, but

Juanito believed in spreading the wealth, especially where the authorities were concerned. They didn't *have* to let you in here, after all. Some days more couriers showed up than there were dinkos, and then the gate guards had to allocate. Overpaying the guards was simply a smart investment.

"Thank you kindly," the android said. "Thank you very much." He hit the scanner override. Juanito stepped through the security shield into the customs tank and looked around for his mark.

The new dinkos were being herded into the fumigation chamber now. They were annoyed about that—they always were—but the guards kept them moving right along through the puffy bursts of pink and green and yellow sprays that came from the ceiling nozzles. Nobody got out of customs quarantine without passing through that chamber. El Supremo was paranoid about the entry of exotic microorganisms into Valparaiso Nuevo's closed-cycle ecology. El Supremo was paranoid about a lot of things. You didn't get to be sole and absolute ruler of your own little satellite world, and stay that way for thirty-seven years, without a heavy component of paranoia in your makeup.

Juanito leaned up against the great curving glass wall of the customs tank and peered through the mists of sterilizer fog. The rest of the couriers were starting to come in now. Juanito watched them going to work, singling out potential clients, cutting them out of the herd. Most of the dinkos were signing up as soon as the deal was explained, but as always there were a few who would shake off all help and insist on setting out by themselves. Cheapskates, Juanito thought. Assholes and wimps, Juanito thought. But they'd find out. It wasn't possible to get started on Valparaiso Nuevo without a courier, no matter how sharp you thought you were. Valparaiso was a free enterprise zone, after all. If you knew the rules, you were pretty much safe from all harm here forever. If not, not.

Time to make the approach, Juanito figured.

It was easy enough finding the blind man. He was very much taller than the other dinkos, practically a giant: a long-limbed massive man some thirty-odd years old, heavy bones, powerful muscles. In the bright glaring light his blank forehead gleamed like a reflecting beacon. The low gravity didn't seem to trouble him much, or his blindness. His movements along the customs track were easy, confident, almost graceful. Like all the rest of the newly arrived passengers, he had the rough, blotchy skin that Earth people tended to have, flaky and reddened from frying all the time in that murderous torrid sunshine of theirs.

Juanito sauntered over and said, "I'll be your courier, sir. Juanito Holt." He barely came up to the blind man's elbow.

"Courier?"

"New arrival assistance service. Facilitate your entry arrangements. Customs clearance, currency exchange, hotel accommodations, permanent settlement papers if that's what you intend. Also special services by arrangement."

Juanito stared up expectantly at the blank face. The eyeless man looked back at him in a blunt straight-on way, what would have been strong eye contact if the dinko had had eyes. That was eerie. What was even eerier was the sense Juanito had that the eyeless man was seeing him clearly. For just a moment Juanito wondered who was going to be controlling whom in this deal.

"What kind of special services?"

"Anything else you need," Juanito said.

"Anything?"

"Anything. This is Valparaiso Nuevo, sir."

"Mmm. What's your fee?"

"Two thousand callaghanos a week for the basic. Specials are extra, according."

"How much is that in Capbloc dollars, your basic?"

Juanito told him.

"That's not so bad," the blind man said.

"Two weeks minimum, payable in advance."

"Mmm," said the blind man again. Again that intense eyeless gaze, seeing right through him. He was silent for a time. Juanito listened to the sound of his breathing, quick and shallow, the way all Earthsiders breathed. As if they were trying to hold their nostrils pinched together to keep the poisons that were in the air from getting into their lungs. But it was safe to breathe the air on Valparaiso Nuevo.

"How old are you?" the blind man asked suddenly.

"Seventeen," Juanito blurted, caught off guard.

"And you're good, are you?"

"I'm the best. I was born here. I know everybody."

"I'm going to be needing the best. You take electronic handshake?"

"Sure," Juanito said. This was too easy. He wondered if he should have asked three kilocallies a week, not two, but it was too late for that now. He pulled his flex terminal from his tunic pocket and slipped his fingers into it. "Unity Callaghan Bank of Valparaiso Nuevo. That's access code 22-44-66, and you might as well give it its own default key, because it's the only bank here. Account 1133, that's mine."

The blind man donned his own terminal and deftly tapped the number pad on his wrist. Then he grasped Juanito's hand firmly in his until the sensors overlapped, and made the transfer of funds. Juanito touched for confirm and a bright green *+cl. 4000* lit up on the screen in his palm. The payee's name was Victor Farkas, out of an account in the Royal Amalgamated Bank of Liechtenstein.

"Liechtenstein," Juanito said, frowning. "That's an Earth country?"

"Very small one. Between Austria and Switzerland."

"I've heard of Switzerland. You live on Liechtenstein?"

"No," Farkas said. "I bank there. *In* Liechtenstein, is what Earth people say. Except for islands. Liechtenstein isn't an island. Can we get out of this place now, do you think?"

"One more transfer," Juanito said. "Pump your entry software across to me. Baggage claim, passport, visa. Make things much easier for us both, getting out of here."

"Make it easier for you to disappear with my suitcase, yes. And I'd never find you again, would I?"

"Do you think I'd do that?"

"I'm more profitable to you if you don't."

"You've got to trust your courier, Mr. Farkas. If you can't trust your courier, you can't trust anybody at all on Valparaiso Nuevo."

"I know that," Farkas said.

Collecting Farkas's baggage and getting him clear of the customs tank took another half an hour and cost about two hundred callies in miscellaneous bribes, which was about standard. Everyone from the baggage-handling androids to the cute snotty teller at the currency-exchange booth had to be bought. Juanito understood that things didn't work that way on most habitat worlds; but Valparaiso Nuevo, Juanito knew, was different from most habitat worlds. In a place where the chief industry was the protection of fugitives, it made sense that the basis of the economy would be the recycling of bribes.

Farkas didn't appear to be any sort of fugitive, though. While he was waiting for the baggage Juanito pulled a readout on the software that the blind man had pumped over to him and saw that Farkas was here on a visitor's visa, six-week limit. He listed his employer as Kyocera-Merck, Ltd. So he was a seeker, not a hider, here to track somebody down who was wanted by one of the biggest of the Earth megacorporations. Well, that was okay. Hider, seeker: it was possible for a courier to turn a profit working either side of the deal. Running traces wasn't Juanito's usual number, but he figured he could adapt.

The other thing that Farkas didn't appear to be was blind. Maybe he had no eyes, but that didn't seem to interfere with his perceptions of his surroundings. As they emerged from the customs tank he turned and pointed back at the huge portrait of El Supremo and said, "Who's that? Your president?"

"The Defender, that's his title. The Generalissimo. El Supremo, Don Eduardo Callaghan." Then it sank in and Juanito said, blinking, "Pardon me. You can *see* that picture, Mr. Farkas?"

"In a manner of speaking."

"I don't follow. Can you see or can't you?"

"Yes and no."

"Thanks a lot, Mr. Farkas."

"We can talk more about it later," Farkas said.

Juanito always put new dinkos in the same hotel, the San Bernardito, four kilometers out from the hub in the rim community of Cajamarca. "This way," he told Farkas. "We have to take the elevator at C Spoke."

Farkas didn't seem to have any trouble following him. Every now and then Juanito glanced back, and there was the big man three or four paces behind him, marching along steadily down the corridor. No eyes, Juanito thought, but somehow he can see. He definitely can see.

The four-kilometer elevator ride down C Spoke to the rim was spectacular all the way. The elevator was a glass-walled chamber inside a glass-walled tube that ran along the outside of the spoke, and it gave you the full dazzling vista: the whole great complex of wheels within wheels that was the Earth-orbit artificial world of Valparaiso Nuevo, the seven great structural spokes radiating from the hub to the distant wheel of the rim, each spoke bearing its seven glass-and-aluminum globes that contained the residential zones and business sectors and farmlands and recreational zones and forest reserves. As the elevator descended—the gravity rising as you went down, climbing toward an Earth-one pull in the rim towns—you had a view of the sun's brilliant glint on the adjacent spokes, and an occasional glimpse of the great blue belly of Earth filling up the sky a hundred fifty thousand kilometers away, and the twinkling hordes of other habitat worlds in their nearby orbits, like a swarm of jellyfish dancing in a vast black ocean. That was what everybody who came up from Earth said, "Like jellyfish in the ocean." Juanito didn't understand how a fish could be made out of jelly, or how a habitat with seven spokes looked anything like a fish of any kind, but that was what they all said.

Farkas didn't say a word about jellyfish. But in some fashion or other he did indeed seem to be taking in the view. He stood close to the elevator's glass wall in deep concentration, gripping the rail, not saying a thing. Now and then he made a little hissing sound as something particularly awesome went by outside. Juanito studied him with sidelong glances. What could he possibly see? Nothing seemed to be moving beneath those shadowy places where his eyes should have been. Yet somehow he was seeing out of that broad blank stretch of gleaming skin above his nose.

It was damned disconcerting. It was downright weird.

The San Bernardito gave Farkas a rim-side room, facing the stars. Juanito paid the hotel clerks to treat his clients right. That was something his father had taught him when he was just a kid who wasn't old enough to know a Schwarzchild singularity from an ace in the hole. "Pay for what you're going to need," his father kept saying. "Buy it and at least there's a chance it'll be there when you have to have it." His father had been a revolutionary in Central America during the time of the Empire. He would have been prime minister if the revolution had come out the right way. But it hadn't.

"You want me to help you unpack?" Juanito said.

"I can manage."

"Sure," Juanito said.

He stood by the window, looking at the sky. Like all the other satellite worlds, Valparaiso Nuevo was shielded from cosmic-ray damage and stray meteoroids by a double shell filled with a three-meter-thick layer of lunar slag. Rows of V-shaped apertures ran down the outer skin of the shield, mirror-faced to admit sunlight but not hard radiation; and the hotel had lined its rooms up so each one on this side had a view of space through the V's. The whole town of Cajamarca was facing darkwise now, and the stars were glittering fiercely.

When Juanito turned from the window he saw that Farkas had hung his clothes neatly in the closet and was shaving—methodically, precisely—with a little hand-held laser.

"Can I ask you something personal?" Juanito said.

"You want to know how I see."

"It's pretty amazing, I have to say."

"I *don't* see. Not really. I'm just as blind as you think I am."

"Then how—"

"It's called blindsight," Farkas said. "Proprioceptive vision."

"What?"

Farkas chuckled. "There's all sorts of data bouncing around that doesn't have the form of reflected light, which is what your eyes see. A million vibrations besides those that happen to be in the visual part of the electromagnetic spectrum are shimmering in this room. Air currents pass around things and are deformed by what they encounter. And it isn't only the air currents. Objects have mass, they have heat, they have—the term won't make any sense to you—*shapeweight*. A quality having to do with the interaction of mass and form. Does that mean anything to you? No, I guess not. But it does to me. And for two-dimensional images: I have a different technique for detecting those. Look, there's a lot of information available beyond what you can see with eyes, if you want it. I want it."

"You use some kind of machine to pick it up?" Juanito asked.

Farkas tapped his forehead. "It's in here. I was born with it."

"Some kind of sensing organ instead of eyes?"

"That's pretty close."

"What do you see, then? What do things look like to you?"

"What do they look like to you?" Farkas said. "What does a chair look like to you?"

"Well, it's got four legs, and a back—"

"What does a leg look like?"

"It's longer than it is wide."

"Right." Farkas knelt and ran his hands along the black tubular legs of the ugly little chair beside the bed. "I touch the chair, I feel the shape of the legs. But I don't see leg-shaped shapes."

"What then?"

"Silver globes that roll away into fat curves. The back part of the chair bends double and folds into itself. The bed's a bright pool of mercury with long green spikes coming up. You're six blue spheres stacked one on top of another, with a thick orange cable running through them. And so on."

"Blue?" Juanito said. "Orange? How do you know anything about colors?"

"The same way you do. I call one color blue, another one orange. I don't know if they're remotely like your blue or orange, but so what? My blue is always blue for me. It's different from the color I see as red and the one I see as green. Orange is always orange. It's a matter of relationships. You follow?"

"No," Juanito said. "How can you possibly make sense out of anything? What you see doesn't have a thing to do with the real color or shape or position of anything."

Farkas shook his head. "Wrong, Juanito. For me, what I see *is* the real shape and color position. It's all I've ever known. If they were able to retrofit me with normal eyes now, which I'm told would be less than fifty-fifty likely to succeed and tremendously risky besides, I'd be lost trying to find my way around in your world. It would take me years to learn how. Or maybe forever. But I do all right, in mine. I understand, by touching things, that what I see by blindsight isn't the 'actual' shape. But I see in consistent equivalents. Do you follow? A chair always looks like what I think of as a chair, even though I know that chairs aren't really shaped at all like that. If you could see things the way I do it would all look like something out of another dimension. It *is* something out of another dimension, really. The information I operate by is different from what you use, that's all. But I do see, in my own way. I perceive objects and establish relationships between them, I make spatial perceptions, just as you do. Do you follow, Juanito?"

Juanito considered that. How very weird it sounded. To see the world in funhouse distortions, blobs and spheres and orange cables and glimmering pools of mercury. Weird, yes, extremely weird. After a moment he said, "And you were born like this?"

"That's right."

"Some kind of genetic accident?"

"Not an accident," Farkas said quietly. "I was an experiment. A master gene-splicer worked me over in my mother's womb."

"Right," Juanito said. "You know, that's actually the first thing I guessed when I saw you come off the shuttle. This has to be some kind of splice effect, I said. But why—why—" He faltered. "Does it bother you to talk about these things?"

"Not really."

"Why would your parents have allowed—"

"They didn't have any choice, Juanito."

"Isn't that illegal? Involuntary splicing?"

"Of course," Farkas said. "So what?"

"But who would do that to—"

"This was in the Free State of Kazakhstan, which you've never heard of. It was one of the countries formed out of the Soviet Union, which you've also probably never heard of, after the First Breakup, a hundred, hundred fifty years ago. My father was Hungarian consul at Tashkent. He was killed in the Second Breakup, what they called the War of Restoration, and my mother, who was pregnant, was volunteered for the experiments in prenatal genetic surgery then being carried out in that city under Chinese auspices. A lot of remarkable work was done there in those years. They were trying to breed new and useful kinds of human beings to serve the republic. I was one of the experiments in extending the human perceptual range. I was supposed to have normal sight plus blindsight, but it didn't quite work out that way."

"You sound very calm about it," Juanito said.

"What good is getting angry?"

"My father used to say that too," Juanito said. "Don't get angry, get even. He was in politics, the Central American Empire. When the revolution failed he took sanctuary here."

"So did the surgeon who did my prenatal splice," Farkas said. "Around fifteen years ago. He's still living here. I'd like to find him."

"I bet you would," Juanito said, as everything fell into place.

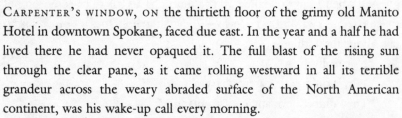

Carpenter's window, on the thirtieth floor of the grimy old Manito Hotel in downtown Spokane, faced due east. In the year and a half he had lived there he had never opaqued it. The full blast of the rising sun through the clear pane, as it came rolling westward in all its terrible grandeur across the weary abraded surface of the North American continent, was his wake-up call every morning.

These days Carpenter earned his living as a desert jockey, a weather forecaster out here in this forlorn drought-stricken agricultural belt. His job involved calculating the odds for the farmers who were betting their livelihoods on trying to guess when the next rainstorm would turn up in eastern Washington—next month, next year, whenever. Inland Washington State was right on the cusp, situated as it was between the moist, fertile agricultural zone of southern Canada and the miserable, perpetually parched wasteland that was the upper west-central United States, and the precipitation was a very chancy thing. Sometimes there was rain and the farmers got fat, and sometimes the rain belt swung far away to the north and east and they all got killed. They depended on Carpenter to tell them weeks or even months in advance how things were going to go for them each season. Their soothsayer, their reader of the entrails.

He had been a lot of other things, too. Before being given the weather gig he had been a cargo dispatcher for one of Samurai Industries' L-5 shuttles, and a chip-runner before that, and before that—well, he was starting to forget. Like a good salaryman Carpenter took whatever assignment was handed him, and made sure to master the skills that were required.

And one of these days, if he kept his nose clean, he'd be sitting in a corner office atop the Samurai pyramid in New Tokyo in Manitoba. That was the Samurai head office, just as New Kyoto down in Chile was the Level One zone of Samurai's arch-competitor, the immense Kyocera-Merck combine. New Tokyo, New Kyoto, it made no difference. One name was simply the other one turned inside out. But you wanted to get yourself into Headquarters. That was the essential thing, to be taken into the Japs' embrace, to become a Headquarters guy, an executiveman, one of their specially favored roundeyes. Once you were in there, you were there for life. It wasn't much of a goal, as ideal visions went, but it was the only one available to him. You played the Company game, Carpenter knew, or else you didn't play at all.

At half past six in the morning on this day in late spring, with the room already flooded with light and Carpenter beginning to wake up anyway, his Company communicator went *beep* and the visor opposite his bed lit up and a familiar contralto voice said, "On your toes, Salaryman Carpenter. Rise and sing the Samurai Industries anthem along with me. *'Our hearts are pure, our minds are true, Our thoughts, our thoughts, are all for you, dear Companeee'*—did I call too early, Salaryman Carpenter? Morning is well along on the West Coast, isn't it? Are you awake? Are you alone? Turn on the visuals, Salaryman Carpenter! Let me see your shining smile. Your beloved Jeanne is calling you."

"For Christ's sake, show some mercy," Carpenter murmured. "I don't have my brain in gear yet." He blinked at the visor. Jeanne Gabel's broad Eurasian face, dark-eyed, strong-featured, looked back at him. A few small alterations around the jaw and the cheekbones and it could have been a man's face. Carpenter and Jeanne had been good friends, never lovers, when they worked out of the same Samurai office in St. Louis. That had been four years back. Now she was in Paris and he was in Spokane: the Company kept you moving around. They talked every once in a while.

He activated the visuals at his end, letting her see the dingy room, the rumpled bed, his bleary eyes. "Is there trouble?" he asked.

"No more than usual. But there's news."

"Good or bad?"

"Depends on how you want to look at it. I've got a deal for you. But go and wash your face, first. Brush your teeth. Comb your hair a little. You look like a mess, you know?"

"You're the one who called at the crack of dawn and then told me to turn on the visuals."

"It's the end of the day in Paris. I waited as long as I could to call. Go on, get yourself washed. I'll sit tight."

"Look the other way, then. I'm not decent."

"Right," she said, grinning, and continued to peer out of the visor at him.

Carpenter shrugged and clambered out of bed, naked, leaving the visuals on. Let her have a peek if she wants, he thought. Do her some good, maybe. He was a lean late-thirtyish man with shoulder-length yellow hair and a brown beard, boyishly proud of his body: long flat muscles, tight belly, hard butt. He padded across the room to the washzone and stuck his head under the sonic cleanser. The instrument purred and throbbed.

In a moment he felt clean and almost awake. The Screen injector was sitting on the toilet counter and he picked it up and gave himself his morning shot, automatically, without even thinking about it. You got out of bed, you washed and peed, and you gave yourself your shot of Screen: it was how everybody started the day. The sun was waiting for you out there in the killer haze of the angry white morning sky and you didn't want to face its marvelous ferocity without your skin armor renewed against the daily onslaught.

Carpenter wrapped a towel around his waist and turned toward the visor. Jeanne was amiably watching him.

"That's better," she told him.

"All right," he said. "You say you have a deal for me?"

"I might. It depends on you. Last time we talked, you said you were going crazy there in Spokane and couldn't wait until you got moved on to another gig. Well, what about it, Paul? Are you still interested in a transfer out of Spokane?"

"What? Damned straight I am!" His heart rate began to climb. He hated being in Spokane. His weatherman gig in this forlorn isolated place seemed to him like a giant life detour.

"I can get you out, if you like. How would you like to be a sea captain?"

"A sea captain," Carpenter repeated, with no expression whatever. "A *sea* captain." But she had startled him. He hadn't expected something like that. It was as if she had asked him how he would like to be a hippopotamus.

He wondered if Jeanne could just be fucking around with him for the fun of it. It was too early in the day for him to find that amusing. But it wouldn't be like her, doing that.

"You're serious?" he asked. "For Samurai, you mean?"

"Of course, for Samurai. A change of career track is something I can't manage for you. But I can get you a transfer, if you want it. Iceberg trawler called the *Tonopah Maru,* getting ready to sail out of San Francisco, commanding officer needed, Salaryman Level Eleven. Came across the Personnel node this morning. You're Level Eleven, aren't you, Paul?"

Carpenter didn't want to seem ungrateful. She was a dear woman and had his interests at heart. But he was baffled by all this.

"What the hell do I know about being commanding officer of an iceberg trawler, Jeanne?"

"What the hell did you know about being a weatherman, or a chip-runner, or all the other things you've done, until you did them? God will provide. God and Samurai Industries. They'll teach you what you need to know. You know that. They give you the proper indoctrination cube, you jack it in, two hours later you're as good a seaman as Columbus ever was. But if you don't like the idea of being a sailor—"

"No. No. Tell me more. Is there grade slope to be had out of this?"

"Of course there's slope. You put in eighteen months aboard your cramped little boat hauling icebergs and keeping your nasty but capable crew in line and you'll make Level Ten for sure. Demonstration of managerial skills under adverse conditions. They'll move you to Europe and stick you on the administrative track and you'll be sitting pretty from then on, straight up the net to New Tokyo. I thought of you the moment this came across the node."

"How come there's a vacancy?" Carpenter asked. Usually any job that held the promise of grade improvement, no matter how disagreeable it might be, was snapped up in-house before it hit any of the general Company nodes. "Why didn't someone in the trawler division take it right away?"

"Someone did," Jeanne said. "Yesterday. Then his lottery number came up two hours later and he bugged out for one of the habitats, just like that, caught a shuttle without even stopping to pack. A job on Outback, I think it was, or maybe Commonplace. The company got caught short and Personnel was asked to fill in with an Eleven, fast. Five names surfaced on the first scoop. Yours was one of them. I thought I'd call you before I ran any checks on the other four."

"Nice."

"Am I wasting my breath?"

"I love you, Jeanne."

"I know that. But do you want the gig?"

"Tell me the time frame?"

"You'd have a five-week transition. Enough time to work up the weatherman specs for your successor in Spokane, get down to Frisco for your indoctrination jacking, and maybe even fit in a few days over here in Paris for fine dining and riotous living, if you could stand it."

Jeanne's face bore the usual ironic glint but there was, it seemed to Carpenter, some wistfulness in it also. When they worked together in St. Louis they had always been flirtatious with each other, and whenever they were with other people they had liked to play at giving the impression that they were sleeping together. But all it was was play. Someone had done some damage to her, emotional, not physical, long ago—Carpenter had never asked for the details—and so far as he knew she was completely asexual. A pity, because he wasn't.

He said, "I'd like that. A few days in Paris. The Seine. The Place de la Concorde. The restaurant on the top of the Eiffel Tower. The Louvre on a rainy day."

"It's always a rainy day here," she said.

"All the better. Water falling from the sky, just dropping right down on your head—it seems like a goddamned miracle to me, Jeanne. I would take off my clothes and dance naked in it, right down the Champs-Elysées."

"Stop showing off. They'd arrest you in two seconds, anyway. There's a cop on every corner here. Androids, very strict. *'Mon Dieu, monsieur— s'il vous plaît, vos vêtements!'*"

"I'll tell him that I don't speak French. Would you dance with me?"

"No. Not naked down the Champs-Elysées."

"In the grand ballroom of the Georges Cinq, then."

"But of course," she said. "The Georges Cinq."

"I love you, Jeanne." He would never see her in Paris, he was sure of that. By the time he was through with the iceberg boat they would have reassigned her to Tierra del Fuego or Hong Kong or Kansas City.

"I love you," she told him. "Keep dry, Paul."

"Not a problem, here," Carpenter said.

The morning that his transfer finally came through—it took about ten days; he was just beginning to doubt that Jeanne had been able to swing it at all—Carpenter had just clocked nineteen straight hours of work at the Samurai Weather Service office in Spokane. Everybody there was working like that these days. A five-alarm toxic emergency had been declared, the worst one in three or four years, and the whole meteorological staff had gone on double overtime, tracking the unusual upper-air movements that might be putting the entire West Coast at risk.

What was going on was that there was a big high-pressure zone sitting over Wyoming, Colorado, Nebraska, and Kansas. That was not exactly news in itself—there was *always* a high-pressure zone sitting on those states, which was why it almost never rained there any more—but this time the entire great mass of heavy dead air had developed a powerful counterclockwise rotation and was starting to pull streams of greenhouse gases out of the blighted Midwest. All the vile poisonous airborne goo—methane, nitrous oxides, and other such things—that was normally salted through the atmosphere over Chicago, Milwaukee, St. Louis, Cincinnati, and Indianapolis was being sucked around the top end of Nebraska and Wyoming and into Idaho.

Ordinarily that would have been no great cause for alarm. It happened once in a while, a river of foul atmospheric bile streaming into the Mountain States and getting whipped right around through the Southwest and back to where it came from. But this time the orbital sensors were showing a line of secondary atmospheric eddy currents along the western edge of the high-pressure zone, currents that had the capacity to peel away the toxic crud as it made its turn southward into Utah and send it drifting toward the Pacific Northwest. Where it would smother Seattle and Portland for a few eye-stinging days, after which the normal north-south winds would catch hold of it and shove it down the coast to torment San Francisco and then Los Angeles and San Diego.

The coast cities had enough toxins of their own to deal with as it was: if a load of extraneous airborne shit got shipped in from the Midwest it would push things well above the tolerance levels as they were now defined. It would hit like a blast of dragon's breath. People would be dropping dead in the streets. They would choke on the sulfurous reek. The deadly smog would excoriate their nostrils and claw at their lungs and blacken their blood. Warnings to stay indoors would have to be issued; industrial production would need to be shut down, maybe for weeks, as would nonessential ground transportation, to avoid aggravating the situation. The economy of the entire region was bound to suffer a terrific short-run setback, and there would probably be long-term environmental damage too, increased uptakes of arsenic, cadmium, and mercury in the water supply, continued infrastructure degradation, severe havoc done to what was left of the West Coast flora and fauna. Redwood trees couldn't go indoors when a five-alarm toxic cloud came drifting westward.

On the other hand, the toxic cloud could still turn around at any minute and go away without doing any harm. Broadcasting premature warning of an oncoming peril that wasn't actually coming could lead to needless factory closings and panic among the civilians: very likely a massive flight of people from the area, which would choke the highways and have environmental consequences of its own. After which would come a bunch of lawsuits demanding damages because the threatened disaster had failed to materialize. People would want to be paid for emotional stress, unnecessary expenses occurred, interruption of trade, any damned thing. Samurai Industries hated being entangled in lawsuits. They had pretty much the deepest pockets around, and everyone knew it.

So the whole situation needed to be monitored in the finest possible detail, minute by minute, and everybody in the Spokane Weather Service office had been placed on round-the-clock duty until the emergency was over. Carpenter, who was considered to have an almost psychic knack for predicting large-scale air movements, was particularly on the spot. He had tanked up on hyperdex and spent the night in front of the computer in a welter of sweat and drug-induced intensity of perception, staring at shifting yellow-and-green patterns of bars and dots, internalizing the dancing data as fast as it arrived in the hope that he would arrive at some mystic sense of the cosmic order of events, some wild gestalt insight that would allow him to see into the future. The night went by like the blink of an eye. And he had grasped it: he had. He was peering around the corner of time into the day after tomorrow, and he saw the deadly stream of toxic atmospherics moving—moving—cutting down past Coeur d'Alene—turning ever so slightly southward and eastward—eastward, really?—yes—maybe—yes—

"Carpenter."

—yes, a shift, a definite shift in the air movement, coming on Tuesday a little after three in the afternoon—

"Carpenter?"

A voice out of the void: thin, high-pitched, annoying. Carpenter waved his hand angrily without looking around. "Fuck off, will you?" He struggled to hold his concentration.

"Boss says, Take a break. He wants to talk to you."

"I've almost got it. I can see—fuck. *Fuck!*" He banged his fist against the edge of the desk. The intrusion had come like a bucket of icy water hurled in his face. It shattered everything and he was unable to see anything any more. The patterns on the visor became a meaningless dance of jiggling blotches. Carpenter glanced up, every nerve in his body twanging and humming. One of the office gofers was standing placidly at his elbow, a pale flimsy girl, Sandra Wong, Sandra Chen, some Chinese name or other, utterly indifferent to his irritation. "What the hell is it?" he asked her furiously.

"I told you," the kid said. "Boss wants you."

"What for?"

"Do *I* know? Tell Carpenter, Take a break, come over here, that's all he said."

Carpenter nodded and stood up. All around the room, people speeding as he had been on hyperdex were staring into their visors with lunatic fixity and babbling back at the computers as torrents of weather data flooded in from space. He wondered why they were so entranced. Their fanatical dedication to their task seemed alien and repugnant to him now. Two minutes ago nothing had mattered more in the universe to him than tracking that vicious cloud of atmospheric crud, but now he was completely out of it, utterly detached, wholly lacking in concern for the fate of Seattle, Portland, San Francisco, Los Angeles, San Diego.

He realized that he had passed into some outer realm of exhaustion without even noticing it. He was no longer speeded up. The hyperdex must have burned out hours ago and he had continued his vigil on sheer mental momentum, doing who knew what damage to his nervous system.

He went into the other room, to the big horseshoe-shaped desk of the department administrator.

"You wanted me?" Carpenter asked.

The office was run by a bleak-souled Salaryman Ten named Ross McCarthy, who despite his name had some slight tincture of Japanese blood in his veins. That had done McCarthy no good whatever in his quest for upward slope, perhaps even had contributed to his stymieing: he had been stuck at the tenth level for years and plainly was going no higher, and he was bitter about it. He was a stocky, flat-faced man with faintly greenish skin and straight, glossy black hair that was starting to thin out across the top.

There was a dispatch printout in his hands. McCarthy fingered it gingerly, as though it were radioactive.

"Carpenter, what the hell is this?" he said.

"How would I know?"

McCarthy made no attempt to let him see it. "I'll tell you what it is. It's the finish of your career that I have right here in my hands. It's a transfer to some goddamn stupid iceberg ship, that's what it is. Have you taken leave of your senses, Carpenter?"

"I don't think that I have, no." Carpenter reached for the printout. McCarthy held it back from him.

"This ship," McCarthy said, "it's an absolute dead end for you. You'll go out into the middle of the Pacific for a couple of years and fry your ass doing stupid manual labor and when you come back you'll find that everybody on your grade level has skipped on past you. Out of sight, off the charts, Carpenter, that's the way things work. Do you follow me? Don't do this to yourself. Take my advice. What you'll do if you're smart is stay right here. You're needed here."

"Apparently the Company thinks it needs me somewhere else," Carpenter said. He was getting annoyed now.

"You stay here, you're bound to move up slope in no time. I'll be going on to a Nine pretty soon now. The word will come down from Yoshida-san any day, that's what I hear. And when I do, you'll slide right into my slot. Isn't that better than hauling fucking icebergs around the ocean?"

McCarthy wasn't going anywhere, Carpenter knew. He had committed some obscure breach of etiquette along the way, perhaps had tried unwisely to pressure some distant and barely acknowledged Japanese fifth cousin of his for promotion, and he was going to rot in Level Ten forever and ever. McCarthy knew that too. And wanted to keep everybody who worked for him trapped here in the same perpetual stasis that enfolded him.

"I think I've achieved as much as I can in weather forecasting," Carpenter told him, controlling himself tautly. "Now I want to try something else."

"An iceberg trawler. Shit, Carpenter. Shit! Turn it down."

"I don't think I will." He took the transfer order from McCarthy and pocketed it without looking at it. "Oh, and you can start to call off your five-alarmer, by the way. The poison cloud is about to break up."

McCarthy's black-button eyes took on sudden feverish brightness.

"You sure of that?"

"Absolutely," Carpenter said, amazed at his own audacity. "The entire system will be heading back east by Tuesday afternoon." If he was wrong, the whole Spokane office would be taken out and shot as soon as the lawsuits began. To hell with them all, Carpenter thought. He would be a thousand miles from here before any trouble could start.

And in any case his forecast was right. He felt it in his bones.

"Show me on the charts," McCarthy said, beginning to look a little suspicious.

Carpenter led him back to the data room. As never before it looked to him like a gaming center in a lunatic asylum, all the hyperdex-zonked crazies grinning fixedly into the bright streams of whorls and loops that were dancing across the faces of their visors. He stood in front of his own computer and pointed to the gaudy yellow-and-green patterns. They made no sense whatsoever to him now. Chimpanzee finger paintings, nothing more. "Here," he told McCarthy, "these isobars here, they indicate the changing gradients." He tapped the screen. "You see, here, along the Idaho border? Definite incipient weakening of the toxic flow. And a clear indication of a retro push coming from Canada, you see, like a giant hand shoving the whole mass the right way." It was all bullshit, every syllable of it. He had unquestionably seen something new taking shape before the girl broke in on him, but whatever it might have been was impossible for him to fathom, now.

McCarthy was staring thoughtfully at the computer visor.

He said, "It'll be a fucking miracle if the damned thing just goes away, won't it?"

"Won't it be, though. But look, Ross—" Carpenter rarely presumed to use McCarthy's first name. "Look here, here, here. And especially here. I know it looks locked tight as a constipated whale's gut right this moment, but when I was clicked into the map a little while ago I could distinctly feel the whole flow shifting, shifting in our favor, definite indications of gradient transform all along the periphery. Look at this. And this."

"Mmm." McCarthy nodded. "Yes. Mmm." He was faking it, Carpenter knew. On Level Ten you didn't need technical ability except of the most superficial kind; you needed managerial skill. Which perhaps McCarthy might have had, once.

"You see?" Carpenter said. "I was flying on intuition, sure. But the substantiating data's already beginning to turn up positive. That toxic mass is as good as out of here. You see that, don't you, Ross?"

McCarthy was still nodding.

"Right. I like it. Right, right, right." And then, abruptly: "Listen, Paul, turn down this transfer, won't you? Stay here with us. We need your kind of mind."

Carpenter had never heard McCarthy plead before. But the pleasure he drew from it was followed immediately by a desolate feeling of contempt.

"I can't, Ross. I've got to move along. Surely you understand that."

"But skipper of an iceberg ship—"

"Whatever. I take what I can get." Carpenter felt dizzy, suddenly. His eyeballs were aching. "Hey, Ross, is it okay if I go home, now? I'm dead on my feet and not worth a damn any more here today. And the crisis is over. I swear to you, it's over. Let me go, okay?"

"Yeah," McCarthy said, absently. "Go on home, if you need to. But if things turn back the wrong way, we'll have to call you back in, no matter what."

"They won't turn back, believe me. Believe me."

"And come in tomorrow. We've got to start setting things up for your replacement. Whoever that is."

"Right. Sure."

Carpenter staggered out of the building, masking up in the vestibule, carefully fastening his face-lung in place to shield his throat and respiratory system from the customary ambient atmospheric garbage. The sky was green and black with broad sickening stripes of dismal crud surrounding the great ugly staring eye of the sun, and the air, hot and moist, clung to the streets like a heavy furry blanket. Even through the mask, Carpenter could feel the pungent atmosphere tickling his nostrils like a fine wire probing upward. He was relieved to see a bubble-bus pull up almost immediately. Quickly Carpenter jumped aboard, shouldering in hard among the other masked figures to make a place for himself, and in ten minutes he was back in his hotel room.

He tossed his face-lung aside and threw himself down fully clothed on his bed, too wound up to go to sleep.

Some world out there, he thought. A kitchen sink full of ecological disasters falling on us for a hundred years, falling and falling and falling. Eutrophication. Red tide. Spontaneous diebacks. Outbursts of mutagenesis, just as spontaneous. Drowned coastlines. Mysterious whirlwinds and thermal upheavals. Fermenting acres of dead vegetation, killed by heat-stroke and pickling now under the merciless sun. Insect hordes on the march across whole continents, gobbling everything in their way, leaving great scars across the land as the mark of their passage. A host of random environmental effects popping out all over the globe, effects whose causes were not immediately apparent any more, were in fact essentially discon-tinuities. The underlying damage had been well and thoroughly done a long time ago. The seeds of a continuing and constantly exfoliating disaster had been planted. And now the crop was coming up everywhere.

It was worst in the middle latitudes, the temperate zone, once so fertile. Rain almost never fell at all there now. The dying forests, the new grasslands taking over, deserts where even the grass couldn't make it, the polar ice packs crumbling, the washed-out bright white hazy sky striped with the gaudy stains of the greenhouse pollutants, the lowlands drowning everywhere, crumbling dead buildings sticking up out of the sea. And of course there were other places where the problem was too much rain instead of not enough. Carpenter thought of that as the revenge of the rain forest: the conquest of places that once had had pleasant warm climates by unending rainfall and stifling wet heat that turned them into humidity-choked jungles, vines sprouting on freeways, monkeys and alligators migrating northward, weird tropical diseases getting loose in the cities.

It occurred to him that if he had been kidding himself about the upcoming movements of the toxic cloud and Seattle and Portland wound up getting trashed next week, McCarthy would have his neck in the noose in two minutes. A scapegoat would be needed and he would be it. And instead of moving up to the iceberg job he'd be sliding downward to some sort of menial crap in a part of the world so dreary it would make Spokane seem like a paradise.

The Company offered you lifetime employment if you toed the line, but any hint of irresponsibility, of nihilistic deviation from proper practice, and you were done for. You didn't get fired, no: firings were very, very rare. But you lost your upward momentum, and once you did that you almost never regained it. So he had gone out on a limb a little, here. A smart slope-seeker would never have been so definite about proclaiming that a favorable shift in air patterns was in the cards: he had completely neglected to cover his ass, he realized.

But what the hell. He had faith in his prediction. You just had to go with your intuitions, sometimes.

Even so, when Carpenter turned up at the office the next day, after lying atop the bed like an off-duty zombie for twelve hours, it was with a certain apocalyptic feeling that he was going to find everybody gathered grim-faced in the doorway, waiting to truss and bind him for execution the moment he walked in. He was wrong. McCarthy was beaming from ear to ear. His eyes were aglow. He absolutely radiated warmth and pride.

"So?" Carpenter asked.

"All's well! You were right on the target, Paul. A direct hit. A genius is what you are, man. A fucking genius, you old son of a whore! Christ, we're going to miss you around here, aren't we, guys? Aren't we?"

It seemed that the weather charts had confirmed Carpenter's intuitive conclusions. Normal cyclonic processes had finally reasserted themselves during the night and all the diabolical Midwestern sky-garbage that had been poisoning the air over the Mountain States was about to be swept back across the Continental Divide to its point of origin. McCarthy couldn't have been happier. He said so in five or six different ways.

But there was no celebration, no champagne. McCarthy wasn't capable of a lot of benevolence; and all too obviously he had had to work himself up with significant effort in order to manage this hearty little display of quasi-paternal delight. Almost at once the warmth drained out of him and Carpenter could see the cold anger that lay just behind it. Was it the envious anger of a stalemated and fucked-up failure over the triumphant achievement of a brilliant underling? Or just his annoyance over the defection of a valuable employee? Whatever it was, McCarthy switched modes quickly, turning chilly and brusque, and the party was over before it had begun.

Time to get back to business as usual, now.

A replacement for him, Carpenter was told, was coming in next week from Australia. Carpenter would have to do up a complete outplacement document, fully outlining the parameters of his official responsibilities here, before he would be free to make the changeover to his new job.

Fine. Fine. One outplacement document, coming right up. He set to work.

Later in the day, when McCarthy was on his lunch break, Carpenter made his first contact with the trawler-division people who were taking him on. A woman named Sanborn, Salaryman Nine at the Samurai Headquarters Pyramid in Manitoba. She had the calm, easy voice of a home-office roundeyes who knew that she had it made: quite a contrast to Ross McCarthy's sour bilious gloom, Carpenter thought.

"You'll have an outstanding crew," Sanborn told him. "And the *Tonopah Maru*'s a fine ship, really up-to-date. She's down in Los Angeles right now undergoing refitting at the San Pedro yards, but they'll be bringing her up the coast around ten days from now, two weeks at the latest. What we want you to do is go down to San Francisco as soon as you've wrapped up everything in Spokane, do your indoctrination course, and then just hang out down there until the ship turns up. Is that all right with you?"

"I can handle it," Carpenter said.

A few weeks of paid idleness in San Francisco? Why not? He had grown up in Los Angeles, but he had always been fond of the cooler, smaller northern city. The sea breezes, the fog, the bridges, the lovely little old buildings, the glittering blue bay—sure. Sure. He'd be glad to. Especially after Spokane. There were people he knew in Frisco, old friends, good old friends. It would be great to see them again.

An exhilarating sense of new beginnings swept through Carpenter like a cooling wind. God bless Jeannie Gabel, he thought. I owe her one, for steering me toward this gig. His first shore leave he would head off to Paris and treat her to the best dinner money could buy. Or the best he could afford, anyway.

The surge didn't last long. Such upbeat feelings rarely did. But Carpenter relished them while they were passing through. You took what joy you could find wherever you found it. It was a tough world and getting tougher all the time.

Getting tougher all the time, yes. Ain't it the truth.

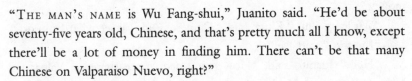

"THE MAN'S NAME is Wu Fang-shui," Juanito said. "He'd be about seventy-five years old, Chinese, and that's pretty much all I know, except there'll be a lot of money in finding him. There can't be that many Chinese on Valparaiso Nuevo, right?"

"He won't still be Chinese," Kluge said.

Delilah said, "He might not even still be a he."

"I've thought of that," said Juanito. "Even so, it ought to be possible to trace him."

"Who you going to use for the trace?" Kluge asked.

Juanito gave him a cool steady stare. Coming from Kluge, who was a consummate pro and constantly wanted to keep everybody else aware of it, the question was virtually a slur on his capabilities as a courier.

"Going to do it myself," Juanito said.

"You?" A quick flicker of a smile.

"Me, myself. Why the hell not?"

"You never did a trace, did you?"

"There's always a first," Juanito said, still staring.

He thought he knew why Kluge was poking at him. A certain quantity of the business done on Valparaiso Nuevo involved finding people who had hidden themselves here and selling them to their pursuers, but up till now Juanito had stayed away from that side of the profession. He earned his money by helping dinkos go underground on Valparaiso, not by selling people out. One reason for that was that nobody yet had happened to offer him a really profitable trace deal; but another was that he was the son of a former fugitive himself. Someone had been hired to do a trace on his own father seven years back, which was how his father had come to be assassinated. Juanito preferred to work the sanctuary side of things.

He was also a professional, though. He was in the business of providing service, period. If he didn't find the runaway gene surgeon for this weird eyeless dinko who had hired him, this Farkas, somebody else would. And Farkas was his client. Juanito felt it was important to do things in a professional way.

"If I run into problems," he said, "I might subcontract. In the meanwhile I just thought I'd let you know, in case you happened to stumble on a lead. I'll pay finders' fees. And you know it'll be good money."

"Wu Fang-shui," Kluge said. "Chinese. Old. I'll see what I can do."

"Me too," said Delilah.

"Hell," Juanito said. "How many people are there on Valparaiso Nuevo altogether? Maybe nine hundred thousand? I can think of fifty right away who can't possibly be the guy I'm looking for. That narrows the odds some. What I have to do is just go on narrowing, right? Right?"

In fact Juanito didn't feel very optimistic. He was going to do his best, sure; but the whole system on Valparaiso Nuevo was heavily weighted in favor of helping those who wanted to hide stay hidden.

Even Farkas realized that. "The privacy laws here are very strict, aren't they?"

With a smile Juanito said, "They're just about the only laws we have, you know? The sacredness of sanctuary. It is the compassion of El Supremo that has turned Valparaiso Nuevo into a place of refuge for fugitives of all sorts from every world, other artificial planets as well as Earth itself, and we are not supposed to interfere with the compassion of El Supremo."

"Which is very expensive compassion, I understand."

"Very. Sanctuary fees are renewable annually. Anyone who harms a permanent resident who is living here under the compassion of El Supremo is bringing about a reduction in El Supremo's annual income, you see? Which doesn't sit very well with the Generalissimo."

They were in the Villanueva Café in the town of San Martin de Porres, E Spoke. They had been touring Valparaiso Nuevo all day long, back and forth from rim to hub, going up one spoke and down the other. Farkas said he wanted to experience as much of Valparaiso Nuevo as he could. Not to see; to *experience*. That was the word he used. And his hunger for experience was immense. He was insatiable, prowling around everywhere, gobbling it all up, soaking it in. He never slowed down. The man's energy was fantastic, Juanito thought. Considering that he had to be at least twice Juanito's age, maybe more. And confident, too. The way he strutted around, you'd think he was the new Generalissimo and not just some strange deformed long-legged dinko who in fact was owned, body and soul, by the unscrupulous Kyocera-Merck combine down there on filthy Earth.

Farkas had never been to one of the satellite worlds before, he told Juanito. It amazed him, he said, that there were forests and lakes here, broad fields of wheat and rice, fruit orchards, herds of goats and cattle. Apparently he had expected the place to be nothing more than a bunch of aluminum struts and grim concrete boxes with everybody living on food pills, or something. People from Earth couldn't quite manage to comprehend that the larger habitat worlds were comfortable places with blue skies, fleecy clouds, lovely gardens, handsome buildings of steel and brick and glass. The way Earth used to be, before they ruined it.

Farkas said, "If fugitives are protected by the government, how do you go about tracing one, then?"

"There are always ways. Everybody knows somebody who knows something about someone. Information is bought here the same way compassion is."

"From the Generalissimo?" Farkas said, looking startled.

"From his officials, sometimes. If done with great care. Care is important, because lives are at risk. There are also couriers who have information to sell. All of us know a great deal that we are not supposed to know."

"I suppose you know a great many fugitives by sight, yourself?"

"Some," Juanito said. "You see that man, sitting by the window?" He frowned. "I don't know, can you see him? To me he looks around sixty, bald head, thick lips, no chin?"

"I see him, yes. He looks a little different to me."

"I bet he does. Well, that man, he ran a swindle at one of the Luna domes, sold a lot of phony stock in an offshore monopoly fund that didn't exist, fifty million Capbloc dollars. He pays plenty to live here. And this one here—you see? With the blond woman?—an embezzler, that one, very good with computers, reamed a big bank in Singapore for almost its entire capital. Him over there, with the mustache—you see?—he pretended to be pope. Can you believe that? Everybody in Rio de Janeiro did."

"Wait a minute," Farkas said. "How do I know you're not making all this up?"

"You don't," Juanito said amiably. "But I'm not."

"So we just sit here like this and you expose the identities of three fugitives to me free of charge?"

"It wouldn't be free," Juanito said, "if they were people you were looking for."

"What if they were? And my claiming to be looking for a Wu Fang-shui just a cover?"

"But you aren't looking for any of them," Juanito said, with scorn in his voice. "Come on. I would know it."

"Right," said Farkas. "I'm not." He sipped his drink, something green and cloudy and sweet. "How come these men haven't done a better job of concealing their identities?" he asked.

"They think they have," said Juanito.

Getting leads was a slow business, and expensive. Juanito left Farkas to roam the spokes of Valparaiso Nuevo on his own, and headed off to the usual sources of information: his father's friends, other couriers, and even the headquarters of the Unity Party, El Supremo's grass-roots organization, where it wasn't hard to find someone who knew something and had a price for it. Juanito was cautious. Middle-aged Chinese gentleman I'm trying to locate, he said. Why do you want to find him? Nobody asked that. Nobody would. Could be any reason, anywhere from wanting to blow him away on contract to handing him a million-Capbloc-dollar lottery prize that he had won last year on New Yucatán. Nobody asked for reasons on Valparaiso. Everybody understood the rules: your business was strictly your business.

There was a man named Federigo who had been with Juanito's father in the Costa Rica days who knew a woman who knew a man who had a freemartin neuter companion who had formerly belonged to someone high up in the Census Department. There were fees to pay at every step of the way, but it was Farkas's money, what the hell, or, even better,

Kyocera-Merck's, and by the end of the week Juanito had access to the immigration data stored on golden megachips somewhere in the depths of the hub. The data down there wasn't going to provide anybody with Wu Fang-shui's phone number. But what it could tell Juanito, and did, eight hundred callaghanos later, was how many ethnic Chinese were living on Valparaiso Nuevo and how long ago they had arrived.

"There are nineteen of them altogether," he reported to Farkas. "Eleven of them are women."

"So? Changing sex is no big deal," Farkas said.

"Agreed. The women are all under fifty, though. The oldest of the men is sixty-two. The longest that any of them has been on Valparaiso Nuevo is nine years."

Farkas didn't seem bothered. "Would you say that rules them out? I wouldn't. Age can be altered just as easily as sex."

"But date of arrival can't be, so far as I know. And you say that your Wu Fang-shui came here fifteen years back. Unless you're wrong about that, he can't be any of those Chinese. Your Wu Fang-shui, if he isn't dead by now, has signed up for some other racial mix, I'd say."

"He isn't dead," Farkas said.

"You sure of that?"

"He was still alive three months ago, and in touch with his family on Earth. He's got a brother in Tashkent."

"Shit," Juanito said. "Ask the brother what name he's going under up here, then."

"We did. We couldn't get it."

"Ask him harder."

"We asked him too hard," said Farkas. "Now the information isn't available any more. Not from him, anyway."

Juanito checked out the nineteen Chinese, just to be certain. It didn't cost much and it didn't take much time, and there was always the chance that Dr. Wu had cooked his immigration data somehow. But the quest led nowhere.

Juanito found six of them all in one shot, playing some Chinese game in a social club in the town of Havana de Cuba on Spoke B, and they went right on laughing and pushing the little porcelain counters around while he stood there kibitzing. They didn't *act* like sanctuarios. There was always an edge of some kind on a sanctuario, a wariness not far below the surface. Not everybody on Valparaiso Nuevo had come here to get away from the law: most, but not all. These just seemed like a bunch of prosperous Chinese merchants sitting around a table having a good time. Juanito hung around long enough to determine that they were all shorter than he was, too, which meant either that they weren't Dr. Wu, who was tall for a Chinese, or that Dr. Wu had been willing to have his legs chopped down by fifteen centimeters for the sake of a more efficient disguise. That was possible but it wasn't too likely.

The other thirteen Chinese were all much too young or too convincingly female or too this or too that. Juanito crossed them all off his list. From the outset he hadn't thought Wu would still be Chinese, anyway.

He kept on looking. One trail went cold, and then another, and then another. By now he was starting to think Dr. Wu must have heard that a man with no eyes was looking for him, and had gone even deeper underground, or off Valparaiso entirely. Juanito paid a friend at the hub spaceport to keep watch on departure manifests for him. Nothing came of that. Then someone reminded him that there was a colony of old-time hard-core sanctuary types living in and around the town of El Mirador on Spoke D, people who had a genuine aversion to being bothered. Juanito went there. Because he was known to be the son of a murdered fugitive himself, nobody hassled him: he of all people wouldn't be likely to be running a trace, would he?

The visit yielded no directly useful result. Juanito couldn't risk asking questions and nothing was visible that seemed to lead anywhere. But he came away with the strong feeling that El Mirador was the answer.

"Take me there," Farkas said.

"I can't do that. It's a low-profile town. Strangers aren't welcome. You'll stick out like a dinosaur."

"Take me," Farkas repeated.

"If Wu's there and he gets even a glimpse of you, he'll know right away that there's a contract out for him and he'll vanish so fast you won't believe it."

"Take me to El Mirador," said Farkas. "I pay for services and you deliver them, isn't that the deal?"

"Right," Juanito said. "Let's go to El Mirador."

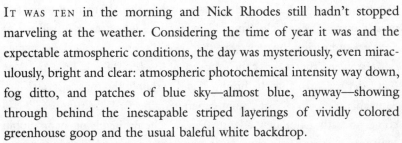

IT WAS TEN in the morning and Nick Rhodes still hadn't stopped marveling at the weather. Considering the time of year it was and the expectable atmospheric conditions, the day was mysteriously, even miraculously, bright and clear: atmospheric photochemical intensity way down, fog ditto, and patches of blue sky—almost blue, anyway—showing through behind the inescapable striped layerings of vividly colored greenhouse goop and the usual baleful white backdrop.

Rhodes had read about blue skies in storybooks when he was a kid, but he hadn't had much of an opportunity for seeing them over the past thirty years or so. Today, though, the air was clean, for some reason. Relatively clean, anyway. From his office on the thirteenth floor of the slender, airy Santachiara Technologies tower, up along the highest ridge of the Berkeley hills a couple of miles south of the University campus, he had a 360-degree view of the whole San Francisco Bay Area: the bridges, the shimmering water, the pretty little toy city across the bay, the rounded inland hills behind him with their serene coats of desiccated lion-colored grass. At this distance you weren't able to see how the surface of practically every structure was spotted and corroded by the unrelenting fumes. And then there was the arching dome of the sky, much of it looking magnificently and improbably blue right now. On a day like this it was impossible to keep your mind on work. Rhodes wandered from window to window, making the full circuit, staring out.

A terrific day, yes. But he knew it couldn't stay that way for long, and he was right.

The annunciator light went on and the calm impersonal androidal voice said, "Dr. Van Vliet is calling on Line Three, Dr. Rhodes. He wants to know if you have a reaction to his report yet."

Rhodes felt a falling-away sensation in the floor of his gut. It was a lot too early in the day to have to cope with Van Vliet and the complications that he represented.

"Tell him I'm in conference and I'll have to get back to him," Rhodes said automatically.

Nick Rhodes was the associate research director of Santachiara Technologies' Survival/Modification Program, which is to say that he earned his living trying to find ways to transform human beings into something that would be either more or less than human, Rhodes still wasn't quite sure which. Santachiara Technologies was a subsidiary of Samurai Industries, the megacorp that owned pretty near all the segments of the universe that weren't the property of Kyocera-Merck, Ltd. And Alex Van Vliet was probably the brightest and certainly the most aggressive of Santachiara's team of hot young genetic engineers. Who supposedly had come up with a hot new adapto plan, a scheme involving hemoglobin replacement, that was said by those who had heard Van Vliet's lunch-hour explanations to have real breakthrough possibilities. That was a new angle, all right, and one that Rhodes found obscurely threatening, without quite understanding why. Just this moment a conversation with Van Vliet was an event that Rhodes wanted very much to avoid.

Not out of cowardice, Rhodes told himself. Merely out of a certain degree of moral confusion. There was a difference, Rhodes liked to think. Sooner or later he would work through the inner contradictions in which he had lately begun to become entangled and then he would deal with Van Vliet. But not just now, please, Rhodes thought. Not just now, okay?

He returned to his desk.

The desk had a very important look, a smooth, sweeping boomerang-shaped slab of highly polished wood, mottled red in color, a fabulous million-dollar chunk of rare wood torn from the heart of some South American rain-forest monarch. And it was importantly cluttered, too: data-cubes stacked in this corner, videos over there, a big pile of virtuals that included Van Vliet's set of simulations and proposals along the far edge. On the left side, below desktop level, was a set of controls for all the room's electronic gadgets; on the right, in a suspended drawer protected by a crystal-tuned privacy lock, was a small collection of cognacs and whiskeys, private stock of Nicholas Rhodes, Ph.D. And in the middle of everything, next to the grille of the annunciator, was the elegant six-sided holochip that Rhodes' girlfriend Isabelle Martine had given him at Christmas, the one that proclaimed in letters of fire (if you held it at the right angle) the six-word mantra that Rhodes had formulated to encapsulate the specific tasks of his department, one word per face:

BONES	KIDNEYS
LUNGS	HEART
SKIN	MIND

Sweet of her. Considering that Isabelle fundamentally despised his work, that she inwardly hoped that it would fail. Rhodes picked it up and turned it over and over in his hand like a giant worry bead. BONES. LUNGS. SKIN. Yes. KIDNEYS. HEART. MIND. He stared for a moment or two at MIND. Ah, that was the real problem, he thought, the true killer. MIND.

The annunciator flashed again and this time the voice said, "Meshoram Enron, calling on Line Two."

"Who?"

"Meshoram Enron," the automaton said again, with great precision. "The Israeli journalist. You've agreed to have lunch with him today."

"Oh. Right." Rhodes hesitated. He wasn't ready for Enron either, just this moment—not, at any rate, one-on-one. "Tell him I can't make lunch, how about dinner?" Rhodes reached without thinking for Van Vliet's virtuals, put them back, pulled them toward him again, stared at them as though they had only just arrived at his office. "And if he says yes, call Ms. Martine for me and put her through when you have her. I'll want her to be joining us."

Back from the android, a few moments later, came the report: Mr. Enron would be happy to make it a dinner meeting. Would Dr. Rhodes care to pick him up at his hotel in San Francisco at half past seven? As for Ms. Martine, she was away from her phone, but a seek-message had been attached to her number. And there was another message from Dr. Van Vliet, who was very much looking forward to the opportunity to discuss his proposals in person with Dr. Rhodes as soon as possible, blah blah, hoping for an early response, blah blah blah—

Yes. Blah blah blah. A busy day, suddenly. Rhodes was starting to feel outnumbered. Van Vliet, turning the pressure on. This Enron, sniffing around wanting to find out God knows what. A spy, no doubt. All Israelis were spies, in one way or another, Rhodes thought. What next? And only ten in the morning. Time for the first drink yet?

No, Rhodes decided crisply. It is not time for a drink yet.

But if it was too soon to have a drink and too soon to deal with Van Vliet's report, then he was making procrastination the order of the day, and that didn't feel good either. With sudden manic decisiveness Rhodes overruled himself on everything he had just been telling himself. Total shift of direction, that was the ticket. Reaching under the desk, he deftly disarmed the privacy lock on the liquor drawer, brought forth the cognac, knocked back a quick shot. Pondered a moment, had another, a smaller nip. Then, as the glow began to spread, he picked up Van Vliet's proposal again and clicked it into the playback slot.

Instantly a virtual Alex Van Vliet stood before him, small as life: trim, wiry little guy, chilly blue eyes, tiny close-clinging goatee, square-shouldered defiant stance that maximized his flimsy frame. Rhodes, a big shambling burly man, mistrusted little agile ones. They made him feel like a beleaguered gorilla surrounded by yapping monkeys. And gorillas were extinct, essentially. Monkeys thrived like mosquitoes in the world's new jungles.

Behind Van Vliet, reaching its arms forward to surround his image like a sort of open-ended nimbus, was a snaking three-dimensional pattern of colored dots which Rhodes recognized almost instantly as a beta-chain hemoglobin molecule. Van Vliet was saying, "They are conjugated proteins and consist of four heme groups and the globin molecule. The heme component is a porphyrin in which the metal ion that is coordinated is iron in the ferrous state, that is, Fe^{+2}. The globin component consists of four polypeptide chains, which are designated alpha, beta, gamma, and so forth, according to their amino-acid makeup."

It was the middle of an elementary lecture on the function of hemoglobin. Rhodes realized that he had somehow activated the visual incorrectly and had missed Van Vliet's introductory remarks. But that was all right. He could pretty well imagine what they were. Best to glide into them in a roundabout fashion.

"—all-important role of the hemoglobin pigment in mammalian respiration is to combine loosely with molecular oxygen, so that it is capable of transporting oxygen from the organism's intake point to the point of utilization. However, hemoglobin has an affinity for many other molecules: for example, it readily unites with carbon monoxide, with disastrous effects to the body. It bonds easily with nitric oxide as well. Sulfhemoglobin, which is hemoglobin plus hydrogen sulfide gas, is another significant pathological form of the pigment. Hematin, which is the hydroxyl compound of heme—"

While he was speaking, Van Vliet moved briskly around the virtual stage, adjusting the molecular patterns behind his simulated figure with quick confident motions of his hands, like a magician rearranging his props. At his deft touch the bright patterns underwent instant metamorphosis to demonstrate each altered form of hemoglobin Van Vliet summoned forth. The colors were very pretty. Rhodes allowed himself another small drink. It took the edge off. Gradually Rhodes' attentiveness diminished, not so much on account of the cognac as simply out of boredom and irritation.

Van Vliet went right on, cruising remorselessly through basic biochemical information. This visual was obviously intended for people on higher managerial levels than Rhodes', where technical expertise was more tenuous. "Ferrous salts—insufficient oxygen supply to the tissues—affinity for carbon, phosphorus, manganese, vanadium, tungsten—iron will form dihalides with all four of the common halogens—"

Yes. Yes. It certainly will.

With a diabolical grin Van Vliet said suddenly, "But of course that will soon be obsolete, so far as the human race is concerned. Since, as I have already indicated, our consensus projections of the makeup of the Earth's atmosphere circa A.D. 2350 indicate significant replacement of oxygen and nitrogen by complex hydrocarbons and sulfur compounds, as well as a continuing increase in the already critical percentage of carbon dioxide, we will need to adjust the body's respiration capacity accordingly. The risks of continuing to use the iron-based pigment hemoglobin as the respiratory system's vital transport protein are manifest. We will have to shatter the human race's dependence on oxygen. A hydrogen-to-methane cycle is one possible alternative, employing a transport protein that utilizes the locking and unlocking of a double sulfur bond, as can be seen in this diagram."

The pattern now was that of a tightly coiled serpent in angry reds and slashing violets, head hovering above the tip of its own tail as though getting ready to strike.

Rhodes put Van Vliet's presentation on hold and backed it up ninety seconds or so.

The risks of continuing to use the iron-based pigment hemoglobin as the respiratory system's vital transport protein are manifest. We will have to shatter the human race's dependence on oxygen.

He's lost his mind, Rhodes thought.

A transport protein that utilizes the locking and unlocking of a double sulfur bond—

Right. Right. The visual, rolling onward, had reached the point where Rhodes had reversed it. Once again Van Vliet, like a capering demigod, built his red-and-purple serpent in midair in front of Rhodes' desk with quick, delicate movements of his hands. Rhodes hunched forward with his chin propped on his fists and watched Van Vliet cruise on to the end of the first capsule, offering more apocalyptic news about the human respiratory system in the coming age of oxygen-deficient air. The second capsule, Van Vliet said by way of teaser, contained the actual technical specifications for the corrective work he proposed to undertake. Rhodes picked up the second capsule but did not insert it for playback.

The backstairs scuttlebutt was true, then.

We will have to shatter the human race's dependence on oxygen—

The little guy was suggesting nothing less than to rearrange the body's whole respiratory-circulatory works to make human beings capable of breathing a sulfur-dioxide/methane/carbon-dioxide mix, and to hell with any need for oxygen. Of all the adapto proposals that had been kicked around the Santachiara labs in the past year and a half, this was by far the most radical. By far, by far, by far. No one had ever envisioned attempting such a total transformation. Rhodes doubted, even after having looked through some of Van Vliet's specs, that the thing could ever be managed. It was wildly out of line with Rhodes' sense of the possible.

Rhodes felt a muscle pulling itself tight in his cheek, like a tiny acrobat getting itself ready for a long-distance leap, and he pressed the tips of two fingers into it, hard, to discharge the tension that was building up there.

Another drink?

No, Rhodes decided. Not just yet.

Could Van Vliet's gimmick work?

Not in a million years, Rhodes thought. You'd have to redesign everything, top to bottom, the entire array of organs—lungs and liver and lights too, whatever the hell lights might be, and right on down to the osmotic capacity of the cell walls—a total makeover, in effect a second creation of humanity. It was an absurdly overambitious scheme that was beyond any imaginable technical capacity Santachiara might be able to develop and which would, if carried somehow to a successful conclusion despite the apparent difficulties, transform the human race beyond all recognition.

Which is exactly the thing, Rhodes thought, that we have been brought together here to come up with, is it not? Which I am paid, and paid well, to achieve. Which I have hired young Alex Van Vliet to help me bring about.

And if Van Vliet is right about the feasibility of his proposal, and I am wrong—

He looked at his hands. They were trembling a little. He spread the fingers wide to regain control over them. Then he hit the button and started Van Vliet over, this time from the actual beginning.

Van Vliet, cocky, self-possessed, grinning at him like an old pal. Twenty-four years old, wasn't he? Young enough to be Rhodes' son, almost. Rhodes, at forty, had never before felt the thunder of the oncoming generation, and he didn't like it.

"What I propose to do in this initial presentation," Van Vliet said, "is to offer a fundamental reevaluation of our adapto efforts thus far, working from the premise that when we are given an extreme situation to deal with, extreme measures are the only appropriate response."

Van Vliet disappeared and was replaced by the virtual image of a lovely female figure in airy robes, a fragile girl, tripping through a forest against a backdrop of bilious green sky thick as soup. She was dainty, elegantly slender, Pre–Raphaelitely Caucasian, with a stunning complexion: the archetypical generic lovely little girl. And all around her the

ghastly air was closing in, fetid, clotted, pockmarked with clusters of what
looked like aerial turds. She didn't seem to care a damn about that. It
didn't trouble her at all. Rhodes saw her precious little nostrils daintily
inputting lungful after lungful of muckosphere as she danced playfully
about, happily singing some sweet little song.

This was, Rhodes knew, by way of being an advertisement for the
New Human Race that Van Vliet meant to create. Would the new and
loathsome Earth to come really be populated by a race of beautiful
faery-maidens like this?

"There can be no significant disagreement with our projection," Van
Vliet continued, "that within four to five generations, six as a maximally
favorable estimate, the air of this planet will become unbreathable for the
human race as it is presently constituted. Despite all corrective measures it
is clear that the buildup of greenhouse gases reached a condition of
irreversibility some time ago and that it is inevitable now that as outgassing
of previously stored pollutants continues we will pass below the oxygen-
ation threshold within the lifetime of the grandchildren of the children
now being born.

"Since we do not have the capability of macro-managing our
atmosphere to return it to its pre-industrial-age mix, in view of the
unavoidable ongoing release into the atmosphere of hydrocarbons that
were locked up in the Earth's oceans and solid matter during the
irresponsible nineteenth and twentieth centuries, we have chosen instead,
here at Santachiara, to attempt to micro-manage the human genome to
meet the coming changes. Various adapto schemes of differing degrees of
complexity are being studied, but it is my considered opinion, after a
thoroughgoing analysis of the entire Santachiara program as it is presently
conceived, that we have allowed ourselves to settle for a program of half
measures which are inevitably doomed to failure and—"

Jesus Christ, Rhodes thought. He says it right to my face, and grins!

Rhodes had had about all that he could take, for the moment. He hit
the button. Van Vliet disappeared.

"Ms. Martine calling on Line One," the annunciator said instantly.

Grateful for the interruption, Rhodes brought her on visor. Isabelle—
head-and-shoulders image—hovered before him, a slim, intense woman
with oddly complex and conflicting features. Fierce glittering gray-violet

eyes; a delicate, finely structured nose; soft, full lips: nothing quite went with anything else. Last spring Isabelle had had her hair turned a volcanic red and Rhodes still was not used to it.

She started right in, her usual brusque headlong approach: "What's this about dinner with some Israeli tonight, Nick? I thought we were going to go to Sausalito and—" Isabelle paused abruptly. "Nick? You look so funny, Nick!"

"Do I? Funny how?"

"Your face is unusually tight. Your pupils are dilated. There's trouble, isn't there?"

Isabelle was always quick to pick up his somatic changes. But that was her business, after all: she was a kinetic therapist. She spoke body language like a native. There was never any sense trying to hide things from her. She and Rhodes had been seeing each other for two and a half years. People were starting to ask him when they would be getting married.

She gave him one of her sensitive, caring therapist looks: Mama Isabelle, eager to relieve him of his anguish. Talk to me, sweet. Tell me about it and you'll feel better.

Rhodes said, "It's been a bad morning, lady. Couple of days ago one of the kids here handed me the goddamnedest far-reaching adapto proposal I've ever seen. A really revolutionary idea. Today's the first chance I've had to play the virtuals he gave me, and I'm halfway through and too upset to go on."

"Why is that?"

"Partly because it's so radical. It would mean the sort of extreme measures you've always been worried about, human somatic adaptation right from the bottom up, not just some kind of quick fix. And partly because his approach is so snotty. He opens it by saying, essentially, that the rest of us are all so hopelessly conservative here that we might as well just quit and let him take over the lab."

"You? Conservative?"

"Around here, yes. Anyway, I'm not yet ready to hear a kid half my age telling me in just about so many words that it's time for old farts like me to step aside and stop obstructing the solution of the problem."

"A solution which he can provide?"

"I didn't get that far. Maybe he can, maybe he can't. I'm inclined to believe that he can't, because what he's proposing is so far out that I don't think it's achievable. There are some built-in technical problems that seem inherently unsolvable to me. But what do I know? I'm only an old fart. He wants us to try a sulfur-based hemoglobin instead of iron-based, so that we can get along without oxygen when push comes to shove a couple of hundred years from now."

"Would that be possible, do you think?"

"I don't know. I doubt it very much. But if it turns out that it is, he'll own this whole lab inside of a year and I'll be out on my ear." Rhodes managed an uneasy smile. "Maybe I ought to have him killed right now, just on the off chance that he's really onto something."

Her expression darkened as he spoke. Her eyes grew steely. The therapist was gone and the face on the screen now was that of the dedicated political activist. Rhodes began to worry. He dreaded that look.

"Is that all you can think about, Nick? That this kid will push you out of your job? What about the human race, for God's sake? Transformation from the bottom up? What does that mean, anyway? Is he going to turn us all into some kind of science-fiction monsters?"

"Isabelle—"

"Sulfur in the blood? It sounds disgusting."

"Yes. Yes, it is. It makes me want to puke, just thinking about it." Rhodes wished he hadn't gone into such detail with her: he had no business sharing company business with anyone on the outside, especially not Isabelle. She had connections to half a dozen reactionary San Francisco humanist groups. She could, if she chose, make real trouble for him. "Listen, let's not get into all that now, okay? Especially over the phone. I'm aware that this is not a proposal you're likely to think highly of. But we can discuss it some other time, all right? About this evening—"

"The Israeli."

"Right." Thinking of the upcoming meeting with Enron, Rhodes regretted more and more having opened up to Isabelle, now. "He's a journalist, he says. Doing one of those uplifting features on the future of the human race, more or less—you know, the Frightening Challenges That We Face, and What Our Finest Minds Mean to Do About Them—for some big slick magazine that has about a billion readers in the

Israeli-Arab world, and he wants to quiz me on the current state of American gene-splicing research. I think he's a spy."

"Of course he is. They all are, those Israelis. Everybody knows that. I'm surprised you've agreed to talk to him."

"I have to. He cleared it with New Tokyo. I'm not supposed to tell him anything that has any substance, naturally, but Samurai wants the PR exposure. It's a *very* big magazine. And the Fertile Crescent is a huge market for Samurai products. We are supposed to position ourselves for their readers as the last best hope for the salvation of humanity. I was supposed to have lunch with him, but I'd rather make it dinner. I want you along to kick me under the table whenever I start veering into classified areas."

"Sure," she said, smiling.

"But—please, Isabelle. No political stuff. No diatribes. You and I have our philosophical differences, and so be it, but tonight, in front of this Enron, is not the time to ventilate them."

Her smile vanished. "I'll try to control myself, Nick. I can be very good. But wouldn't it help give his article a broader perspective if it were to reflect American diversity of opinion on the whole subject of human adapto work?"

"Please."

"All right," she said. Her tone was cool. Rhodes wondered whether she really would keep quiet this evening. Isabelle meant well, but she was a very volatile woman. Probably it had been a mistake to ask her along. But, then, probably the whole relationship with Isabelle was a mistake, and he had never let that interfere with anything up till now.

"I'll pick you up at seven," he said. "He's staying in the city, and we didn't discuss where we would eat. Maybe we'll go over to Sausalito after all." He blew her a kiss, through the visor. The thought came to him suddenly of the other end of the evening, when all the babble was done with and over and Meshoram Enron was out of his hair, and he and Isabelle were alone together at midnight in his flat high up above the bay—the lights low, soft music tinkling, maybe a little brandy, then on the couch with Isabelle in his arms, her sweet fragrance rising to dizzy him, his head swooping down to nestle between her breasts—

Yes. Yes. To hell with Alex Van Vliet and his red-and-purple snakes, to

hell with Meshoram Enron, to hell with the whole doomed withering
pollution-choked world. What mattered was to carve out an island of
safety for yourself in the night.

Christ, that my love were in my arms, and I in my bed again!

There was the annunciator light again.

Jesus. Rhodes glared at the machine. "If it's Van Vliet, you can tell
him—"

"Mr. Paul Carpenter is calling on Line One," said the android
blandly.

"Paul Carpenter?" Rhodes was astounded. He jabbed at the button
and there was old Paul, all right, square in the middle of the visor, the
unmistakable Paul, looking a little older, maybe more than a little, and
with a dark shaggy beard covering the whole lower half of his face instead
of the trim little Vandyke that he once had affected. His coarse blond hair
was very much longer than Rhodes remembered it and he was tanned and
weather-beaten and crows'-footed, as though he might have been outdoors a little too much for his own good, lately. It was five years since
Rhodes last had any contact with him.

"Well," Rhodes said. "The prodigal returns. Where the hell are you
calling from, man?"

"Right over here next door to you in San Francisco. How are you,
Nick? Splicing a lot of interesting genes these days?"

Rhodes stared. "San Fran*cisco?* You're in *town?* Why? What for? Why
didn't you give me a little notice that you were coming in?"

"I didn't think I needed to. I'll be here for a few weeks, and then the
Company's shipping me out to the fucking South Pacific. Skipper of an
iceberg trawler, I am. Call me Ahab. Do you think you could manage
lunch with an old friend sometime next week?"

"Next week?" Rhodes said. "What about today?"

Carpenter looked surprised. "Can you do it on such short notice?
Important man like you?"

"I'd love to. A chance to get out of this goddamned bughouse for a
couple of hours."

"I could catch a pod across the bay and be over there in thirty
minutes. Go straight up to your lab, get the grand tour before we
eat—how's that?"

"Not good," Rhodes said. "All the interesting work areas are under security seal and the rest is just offices. Anyway, there's someone here I'm trying to duck this morning and I don't dare come out into view before lunchtime." He looked at his watch. "Meet me at noon at a place called Antonio's, along the Berkeley waterfront, right on the seawall. Any cabbie will know where that is. Jesus, it'll be good to see you, Paul! Jesus! What a goddamned surprise!"

▼　　　▼　　　▼

FARKAS SAID, "I think we've located our merchandise."

He was in his hotel room, alone, talking by scrambled telephone to Colonel Emilio Olmo, the number-three man in Valparaiso Nuevo's Guardia Civil. Colonel Olmo was very high up in the confidence of Don Eduardo Callaghan, the Generalissimo, El Supremo, the Valparaiso Nuevo habitat's Defender and Maximum Leader. More significantly for Farkas's purposes, though, Olmo was Kyocera-Merck's chief point man on Valparaiso Nuevo. It was Kyocera-Merck's long-range plan, so Farkas understood, to bring Olmo forward as the successor to El Supremo whenever it seemed appropriate for Don Eduardo's long reign to come to an end. Drawing pay from both sides, Olmo was in a nice position and it might be considered unwise to trust him in any major way, but his long-term interests plainly lay with K-M and therefore Farkas deemed it safe to deal with him.

"Who's your courier?" Olmo asked.

"Juanito Holt."

"Nasty little spic. I know him. Very clever kid, I have to say. How'd you find him?"

"He found me, actually. Five minutes off the shuttle, and there he was. He's very quick."

"Very. *Too* quick, sometimes. Father was mixed up in the Central American Empire thing—you remember it? The three-cornered revolution?—working both sides against the middle. Very tricky *hombre*. He was either a socialist or a fascist, nobody could ever be quite sure, and in the end when things fell apart he skipped out and continued his plotting from up here. He made himself troublesome and after a time the right and the left found it best to team up and send a delegation here to get rid of him. The kid is tricky too. Watch him, Victor."

"I watch everything," Farkas said. "You know that."

"Yes. Yes, you certainly do watch."

Farkas was watching the telephone visor, now. It was mounted flush against the wall, and to Farkas it looked like an iridescent yellow isosceles triangle whose long, tapering upper point bent backward into the wall as though it were trying to glide into some adjacent dimension. Olmo's head-and-shoulders image, centered near the base of the triangle, impinged on Farkas's sensorium in the form of a pair of beveled cubes in cobalt blue, linked by a casual zigzag of diamond-bright white light.

The air in the room was unnervingly cool and sweet. Breathing it was like breathing perfume. It was just as artificial as the air you breathed indoors anywhere on Earth, in fact even more so: but somehow it was artificial in a different way. The difference, Farkas suspected, was that on Earth they had to filter all sorts of gunk out of the air before they could let it come into a building, the methane, the extra CO_2, all the rest of the greenhouse stuff, so that it always had a sterile, empty quality about it once they were done filtering. You knew it was air that had needed to be fixed so you could breathe it, and you mistrusted it. You wondered what they had taken out of it besides the gunk. Whereas on an L-5 satellite they manufactured the atmosphere from scratch, putting together a fine holy mix of oxygen and nitrogen and carbon dioxide and such in the proportions God had originally intended, in fact better than God had designed things, since there was less of the relatively useless nitrogen in the air than there was on Earth and a greater proportion of oxygen; and there was no need to filter anything out of it, since it contained nothing in the first place that wasn't supposed to be there.

So the completely synthetic air of the habitats was richer and fuller in flavor than the denatured real air of Earth's sealed buildings. Headier. Too heady for him. Farkas knew that it was better air than the indoor air on Earth, but he had never been able quite to get used to it. He *expected* air to taste dead, except when you were outdoors without a mask, filling your lungs with all those lovely hydrocarbons. This bouncy, springy stuff was holier than he needed his air to be.

But give me a little more time, Farkas thought. I'll get to like it.

He said to Olmo, "The merchandise is said to be stored in a place called El Mirador. My courier will be taking me there later in the day to inspect the warehouse."

"*Bueno*. And you are confident you will find everything in order?"

"Very."

"Do you have any reason to think so?" Olmo asked.

"Just intuition," said Farkas. "But it feels right."

"I understand. You have senses that are different from our senses. You are a very unusual man, Victor."

Farkas made no reply.

Olmo said, "If the merchandise is to your satisfaction, when will you want to make shipment?"

"Very soon, I think."

"To the home office?"

"No," said Farkas. "That plan has been changed. The home office has requested that the merchandise be sent directly to the factory."

"Ah. I see."

"If you would make certain that the cargo manifests are in proper order," Farkas said, "I'll let you know as soon as we're ready to transfer the goods."

"And the customs fees—"

"Will be taken care of in the usual manner. I don't think Don Eduardo will have reason to complain."

"It would be very embarrassing if he did."

"There won't be any problem."

"*Bueno*," Olmo said. "Don Eduardo is always unhappy when valuable merchandise is removed from Valparaiso Nuevo. His unhappiness must always be taken into account."

"I said there'd be compensation, didn't I?"

There was sudden new force in Farkas's tone, and Olmo's image responded by changing color ever so slightly, deepening from cobalt blue almost to black, as though he wanted Farkas to understand that the possibility that the necessary bribes might somehow fall through was disturbing to him and that the eyeless man's implied rebuke was offensive. But Farkas saw Olmo's color return to its normal shade after a moment, and realized that the little crisis had passed.

"*Bueno,*" Olmo said once more. And this time he seemed to mean it.

El Mirador was midway between hub and rim on its spoke. There were great glass windows punched in its shield that provided a colossal view of all the rest of Valparaiso Nuevo and the stars and the sun and the moon and the Earth and everything. A solar eclipse was going on when Juanito and Farkas arrived, not a great rarity in the satellite worlds but not all that common, either: the Earth was plastered right over the sun with nothing but one bright squidge of hot light showing down below like a diamond blazing on a golden ring. Purple shadows engulfed the town, deep and thick, a heavy velvet curtain falling over everything.

Juanito tried to describe what he saw. Farkas made an impatient brushing gesture.

"I know, I know. I feel it in my teeth." They stood on a big peoplemover escalator leading down into the town plaza. "The sun is long and thin right now, like the blade of an ax. The Earth has six sides, each one glowing a different color."

Juanito gaped at the eyeless man in amazement.

"Wu is here," Farkas said. "Down there, in the plaza. I feel his presence."

"From five hundred meters away?"

"Come with me."

"What do we do if he really is there?"

"Are you armed?" Farkas asked.

"I have a spike, yes." Juanito patted his thigh.

"Good. Tune it to shock intensity, and don't use it at all if you can help it. I don't want you to hurt him in any way."

"I understand. You want to kill him yourself, in your own sweet time. Very slowly and in the fullest enjoyment of the pleasure."

"Just be careful not to hurt him, that's all," Farkas said. "Come on."

* * *

It was an old-fashioned-looking town, a classic Latin American design, low pastel buildings with plenty of ironwork scrolling along their facades, cobblestone plaza with quaint little cafés around its perimeter and an elaborate fountain in the middle. About ten thousand people lived there and it seemed as if they were all out in the plaza right this minute sipping drinks and watching the eclipse. Juanito was grateful for the eclipse. It was the entertainment of the day. No one paid any attention to them as they came floating down the peoplemover and strode into the plaza. Hell of a thing, Juanito thought. You walk into town with a man with no eyes walking right behind you and nobody even notices. But when the sunshine comes back on it may be different.

"There he is," Farkas whispered. "To the left, maybe fifty meters, sixty."

He indicated the direction with a subtle movement of his head. Juanito peered through the purple gloom down the way, focusing on the plazafront café that lay just beyond the one in front of them. A dozen or so people were sitting in small groups at curbside tables under iridescent fiberglass awnings, drinking, chatting, taking it easy. Just another casual afternoon in good old cozy El Mirador on sleepy old Valparaiso Nuevo.

Farkas stood sideways, no doubt to keep his strange face partly concealed. Out of the corner of his mouth he said, "Wu is the one sitting by himself at the front table."

Juanito shook his head. "The only one sitting alone is a woman, maybe fifty, fifty-five years old, long reddish hair, big nose, dowdy clothes ten years out of fashion."

"That's Wu."

"How can you be so sure?"

"It's possible to retrofit your body to make it look entirely different on the outside. You can't change the nonvisual information, the data I pick up by blindsight. What Dr. Wu looked like to me, the last time I saw him, was a cubical block of black metal polished bright as a mirror, sitting on top of a pyramid-shaped copper-colored pedestal. I was nine years old then, but I promised myself I wouldn't ever forget what he looked like, and I haven't. That's exactly what the person sitting over there by herself looks like."

Juanito stared. He still saw a plain-looking woman in a rumpled old-fashioned suit. They did wonders with retrofitting these days, he knew: they could make almost any sort of body grow on you, like clothing on a clothes rack, by fiddling with your DNA. But still Juanito had trouble thinking of that woman over there as a sinister Chinese gene-splicer in disguise, and he had even more trouble seeing her as a polished cube sitting on top of a coppery pyramid.

He could practically feel the force of the hatred that was radiating from Farkas, though. So he knew that this must really be the one. The eyeless man was going to exact a terrible vengeance for the thing that had been done to him at birth, the thing that had set him apart from all the rest of the human race.

"What do you want to do now?" Juanito asked.

"Let's go over and sit down alongside her. Keep that spike of yours ready. But I hope you don't need to use it."

"If we put the arm on her and she's not Wu," Juanito said uneasily, "it's going to get me in a hell of a lot of trouble, particularly if she's paying El Supremo for sanctuary. Sanctuary people get very stuffy when their privacy is violated. She could raise a stink and before she's finished with us you'll be expelled and I'll be fined a fortune and a half and I might wind up getting expelled too, and then what? Where would I live, if I had to leave here? Have you thought about that?"

"Don't worry so much," Farkas said. "That's Dr. Wu, all right. Watch him react when he sees me, and then you'll believe it."

"We'll still be violating sanctuary. All he has to do is yell for the Guardia Civil."

"We would need to make it clear to him right away," said Farkas, "that that would be a foolish move. You follow?"

"But I'm not supposed to hurt him," Juanito said.

"No. Not in any fashion do you hurt him. All you do is demonstrate a willingness to hurt him if that should become necessary." Farkas nodded almost imperceptibly toward the woman at the front table of the café. "Let's go, now. You sit down first, ask politely if it's okay for you to share the table, make some little comment about the eclipse. I'll come over maybe thirty seconds after you. All clear? Good boy. Go ahead, now."

* * *

"You have to be insane," the red-haired woman said, sounding really testy. But she was sweating in an astonishing way and her fingers were knotting together like anguished snakes. "I'm not any kind of doctor and my name isn't Wu or Fu or whatever it was that you said, and you have exactly two seconds to get yourself away from me." She seemed unable to take her eyes from Farkas's smooth blank forehead. Juanito realized that he had grown used to the strangeness of that face by this time, but to other people Farkas must seem like a monstrosity.

Farkas didn't move. After a moment the woman said in a different tone of voice, sounding more calm, merely curious now, "What sort of thing are you, anyway?"

She isn't Wu, Juanito decided.

The real Wu wouldn't have asked a question like that. The real Wu would have *known*. And fled. Besides, this was definitely a woman. She was absolutely convincing around the jaws, along the hairline, the soft flesh behind her chin. Women were different from men in all those places. Something about her wrists, too. The way she sat. A lot of other things. There weren't any genetic surgeons good enough to do a retrofit this convincing. Juanito peered at her eyes, trying to see the place where the Chinese fold had been, but there wasn't a trace of it. Her eyes were blue gray. All Chinese had brown eyes, didn't they? Not that that would have been hard to fix, Juanito thought.

Farkas said in a low, taut voice, leaning in close and hard, "You know exactly what sort of thing I am, doctor. My name is Victor Farkas. I was born in Tashkent during the Second Breakup. My mother was the wife of the Hungarian consul, and you did a gene-splice job on the fetus she was carrying. That was your specialty back then, tectogenetic reconstruction. You don't remember that? You deleted my eyes and gave me blindsight in place of them, doctor."

The woman looked down and away. Color came to her cheeks. Something heavy seemed to be stirring within her. Juanito began to change his mind again. Maybe there really were some gene surgeons who could do a retrofit this good, he thought.

"None of this is true," the woman said. "I've never heard of you and I was never in whatever place it was you mentioned. You're nothing but a lunatic. I can show you who I am. I have papers. You have no right to harass me like this."

"I don't want to hurt you in any way, doctor."

"I am not a doctor."

"Could you be a doctor again? For a price?"

Juanito swung around, astounded, to look at Farkas. This was a twist he hadn't expected.

The tall man was smiling pleasantly. Leaning forward, waiting for an answer.

"I will not listen to this," the woman said. "You will go away from me this instant or I summon the patrol."

Farkas said, "Listen to me very carefully, Dr. Wu. We have a project that could be of great interest to you. I represent an engineering group that is a division of a corporation whose name I'm sure you know. Its work involves an experimental spacedrive, the first interstellar voyage, faster-than-light travel. The estimate is that the program is three years away from a launch. Perhaps four."

The woman rose. "This madness is of no importance to me."

"The faster-than-light field distorts vision," Farkas went on. He didn't appear to notice that she was standing and looked about ready to bolt. "It disrupts vision entirely, in fact. Perception becomes totally abnormal. A crew with normal vision wouldn't be able to function in any way. But it turns out that someone with blindsight can adapt fairly easily to the peculiar changes that the field induces. As you see, I would be ideally fitted for a voyage aboard such a vessel, and indeed I have been asked to take part in the first experimental trip."

"I have no interest in hearing about—"

"The spacedrive has been tested, actually. Ground tests, strictly preliminary, no distance covered, but the theoretical results are extremely encouraging. With me as the subject. So we are quite confident that the project is going to work out. But I can't make the voyage alone. We have a crew of five and they've volunteered for tectogenetic retrofits to give them what I have. We don't know anyone else who has your experience in that area. We'd like you to come out of retirement, Dr. Wu."

This was not at all the way Juanito had expected the meeting to go. He was altogether off balance.

Farkas was saying, "We've set up a complete lab for you on a nearby habitat, already containing whatever equipment you're likely to need, though anything else you want, you just have to ask. We'll pay you very well, of course. And ensure your personal safety all the time you're gone from Valparaiso Nuevo. What do you say? Do we have a deal?"

The red-haired woman was trembling and slowly backing away. Farkas didn't seem to notice her movements.

"No," she said. "It was such a long time ago. Whatever skills I once had, I have forgotten, I have buried."

So Farkas had been right all along, Juanito thought. No question about it. This was his Dr. Wu.

"You can give yourself a refresher course," Farkas said. "I don't think it's possible really for a person to forget a great gift like yours, do you?"

"No. Please. Let me be."

Juanito was amazed at how cockeyed his whole handle on the situation had been from the start. He had had it all wrong, that entire scenario of revenge. He had rarely been so wrong in his life. Farkas hadn't come here with the idea of evening the score with Wu, Juanito saw now. Just to cut a deal, apparently. On behalf of Kyocera-Merck. Farkas didn't give a shit about revenge. He wasn't at all angry about what the gene surgeon had done to him long ago, no.

He was even more alien than Juanito had thought.

"What do you say?" Farkas asked again.

Instead of replying, the woman—Wu—took a further couple of steps backward. She—he—whatever—seemed to be poised, getting ready to bolt in another second or two.

"Where's he going?" Farkas said suddenly. "Don't let him get away, Juanito."

Wu was still retreating, moving faster now, not quite running but sidling away at a steady pace, back into the enclosed part of the café. Farkas gestured sharply and Juanito began to follow. The spike he was carrying could deliver a stun-level jolt at fifteen paces. But he couldn't just spike Wu down in this crowd, not if she had sanctuary protection, not in El Mirador of all places. There'd be fifty sanctuarios on top of him in a minute. They'd grab him and club him and sell his foreskin to the Generalissimo's men for two and a half callies.

The café was crowded and dark. Juanito caught sight of the woman somewhere near the back, near the rest rooms. Go on, he thought. Go into the ladies' room. I'll follow you right in there if you do. I don't give a damn about that.

But she went on past the rest rooms and ducked into an alcove near the kitchen instead. Two waiters laden with trays came by, scowling vehemently at Juanito, telling him to get out of the way. It took him a moment to pass around them, and by then he could no longer see the red-haired woman. He knew he was going to have big trouble with Farkas if he lost her in here. Farkas was going to have a fit. Farkas would try to stiff him on this week's pay, most likely. Two thousand callies down the drain, not even counting the extra charges.

Then a hand reached out of the shadows and seized his wrist with surprising ferocity. Juanito was dragged a little way into a claustrophobic games room dense with crackling green haze coming from some bizarre machine on the far wall. The red-haired woman glared at him, wild-eyed.

"He wants to kill me, doesn't he? That's all a bunch of shit about having me do retrofit operations, right?"

"I think he means it," Juanito said.

"Nobody would volunteer to have his eyes replaced with blindsight."

"How would I know? People do all sorts of crazy things. But if he wanted to kill you I think he'd have operated differently when we tracked you down."

"He'll get me off Valparaiso and kill me somewhere else."

"I don't know," Juanito said. "He keeps his plans to himself. I'm just doing a job."

"How much did he pay you to do the trace?" Savagely. "How much?" A quick darting glance downward. "I know you've got a spike in your pocket. Just leave it there and answer me. How much?"

"Three thousand callies a week," Juanito muttered, padding things a little.

"I'll give you five to help me get rid of him."

Well, that was a switch. But Juanito hesitated. Sell Farkas out? He didn't know if he could turn himself around that fast. Was it the professional thing to do, to take a higher bid?

"Eight," he said, after a moment.

Why the hell not? He didn't owe Farkas any loyalty. This was a sanctuary world; the compassion of El Supremo entitled Wu to protection here. It was every citizen's duty to shield his fellow citizens from harm. And eight thousand callies was a big bundle of money.

"Six five," Wu said.

"Eight, or no deal. Handshake right now. You have your glove?"

The woman who had been Dr. Wu Fang-shui made a sour muttering sound and pulled out her flex terminal. "Account 1133," Juanito said, and they made the transfer of funds. "How do you want to do this?" Juanito asked.

"There is a passageway into the outer shell just behind this café. You will catch sight of me slipping in there and the two of you will follow me. When we are all inside and he is coming toward me, you get behind him and take him down with your spike. And we leave him buried in there." There was a frightening gleam in Wu's eyes. It was almost as if the cunning retrofit body was melting away and the real Wu beneath was emerging, moment by moment. "You understand?" Wu said. A fierce, blazing look. The face of a dithering old woman, but the eyes of a devil. "I have bought you, boy. I expect you to stay bought when we are in the shell. Do you understand me? Do you? Good."

▼   ▼   ▼

CARPENTER WAS THE first to reach the restaurant. The trip across the bay had been quicker than he expected. He waited out in front for Rhodes, pacing up and down in the white midday glare. The restaurant was a series of small perspex domes nestling along the rim of the seawall that protected lowland Berkeley from further incursions by the bay. They looked like clumps of gleaming fungi.

Half the Berkeley flatlands had been gobbled by the rising water in the first big surges forty or fifty years back, and at low tide, so Carpenter understood, it was possible to glimpse the tops of the old drowned buildings sticking up out of the glistening microorganism-stained surface of the bay. But there hadn't been any serious new flooding here since the seawall had been put in. The West Coast had come off pretty well, generally speaking, in the great drowning of the shorelines, which had happened in a highly erratic way around the world: catastrophic in China and Japan and Bangladesh, and also the eastern United States, especially Florida, Georgia, the Carolina coast, but only a minor annoyance in Western Europe—except in Holland, Denmark, and the Baltic countries, which were pretty much gone—and no big deal along the Pacific side of the Americas, either. Now they said that the present phase of the melting of the polar ice caps was essentially complete: what remained of them was going to stay frozen, at least for the immediate future, so there was nothing more to fear from the rising of the planetary water levels. That was always nice to hear, Carpenter thought, that there was nothing more to fear. In any context at all. Even if it wasn't true.

The noon sun was fierce and big and the air was, as usual, like thick soup. Rhodes was late, not unusual for him. Carpenter, fidgeting in the sticky heat, walked up the ramp leading up to the seawall, flapping his shirt to cool himself and tugging at his face-lung where it was clinging, warm and clammy, to his cheek.

He stared out at the fine old bridges and the broad bay, green and blue and violet with its skin of tropical pond scum, and at the glistening elegance of San Francisco across the way, and the dark heavy bulk of Mount Tamalpais off to the north. Then he looked around the other way, at the Berkeley-Oakland hills, heavily built over but still showing big grassy areas.

All the grass was brown and withered and dead looking, but Carpenter knew from childhood experience that it would spring up in fresh green life within a week or two, once the winter rains came. The trouble was that the winter rains didn't seem to come here very often, any more. It was an endless summer all up and down the coast, year in, year out. Whereas former deserts like those in the Middle East and northern Africa were blessed now with sweet downpourings of precipitation as never before, and the whole southeastern arc of the United States from East Texas to Florida had turned into one enormous rain forest, strangling under a phantasmagorical burden of colossal furry vines and great clumps of orchids and gigantic creeping plants with shiny leaves.

"There you are," said a deep, husky voice behind him. "I've been looking all over the place."

Nick Rhodes grinned at him from the foot of the seawall ramp. He had risen up out of nowhere, it seemed. Rhodes was maskless, wearing an airy-looking white cotton djellaba imprinted with bold Egyptian motifs. His tight, curling brown hair had begun to turn gray and had receded considerably at his temples since Carpenter had last seen him, and he looked tired and eroded. His round face had become fleshy, almost puffy. There was a feeling of forced exuberance about his grin, Carpenter thought. Something was wrong. Definitely wrong.

"Herr Doktor," Carpenter said. "Here at last. The soul of punctuality, as ever." He descended to Rhodes and put out his hand. Rhodes caught it and reeled him in and gave him an effusive bear hug, cheek to cheek. Carpenter was a tall man, but Rhodes was a little taller and very much broader and deeper, and the hug was a crusher.

They stepped back, then, and surveyed each other. They had known each other all their lives, more or less. Rhodes, two years older, had been an early friend of Carpenter's slightly older brother, originally, in their distant Southern California boyhoods. By the time they had reached adolescence Rhodes had become a little too dreamy, a little too vulnerable, for the older Carpenter, but he had clicked in some mysterious way with Paul.

They had followed parallel tracks all through life, both entering the giant Samurai Industries combine soon after college, the one difference being that Rhodes had real scientific ability and Carpenter's main areas of intellectual interest lay in soft fields like history and anthropology, where there were no real career possibilities at all. So Rhodes had gone in for genetic bioengineering, a potent fast-slope path for which the Company would underwrite his graduate work and subsequent research, and Carpenter had signed on as an unspecialized executive trainee, which he knew would carry him to an unpredictable, constantly shifting series of enterprises, completely at the whim of his employer. Through all the twists and turns of their lives ever since they had managed to maintain a tenuous but nevertheless tenacious sort of friendship.

"Well," Carpenter said. "It's been quite a while."

"So it has, Paul. What a treat this is. I have to tell you, you look great."

"Do I? Life in fabulous Spokane. The wine, the women, the fragrance of the flowers. And you? Everything going well? The life, the work?"

"Wonderful."

Carpenter couldn't tell if there was irony in that. He suspected there was.

"Let's go inside," he said. "You must be crazy, coming out without a breathing-mask. Or else you've had your lungs retrofitted with vanadium steel."

"This isn't your Inland Empire, Paul. We have actual sea breezes here. It's safe to let unfiltered air into your lungs."

"Is it, now?" Carpenter unclipped his face-lung and pocketed it, with some relief. The whole mask thing, he suspected, was a paranoid overreaction, anyway. Places like Memphis, yes, Cleveland, St. Louis, you wanted to hide behind as much filtering as you could, if you had to be outdoors. The ruinous air there hit you like a knife, scalpeling right down through your lungs into your gut. But the Bay Area? Rhodes was right. The whole world hadn't quite become unlivable yet. Not quite.

Rhodes seemed well known in the restaurant. The place was busy, but the maître d', a silky-voiced android of vaguely Oriental appearance, greeted him with a stagy overabundance of warmth and led them at once to what must have been a choice table, high up in the middle dome with a terrific view of the water. "What will you drink?" Rhodes asked, the moment they were seated.

Carpenter, caught by surprise, asked for a beer. Rhodes ordered a whiskey on the rocks. Both drinks came almost at once and Carpenter noticed with interest how quickly Rhodes went to work on it, and how rapidly he proceeded to put it away.

"An iceberg skipper," Rhodes said, bringing up menus for them both on the table visor. "Whatever gave you the idea of doing that?"

"It was handed to me. Woman I know in Personnel, working out of Paris. She said there was slope in it. Hell, even if there wasn't, Nick. I hated Spokane. So I move along. I do this, I do that, whatever the

Company says. Your basic uncomplaining salaryman. Jack of all trades, master of each, sooner or later."

"Weather forecaster, weren't you, this last time?"

Carpenter nodded. Somehow a second round of drinks had arrived. He hadn't seen Rhodes order them. He still hadn't finished his first beer.

"What about you, Nick? Continuing to steam away on Project Frankenstein, are you?"

"Easy," Rhodes said. He looked hurt. "Cuts a little close."

"Sorry."

"I hear enough crap from my humanist friends here about the diabolical implications of my research. It gets a little tiresome, being a villain to your friends."

"I don't understand," said Carpenter. "Why a villain?"

Rhodes made quotation marks in the air with his fingers. " 'Changing the human race into something grotesque and hideous, something that can scarcely be deemed human at all. Creating a new species of sci-fi monsters.' "

Carpenter took a long, reflective pull of the first beer, finishing it, and contemplated the second one. He began to think it would be a good idea to shift to something stronger for the next round.

Carefully he said, "You aren't doing any such thing, though. You're simply trying to develop some useful anatomical modifications to meet the really heavy conditions that are waiting for us somewhere down the road. Right?"

"Right."

"Then why—"

"Do we have to talk about this?" Rhodes said, a little snappishly. "I just want to relax, to get the fuck away from—" He looked up. "I'm sorry. You were just asking questions. And the answer is, no, I'm not actually setting out to create monsters in human form. Or even inhuman form. I'm just trying to use my knowledge for the good of humanity, pretentious as that may sound. The monsters are already here, anyway. Out there."

He pointed through the curving perspex, toward the bay.

"I don't get you," Carpenter said.

"You see those low green humps just off shore? Monster algae, is what they are. Something new, some kind of mutant species, a foot wide and God knows how many yards long. They arrived a couple of years ago, from Monterey. The bay is choked with them. They grow a yard a month. The Bay Environmental Commission has brought in dugongs to feed on them in the hope of clearing the waterway a little."

"Dugongs?"

"Herbivorous aquatic mammals, from the Indian Ocean. Ugly as shit, but harmless. They're stupid looking and practically blind. They eat seaweed as if it was candy. You can see them lying around in the algae beds gobbling like pigs in clover. The trouble is that the crocodiles like to eat *them* a whole lot."

"Crocodiles," said Carpenter dully.

"In San Francisco Bay, yes. They finally made it up here from Los Angeles, and they love it."

"I can't believe it. Crocodiles up here!"

"You better believe it. They'll be in Puget Sound next."

Carpenter stared. He knew that crocodiles had been making a comeback as the global climate warmed. Even when he was a boy they had started crawling up out of Mexico toward San Diego. In a world where most wildlife was on the skids, practically everything desperately sliding toward extinction, there was a sudden bizarre boom in obsolete Mesozoic reptiles.

They were all over sweltering super-tropical Florida, of course—what little had survived of it after the sinking of the shoreline. You couldn't pee in Florida without seeing a crocodile grinning up at you out of the bowl. But California? Crocs in San Francisco Bay? It had never been that way. It was an abomination.

"And then we get tyrannosaurs?" Carpenter asked.

"I doubt that very much. But what we do have is nutty enough as it is. The bay is full of giant seaweed and giant seaweed-eating dugongs and giant dugong-eating crocodiles, and here they have the gall to tell me that *I'm* making monsters. With monsters all around us and more arriving every day. Jesus Christ, Paul, it drives me crazy!" Rhodes smiled almost sheepishly, as though to take the impetus out of his outburst. He had always been a very self-effacing man, Carpenter thought. Something must really be eating at him to make him complain like this.

Neither of them had glanced at their menus, yet.

"It's been a shitty day," Rhodes said, after a moment, in a quieter tone. "A little problem in my department. One of those steely little completely amoral kids who happens to be a genius, got his doctorate at nineteen, that sort of kid, and he's come up with something now, or says he has, a substitute for hemoglobin that'll thrive on lethal metallic salts. His scheme as currently set forth is full of huge assumptions and speculative leaps. But if it works, it'll lead the way to a total redesign of the body that'll enable us to cope with almost any sort of environmental crap that's heading our way."

"And what's the problem? Isn't it going to work?"

"The problem is that it just might. I figure the odds against it are ninety-nine to one. But long shots sometimes do come through, don't they?"

"And if this one does—?"

"If it does," Rhodes said, "we really *will* wind up with a world full of sci-fi monsters instead of human beings. You change the hemoglobin, that means changing the basic chemical makeup of the blood, and then the heart-lungs interface has to be modified, and the lungs need to go some other route anyway because of the atmospheric changes, maybe turn them into book-lungs like spiders have, and then too the kidneys will need rearrangement, and that leads to modification of the skeletal structure because of calcium differentials, and then—" Rhodes caught his breath. "Oh, shit, Paul, when it's all done we have a creature that may be very nicely adapted to the new conditions, but what kind of thing is it, really? Can you still call it human? I'm scared. I'm tempted to have this kid transferred to Siberia to raise cucumbers, before he can fill in the missing pieces in his puzzle and bring his goddamn idea off."

Carpenter felt confused. But the confusion, he sensed, was really in Nick Rhodes.

"I don't want to bug you about any of this," he said. "But you told me five minutes ago that your goal is to work for humanity as the planet changes around us."

"Yes. But I want us to stay human."

"Even if the world becomes unfit for human life?"

Rhodes looked away. "I see the contradiction. I can't help it. All this is making me very uneasy. On the one hand I believe that what I'm doing is fundamentally necessary for human survival, and on the other hand I'm frightened of the deeper implications of my own work. So I'm really marching in two directions at once. But I go along like a good soldier, doing my research, winning little victories and trying not to ask the big questions. And then a kid like this Alex Van Vliet breaks through to the next plateau, or seems to, or at any rate claims that he has, and forces me to contemplate the ultimate issues. Shit. Let's order lunch, Paul."

Almost at random, Carpenter punched out things on the table computer. A hamburger, some fries, coleslaw, nice antique food, probably all of it synthetic or recycled out of squid and algae, but that didn't matter to him just now. He wasn't very hungry.

Rhodes, he observed, had conjured up yet another set of drinks. He seemed to take in alcohol at a steady-state clip, inhaling it like air, without ever showing much effect.

So he was a drinker now. Too bad. Basically, though, nothing had changed for Rhodes, Carpenter saw, in all the time that had gone on since their school days. Back then, Rhodes had often come to Carpenter for advice and a sort of protection from his tendency to fuck up his own head. Though Carpenter was younger than Rhodes, he had always felt like the older of the two, the more capable at meeting the problems of daily living. Rhodes had a way of entangling himself in intricate moral complexities of his own making—involving girls, his developing political consciousness, his teachers, his hopes and plans for the future, a million and one things—and Carpenter, pragmatic and direct, had known how to lead the older boy through the mazes he could not stop weaving about himself. Now Rhodes was a famous scientist, high in the esteem of the Company bigwigs, rising in grade on the steepest of slopes, probably earning ten times what Carpenter made; but Carpenter sensed that inwardly everything was pretty much the same for Rhodes as it had been when they were in their teens. Just a big helpless kid blundering through a world that was always a little too complicated for him to handle.

It seemed like a good idea to change the subject to something lighter. Carpenter said, "How's your social life? You haven't gotten married again, have you?"

Mistake, he realized instantly. Dumb.

"No," Rhodes said, and it was obvious how much the question

troubled him. Carpenter saw too late that the collapse of Rhodes' marriage, which had injured him so deeply eight years back, still must be a bleeding wound for him. Rhodes had been terribly in love with his wife, and he had taken a terrible beating when she left him. "I'm in a relationship. A somewhat difficult one. Beautiful, intelligent, sexy woman, very articulate. We don't agree on everything."

"Does anyone?"

"She's a radical humanist. Old San Francisco tradition, you know. Hates my work, fears its potential, would like to see the laboratory shut down, etc., etc. Not that she sees any alternative, mind you, but she's against it all the same. The pure reactionary trip, the complete know-nothing antiscientism, absolutely medieval. And yet we managed to fall in love. Aside from the politics, we do just fine. I wish you could get a chance to meet her while you're in town."

"I'm sure we could work that out," Carpenter said. "I'd like that very much."

"I would too." Rhodes thought for a moment. "Hey, how about tonight? Isabelle and I are having dinner with some pest of an Israeli newsman who wants to ask me nosy things about my work. I could pick you up over in the city somewhere around quarter to eight, at your hotel. Or wherever. How does your schedule look?"

"I've got to get back across to Frisco and over to the Samurai office at half past three to receive some of my indoctrination material," Carpenter said. "That should take me until around five. After that, nothing."

"You want to join us, then?"

"Why not? I'm at the Marriott Hilton in China Basin: you know where that is?"

"Sure."

"One thing, though. If this is an interview, are you certain that I won't be in the way?"

"It might be helpful if you were, actually. The truth is, I'm scared stiff of telling the Israeli things I shouldn't say. He's probably damn good at worming them out. Having friends around will dilute the conversation. The more the merrier, I figure, to keep things from getting down to real stuff. That's why I'm bringing Isabelle along. And now you." Rhodes put his glass down and shot Carpenter a curious look. "For that matter I could get you a date, if you like. Friend of Isabelle's, very attractive, somewhat screwed-up woman named Jolanda Bermudez. A dancer, I think, or a sculptor, or both."

Carpenter chuckled. "Last time I had a blind date was when I was thirteen."

"I remember. What was her name? With the freckles?"

"I don't recall."

"Shall I see if Jolanda wants to come along also?" Rhodes asked.

"Sure," said Carpenter. "Why not? The more the merrier, as you say."

THE SHELL OF the El Mirador segment of Valparaiso Nuevo was actually a double one, a huge hollow crawl space entirely surrounding the globe that was El Mirador. Around the periphery of the shell's spaceward face was a deep layer of lunar slag held in place by centrifugal forces, the tailings that had been left over after the extraction of the gases and minerals that had been needed in the construction of the satellite world. On top of that was a low open area for the use of maintenance workers, lit by a trickle of light from a faint line of incandescent bulbs; and overhead was the inner skin of El Mirador itself, shielded by the slagpile from any surprises that might come ricocheting in from the void. Juanito, who was compactly built, was able to move almost upright within the shell, but long-legged Farkas, following along behind, had to bend double, scuttling like a crab.

"Can you see him yet?" Farkas asked.

"Somewhere up ahead, I think. It's pretty dark in here."

"Is it?"

Juanito caught a glimpse of Wu off to the right, edging sideways, moving slowly around behind Farkas now. In the dimness the doctor was barely visible, just the shadow of a shadow. Wu had scooped up two handfuls of tailings. Evidently he was going to fling them at Farkas to attract his attention, and then when Farkas turned toward Wu it would be Juanito's moment to nail him with the spike.

Juanito stepped back to a position near Farkas's left elbow. He slipped his hand into his pocket and rested his fingertips on the butt of the cool sleek little weapon. The intensity stud was down at the lower end, shock level, and without taking the spike from his pocket he moved the setting up to lethal. Across the way, Wu nodded.

Time to do it.

Juanito began to draw the spike.

At that moment, before Juanito could manage to pull the weapon out, before Wu even could hurl his tailings, Farkas let out a roar like a wild creature going berserk. Juanito grunted in shock, stupefied by that terrible sound. This is all going to go wrong, he realized. In that same instant Farkas whirled and seized him around the waist in a powerful grip, lifting him off his feet with no apparent effort at all. In one smooth and almost casual motion Farkas swung him as if he was a throwing-hammer and released him, sending him hurtling on a rising arc through the air to crash with tremendous impact into Wu's midsection.

Wu crumpled, gagging and puking, with Juanito sprawled stunned on top of him.

Then the lights went out—Farkas must have reached up and yanked the conduit loose—and then Juanito found himself lying with his cheek jammed into the rough floor of tailings, unable to move. Farkas was holding him face-down with a hand clamped around the back of his neck and a knee pressing hard against his spine. Wu lay alongside him, pinned the same way.

"Did you think I couldn't see him sneaking up on me?" Farkas asked. "Or you, going for your spike? It's 360 degrees, the blindsight. Something that Dr. Wu must have forgotten. All these years on the run, I guess you start to forget things."

Holy Mother of Jesus, Juanito thought.

Couldn't even get the drop on a blind man from behind him. And now he's going to kill me. What a goddamned stupid way to die this is.

He imagined what Kluge might say about this, if he knew. Or Delilah. Nattathaniel. Decked by a blind man. Jesus! Stupid. Stupid. Stupid. But he isn't blind, Juanito thought. Not really. He isn't blind at all.

Farkas said, in a low harsh voice thick with anger, "How much did you sell me to him for, Juanito?"

The only sound Juanito could make was a muffled moan. His mouth was choked with sharp bits of slag.

Farkas gave him a poke with his knee. "How much? Five thousand? Six?"

"It was eight," said Wu quietly, from below.

"At least I didn't go cheaply," Farkas murmured. He reached into Juanito's pocket and withdrew the spike. "Get up," he said. "Both of you. Stay close together. If either of you makes a funny move I'll kill you both. Remember that I can see you very clearly. I can also see the door through which we entered the shell. That starfish-looking thing over there, with streamers of purple light pulsing from it. We're going back into El Mirador now, and there won't be any surprises, will there? Will there? You try to bolt, either one of you, and I'll spike you on lethal and take it up with the Guardia Civil afterward."

Juanito sullenly spit out a mouthful of slag. He didn't say anything.

"Dr. Wu? The offer still stands," Farkas continued. "You come with me, you do the job we need you for. That isn't so bad a deal, considering what I could do to you for what you did to me. But all I want from you is your skills, and that's the truth. You are going to need that refresher course, aren't you, though?"

Wu muttered something indistinct.

Farkas said, "You can practice on this boy, if you like. Try retrofitting him for blindsight first, and if it works, you can do our crew people, all right? He won't mind. He's terribly curious about the way I see things, anyway. Aren't you, Juanito, eh? So we'll give him a chance to find out firsthand." Farkas laughed. To Juanito he said, "If everything works out the right way, maybe we'll let you go along on the voyage with us, boy." Juanito felt the cold nudge of the spike in his back. "You'd like that, wouldn't you? The first trip to the stars? You'd go down in history. What do you say to that, Juanito? You'd be famous."

Juanito didn't answer. His tongue was still rough with slag, and he was so far gone, altogether lost in fear and chagrin, that he did not even attempt to speak. With Farkas prodding him from behind, he shambled slowly along next to Dr. Wu toward the door that Farkas said looked like a starfish. It didn't look at all like a fish to him, or a star, or like a fish that looked like a star. It looked like a door to him, as far as he could tell by the feeble light of the distant bulbs. That was all it looked like, a door that looked like a door. Not a star. Not a fish. But there was no use thinking about it, or anything else, not now, not with Farkas nudging him between the shoulder blades with his own spike. He let his mind go blank and kept on walking.

Emerging from the habitat's shell into the plaza of El Mirador again, Farkas very quickly took cognizance of everything around him: the ring of jolly little cafés, the flowing fountain in the middle, the statue of Don Eduardo Callaghan, El Supremo, benignly looming down to the right. Seeing everything in its blindsight equivalent, of course: the cafés as a row of jiggling point-sources of shifting green light, the fountain as a fiery spear, the monument to Don Eduardo as a jutting white triangular wedge that bore the distinctively massive, craggy features of the Generalissimo.

And of course there were his two prisoners, Wu and Juanito, just in front of him. Wu—the shining polished cube atop the copper-hued pyramid—seemed calm. He had come to terms with the event that had just occurred. Juanito—half a dozen blue spheres tied together by an orange cable—was more agitated. Farkas perceived his agitation as an up-spectrum shift in the color of what Farkas called the boundary zone, which marked the Juanito-object off from the surrounding region.

"I have a call to make," Farkas told them. "Sit here quietly with me at this table. The spike is tuned and ready to use if you force me to do so. Juanito?"

"I didn't say nothing."

"I know that. I just wanted you to tell me how cooperative you intend to be. I don't want to have to kill you. But if you try something funny, I will. I'm way ahead of you on every move. You know that, don't you?"

"Yes."

"So be a good boy and sit right there, and if you see any of your little friends come through the plaza, don't try to send any sort of signals to them. Because I'll notice what you're doing and it'll be the last thing you ever do. Clear?"

"Look," Juanito said miserably, "you can just let me get up and walk out of here and we don't ever need to have anything to do with each other ever again. I got no interest in making any trouble for you."

"No," Farkas said. "You tried to fuck me, boy. You were working for me and you sold me out. I make it a rule to punish behavior like that very severely. You aren't walking away from this in one piece." He looked toward Wu. "And you, doctor? I'm willing to make an exception for you to my general rule of retribution, for you, if you cooperate. Of course, I'll leave the choice up to you, but I think I know how you would prefer matters to go. You would rather work for Kyocera-Merck for a short time at a fine salary in a nicely furnished laboratory, wouldn't you, than have me show you in great detail how displeased I am at what you did to my eyes when I was still a fetus, and how extremely vindictive I'm capable of being. Wouldn't you, doctor?"

"I told you already," Wu muttered. "We have a deal."

"Good. Very good."

A public communicator wand in a clip was fastened to the side of the table. Without taking his attention off Wu and Juanito, Farkas picked the wand up, using his left hand because his right was holding the spike, and punched in the number of Colonel Emilio Olmo of the Guardia Civil. There was a certain amount of hunt-and-seek action while the central computer tried to find him; and then an androidal voice asked for Farkas's caller identification code. Farkas gave it, adding, "This is a Channel Seventeen call." That was a request for a scrambled line. There was another little stretch of silence broken occasionally by screechy bits of electronic noise.

Then:

"Victor?"

"I just want to let you know, Emilio, that I have the merchandise in hand."

"Where are you calling from?" Olmo asked.

"The plaza in El Mirador."

"Stay there. I'll come as soon as possible. I have to talk to you, Victor."

"You *are* talking to me," Farkas said. "All I need is a couple of Guardia men to collect the consignment, right away. I'm sitting here with it right in the plaza, and I don't like having to be a cargo superintendent out in public."

"Where are you, exactly? The specific location."

To Juanito, Farkas said, "What's the name of this café?" Reading signs was often difficult for him: seeing by blindsight was not an exact equivalent of seeing by ordinary vision, a fact of which Farkas was reminded a thousand maddening times a day.

"Café La Paloma," Juanito said.

"La Paloma," Farkas told Olmo.

"*Bueno.* I'll have the plaza patrol make the pickup within two minutes. We'll collect the shipment and transfer it to the depot as arranged."

"Something you ought to know. There's an extra item of merchandise," said Farkas.

"Oh?"

"I'm sending the courier along to the depot too. Don't worry. I'll provide you with the bill of lading in proper order."

"Whatever you want, my friend," said Olmo, with a touch of mystification in his voice. "He is yours, whatever you want to do with him, and good riddance. I give him to you freely. But not free, you understand. You are aware that there may be extra shipping charges, yes?"

"That doesn't worry me."

"*Bueno.* The pickup will be made quite swiftly. You stay right there. I will come to you in person in a very little while so that we can speak. A serious matter has developed that must be discussed."

"Scrambler call isn't good enough?" Farkas asked, puzzled and a little alarmed.

"Not nearly, Victor. This must be in person. It is very delicate, very. You will stay? Café La Paloma?"

"Absolutely," Farkas said. "You can recognize me by the red carnation in my lapel."

"What?"

"A joke. Get the goddamned pickup taken care of, Emilio, will you?"

"Immediately."

"Bueno," Farkas said.

Olmo rang off. Farkas put the wand back in its slot.

Juanito said, "Was that Colonel *Olmo* you were talking to?" He sounded awed.

"Why would you think that?"

"You called him 'Emilio.' You asked for Guardia men to be sent. Who else could it have been?"

Farkas shrugged. "Colonel Olmo, yes. We occasionally do business with each other. We are friends, in a way."

"Holy Mary Mother of God," said Juanito hoarsely, and made the gesture that Farkas recognized as the sign of the cross, a lateral trembling and bucking of the middlemost pair of the six blue spheres that made up Juanito's apparent body. "You and Olmo are *friends*! You call him up just like that and he talks to you. And so I am really fucked."

"Yes. You really are," said Farkas. "*Todo jodido,* isn't that the phrase?"

"*Sí,*" Juanito said ruefully. "*Estoy jodido,* completely. Completely." He turned away and looked into the distance. A thin chuckle came from Wu. Good for him, Farkas thought. He is capable of being amused by Juanito's distress. That meant he had stopped caring about his own predicament. Farkas liked the idea that the person who had so casually and gratuitously transformed his life beyond repair, long ago, was fundamentally indifferent to circumstances, an impassive technician, a pure force of nature.

Within moments Farkas saw two shapes moving purposefully toward him from the direction in which Juanito was looking: a red tetrahedron on spiny little legs and a pair of upright emerald columns joined by three parallel golden bars. They had to be the local Guardia Civil patrol, Farkas knew. Olmo was quick. Of course, K-M paid Olmo very well for his cooperation. And Valparaiso Nuevo was a very efficient police state, and the Guardia probably had outstanding communications techniques.

"Mr.—Farkas?" The tetrahedron speaking. A little hitch in the voice, a kind of verbal flinch. Farkas knew what that was: the first sight of the eyelessness, the blank forehead, often did that to people. "Colonel Olmo sent us. Two men, he said, we were supposed to get." He sounded confused.

"I wasn't that specific with him. Two people is all that I indicated. A boy and an old woman, as it happens," said Farkas. "These two."

"Yes, sir. Glad to be of service, sir."

"Olmo made it clear to you that you aren't supposed to hurt them, right? I don't want you to hurt them. Just put them in storage until the procedures for their deportation are completed. Is that understood?"

"Yes, sir. Of course, sir."

Farkas watched them lead Juanito and Wu away.

Now that he was no longer obliged to be guarding two prisoners at once, Farkas allowed himself to relax. He sat back, stared around the cobbled plaza.

An odd emptiness came upon him.

His mission had been satisfactorily completed, yes, and with striking ease. But it was strange, having had Wu in his possession after all these years of imagining what he would do to him if he ever caught him, and doing nothing at all.

Disguised as a woman, an old dowdy woman. Well, well, well.

It would have been easy enough, back there in the musty slaggy confines of the habitat shell, to have put his thumbs on Wu's eyeballs and pushed. But of course Farkas knew that doing that would not thereby give him the normal vision that had been denied him before his birth. He wasn't even sure that he wanted normal vision, anyway, not any more; but paying Wu back would have brought him a certain degree of pleasure.

But it was also necessary to consider that that one little moment of gory self-indulgence would have destroyed his career, and his career was a very fine one, extremely rewarding in a number of ways. It wouldn't have been worth it.

And the boy—

Farkas felt no remorse about that. The boy would suffer: good. He was a treacherous little bastard who had behaved exactly as Farkas had expected him to, peddling his loyalties to the highest bidder, just as his father had done before him, apparently; and he needed a lesson. He would get one, a good one. Farkas brushed him from his mind and signaled to the waiter.

He asked for a small carafe of red wine, and sat patiently sipping it, waiting for Olmo.

It wasn't a long wait.

"Victor?"

Olmo was hovering by his shoulder. By the color he was radiating, he seemed very tense.

"I see you, Emilio. Sit down. You want some wine?"

"I never drink." Olmo arranged himself ponderously at the table, sitting at a ninety-degree angle from Farkas. It was the first time they had actually met: all their previous dealings had been by scrambled data-link. Olmo was shorter than Farkas expected him to be, but very stocky. The upper cube of the two that made up his body was wider than the lower one in a way that indicated broad shoulders and powerful forearms. When he was sitting down Olmo seemed to be quite tall, a massive presence.

Farkas imagined him at some earlier phase of his career sweatily working over the enemies of the Generalissimo in a basement room with a pliant strip of hemp: rising to his present eminence on this world from the humble ranks of the official torturers. Did El Supremo torture his enemies? Farkas wondered. Of course. All petty tyrants did. He would ask Olmo about it some time or other; but not now.

Farkas took a thoughtful sip of his wine. Local product, he supposed. Not bad at all.

He said, into an awkwardness that he was certain was caused by Olmo's discomfort over the realities of his physical appearance, "You arouse my curiosity, Emilio. Something so delicate that you won't even risk telling me about it by scrambler?"

"Indeed. I think I will have some water. It will look more casual to those who are watching us, and I know that they are, if I am drinking something too."

"Whatever you say." Farkas beckoned to the waiter.

Olmo hunched forward, cupping his glass in his hand. In a very quiet voice, more than a whisper but less than a normal conversational tone, he said, "This is strictly hearsay. The reliability of the source is questionable and the content of the rumor is so surprising that I am extremely skeptical. But I want to check it with you nonetheless. We did not, of course, have this discussion, if anyone asks."

"Of course," said Farkas impatiently.

"*Bueno.* So, then, this is the news. The possible news. Word has reached me, by, as I say, highly irregular and somewhat untrustworthy sources, that a group of criminals based in South California is getting ready to launch an insurrection against the existing authority here on Valparaiso Nuevo."

"Southern California," Farkas said.

"What?"

"*Southern* California. That's what they call it. You said *South* California."

"Ah."

"An insurrection."

"They intend to invade this world and overthrow the Generalissimo by force. Then they intend to establish their own government here, and round up all the fugitives who have taken sanctuary. And then they will sell them, for many billions of Capbloc dollars, to the various agencies and forces on Earth who would like to have them back."

"Really?" Farkas said. It was a fascinating idea. Crazy, but fascinating. "Someone actually plans to do this?"

"I have no idea. But it is something that perhaps could be done, and it would be very lucrative if it was managed in the right way."

"Yes. No doubt it would." Valparaiso Nuevo was an absolute treasure trove, a gold mine of expensively wanted fugitives. But Callaghan had to have it well defended, and himself also. Especially himself. They didn't call him the Defender for nothing. The only way to overthrow him would be to blow the whole place up. "I see why you called it a delicate matter," Farkas said. "But why are you telling me this, Emilio?"

"For one thing, if there is a threat against the life of the Generalissimo, it is my responsibility to take preventive action."

"I understand that. Still, why bring me in? Do you think I can lead you to the conspirators?"

"Perhaps."

"For God's sake, Emilio. I thought you were an intelligent man."

"Intelligent enough, I think."

"If I were involved with this thing, would I be likely to want to tell you word one about it?"

"That depends," said Olmo. "Let us look at some other factors. I have not only the Generalissimo's security to be concerned with, but also my own."

"Naturally."

"I am useful to you, or at least to your employer. Your employer is

Kyocera-Merck, Victor. You make no secret of that. Why should you? I work for K-M too, of course, although not quite so openly. Indeed, not openly at all."

"True."

"The Generalissimo has ruled Valparaiso Nuevo for thirty-seven years, Victor. He was not young when he seized power here and he is quite old now. When he goes, the Company sees it to be in its interest for me to succeed him. You knew this, didn't you?"

"More or less." Farkas was getting tired of Olmo's circuitous manner. The fracas in the outer shell had wearied him and he wanted to go back to his hotel. "Would you mind getting to the point, Emilio?"

"I've given you a great deal of help in carrying out the project the Company sent you here to do. Now you help me. It is only reasonable, one K-M man to another. Tell me the truth. Do you know anything whatsoever about this takeover conspiracy?"

Farkas found this hard to believe. He hadn't imagined Olmo to be so dumb.

"Not a thing," he said. "This is the first I've heard about it."

"You swear that?"

"Don't be stupid, Emilio. I could swear to whatever you wanted me to, and what would it matter?"

"I trust you."

"Do you? Yes, I suppose you do. You shouldn't trust anybody, but all right. If it'll make you feel any better, here: the holy truth is that I really don't know a thing about any of this. God's sacred truth. By the archangels and apostles, this is absolutely the first that I've heard of it. And I suspect that there's nothing to the rumor at all."

"No. I believe that you have spoken honestly. But what I am afraid of," said Olmo, "is that there actually is such a conspiracy, and Kyocera-Merck may be behind it. Perhaps using these California people as proxies. And that when Don Eduardo goes, I will go with him. That I have become irrelevant to the Company; that the Company has decided to discard me."

"This sounds crazy to me. So far as I know, you're as important to the Company as you've ever been. And your role in facilitating the Wu business will strengthen your position in their eyes even more."

"And the coup? Let's say that the stories I have heard have substance behind them, this South California group. Let us assume that such a group exists, and such a plan. It is your belief that they have nothing to do with K-M, then?"

"How would I know? Am I Japanese? Use your brain, Emilio. I'm just a Company expediter, Level Nine. That's pretty high up the slope but it's nowhere near policy level. The boys in New Kyoto don't call me in to share their secret plans with them."

"You think, then, that the plotters of this coup are merely a gang of free-lance criminals from South California, acting completely on their own. *Southern* California."

"God in heaven," Farkas said, exasperated now close to his limit of tolerance. "Haven't I made it sufficiently clear that all I know about this idiotic coup is the stuff you've just told me? I have no evidence that it exists at all, and apparently you don't have much yourself. But all right. All right. If it'll reassure you, Emilio, let me tell you that in my estimation the plotters, if there are any and whoever they may be, are more likely to want to cooperate with you than to put you down, if they have any sense at all, and when and if they get close to making their move on this place, the smartest thing they could possibly do would be to get in touch with you and hire you to help them overthrow the Generalissimo. You will furthermore have the backing of Kyocera-Merck in whatever happens, because K-M is interested, God knows why, in bringing this foul little orbiter into its sphere of influence and has already tapped you to be the next Generalissimo, so they are not likely to sit by idly while a bunch of free-lance gangsters from California push their chosen man out the window. Okay, Emilio? Do you feel better, now?"

Olmo was silent for a time.

Then he said, "Thank you. If you learn anything more about any of this, you will tell me, Victor?"

"Of course."

"Bueno," Olmo said, a fraction of a second before Farkas could say it for him. "I do trust you, my friend. As much as I trust anyone."

"Which is not at all, correct?"

Olmo laughed heartily. He seemed suddenly much more at his ease, after Farkas's long and irritable outburst. "I know you will do nothing to harm me unless you find it absolutely unavoidable, for your own sake, to turn against me."

"That sounds right enough."

"Yes. Yes."

"So you will let me know, if you hear from anyone about this plot?"

"Jesus! I've already said I would. Under the terms you've just laid out. Does that satisfy you?"

"Yes."

"Then we can get back to the business at hand, all right? You agree to see to it that Wu and Juanito get shipped off promptly to the K-M lab satellite, as the Company has directed us to arrange. Yes?"

"Absolutely."

"*Bueno*," Farkas said. And they both laughed.

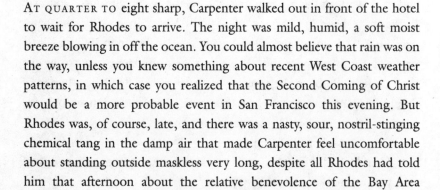

AT QUARTER TO eight sharp, Carpenter walked out in front of the hotel to wait for Rhodes to arrive. The night was mild, humid, a soft moist breeze blowing in off the ocean. You could almost believe that rain was on the way, unless you knew something about recent West Coast weather patterns, in which case you realized that the Second Coming of Christ would be a more probable event in San Francisco this evening. But Rhodes was, of course, late, and there was a nasty, sour, nostril-stinging chemical tang in the damp air that made Carpenter feel uncomfortable about standing outside maskless very long, despite all Rhodes had told him that afternoon about the relative benevolence of the Bay Area atmosphere. He went back inside and stood there peering out through the lobby portholes. Rhodes finally showed up around ten after eight.

He was driving a big, broad-nosed car, an antiquated-looking job extremely full of people. Carpenter got in back, next to a hefty Latin-looking woman with an immense mass of dark, tumbling hair, who flashed him a huge, beacon-bright, improbably glossy smile. Her eyes had a sheen and protrusiveness that said immediately to Carpenter that she was a heavy hyperdex user. She seemed about to introduce herself; but before she could say a thing a stocky, swarthy-faced man on the other side of her reached his hand across her, seizing Carpenter's with a startlingly aggressive grip, and said loudly, in a deep, robust voice, faintly tinged with a European accent of some unspecifiable sort, "I am Meshoram Enron. I am from Israel."

As if I couldn't guess, Carpenter thought.

"Paul Carpenter," he said. "Friend of Dr. Rhodes. Childhood friend, in fact."

"Very good. I am extremely pleased to make your acquaintance, Dr. Carpenter. I write for *Cosmos,* on scientific and technological matters. You know this magazine? It is one of the biggest. I am with the Tel Aviv office. I have arrived from Israel only the day before yesterday, especially to talk with your friend."

Carpenter nodded, wondering how often Enron began a sentence with anything except the first-person-singular pronoun. One out of three? One out of five?

"And I'm Jolanda," said the big woman with the hair and the smile and the hyperdex eyes, now that Enron had subsided for the moment.

Her voice was a trained theatrical one, rich and husky, straight from the diaphragm. A cloud of pheromonal fragrance seemed to burst from her as she spoke, and Carpenter felt an immediate response in his groin. But he was too experienced to build any happy assumptions on that. Most likely she greeted everyone that way, plenty of voltage up front, nothing in particular behind it.

Rhodes said without looking back, "Paul, this is Isabelle."

The woman sitting next to Rhodes up front swiveled and flashed the swiftest of how-d'ye-do grins, a mere chilly flicker. Carpenter found himself taking an immediate irrational dislike to her. She was very attractive, he saw, in the moment before she turned away from him again; but attractive in an oddly discordant way, too much force in the eyes and too little in the rest of the face, and her great corona of wild, frizzy scarlet hair was like a shriek of disdain for the conventions of ordinary beauty. She was probably a handful and a half, Carpenter thought, on scarcely any evidence at all: an unpredictable mix of tenderness and ferocity.

He shook his head. Poor Nick. He never did have any luck with women.

"We're going over to Sausalito," Rhodes said. "Nice restaurant with a wonderful view. Isabelle and I go there a whole lot."

"Our special place," she said. Her tone was a little grating. She sounded as though she might be being sarcastic, but perhaps not. Carpenter wasn't at all sure.

But it turned out to be a fine romantic place indeed, when they finally reached it an hour later, after a harrowing drive all the way across the heart of the city and over the Golden Gate Bridge. Carpenter had forgotten how ghastly a driver Rhodes was; he kept overriding the car brain, imposing his own goofy judgment at every traffic interchange, and left a trail of astounded fellow drivers in his wake, honking madly as he passed. Hard to see how you could get lost between Frisco and Sausalito, Carpenter thought, a straight shot right across the bridge, but Rhodes kept managing to do it. The glowing colored map on his dashboard would say one thing, Rhodes persisted in saying another. The car didn't like that and the dash lit up with warning lights. Rhodes overrode them. His little expression of power.

Rhodes was smart, yes, and had lived in Berkeley long enough to believe that he knew his way around in the bigger city across the bay: but the car, old as it was, really was smarter, within its special area of competence, and it had an utterly accurate San Francisco grid in its memory tank. It went on patiently guiding Rhodes out of the western ends of the city into which he constantly seemed to be compulsively drifting, and back toward the bridge. And somehow they all survived the trip, even the overloaded and doubtless exasperated car brain; and the restaurant, nestled cozily away on a hillside above the walled-in Sausalito waterfront, gave them the warm welcome of regular customers.

Indeed the view *was* spectacular: the whole northern side of San Francisco, rising out of the bay in a dazzling brilliance of a million lights, and the floodlit splendor of the bridge.

Drinks arrived almost at once. Rhodes was very good at arranging for that, Carpenter was discovering.

"I want to make it understood," said Enron, "that the magazine is paying for this, for everything, tonight. You should not stint yourselves at all." As the foreign guest, he had a seat facing the picture window. "What a beautiful city, your San Francisco. It reminds me very much of Haifa: the hills, the white buildings, the foliage. But of course it is not so dry and dusty in Haifa. Not nearly. You have ever been in Israel, Dr. Carpenter?"

"Just *Mr.* Carpenter, please. And no, no, never."

"So beautiful. You would love it. Flowers everywhere, trees, vines. Of course all of Israel is beautiful, one big garden. A paradise. I weep when I must leave it for another place." Enron gave Carpenter a look of astonishingly intense scrutiny. His eyes were dark and fathomless and glittering with curiosity, his face angular and taut, closely shaven, the earliest black bristles of what was surely a dense Assyrian beard already poking through the carefully and recently scraped skin. "—You are with Samurai Industries also, I understand? In what capacity, may I ask?"

"Salaryman Eleven," Carpenter said. "Hoping to make Ten, one of these days. I've been up north, working as a weatherman, and now I'm about to ship out as captain of a trawler that brings icebergs to shore for the San Francisco Public Utility District. San Francisco doesn't have all the rainfall that you people in the Middle East do."

"Ah," Enron said. Carpenter saw something click shut behind his eyes. The glitter of curiosity left them. End of Enron's moment of interest in Mr. Salaryman Eleven Carpenter of Samurai Industries.

The Israeli turned to Jolanda, who was sitting between him and Carpenter. "And you, Ms. Bermudez? You are an artist, is this correct?"

Enron was interviewing everybody, it seemed.

"Mainly a sculptor, yes," she said, giving Enron another tremendous smile. She must have had fifty teeth just in front. Her face was round, full, pretty, with a wide mouth and those great bulging hyperdexy eyes standing out wondrously. "I work in bioresponsive materials, mainly. The viewer and the work of art are linked in a feedback loop, so that what you see is modified by who you intrinsically are."

"How fascinating," said Enron, all too plainly not meaning it. "I hope to experience your work very closely."

"I also do modern dance," she said. "And I've written a little poetry, though I wouldn't really call it very good, and of course I've acted. I was in *Earth Saga* in Berkeley last summer, outdoors, along the seawall. It was quite a great event for all of us, as much of an incantation as it was a theatrical performance. An incantation designed to protect the planet, I mean. We were attempting to place the audience in tune with the deeper cosmic forces that hold us in their grasp at every moment but which are so rarely apparent to us. I hope to perform it again in Los Angeles during the winter." Another wondrous smile, and she leaned toward Enron, giving him the full pheromonic blast.

"Ah," Enron said again, and Carpenter saw a second click of disengaged attention. Doubtless the Israeli would be able to find Jolanda Bermudez of interest in one obvious way or another, but he clearly had heard all he needed to about her artistic endeavors. Carpenter's own heart sank a little too. Jolanda was full of passion and energy, obviously, drug-induced or otherwise, and the notion that she might actually be a talented artist had cast a momentary aura of intense glamour over her; but Carpenter realized now that there was probably no talent here at all, very likely not even any basic ability of any sort, certainly not any common sense, just the old-fashioned nutty artiness that seemed to be a Bay Area tradition going back into the remote past. And the part about the incantation to protect the planet gave him a queasiness in the gut. Here was the future erupting about them at a mile a minute and she was still mumbling mantras out of an earlier century.

She was, all the same, a handsome woman. But Rhodes had warned him that she was screwed up, and Rhodes was probably in a position to know.

Isabelle jumped in, while Rhodes was signaling—already—for the second round of drinks, wanting to be told about Enron's magazine, whether it was published in Israeli or Arabic, or both. Enron explained to her, with what was probably great restraint, for him, that the language spoken in Israel was called *Hebrew,* not *Israeli,* and went on to let her know that *Cosmos* was, of course, published primarily in English, like all important magazines throughout the world. But its readers, he said, always had the option, with a single keystroke, of having Arabic or Hebrew text come up on the visor instead. Unbelievable as it might seem, said Enron, there were still some people in the remote reaches of the vast Judaeo-Islamic world who had not yet achieved full reading comprehension in English.

"Mostly Arabs, I suppose," Isabelle said. "There still are a lot of backward Arabs, aren't there? Like medieval people in a high-tech world?"

It was too obvious an attempt at flattery. Enron responded with a flash of contempt in his eyes and the quickest, bleakest of smiles. "Actually, no, Ms. Martine. The Arabs proper are all quite sophisticated. You must really learn to distinguish between Arabs and speakers of the Arabic language, you see. I was referring specifically to our readers in the agricultural regions of the northern Sudan and the Sahara, who are Arabic-speaking Islamics, but certainly not Arabs in any true way."

Isabelle looked flustered. "We know so little, here, of what things are really like in other parts of the world."

"Indeed," said Enron. "This is true. A great pity, the insularity of this country. I feel sorry for America. Ignorance is dangerous, in such difficult times as these. Especially the kind of ignorance that displays itself in triumphant complacency."

"Perhaps we ought to order dinner," Rhodes put in, sounding strained. "If I might make a few recommendations—"

He made more than a few. But Carpenter observed that Enron was paying almost no attention to anything Rhodes was saying. His eyes were already on the menu; he had punched choices of his own into the restaurant's data system long before Rhodes had finished. There was a certain abrasive charm about the fellow, Carpenter decided: he was gloriously offensive, all the bad things you had heard about Israeli rudeness and arrogance rolled into one—practically a stage Israeli, a ballsy little guy with such totally excessive self-esteem that you began to think it had to be an act. And yet you had to respect the intelligence, the quicksilver Darwinian adaptability, the dry playful Darwinian wit of him. A bastard, sure, but an amusing bastard, if you could be amused by someone like that. Carpenter could.

A bastard all the same, though. Playing like a cat among mice with poor beleaguered Nick and poor edgy Isabelle and poor silly Jolanda. Enjoying his domination of them a little too much. Perhaps back in Tel Aviv, among his own people, Enron might be considered a tactful and courteous guy, easygoing, even; but here, among the *goyim*, the barbarian Americans, he felt it was necessary to score points with every word he uttered. You would think that Israelis, a people who had turned up one of the few winning hands in this era of the intensifying uninhabitability of the

Earth, would be able to relax and enjoy their position of dominance, without rubbing your face in it. Not this one, apparently.

"But we should get down now to the topic of our chief concern, the great issue that has brought me here tonight," Enron said, while the others were still tapping out their dinner orders. He placed a tiny crystalline recording cube beside his plate, and activated it with a quick touch of his thumb. Then he looked slowly around the table, letting his eyes linger contemplatively on each one in turn for a long disturbing moment before they came to rest on Nick Rhodes. "My magazine," he began in a new and more formal tone, "wishes to address itself early next year to the tremendous problem that the world faces: that is, of course, the problem of the continued deterioration of our environment that is occurring despite all the palliatory measures that have been taken. A problem that is more intense in some regions than in others, but will ultimately involve us all. For there is really no hiding place, is there, anywhere on Earth? It is one small planet, is it not? And we have made it very difficult and uncomfortable for ourselves."

"More difficult for some than for others," Carpenter said.

"At present, Mr. Carpenter. At present. I agree, the shift of global rainfall patterns in my part of the world has delivered great and unexpected economic advantages to my country."

That and the general ban on fossil fuels, Carpenter thought, which had wiped out such wealth as the Arab world had been able to accumulate during the years of the world's dependence on oil and forced them to turn in desperation to their old enemies the Israelis for technological guidance.

"But it is a short-run advantage," Enron continued. "For us to say that we of the Middle East have not been harmed by the environmental challenges that are presently afflicting other areas—in fact, have greatly benefited from them—is like the passengers on the top deck of a sinking ocean liner telling each other that they have nothing to worry about, because it's only the other end of the ship that's going down, and when the people down there have drowned there'll be that much more caviar on board for us to eat." Enron, obviously pleased with his own well-worn simile, laughed enthusiastically. "Only the other end sinking! Do you see, do you see? We all breathe the same air, is that not so? Solutions must be found or we will all sink together. And so my magazine will devote an entire issue to the situation, and to the possible solutions. And you, Dr. Rhodes—your work, the extraordinary potential of your work—" Enron's eyes were glittering again. His narrow, strong-featured face was alive with predatory intelligence. Clearly he was zeroing in on his real prey, now. "We believe that your work, if we understand its purposes correctly, may hold the only answer to the salvation of the human race on Earth."

Isabelle Martine said suddenly, very loudly, "Christ, no! *No!* May God help us all if what you just said is true! Nick's work the only solution? Christ! Don't you see, his work is the fucking *problem,* not any kind of solution!"

Carpenter heard Rhodes gasp. Rhodes turned toward Isabelle in a slow numb way and gave her a sad-eyed look, as though he might be about to break into tears.

No one said anything. Even the Israeli had been startled into speechlessness by her outburst. For the first time all evening his impermeable composure seemed broken. The taut planes of his face seemed to dissolve momentarily in confusion, as though Isabelle's outburst was entirely beyond his comprehension. He blinked a couple of times and gaped at her as though she had picked up the wine bottle and sent its contents spilling forth across the middle of the table.

Finally Rhodes said, mildly, into the twanging silence of rising tension, "Ms. Martine and I have some political differences, Mr. Enron."

"Ah. Yes. Yes. So I see." The Israeli continued to seem mystified. Such a vehement public display of disloyalty to one's companion must violate even an argumentative Israeli's sense of the permissible. "But surely it is not a political matter, the saving of the human species," Enron said. "It is a matter only of doing what must be done."

"There are ways and then there are ways," said Isabelle, pointedly ignoring Rhodes' plaintive stare.

"Yes. Of course." Enron sounded bored, offended, even, by her contentiousness. He gave her another of his dismissive looks. Carpenter saw the gleam of barely suppressed fury in the Israeli's eyes. Doubtless Enron was thinking that Isabelle was going to be an obstacle to his gathering the information he needed. A pain in the ass for him, nothing more. Rhodes, who had taken on an unnerved and disconsolate air, was studying the tablecloth and industriously working on his next drink.

Carefully, controlling himself with a visible effort, Enron said to no one in particular, "Let me make the thinking of myself and my editors clear, if you will." He took a deep breath. A prepared speech was coming up, Carpenter knew. Enron was speaking for the record. "We accept the generally held scientific position that the damage to the world's environment during the industrial age is irreversible: that the uncontrolled burning of fossil fuels over a period of two or three hundred years created degrees of carbon-dioxide and nitrogen-oxide emission far beyond proper tolerance, that this has caused gradual but eventually significant global warming; that the changes in ocean temperature and pressure which have resulted from that warming have caused release of oceanic methane into the atmosphere, further exacerbating the warming patterns; and that the buildup of the so-called greenhouse gases in the atmosphere plus the locking away of additional quantities of such pollutants in ground storage and in the form of hypertrophied vegetation stimulated by a CO_2 surplus has been such that things are destined to get worse before they get better, because the stored gases that were locked away in the period of environmental abuse are destined to emerge inescapably from storage over the course of time and are in fact being released even now through ground outgassing and the decay of vegetable matter. I think this is a fair statement of the situation."

"The ozone," Carpenter said.

"Yes, of course. That, too. I should not have neglected to add that the damage to the ozone layer through the use of chlorofluorocarbons and similar substances in the twentieth century has brought about a serious intensification of incoming solar radiation, adding to the problem of global warming. Et cetera, et cetera. But I think I have sufficiently set the ground for our discussion. I need hardly go further with this summary of our many problems—to list, eh, the many various feedback mechanisms that have operated to make a bad situation worse, for example? All this is old news to you. There is no disagreement that we are entering a time of great peril."

"Completely true. The planet must be protected," said Jolanda Bermudez in a spacy voice, as though delivering news bulletins from Venus.

"I agree absolutely with Jolanda," said Isabelle Martine. "We have to come to our senses. The whole planet is in jeopardy! Something must be done to save it!"

Enron smiled icily. "I beg to disagree. The planet, Ms. Martine, is not what is in danger. It makes no difference to the planet, does it, whether the rain falls in the Sahara Desert or in the agricultural plains of the middle of North America? So the Sahara ceases to be a desert and your Kansas and Nebraska become one instead. That is very interesting for the farmers of Kansas and Nebraska and for the nomadic herdsmen of the Sahara, yes. But what is it to the planet? The planet has no use for the wheat that used to be produced in Kansas and Nebraska. The atmosphere contains much less oxygen and nitrogen than it did a century ago, and a great deal more carbon dioxide and hydrocarbons. Why should the planet be concerned? There was a time when there was no oxygen in Earth's atmosphere at all. The planet survived it quite well. The polar ice caps melt and much of the low-lying shoreline of the world is drowned. The planet is indifferent. It is all the same thing to the planet whether the Japanese live along the coast of certain islands at the edge of Asia or are forced to take refuge in other, higher places. The planet does not care about the Japanese. Nor does the planet need saving. People have been parroting this nonsense about saving the planet for I don't know how long, a hundred, a hundred fifty years. The planet will be okay. *We're* in trouble. The issue, Ms. Martine, Ms. Bermudez, is not saving the planet: it is saving ourselves. Earth will go serenely on, with or without oxygen. But we will die." Enron smiled as though he were speaking of the outcome of some sports event. "We are, of course, taking certain steps to save ourselves." He held up the fingers of his right hand and ticked items off with the index finger of his left. "Firstly, we have tried to limit our emission of the so-called greenhouse gases. Too late. They continue to emerge from their storage places in the oceans and the land surface, and nothing can hold that process back. Our air grows steadily less breathable. We are faced with the possibility that before very long we will have to evacuate Earth entirely."

"No!" Isabelle Martine cried. "What a cowardly solution that would be! The thing we need to do is to stay here and regain control of our own environment!"

"But there are those," said Enron with merciless restraint, "who are convinced that evacuation is our only recourse. And so—secondly, if I may continue, Ms. Martine—we have filled the nearby zones of outer space with dozens, hundreds, of artificial satellite worlds with agreeable artificial climates, and built a few domed encampments on Mars and the moons of Jupiter."

"I do sometimes think the habitats are really the only answer," Jolanda Bermudez said, dreamily cutting in once again. "I've often considered moving up there myself, if all else fails. Some friends of mine in Los Angeles are very interested in L-5 resettlement." She seemed to be speaking entirely to herself.

Enron, caught up in the momentum of his own monologue, ignored her. "The orbital settlements are a notable achievement; but each one has extremely limited capacity, and they are very costly to construct. Obviously we could never afford to transport the entire population of Earth to those small refuges in space. There is still another evacuation option, however, one which at the moment seems even less feasible: the proposal to discover and colonize a New Earth of planetary size in some other solar system, where human life can get a second chance."

Isabelle snorted. "That's just foolishness. A dumb crazy fantasy."

"Indeed, so it appears," said Enron reasonably. "As I understand it, we have no workable stardrive, nor have we yet been able to discover any extrasolar planets, let alone one that would be suitable for human life."

"I'm not so sure of that," Rhodes said, just barely at the threshold of audibility.

Everyone turned to look at him. Rhodes, obviously disconcerted by the attention he had drawn to himself, hastily gulped the dregs of his most recent drink and signaled for yet another.

"We have found a planet, you say?" Enron asked.

"We have a stardrive," Rhodes said. "*May* have, that is. I understand some considerable breakthroughs have been achieved lately, and that important tests are coming up."

"This stardrive—you say 'we.' It is a project of Samurai Industries, then?" Enron asked. He was perspiring, suddenly. His eyes revealed a greater degree of interest, perhaps, than he might have wanted to display.

Rhodes said, "No, actually, I was using 'we' collectively, to mean the human race in general. In fact the rumor going around is that it's

Kyocera-Merck that is well along on some sort of a starship project. Not us."

"But surely Samurai would want to be involved in a similar project too," said Enron, "if only to remain competitive."

"As a matter of fact, you're probably right," Rhodes said. And winced, as though someone had kicked him under the table. Carpenter saw him glower briefly at Isabelle. "I mean, there's a rumor to that effect going around as well," he said, after a moment, sounding newly evasive. "I wouldn't really know whether there's any substance to it. We hear things like that all the time. —Of course you understand that any kind of Samurai stardrive research would involve a completely different division of the company from mine."

"Yes. Yes, of course," said Enron. He was silent for a while, poking purposelessly at the food on his plate, obviously considering the thing that Rhodes had allowed to slip out.

Carpenter wondered whether there could be any truth to it. A stardrive? An expedition to some other solar system, a New Earth to be founded fifty light-years away? A fresh start, a second Eden. The notion momentarily dazzled him with its vastness.

But Isabelle was right, for once: there was no solution in that for Earth's problems. The idea was too wild. It would take centuries to get to any of the other stars, even if another Earth-like planet could be found somewhere; and even if one were to be found, no significant fraction of Earth's billions could be transported there. Forget about it, Carpenter told himself. It made no real sense.

Enron, recovering his poise, said, "That is very interesting, the hope of an effective stardrive. I must look into it at another time, Dr. Rhodes. But for now let us turn our attention to the final option that humanity has—the one that I have come here tonight to discuss with you. I mean, doctor, the use of gene-splicing techniques to adapt newborn children to the ever-more-poisonous atmosphere that the people of Earth will be facing."

"Not only newborns," said Rhodes. He appeared animated for the first time since they had reached the restaurant. "We're looking also into ways of retrofitting adult humans to cope with the conditions that will lie ahead."

"Ah," said Enron. "Very interesting indeed."

"We can all be monsters together," Isabelle said. "'O brave new world, that has such people in it!'"

Carpenter realized that he had been matching Rhodes drink for drink, and was very much less good than Rhodes was at dealing with that quantity of liquor.

"If I may, Ms. Martine," Enron said smoothly. He turned again toward Rhodes. "What is your timetable, doctor, for Earth's atmosphere to reach the point where the world becomes uninhabitable for human beings as they are presently constituted?"

Rhodes did not answer right away.

"Four or five generations," he said, at last. "Six at the outside."

Enron's dark eyebrows rose. "You are saying, one hundred fifty years, perhaps two hundred?"

"More or less. I wouldn't want to try to be too precise. But the figures are there. The encircling layer of greenhouse gases that surrounds us is still letting the ultraviolet come in and preventing the infrared from going out, so we bake and fry as the heat builds up. On top of that we continue to lose our ozone insulation. Strong sunlight is pouring through the hole, cooking the planet like a giant laser, accelerating all of the deleterious processes that have been under way the past couple of centuries. The seas are belching methane like a son of a bitch. The plant biota, which we used to count on to *remove* CO_2 from the atmosphere through photosynthesis, is now actually providing us with a net annual gain of the stuff, from the rapid decay of dead vegetable matter in the humid new jungles all over the planet. Every year the substance we breathe gets further and further away in its chemical makeup from what we were evolved to deal with."

"And there is no likelihood that we will continue to evolve to meet these changing conditions?" Enron asked.

Rhodes laughed, a harsh explosive burst of sound. It was the strongest sign of vitality he had shown all evening.

"Evolve? In five generations? Six? Evolution doesn't work that fast. Not in nature, anyway."

"But evolution can be artificially brought about," said the Israeli. "In the laboratory."

"Exactly."

"Would you tell us, then, what the specific goals of your research are? Which aspects of the body you are attempting to modify, and what progress you have made thus far?"

"Don't tell him a fucking thing, Nick," Isabelle Martine said. "He's a spy from Kyocera or maybe some company we don't even know about, some operation working out of Cairo or Damascus, don't you see?"

Rhodes reddened. "Please, Isabelle."

"But it's true!"

Enron, less bothered this time, glanced at her and said, almost jovially, "I have been cleared for this interview by Dr. Rhodes' employer, Ms. Martine. If they are not afraid of me, is there any reason why you should be?"

"Well—"

Rhodes said, "She didn't really mean to cast aspersions on your credentials, Mr. Enron. She just doesn't like to hear me speak of any aspect of my research."

Enron looked at Isabelle as though she were some strange life-form that had just emerged from the carpet.

"What is it, exactly, about Dr. Rhodes' work that causes you such distress?" Enron asked her.

She hesitated. She seemed, Carpenter thought, a little abashed now by her own vociferousness.

Softly she said, "I don't mean to be as critical of Nick as I may have sounded. He's a genius and I admire him tremendously for what he's accomplished. But I just don't want to see the whole world turned into a zoo full of weird adaptos. There's been enough genetic fooling around already, all the retrofitting and baby-splicing and everything. The sex-changing stuff, the cosmetic body-modeling. And now to have every fetus automatically altered into some grotesque kind of creature with gills and three hearts and I don't know what—" Isabelle shook her head. "For one thing, we can't afford to do it. There are too many other problems that we need to solve for us to have the luxury to go into any project as far out as that. For another, I think it's horrible. It would mean the end of humanity as we know it. You change the body, you change the mind. That's a law of nature. It'll be a new species coming forth, God only knows what. Not human any more. Some kind of hideous, evil, bizarre thing. We can't do that to ourselves. We just can't. I love Nick, sure, but I hate what he and his people want to do to the human race."

"But if the human race is no longer able to survive on Earth as we are presently designed—?" Enron asked.

"Fix the world, then. Not the species."

"I wonder, Isabelle," said Jolanda Bermudez in the same dreamy lady-from-space voice as before. "It just may be too late for that, I sometimes think. You know, sweet, I don't really care for Nick's research any more than you do, and I agree with you that it ought to be stopped. But not because it's evil, only because it's a waste of time and money. There's no reason for us to turn ourselves into things with gills, or whatever. Our real hope, I do believe, is in the habitat worlds."

"Ms. Bermudez—" Enron said.

But she rolled right on. "Personally I've done everything I can think of to protect the Earth, through my work, my art, and I don't intend to give up the effort now. But I've started to realize that possibly it's no use, that we may have damaged it beyond repair. So we may have to leave, and that's the honest truth. Like the expulsion from Eden, you know? I think I mentioned that I know people who are very deeply involved in the whole habitat culture that has evolved up there in orbit. L-5 is the coming place. I hope to emigrate there myself, before long."

Isabelle said, "You never told me—"

"Oh, yes. Yes."

"Ladies, please," Enron said.

But it was all beyond the Israeli's control. Jolanda, who seemed to be able to hold three or four contradictory beliefs at the same time without the least difficulty, had tossed a new ball into play. They went on and on, arguing with Enron, with each other, with the environment, with destiny. Carpenter, watching as though from a great height, had to fight back laughter. The women were beating their various political tom-toms and Rhodes, drinking steadily, had passed into a kind of impassive stupor, not actually drunk—did he ever really get *drunk?* Carpenter wondered—but simply glazed, detached, absent; and Enron was looking on in horror, undoubtedly having come to realize by now that he was going to get nothing useful out of this evening.

Carpenter felt sorry for Rhodes, mixed up with this ferocious and badly confused Isabelle: poor sad Nick, pussywhipped yet again. He almost felt sorry for Enron, too. Whatever he had hoped to learn from Rhodes tonight was shrouded now in a haze of fuzzy polemic. It was nearly midnight. The Israeli made one last attempt to pin Rhodes down on the kind of genetic modifications his lab was working on; but Rhodes, vanishing fast into alcoholic nebulosity, offered him nothing but vague talk about restructuring the respiratory and circulatory systems.

"Yes, but how? *How?*" Enron kept asking. And got no coherent answers. The whole thing was hopeless.

Angrily the Israeli called up the check and clicked it with his flex terminal, and they all went out into the sticky night, wobbling a little from all the wine.

Even at this late hour, tangible bands of blast-furnace heat seemed to be pulsing out of the sky. A kind of chemical fog had settled over Sausalito, a dense pungent glop. It smelled like vinegar with an undertone of mildew and disinfectant. Carpenter lamented not having taken his face-lung with him tonight.

The dinner conversation resonated in his mind. The poor fucked-up world! All of human history seemed to rise up before him: the Neolithic world, the little farms and settlements, and Babylon and Egypt, Greece and Rome, Byzantium and Elizabethan England and the France of Louis XIV. All that striving, all that arduous movement up from the ape, and where had it ended up? In a civilization so highly advanced, Carpenter thought, that it had been able to make its own environment unlivable. A species so intelligent that it had invented a hundred brilliant ways of fouling its own nest.

And so—the grime, the pollution, the heat, the poisons in the air, the metals in the water, the holes in the ozone layer, the ruined garden that was the world—

Shit! What a marvelous achievement it all was! For a single species of fancy ape to have wrecked an entire planet!

While they waited at the end of the restaurant pier for Rhodes' car to be brought out, Carpenter went over to him and said quietly, "I can drive, Nick, if you don't feel up to it." Rhodes was looking none too steady.

"That's okay. I'll just let the car take care of things. It'll be all right."

"If you say so. You can drop me off at the Marriott after you take Enron back to his hotel, I guess."

"And Jolanda?"

"What about her? She lives in the East Bay, doesn't she?"

"You could let her take the pod home by herself in the morning. That'll be okay with her."

"Nick, I haven't arranged anything at all with her. I've hardly said a word to her all evening."

"You don't want her? She's expecting it, you know. She's your *date*."

"Does that automatically mean—"

"With her it does. She'll be very hurt. Of course, I can always explain that you've taken homosex vows since I last saw you, or something, and I can run her back to Berkeley tonight. But you'd be making a mistake. She's a lot of fun. What's the matter, Paul? Are you tired?"

"No. Just—ah, to hell with it. Don't worry, I'll gallantly play my part. Here's your car coming up, now."

Carpenter glanced around for Jolanda. She was standing at the water's edge with Enron, gazing out at the shining track of light that led across the bay to San Francisco, and from the close way they were standing Carpenter suspected that he might be off the hook. She stood half a head taller than the short, powerfully built Israeli, but he was whispering to her in an urgent, intimate way, and her stance was certainly a responsive one. But then she turned away from him and gave Carpenter an expectant look, and he knew that whatever Enron had been up to just then did not involve this evening.

So he played out the familiar ritual, asking her if she'd like to stop off at his hotel for a late drink, and she fluttered her eyelids at him and gave him a little quiver of acceptance, and that was that. Carpenter felt foolish. And vaguely whorish, too. But what the hell, what the hell: he'd have plenty of time to sleep alone when he was out in the Pacific fishing for icebergs.

Rhodes put the car on autopilot and it got itself across into San Francisco without any problems. Jolanda nestled up comfortably against Carpenter during the drive as though they had spent all evening steadily building up to the consummation that awaited them. Perhaps they had, Carpenter thought, and he had simply failed to notice.

When the car reached Enron's hotel, a venerable Gothic pile in Union Square, the Israeli took Jolanda's hand before he got out, held it a long moment, kissed it flamboyantly, and said to her, "It has been a highly pleasant evening. I look forward very much to seeing you again." He thanked Rhodes and even Isabelle, nodded to Carpenter, and bounded away.

"What a remarkable man," Jolanda murmured. "Not nice, no, but certainly remarkable. So very dynamic. And such a grasp of world problems. I find Israelis to be fascinating people, don't you, Paul?"

"Marriott Hilton next," said the car. Rhodes seemed to have fallen asleep up front, his head on Isabelle's shoulder. Carpenter wasn't sleepy at all, but his eyes felt raw and achy, from the air, the tensions of the evening, the lateness of the hour. This was going to be a night of no sleep for him, he suspected. Well, not the first one. Probably not the last.

"Let's not bother with the drink," Jolanda said, in the Marriott lobby. "Let's just go right upstairs."

In Carpenter's hotel room, as they were undressing, she said, "Have you known Nick Rhodes a long time?"

"Only about thirty years."

"You grew up together?"

"In Los Angeles, yes."

"He envies you tremendously, you know." She tossed her underwrap aside, stretched, inhaled, enjoying her nakedness. Heavy breasts, heavy thighs, dimples everywhere, a torrent of dark fragrant curling hair: the torrid Latin look, Carpenter thought. Voluptuous. Nice.

"Envies me?"

"Totally. He told me all about you. How much he admires your freewheeling intellectual outlook, the way you aren't tied down by all sorts of moral qualms."

"You're telling me that he thinks I'm amoral?" Carpenter asked.

"He thinks you're *flexible*. That isn't the same. He admires your willingness to adapt quickly to difficult situations, to moral complexities. He wishes he could do that as easily as you do. He ties himself up in knots all the time. You seem to cut right through them."

"I hadn't thought of myself as such a free spirit," said Carpenter. He came up alongside her and ran his hand lightly down her spine. Her skin was amazingly smooth. He found that pleasing. Many people, lately, had had their skins retrofitted to help them cope with the killer crackle of the ozone-deficient air. It usually didn't help them much; and they came out of it looking and feeling like lizard-hide luggage. But Jolanda Bermudez had skin that felt like the skin of a genuine female human. Carpenter liked it very much. And the soft resilient flesh beneath it, too.

She said, "What a great man Nick is, isn't he? So brilliant, so serious-minded. How devoted he is to the task of finding a solution to the terrible problems the world faces! Isabelle gives him an awfully hard time."

"I think he may prefer women who give him a hard time."

She didn't take any notice of that. "And I try not to let her see it, but there are times when I disagree with Isabelle's condemnation of Nick's research program. It may just be our only way out, much as I hate to admit it. Even though I do think that emigrating to L-5 is probably our best bet, I privately hope and pray that it'll be possible for the human race to stay here on Earth, don't you? And Nick's answer may be the only one. That is, if we can't find some way of reversing the terrible damage that we've done to the ecology. The work that Nick is doing—"

She was wide-awake, full of verbal energy. Carpenter was afraid that she was going to start in on the need to protect the planet all over again. The hyperdex, he thought. It must keep her jazzed up all the time. He saw that he would have to fuck her in self-defense, before she became too oratorical. With gentle insistence he drew her down on the bed, and eased himself up against the cradle of her soft and creamy body, running his hands up her sides and over her breasts, and covered her mouth with his. It proved to be an effective way of changing the subject.

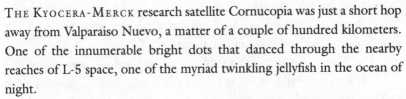

THE KYOCERA-MERCK research satellite Cornucopia was just a short hop away from Valparaiso Nuevo, a matter of a couple of hundred kilometers. One of the innumerable bright dots that danced through the nearby reaches of L-5 space, one of the myriad twinkling jellyfish in the ocean of night.

Farkas was supposed to go over to Cornucopia to pick up the details of his next assignment, and in any case he wanted a chance to talk with Dr. Wu a little before he left the satellite zone. Surely they would let him have a little chat with Dr. Wu, he thought. He figured they owed him that much; but just to be safe Farkas put it on a need-to-know basis, as though what he wanted to learn from Wu was something that another division of K-M had asked him to find out. That was more likely to produce results than a simple request for a personal favor.

He waited on Valparaiso Nuevo a couple of days, to give them a chance to get their new acquisition properly settled in over there. Then he booked a flight across to Cornucopia for himself, taking the midday shuttle that made a regular daily daisy-chain circuit through the neighboring group of habitat worlds.

No nonsense about visas here. Authorized personnel only: you couldn't get a ticket to Cornucopia in the first place unless you were going there on legitimate Company business and they were expecting you. Even then, you weren't allowed off the shuttle until the passenger manifest had been checked at the Cornucopia end and they had formally agreed to receive you.

A reception committee was waiting for Farkas in the docking bay: a short man and a tall woman. The man looked, to Farkas, like a series of yellow spirals arranged around an inverted green cone; the woman was a single vertical flow of soft-textured blue fabric. Farkas didn't quite catch their names, but decided it didn't matter. The man was something on the technical side, but obviously nothing very important, and the woman introduced herself as a Level Twenty administrative executive. You didn't need to bother learning the names of Level Twenties, Farkas had discovered long ago.

"There's an assignment document waiting for you, Mr. Farkas," the Twenty said right away. "It's in your logistics box. You can access it from your accommodation chamber." She seemed to be fighting to keep from flinching at his strangeness.

"Thank you," Farkas said. "I also requested an interview with Dr. Wu. Do you have any information about that?"

The Twenty looked uncertainly at the technical-side guy. "Paolo?"

"Affirmative. Subject Wu is to be made available for a meeting with Expediter Farkas upon his demand."

"Good," Farkas said. "I so demand. Now."

The Twenty seemed troubled by the swiftness of his response. "You want to see Dr. Wu *now*? Before we even take you to your accommodation chamber?"

"Yes," he said. "If you don't mind."

"Well," the Twenty said. "Of course. No problem, Mr. Farkas. She's in a security dorm, you understand. I'll need to do an access notification. It'll take just a minute, though."

She, Farkas thought. Well, yes. To these people, Wu was a *she*. He would have to reprogram his own way of thinking about him, he saw, or there would be confusion.

The Twenty had walked a little distance off and was busy with a terminal, tapping in codes. Obtaining immediate access to Wu for him took a little longer than she had promised. There were complications, evidently. But eventually she got it.

"If you'll come this way, Mr. Farkas—"

Cornucopia was very different from Valparaiso Nuevo: stark, functional, a place of pure industrial texture, a lot of bare girders and struts and other such structural things showing everywhere. Even by way of blindsight, Farkas could see and feel the difference at once. No fountains here, no waterfalls, no lush vines and banana trees, just lots of austere Company hardware at work. All sorts of research went on up here. It was cheaper to build an entire space satellite from scratch than to try to provide a properly clean laboratory on Earth. Scientific research required pure air and water. And of course there was the advantage of variable gravity aboard a satellite world, very useful, so Farkas had heard, in certain areas of scientific work.

Paolo and the Level Twenty led Farkas through a series of security locks and barrel-shaped vaulted corridors and finally to a sort of vestibule where an android guard asked Farkas for a drop of blood in order to check his serum print against the Company archive, apparently to make sure that he was really who he claimed to be, and not some impostor who had had his eyes removed in order to get in where he didn't belong. The android didn't give a damn how unlikely that might be, or that Farkas was a Nine, with all the prestige that that carried. He had his orders. Your finger, please, sir.

Well, so be it, Farkas thought, obligingly offering his finger. He was used to surrendering drops of blood for identification purposes. The usual Company mode of identification check was by way of retinal-print scanning. But they couldn't very well do that with him.

The android drew Farkas's blood in a brusque and businesslike way and put it under a scanner.

"Identification confirmed," the android reported, in a moment. "You may go inside, Expediter Farkas."

Wu was being kept in a containment area that seemed to be something more lavish than a prison cell, something less comfortable than a hotel room. When Farkas entered the room she remained where she was, seated at a desk along the far wall.

Farkas glanced at the Twenty, who was standing right behind him, with Paolo the technician next to her.

"I'd like to talk to Dr. Wu privately."

"I'm sorry, Expediter Farkas. A private interview hasn't been authorized."

"Oh?"

"We have been instructed to be present during the interview. I'm sorry, Expediter Farkas."

"I don't intend to murder him, you know. Her, I mean."

"If you'd like, we could file a formal application for an exception from the instructions, but it would probably take—"

"Never mind," Farkas said. What the hell. Let them listen. He turned toward Wu. "Hello again, doctor."

"What do you want with me?" Wu asked, not sounding especially charmed.

"Just a visit. A social visit. I asked permission to have a little talk with you."

"Please. I am an employee of Kyocera-Merck now. I have the right not to be bothered when I am off duty."

Farkas took a seat on a kind of low sofa next to the desk. In a quiet voice he said, "I'm afraid you don't have the option of refusing, Dr. Wu. I've requested this meeting and the request has been granted. But I do want it to be a friendly visit."

"Friendly."

"Friendly, yes. I mean that sincerely. We aren't enemies. As you said, we are both employees of Kyocera-Merck."

"What do you want with me?" Wu said again.

"I've told you. A social visit. Bygones are bygones, do you understand what I'm saying?"

Wu did not reply.

Farkas said, "So tell me: how do you like your new accommodations? Everything to your satisfaction? What do you think of the laboratory that's been fixed up for you?"

"The accommodations are as you see. I have lived in worse places, and also better ones. As for the laboratory, it is a very fine one. Most of the equipment is beyond my understanding." Wu's voice was all on the same pitch, flat and dull and dead, as though modulating the tone a little would be too expensive.

"You'll learn how to use it," Farkas said.

"Perhaps. Or perhaps not. My knowledge of the field is years out of date. Decades. There's no assurance that I can do the work you people are expecting from me."

"Nevertheless," Farkas said. "Here you are. Here you'll stay, being comfortably looked after, until you accomplish something worthwhile or the Company decides that you really aren't going to be of any use. My hunch is that as you familiarize yourself with the equipment in your new lab, you'll become very excited by the progress that's been made in your field since you left it, and that you'll relearn your old skills very fast and pick up all the new ones. After all, there's no risk for you, is there, doctor? Your work here will be strictly legal."

"My work was always strictly legal," Wu said, in the same sullen robotic monotone.

"Ah. Ah, now. That's what I wanted to talk about."

Wu was silent.

Farkas said, "Did you ever think, Dr. Wu, that your experimental subjects in the Tashkent laboratory didn't especially want their genetic material altered?"

"I am not required to discuss this. You indicated that bygones would be bygones."

"Not required, no. But I'd like you to. I don't feel any vindictiveness, but I do have some curiosity. Quite a lot of curiosity, in fact, things I really want to learn from you about yourself."

"Why must I answer you?"

"Because you did a monstrous thing to me," Farkas said, still keeping his voice quiet but for the first time putting an edge on it, a whiplash crackle. "That gives me the right to get some answers out of you, at the very least. Tell me a few things, out of simple human compassion. You *are* human, aren't you, Dr. Wu? You're not just some kind of soulless thing, some clever sort of android?"

"You will kill me, is that not so, when I am finished with my work in this place."

"Will I? I don't know. I don't see where it would do me any good, and it seems like a petty thing to do. Of course, if you happen to *want* me to kill you—"

"No. No."

"Well, then." Farkas smiled. "If I really wanted to kill you, Dr. Wu, I would have done it on Valparaiso Nuevo. I'm not so completely the creature of Kyocera-Merck that I would put the Company's interests ahead of my own to that extent. So obviously I saw no point in killing you when I had the chance. I was content instead just to carry out the assignment that I had been sent to Valparaiso Nuevo to do, which was to deliver you to Cornucopia so that you could perform certain research on behalf of the Company, research for which you had unique qualifications."

"You did your job, yes. It matters a great deal to you, to do your job.

And when the Company is through with me, *then* you will kill me. I know that, Farkas. Why should I talk with you?"

"To give me reasons for not killing you when the Company is finished using you."

"How could I possibly do that?"

"Well," said Farkas. "Let's see, shall we? Perhaps if I could come to understand your side of the event a little better I'd be more inclined toward being merciful. For instance: when you were doing your experiments on fetuses in Tashkent, what exactly did you feel, in here, in your heart, about the nature of your work?"

"It was all such a long time ago."

"Almost forty years, yes. Some of those fetuses have since turned into large grown men without eyes. But you must remember a little about it. Tell me, doctor: did you experience any hesitation at all, any kind of moral qualms, when you set about working on me in my mother's womb? Any kind of ethical queasiness? Or pity, say?"

Wu said stolidly, "What I felt was intense scientific curiosity. I was trying to learn things that seemed important to discover. We learn by doing."

"Using human victims."

"Human subjects, yes. That was necessary. The human genome is different from that of animals."

"Ah, not true, not true! Not really. You could have experimented with chimpanzee fetuses and had pretty much the same set of genes to work with. You know that, doctor."

"The chimpanzees would not have been able to report to us verbally on the nature of the extended perceptions they could attain using blindsight."

"I see. Only humans could do that."

"Exactly."

"And a supply of humans was readily available while you were in Tashkent, thanks to the chaos of the Breakup. Unborn humans, highly suitable for genetic experimentation. Your intense scientific curiosity therefore was going to be satisfied, and you were very happy about that. But even so, it would have been more ethical if you had asked the mothers of the unborn humans for permission to operate, wouldn't it? My mother, for example, not only gave no permission, but was in fact a foreigner, a foreigner with diplomatic immunity. Nevertheless—"

"What do you want me to say?" Wu cried. "That I did a terrible thing to you? Yes. Yes. I admit it. I did a terrible thing. I took advantage of helpless people in a time of war. You want me to say that I'm evil? That I feel remorse for my crimes? That I am willing to have you kill me for the crime I committed against you? Yes. I acknowledge that I am evil. I am racked with remorse. I feel unbearable guilt and I know that I deserve to be punished. What are you waiting for? Kill me right now! Go ahead, Farkas, wring my miserable neck and be done with it!"

The Level Twenty girl said uneasily, from where she stood near the door, "Mr. Farkas, it's probably not a good idea for this conversation to continue. Perhaps we ought to go now. I can show you to your accommodation chamber, and—"

"Give me another minute," Farkas said. He turned back to Wu, who had subsided again into sullen stillness. "You didn't mean a word of that, did you, doctor? You continue to feel to this day that what you did to me and the others like me in Tashkent was perfectly justifiable in the holy name of science, and you don't have a contrite bone in your body. Isn't that so?"

"That is so. I would do it all over again, if I had the chance," Wu said.

"Ah. Yes, that's what I thought."

"So now you know what you already knew. Will you kill me now? I think your Kyocera-Merck will be displeased if you do."

"No," Farkas said. "I'm not going to kill you now, or later either, for that matter. I just needed to hear you say what you just said. Now I want to hear one thing more. Did you get any *pleasure* out of what you were doing?"

"Pleasure?" Wu sounded utterly baffled. "It was not something I was doing for pleasure. The concept of pleasure never entered into it at all. It was research, do you understand? It was a thing that I did because I needed to know if it could be done. But pleasure? The word has no application."

"A pure technician. A dispassionate seeker after truth."

"I am not required to listen to your mockery. I will ask them to take you out of here."

"But I'm not mocking you," Farkas said. "You really have integrity, don't you, doctor? Defining 'integrity' as the quality of being of a single consistency, of being of an undiluted substance, a oneness. You are completely and totally what you are. That's good. I understand you a lot better, now."

Wu was utterly motionless, scarcely seeming even to be breathing. Shining cubical block of black metal, rising out of pyramidal copper-colored pedestal.

Farkas said, "You had no emotional involvement at all in what you did to me. You got no kind of sadistic joy out of it. As you said: there was a thing you needed to find out, so you simply did what you had to do to get your answers. And so there's no reason why I should take it personally. Right? Right? I never existed as a person in your eyes at all. I was only a hypothesis. I was a problem in biological algebra to you, something that had to be solved, an abstract intellectual challenge. For me to want to get revenge against something like you would be like wanting to get revenge against a hurricane or an earthquake or a landslide or any other impersonal force of nature. They just come along and do to you what they do, but there's nothing personal in it, and no reason why you should get angry at them for wiping you out. You can't forgive a hurricane either, though, can you? The memory of what happened sticks with you. But you have to just pick yourself up and dust yourself off and tell yourself that you had the bad luck to be in the wrong place at the wrong time, and then you go on with your life."

It was perhaps the longest speech Farkas had ever made. His voice was in ragged shreds by the time he was finished; and he wanted nothing more than to go somewhere and lie down.

Wu was still staring at him in that frozen way. Farkas wondered if Wu understood. If Wu cared.

He said to the Level Twenty, "All right, I'm done here now. You can take me to my chamber."

A chamber was what it was, too, a palatial cubicle about three meters long and a meter and a half high, suitable only for lying down and stretching out. But that was all he wanted to do now anyway.

An icon was flashing, telling him that there was a coded message waiting for him in the message niche. He accessed it and discovered that he was being assigned right back to Valparaiso Nuevo. To investigate, it said, the rumors of a coup d'état, a plot to overthrow Generalissimo Callaghan.

Don't say anything to anybody, he was told. *Just drift around the place and listen to things, and let us know what's going on, if in fact anything is.*

The message didn't name any source for the rumor. The most probable one was Colonel Olmo, who after all was K-M's main man on Valparaiso Nuevo, but why, then, hadn't the Company instructed Farkas to check in with Olmo first thing? Did the Company no longer trust Olmo, or had the coup rumor reached them from some other direction, or was it just a case of the right hand not giving a damn about the left? In any event, there didn't seem to be much substance to Olmo's notion that the Company was somehow involved in the plot itself. The Company seemed to be as much in the dark about it as Olmo was himself.

Hi-ho. The most likely possibility, Farkas thought, was that there was no coup conspiracy at all, just some vaporous cloud of disinformation floating around the system. Or else that it really was being put together by a bunch of free-lancers from Southern California with no corporate affiliation of any kind, as Olmo had been told. Well, maybe so. A crazy scheme, all right. But there would be billions in it if it worked.

Farkas caught the morning shuttle back to Valparaiso Nuevo. A horde of eager couriers came swarming around him when he arrived, but Farkas amiably shook them all off and made his own way back to the San Bernardito Hotel in Cajamarca, where he was able to check back into the room he had vacated the day before. He liked the view there, that rim-side room, facing out toward the stars. And the Earth-one gravity pull that the town of Cajamarca enjoyed was very pleasing to his Earth-one-type musculature.

He took a long shower and went out for a stroll.

What a nice place this is, Farkas thought. He was getting used to the atmosphere of it, now. All that bright, clean air, giving you that terrific oxygen zap with every inhalation. You could get drunk on air like this. He pulled it deep into his lungs, playing with it, trying to analyze it with his alveoli, separating out the individual molecules of CO_2 and nitrogen and oxygen.

This stuff could spoil you fast, he knew. It wasn't going to be easy, going back to Earth and Earth's poisonous, corrupting air. To return to life as a dinko, a mudcrawler, a shitbreather, whatever the L-5 people called those who were condemned to live out their lives on the unfortunate mother world. But no one seemed to be in any hurry for him to head back to Earth just yet.

That was good. Good. Take your time, enjoy yourself, have a little holiday in outer space. Carry out an extremely thorough investigation of the supposed conspiracy against the government of Generalissimo Callaghan.

There was a cheerful café at the upside end of Cajamarca not far from the hotel. It was right under one of the shield windows, with a fantastic view of Earth and moon that afternoon. Farkas took a seat out front and ordered a brandy, and sat back, drinking slowly. Maybe one of the conspirators would come up to him while he sat here and offer to sell him some useful information.

Sure. Sure.

He sipped his brandy. He sat and waited. Nobody offered to sell him anything. After a while he went back to his room. Put some soft music on. Made the subtle mental adjustments that were his private equivalent of closing his eyes. It had been a pretty full few days, and he was tired. A little downtime was in order, Farkas told himself. Yes. Yes, definitely, a little downtime.

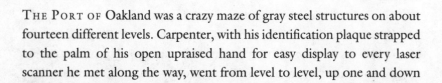

THE PORT OF Oakland was a crazy maze of gray steel structures on about fourteen different levels. Carpenter, with his identification plaque strapped to the palm of his open upraised hand for easy display to every laser scanner he met along the way, went from level to level, up one and down the next, following the portentous instructions of invisible metallic voices, until at last he came to the waterfront itself, ashimmer in a bright green haze of midday heat. He saw dozens of vessels sitting placidly atop the tranquil slime-covered estuary like sleeping ducks drifting in the shallows.

His own ship, the *Tonopah Maru,* had reached San Francisco this very morning after its journey up the coast from the San Pedro shipyard in Los Angeles. It was in port over here on the Oakland side of the bay—San Francisco's own piers had been purely tourist arcades for a century or more—and on this hot grimy afternoon of near-lethal atmospheric inversions, greenish-brown air pressing down like a fist out of a concrete sky and breathing-masks mandatory even in wonderful San Francisco, Carpenter had taxied over there to meet his crew and take formal command.

On the waterfront level he found not merely the expectable array of blinking laser scanners, but an immense square-headed robot guarding the approach to the piers like Cerberus before the gates of hell. It turned slowly to face him.

"Captain Carpenter checking in," he told it. "Commander of the *Tonopah Maru.*" It all sounded so terribly self-important that he had to fight to keep from laughing at his own pomposity. He felt like a character out of Joseph Conrad: the earnest young skipper, taking command for the first time, confronting the bored old salt who had seen it all a thousand times and didn't give the slightest fraction of a damn.

And indeed the robot, who probably knew nothing about Conrad, was neither amused nor awed by Carpenter's announcement of his new status. In somber silence it ran one more laser check on Carpenter's credentials, found them in order, scanned his eyeballs for absolute certainty, and sent him out into the sizzling sunshine beyond the security shed to look for his ship.

His indoctrination course had taken about a week. It was straight subliminal, an hour a day jacked into the data flow, and now Carpenter knew, or hoped he did, about as much as was necessary for him to know about being the captain of an iceberg trawler that would sail the South Pacific. Any aspects of the job that were missing from his shoreside education would have to be picked up at sea, but that didn't trouble him. He would manage. Somehow he always did.

He spotted the *Tonopah Maru* right away, by the bulge of the giant rack-and-pinion gear that powered its grappling hooks, and by the great spigots that occupied most of the deck space. Those, as he had learned only the day before, were used to spray the captured icebergs with a sintering of melt-retardant mirror-dust. The ship was a long, slim, cigar-shaped vessel, elegant and almost disturbingly narrow in outline. It was sitting oddly high up out of the water amidst a cluster of other specialized ships that bore Samurai Industries' familiar sun-and-lightning-bolt monogram. Carpenter had no idea what the other ships might be: seaweed collectors, shrimpers, squid-hunters, whatever. There were a million kinds of ships at work in the sea these days, desperately harvesting the ocean's remaining bounty. Each type was good for only one thing and one thing only, but very good at that one thing.

A big flat-nosed grizzled-looking man whose Screen-induced body-armor coloring gave his skin a remarkable midnight look was standing on deck, squinting through the eyepiece of some sort of navigational device that he seemed to be trying to calibrate. The gadget afforded Carpenter some notion of who the man might be—his oceanographer/navigator, his number two, essentially—and he called down to him:

"Are you Hitchcock?"

"Yeah?" Wary, a little hostile.

"I'm Paul Carpenter. The new captain."

Hitchcock gave him a look of appraisal, a long steady stare. His eyes had a considerable bulge to them and they were rimmed with ribbons of red.

"Well. Yeah. Come on aboard, Cap'n."

No real warmth in the invitation, but Carpenter hadn't expected any. He understood that he was the enemy, the representative of the managerial class, placed in a position of temporary superiority over the crew of the *Tonopah Maru* purely by grace of some random twitch of the vast corporate bureaucracy far away. They had to take his orders but that didn't mean they had to like him, or respect him, or be in any way impressed with him.

Still, there were appearances that had to be honored. Carpenter came down the catwalk, dropped his bag on the deck, and waited calmly for Hitchcock to approach him and offer him his hand.

But the handshake seemed ungrudging enough. Hitchcock moved slowly but his grip was powerful and straightforward. Carpenter even got a smile out of him.

"Good to know you, Cap'n."

"The same. Where are you from, Hitchcock?"

"Maui."

That accounted for the color, then, and the face, and the grizzled hair. An Afro-Hawaiian mix, and plenty of Screen to deepen the hue. He was bigger than he had looked from above, and older, too, easily into his fifties.

"Beautiful place," Carpenter said. "I was there a few years back. Place called Wailuku."

"Yeah," Hitchcock said. He didn't seem very interested. "We sail tomorrow morning, right, Cap'n?"

"Right."

"You ever been on board one of these before?"

"Actually, no, I haven't," said Carpenter levelly. "This is my first time out. You want to give me a tour? And I'd like to meet the rest of the crew."

"Sure. Sure. There's one now. Nakata! Hey, Nakata! Come say hello to the new cap'n!"

Carpenter narrowed his eyes into the sun-blink and saw a tiny figure outlined high up along the superstructure on the far side of the ship, doing something near the housing of the grapple gear. He looked no bigger than a midget against the immensity of the bulging gear, the huge silent mechanism that was capable of hurling the giant grappling hooks far overhead and whipping them down deep into the flanks of even the biggest bergs.

Hitchcock waved and Nakata came scrambling down. The grapple technician was a sleek beady-eyed catlike little guy with an air of tremendous self-confidence about him. He seemed a little higher up the class ladder than Hitchcock. Unhesitatingly he put out his hand, as though equal to equal, for Carpenter. The usual Japanese cockiness, Carpenter figured. Not that being Japanese-American got you anywhere particular in the Samurai hierarchy, any more than being Polish-American or Chinese-American or Turkish-American would. The *real* Nips awarded no extra points to their cousins of diluted blood. Having a Japanese name didn't necessarily make you Japanese, in their eyes. A tough bunch.

Grinning, Nakata said, "We going to go get ourselves some monster bergs, huh, skipper? To keep San Francisco from getting too thirsty." He giggled.

"What's funny about San Francisco?" Carpenter asked.

"Everything," Nakata said. "Damn silly place. Always has been. Weirdos and fairies and dataheads and everything. You aren't from Frisco yourself, are you, skipper?"

"Los Angeles, in point of fact. West L.A."

"All right, then. I'm from Santa Monica. Right down the road from you. I never liked it up here for shit. Samurai had this ship chartered to L.A., you know, until Frisco hired it last month." He gestured vaguely at the bay behind him, the lovely hilly city on the far shore. "I think it's funny as hell, me working to bring water for Northern California. But you do what they pay you for, right, skipper?"

Carpenter nodded.

"Right," he said. "That's the system."

"Show you around the ship now?" Hitchcock asked.

"Two more crew still to meet, aren't there?"

"Caskie, Rennett, yeah. They went into town. Should be along a little later."

Rennett was maintenance/operations, Caskie was the communications operator. Both women. Carpenter was mildly annoyed that they weren't on hand to give him his official welcome, but he hadn't sent word ahead that he was coming at this precise time. The official welcome could wait, he figured.

Hitchcock took him on a tour of the ship. First the deck spigots and the grapple gears, with a view of the stupendous grappling hooks themselves, tucked away in their niche in the ship's side; and then belowdeck to peer at the powerful fusion-driven engine, strong enough to haul a fair-sized island halfway around the world.

"And these here are the wonderful cabins," Hitchcock announced.

Carpenter had been warned not to expect lavish accommodations, but he hadn't expected anything quite like this. It was as though the ship's designers had forgotten that there was going to be an actual crew, and had made a bit of space for them amidst all the machinery purely as an afterthought. The living quarters for Carpenter and the others were jammed into odd little corners here and there. Carpenter's cabin was a whisker bigger than the other four, but even his wasn't a whole lot more roomy than the coffin-sized sleeping capsules you got at an airport hotel, and for recreation space they all had to share one little blister dome aft and the pacing area on the foredeck where Carpenter had first spotted Hitchcock checking out his equipment.

A sardine-can kind of life, Carpenter thought.

But the pay was decent and there was hope of slope for him. And at least he would be able to breathe fresh air at sea, more or less, instead of the dense gray-brown-green murk that hovered over the habitable parts of the West Coast most of the time.

"You got the route specs with you, Cap'n?" Hitchcock asked him, when he had seen all that there was to see.

Carpenter tapped his breast pocket. "Right here."

"Mind if I get to work on them, then?"

He handed over to Hitchcock the little blue data-cube that they had given him at the briefing center that morning. It was, Carpenter knew, a kind of formal ceremony of taking charge: officially giving his navigator the route software, the defining program for their voyage. Of course Hitchcock must already know approximately where they were supposed to go, and was probably capable of getting them there the way mariners had been getting around in the Pacific since the time of Sir Francis Drake and Captain Cook. They hadn't needed computers, and most likely neither did Hitchcock. But turning over the data-cube to the navigator was the modern-day equivalent of the conference before the mast on the eve of sailing, and that was okay with Carpenter: he took some mild pleasure out of being the inheritor of ancient tradition.

A sea captain. Odysseus, Vasco da Gama, Columbus, Magellan. Captain Kidd. Captain Hook. Captain Ahab.

Hitchcock went away and left him alone in his tiny cramped cabin. Carpenter stowed his gear, jamming things into the storage holds as efficiently as he could. When he was done with that he put through a ship-to-shore call to Nick Rhodes at the offices of Santachiara Labs.

"You can't imagine the luxury of my quarters," he told Rhodes. "I feel like J. P. Morgan aboard his yacht."

"I'm very happy for you," Rhodes said bleakly.

The visor screen on Carpenter's cabin communicator wasn't much bigger than a postage stamp, and the resolution was low-grade black-and-white, like something out of electronic antiquity. Even so, Carpenter could see that Rhodes' face looked dour and disheartened.

"Actually, I'm lying absolutely and totally," said Carpenter. "The place is claustrophobia city. If I had a hard-on I wouldn't be able to turn around in here. —What's wrong, Nick?"

"Wrong?"

"Plain as the nose on your face on my visor. Come on, you can be straight with me."

Rhodes hesitated.

"I've just been talking to Isabelle."

"And?"

Another little pause. "What do you think of her, Paul? Really."

Carpenter wondered how far he wanted to get into this. Carefully he said, "A very interesting woman." Rhodes seemed to want more. "Probably extremely passionate," Carpenter added, after a bit.

"What you really think, I said."

"And deeply dedicated to her beliefs."

"Yes," said Rhodes. "She certainly is that."

Carpenter paused one moment more, then decided to drive on forward. *You owe your friends the truth.* "Her beliefs are all fucked up, though. Her mind is full of dumb messy ideas and she's spilling them out all over you. Isn't that the problem, Nick?"

"That's it exactly. —She's driving me crazy, Paul."

"Tell me."

"Last night, we get in bed, I reach for her—I *always* reach for her, it's as natural as breathing for me when I'm with her—but no, no, she wants to talk about The Relationship. Not about me, not about her, but The Relationship. Right at that very moment, no other time will do. Says that my work is endangering The Relationship."

"I'd say that that might be true. Which is more important to you?"

"That's the whole thing, Paul. They're equally important. I love my work, I love Isabelle. But she wants me to leave Santachiara. Doesn't quite put it on a basis of either-you-quit-or-we-break-up, but the subtext is there."

Carpenter tapped the front edge of his teeth with his fingernails.

"Do you want to marry her?" he asked, after a little while.

"I'm not sure. I don't think much in terms of marrying again, yet. But I want to stay with her, that's for absolutely sure. If she insisted on my marrying her, I probably would. I've got to tell you, Paul, the physical side of this thing is like nothing I've ever experienced before. I start to tingle all over as soon as I come into the room where she is. My crotch, my fingertips, my ankles. I can feel something like a kind of radiation coming from her, and it sends me right into heat. And when I touch her—when we start to make love—"

Carpenter studied the visor gloomily. Rhodes sounded like a lovesick college kid. Or, worse, like a screwed-up obsessive erotomaniac adult.

"I tell you, when we make love—you can't imagine—you simply can't imagine—"

Sure. He listened to Rhodes going on and on about Isabelle Martine's fantastic sexual appeal, and all he could think of was that huge frizz of uncouth red steel-wool hair and those hard, implacable, neurotically fierce eyes.

"All right," Carpenter said finally. "So you have the serious hots for her. I can understand that, I guess. But if she wants you to give up your work—" Carpenter frowned. "Because it's evil, I suppose? All that bilge about turning the human race into nasty, spooky Frankenstein monsters?"

"Yes."

Carpenter felt anger beginning to rise in him. "You know as well as I do that that's just standard antiscientific bullshit of the kind that people of her nitwit mind-set have been handing out since the beginning of the industrial revolution. You told me yourself that she admits she doesn't see any alternatives to adapting. And yet she continues to lambaste you for working for Santachiara. Jesus, Nick. Brilliant scientists like you ought to have more sense than to get emotionally involved with people like that."

"It's too late, Paul. I already am."

"Right. She's cast a spell over you with her magic vagina, which is of utterly fantastic pleasure-giving ability and unique and irreplaceable, so that you could never find its equal if you were to search the whole length and breadth of the female sex, and therefore you're incapable of—"

"Please, Paul."

"Sorry," Carpenter said.

Rhodes smiled sheepishly. "I admit that I'm hung up on her in a stupid way. I am, and that's the shape of things, and so be it. I also understand very clearly that her political ideas are simplistic know-nothing nonsense. The trouble is, Paul, that in a certain sense I agree with her."

"What? You really have fucked yourself up, haven't you? You *agree* with her?"

"Not that it's wrong to be using genetic engineering to help us cope with all the bad stuff that's heading our way, no. Isabelle's completely full of crap if she thinks that we can go on living on Earth without modifying the human race. It *has* to be done. We don't have any option."

"So where are you in agreement with her, then?"

Rhodes said, "Here's the thing. The gene work that's going on at Santachiara Labs is already far ahead of any research that's being done elsewhere. Samurai has its corporate espionage division just like anybody else and the reports that I'm getting have me altogether convinced that we're way out front. And the new work that I told you about last week that this kid Alex Van Vliet wants to do would be the clincher. I hate to say this, but Van Vliet's notion, wild as it is, seems to hold better promise of helping the race cope with the environmental problems of the upcoming century than any scheme I've ever seen."

"The hemoglobin idea."

"That's the one. It's still missing a couple of critically important breakthroughs, but who's to say that the problems can't be overcome? As you know, I'd simply like to deep-six his whole project, because it scares me, but I can't. I simply can't. Not without running decent simulations and some actual lab work. It sounds corny, but my conscience won't let me kill it a priori, without testing."

"That's all right. It's okay to have a conscience, Nick."

"I have some reservations about his concept, not just the moral ones I was telling you about, but technical ones too. I'm not at all sure it's really doable, or, even if it is, whether it *ought* to be done. But I'm very conservative in these things. I'm getting a little elderly for making big

speculative jumps. It's possible that I'm a hopeless stick-in-the-mud and
Van Vliet is a true genius. The only way to find out whether he is or not
is to give his proposal a proper checking out. Okay, so that's what we're
going to do. I dithered around for a couple of days and then this morning
I called Van Vliet in to see me and I told him that I was going to
requisition an expansion of his research funds."

"The only honorable course," Carpenter said.

"But if it turns out that he's actually got something workable, and
Santachiara successfully develops it, it'll give Samurai Industries essential
control over all human survival on Earth. A monopoly on staying alive,
Paul, do you see that?"

"Jesus."

"You want to go on breathing, you get yourself retrofitted by
Samurai. You want to bring kids into the world that are capable of
surviving outside of a sealed room, you get your genes remodeled by
Samurai. It'll be a world empire, Paul. Absolute control. And here I am
taking the first steps toward wrapping the package up and delivering it to
New Tokyo. How do you think I feel about that, with or without
Isabelle's rhetoric ringing in my ears?"

"And if you quit the Company now?" Carpenter asked. "Wouldn't it
turn out just the same? Someone else would deliver the package instead of
you."

"It would be someone else. That's the whole point."

"And what would you do?"

"I could get a job anywhere. With Kyocera, with IBM/Toshiba, with
one of the Swiss megacorps."

"And four generations from now Samurai Industries will own the
world."

"I won't be here in four generations. And at least nobody will curse
my name for having helped hand the world over to them."

"You sound like one of those twentieth-century physicists who
refused to work on developing the atomic bomb, because it was a weapon
too deadly to use. But it got developed anyway, without their help. There
were other people willing enough to work on it. In the long run, what
difference did it make whether Scientist A had moral qualms or not, if the
thing was needed and Scientist B and C were available to do the work?"

"It might have made a difference to Scientist A," Rhodes said. "How he slept at night. How he saw himself in the mirror. But it's a false analogy, Paul. There was a war going on then, wasn't there? You had to be loyal to your country."

"There's a war going on now," Carpenter said. "A different kind of war, but a war nonetheless. And we're likely to lose it if we don't do something drastic. You said so yourself."

Rhodes stared at him sadly. Interference waves somewhere high above the Earth carved blurry gray streaks across his face.

"I'm not very tough, Paul. You know that. Maybe I just can't face the moral responsibility of being the man who gives Samurai Industries that much power over the world. If we have to transform the whole human race, it shouldn't be done for the profit of a single megacorp."

"So you're really going to quit, then, Nick?"

"I don't know. This whole too-much-power-for-Samurai angle is tremendously confusing. I've never had to deal with stuff like this before. And I love my work. I love being at Santachiara. Most of the time I think what we're doing is important and necessary. But of course Isabelle's turning terrible pressure on me, and it's messing up my head. And if she understood what I'm really worried about here, she'd never let up on me for a minute. She already thinks the megacorps are menaces. Especially Samurai."

"She's a disturbed woman, Nick."

"No, she's simply deeply committed to—"

"Listen to me. She's emotionally disturbed. So is her friend Jolanda, who you were kind enough to toss into my bed the other night. These are very sexually gifted women, and we who wander around looking for the solace of a little nookie are highly vulnerable to the mysterious mojo that throbs out at us from between their legs, but their *heads* are all full of stupid shit. They have no educations and no real knowledge of anything and they aren't able to think straight: they just buy into whatever hysterical the-sky-is-falling garbage happens to be making the rounds, and they go around screaming and demonstrating and trying to change the world in five different internally inconsistent ways at once."

"I'm unable to see how that justifies your calling her emotionally disturbed," Rhodes said stiffly.

"Of course you're unable to see it. You're in love with her and she can do no wrong. Well, if Isabelle loved *you* she'd be capable of meeting the implications of your work halfway instead of handing you all this paranoid jealousy of it, this hatred of your devotion to the cause of saving the human race. Instead she loves the power she holds over you and hopes to enjoy the sublime thrill of rescuing you from grave error. She's incapable of grasping the inherent contradictions in her loathing of adapto research, and she's succeeding now in exporting those contradictions into your own head. You've entangled yourself with an extremely inappropriate person, Nick. If I were you I'd walk away from her in two seconds flat."

"I keep hoping she'll come around to my viewpoint."

"Right. Reason will triumph, as it always does. Except in my experience reason hardly ever triumphs, really. And what *is* your viewpoint, anyway? You want to succeed in your work but you're uneasy about Van Vliet and you're terrified that you'll ultimately hand Samurai the key to world dominion." Carpenter took a deep breath. He wondered if he was bearing down too hard on Rhodes. "You want some quick and cheap advice? Don't leave genetic engineering. You fundamentally believe in the importance and necessity of what you do. Don't you?"

"Well—"

"Of course you do. You may have some doubts about handing all this power to Samurai Industries, and I can certainly understand where you're coming from there; but you basically believe that adapting the human race to the coming changes in the atmosphere is the only way to keep civilization alive on Earth."

"Yes. I do believe that."

"Damned right you do. Your work is the one thing that keeps you sane in this crazy miserable greenhouse of a world. Don't even think of abandoning it. Immerse yourself in it as deeply as you can, and if Isabelle won't put up with it, get yourself a different girlfriend. I mean it. You'll feel like you've been through an amputation for a little while, and then you'll meet someone else—people always do—and maybe it won't be quite as magical as it was with Isabelle, but it'll be okay, and after a time you'll wonder what the magic was all about anyway."

"I don't know. I don't think I—"

"Don't think. *Do.* And as for your worrying about giving the world

to Samurai on a silver platter, that's easy too. Quit Santachiara and go over
to somebody like Kyocera-Merck. Take your whole department with you.
Turn your gene technology over to the competition. Let Samurai and
K-M fight it out for world domination. But at least the technology will be
in place when the race needs it."

"I couldn't do that. It would violate my contract. They'd hunt me
down and kill me."

"People have been known to change companies and survive, Nick.
You could get protection. Just go public with your desire to see that more
than one megacorp has the secret of human adapto work. And then—"

"Look, this conversation is getting pretty dangerous, Paul."

"Yes. I know."

"We'd better stop. I need to think about everything you've said."

"I'm sailing tomorrow. I'll be out in the Pacific for weeks."

"Give me a number where I can reach you aboard the ship."

Carpenter thought about that a little. "No. Ungood idea. Samurai
ship, Samurai radio channels. We'll talk when I get back to Frisco."

"Okay. Fine." Rhodes sounded very nervous, as though he had
begun to imagine this conversation already being discussed on the highest
Company levels. "Hey, Paul, thanks for everything you've said. I know
that you were telling me things that it was important for me to hear. I just
don't know if I can act on them."

"That's up to you, isn't it, fellow?"

"I suppose it is." A wan smile crossed Rhodes' face. "Listen, take care
of yourself out there on the high seas. Bring back an iceberg for me, will
you? A little one."

"This big," Carpenter said. He held up his thumb and forefinger, a
couple of inches apart. "Good luck to you, Nick."

"Thanks," said Rhodes. "For everything."

The visor went blank. Carpenter shrugged, shook his head. A burst of
pity for Nick Rhodes suffused him, and an inexorable sense of the futility
of all he had just said. Rhodes was suffering, yes; but he was too weak,
really, too muddled, too wounded, to be able to walk away from the things
that were hurting him. The breakup of his marriage had damned near

killed him; and so on the rebound he had tied himself up with one of your basic airbrained San Francisco radicals, and here he was, hopeless prisoner of Isabelle Martine's enchanted pussy, coming home from his adapto lab each night to listen to her wild screeds against gene-splicing. Terrific. And in the midst of all that, worrying that the work of his research group might actually be successful, and by its very success give Samurai Industries a deathgrip on the world economy. It all bespoke an element of masochism in Rhodes' psychic makeup that Carpenter had never consciously noticed before.

Shit, Carpenter thought. Rhodes worries too much, that's the real truth. He'll worry himself right into an early grave. But he seems to *like* to worry. That was a difficult thing for Carpenter to understand.

He went upstairs to see if the rest of his crew had shown up.

Apparently they had. As Carpenter came up the ladder he heard voices, Hitchcock's gruff rasping one and Nakata's light tenor, but also two female ones. Carpenter paused to listen.

"We'll make out all right anyway," Hitchcock was saying.

"But if he's just a dumb Company asshole—" Female voice.

"Asshole, yes. Probably not dumb." That was Nakata. "You don't get to be an Eleven, being dumb."

"What I don't like," Hitchcock said, "is how they keep sending up these fucking salarymen instead of picking a real sailor to be captain. Just because they've sort of learned which buttons to push don't mean goddamn shit, and they ought to understand that."

"Look, as long as he does his job right and lets us be—" Woman's voice, different one.

Yeah, Carpenter thought. I'll push the buttons I'm supposed to push and I'll let you be so long as you push yours, and we'll all be happy. Okay? Do we have a deal?

Their grousing didn't trouble him. It was what they were supposed to do, when a new boss came on board. Any other reaction would have been surprising. They had no reason to love him at first sight. He would simply have to make them see that he was just doing his job, same as them, and that he didn't want to be here any more than they wanted him to. But he *was* here. For a while, anyhow. And all the responsibility for running this ship fell to him. He was the one whose feet the Company would put to the fire, if anything went wrong on the voyage.

But what could go wrong? This was just an iceberg trawler.

Carpenter clambered the rest of the way to the deck, doing it noisily enough to give them some warning he was coming. The decktop conversation died away as soon as the clattering echoes of his approach could be heard.

He emerged into the blaze of afternoon. The humid air was thick and gross and a swollen greenish sun stood speared atop one of San Francisco's pointy high-rises across the bay.

"Cap'n," Hitchcock said. "This here's Caskie, communications. And Rennett, maintenance/ops. Cap'n Carpenter."

"At ease," Carpenter said. It sounded like the right thing to say.

Caskie and Rennett were both on the small side, but that was where their resemblance ended. Rennett was a husky, broad-shouldered little kid, less than chest-high to him, who looked very belligerent, very tough. Most likely, Carpenter figured, she had come out of one of the dust-bowl areas of the Midwest: they all had that chip-on-the-shoulder look back there. She kept her scalp shaved, the way a lot of them did nowadays, and she was brown as an acorn all over, with the purple glint of Screen shining brilliantly through, making her look almost fluorescent. But for her height you might not have thought she was female at all.

Brown eyes bright as marbles and twice as hard looked back at him. "Sorry I was late getting back," she said, not sounding sorry at all.

Caskie, the communications operator, was slight and almost dainty, with a much softer, distinctly more feminine look about her: glossy black hair and lots of it, no bare scalp for her. Her face was on the plain side, with a wide mouth and an odd little button of a nose, and her skin was spotty and flaked from too much sun, but despite all that there was an agreeable curvy attractiveness to her.

Carpenter had wondered, upon first hearing that he was getting a crew of two men and two women, how you kept sexual tensions from becoming a problem aboard ship, and now, looking at Caskie, he thought about that once more. But the answer came to him in another moment, and it was so obvious he reproached himself for not having seen it instantly. These two, Caskie and Rennett, were a couple, a closed system. There wouldn't be any flirtations on the *Tonopah Maru,* any sort of sexual rivalries, to make life complicated for him.

He said, "As I think all of you know, this is my first time at sea. That doesn't mean I'm ignorant of a captain's duties and responsibilities, though, only that I haven't exercised them before. You're an experienced crew and you have a record of working well together, and I'm not going to pretend that I know your jobs better than you do. Where I need practical advice and have only theoretical data to fall back on, I won't be ashamed to ask for your help. I just want you to remember two things: that I'm a fast learner, and that ultimately I'm the one who will have to stand up and account for the voyage before the Company if our performance isn't up to mode."

"Do you think we'd slack off, just because we've got a new man in charge?" Rennett asked. Midwest, yes: he could hear it in her voice, the dry flat tone. Raised in dust-bowl poverty, vile dirty air, crumbling shanties, broken windows, the endless uncertainty of the next meal.

"I didn't say that you would. But I don't want you telling yourselves that this is going to be anything less than a profitable voyage because of my supposed inexperience. We're going to be okay. We'll do our work properly and well and we'll get damned fine bonuses when we get back to San Francisco." Carpenter snapped them a formal smile. "I'm glad to have met you and I'm damned pleased to be shipping out with such a capable crew. That's all I have to say. We'll clear port at 1800 hours. Dismissed."

He saw them exchange glances with one another before they broke ranks, but he was unable to interpret their expressions. Relief, that the new captain wasn't an absolute jerk? Confirmation of their suspicion that he was? Formation of an alliance of the true workers against the loathed parasitic eleventh-level salaryman?

No sense trying to read their minds, Carpenter told himself. Take the voyage day by day, do the work as it comes, stay on top of things, and all will be well.

His first order of duty was to file the official notice of embarkation with the harbormaster. He went down to his cabin to take care of that, making his way with difficulty through the narrow, cramped, and unfamiliar belowdecks spaces, jammed everywhere as they were with matériel and instruments.

As he picked up the phone he thought of calling Nick Rhodes back and trying to take some of the sting out of what he had said earlier. Telling a man that the woman he loves is a dangerous nutcase who ought to be jettisoned is a heavy thing to do, even if he is your closest friend. Rhodes might be brooding right now about that, angry, resentful. It might be best to attempt some retroactive softening.

No, Carpenter thought. Don't.

What he had said was the truth as he saw it. If he was wrong about Isabelle—and he didn't think he was—Rhodes would forgive him for having spoken out of turn: their friendship had survived worse things than that over the years. They were inextricably bound by time and history and nothing they could say to each other could do permanent damage to that bond.

But even so—

The poor unhappy bastard. Such a nice, gentle guy, such a brilliant man. And always drifting into some kind of anguish and grief. Rhodes deserved better of life, Carpenter thought. But instead he kept finding women who were more than he could handle; and even in the one area of his life where he was a true genius, his research, he was managing now to fuck himself over with the tormenting qualms of profound moral uneasiness, gratuitously self-generated. No wonder he drank so much. At least the bottle didn't engage him in philosophical discussions. It just offered him a little solace, an hour or so at a time. Carpenter wondered what would happen to Rhodes when the drinking too got out of hand, and began to erode the parts of his life that actually worked.

A rough business, he thought sadly.

Best not to call him again now, though.

"Harbormaster's office," said an androidal voice out of the visor.

"This is Captain Carpenter of the *Tonopah Maru*," Carpenter said. "Requesting port clearance, 1800 hours—"

Enron said, "It is a beautiful place, where you live. Is it very old?"

"Mid-twentieth century," Jolanda Bermudez told him. "Old, but not exactly ancient. Not like the old world, where everything's five thousand years old. You like it?"

"So beautiful, yes. A quaint little cottage."

So it was, in a way, Enron thought. A small ramshackle building on a narrow winding street high up on the hillside not far north of the university campus. It was definitely charming, with its little decks and odd outcurving windows and its mitre-saw filigree decorations along the roofline. Charming, yes: even though the paint was pocked and peeling from the constant onslaught of the chemical-laden air and the windows were so degraded for the same reason that they were starting to look like stained glass and the decks were swaybacked and lopsided and the shingles were coming loose and the garden in front was a shameless withered tangle of dry knotty weeds.

This was the third evening Enron had seen Jolanda in the past week, but he hadn't come to her house before; she had preferred to go with him to his hotel in the city. His little fling with her had greatly enlivened his week in the United States. Of course she would undoubtedly begin to bore him, over any considerable span of time. But he wasn't expecting to marry her, and he would be going back to Israel very soon now anyway. In the short run she had been just what he needed here, an undemanding companion and a complaisant, eager playmate in bed; and there was always still the possibility that he might actually learn something useful from her, on this otherwise largely wasted trip. A slender possibility, but it was there.

"Well? Shall we go in? I'm dying to have you experience my work."

She was like a big prancing dog, Enron thought. Not very bright, in fact not intelligent at all, but extremely friendly and lively, and good company for a romp. A warmhearted, easy-natured person. Very different from most of the shrewd, hard-edged, keen-eyed Israeli women he knew, who prided themselves on being utterly clear-minded, who always had everything in its absolutely proper perspective, not caring that their souls had turned to ice.

He followed her through a dimly lit vestibule. The interior of the place was dark and cluttered and confusing, a murky maze of little rooms filled with wall hangings, sculptures, statuettes, weavings, brassbound chests, intricate veils dangling from pegs, tribal masks, posters, books, African spears, pieces from a suit of medieval Japanese armor, coiled loops of fiber-optic cable, stacks of data-cubes, carved screens, bells, old wine bottles festooned with colored wax, iridescent strips of hologram tape that stretched from wall to wall, odd ceramic things of uncertain function, items of antique clothing giddily scattered all about, bird cages with actual birds in them, visors flashing abstract patterns: a stupefying, overwhelming plenitude of bric-a-brac. All of it, so far as Enron could see, tasteless and absurd. He could smell the stale odor of burned incense in the air. Cats were meandering around everywhere, five, six, a dozen cats, a couple of Siamese and a couple of Persian and some that were of kinds he could not identify at all. Like their owner, they seemed afraid of nothing: they pushed up against him, sniffed him, nuzzled him, sharpened their claws on his leg.

"Well? What do you think?" Jolanda asked.

What could he say? He beamed at her.

"Fascinating. Delightful. Such a wonderful collection of unusual things."

"I knew you'd love it. I don't bring *everybody* here, you know. A lot of men, they simply don't *understand*. They'd be turned off. But you—a man who's traveled so widely, a cultured man, who appreciates the arts—" She flung her arms wide in her joy. Enron was afraid she would knock one of her artifacts flying across the room. She was a big woman: he might almost say intimidatingly big, if he were capable of being intimidated by anything, especially a woman. Ten centimeters taller than he was, at least, and probably twenty kilos heavier. Enron suspected that she was a hyperdex user: she had that overwrought look about the eyes. Drug use of any kind disgusted Enron. But what this woman did was no business of his, he told himself. He wasn't her father.

"Come," Jolanda said, taking him by the wrist and pulling him along. "My studio is next."

It was a long low-ceilinged room in back, windowless, jutting into the hillside, no doubt something that had been added to the original structure. The clutter of her living area was not replicated here. The studio was empty except for three mysterious objects, large and of indeterminate shape, standing in a triangular array in the middle of the floor.

"My latest sculptures," she said. "This one on the left is *Agamemnon*. On this side, *The Tower of the Heart*. And the one in back I call *Ad Astra Per Aspera*."

"I have never seen such work as this," said Enron truthfully.

"No. I don't think anything like it is being done anywhere else yet. It's a new art form, strictly American so far."

"And it is called—what did you say?—bioresponsive art? How does it work?"

"I'll show you," she said. "Here. You have to put the receptors on, first." From a cupboard he had not noticed she produced an ominous handful of electrodes and bioamplifiers. "Let me do it," she said, quickly taping things to him, putting some small device on his left temple, another right on the top of his head, reaching down into his shirt to stick one on his breastbone.

Go on, Enron thought. Put one between my balls, now.

But she didn't. She affixed the fourth and last one at the midpoint of his shoulder blades. Then she was busy for a time with some sort of electronic rig in the cupboard. He studied her thoughtfully, watching the movements of her unfettered breasts and meaty buttocks within the thin wrap that was all she was wearing, and wondered how long this demonstration of her art was likely to take. There were other things to do tonight and he was ready to get on to them. He could be patient indeed in the pursuit of a goal, but he didn't want to consume the whole evening in these absurdities.

In a very minor way, too, Enron was uneasy about the electrodes and bioamplifiers. Unless he had completely lost his capacity for judging human beings, this woman was harmless, a mere silly innocent with ridiculous taste and a slipshod mind and the morals of a she-camel. But what if he was wrong? If she was in fact a functionary of Samurai counterintelligence, and had cunningly set him up with the uninhibited use of her lusty energetic hips and dark musky loins for the sake of administering a brainburning here this evening?

Paranoia, he told himself. Idiocy.

"All right, now. We're ready to go. Which one first?"

"Which what?" Enron asked.

"Sculpture."

"The one in back," he said at random. *"Ad Astra Per Aspera."*

"A good choice to begin with," she said. "I'll count to three. Then you start walking toward it. One—two—"

At first he saw nothing except the sculpture itself, an ungainly, unappealing-looking assemblage of wooden struts arranged at awkward angles with some sort of metallic armature visible within. But then something began to glow in the sculpture's depths, and in another moment he became aware of a distinct psychogenic field beginning to kindle within him: a pulsation at the back of his neck, another in his belly, a sensation of odd disorientation everywhere. As though his feet were beginning to leave the ground, almost as if he was starting to float upward and outward, through the doorway that led to the main part of the house, up through the ceiling, into the hot muggy night—

Well, it was *Ad Astra Per Aspera,* wasn't it? So probably he was supposed to be experiencing a simulated star voyage, then. Upward and outward to the far galaxies.

But all Enron felt was the initial sense of rising. He went nowhere, he experienced nothing beyond a certain queasy strangeness in his nervous system. It was as if his starward impetus was limited, that he could journey only so far and no farther before he hit some kind of psychic wall.

"There," Jolanda said. The sensations went away. "What did you think?"

He was ready, as always. "Magnificent, wholly magnificent. I was scarcely prepared fully enough for the intensity of it. What I felt was—"

"No! Don't tell me! It has to stay private—it's your personal experience of the work. No two are alike. And I wouldn't presume to ask you to put the essentially nonverbal into words. It would spoil it for you, don't you think?"

"Indeed."

"Shall we do *Tower of the Heart* next?"

"Please."

She touched each electrode, as if adjusting the receptors in some minor way, and went to the cupboard again.

Tower of the Heart was wide, squat, not in any way towerlike that Enron could see. The glow of its internal workings was of a deeper hue than the other's, violet blue rather than golden pink. Approaching it, he felt very little at first, and then came some of the queasiness he had felt with the first sculpture, indeed pretty much the same sensation. So it is all foolishness, he thought, a mild electric current that gives you the twitches and some gentle discomfort, and then you pretend that you have had a deeply moving aesthetic experience which—

Suddenly, without warning, he found himself on the verge of an orgasm.

It was immensely embarrassing. Not only was it his intention to save that orgasm for better use a little later in the evening, but the whole idea of losing control this way, of staining his clothes like a schoolboy, was infuriating to him. He fought it. The emanations coming from the second sculpture were far stronger than those of the first, and it was a struggle for him. His face, he knew, must be ablaze with shame and rage, and his erection was so powerful that it made him ache. He didn't dare look down to see if it showed. But he fought. It had probably been thirty years since he had had to fight so desperately against the release of pleasure: not since the hairtrigger days of his hot adolescence. His mind was filled with thoughts of Jolanda Bermudez's overflowing body, her immense swaying breasts, her hot slippery throbbing hole. She was devouring him, she was engulfing him, carrying him away on a tide of ecstasy. Think of anything, he ordered himself sternly. Think of the Dead Sea, the harsh metallic taste of its water, the thick slimy coating on your skin after you emerge from it. Think of the Mosque of Omar's golden dome shining in the noon sun. Think of the nauseating ball of greenhouse gases that surrounds the spinning globe of Earth. Think of yesterday's stock-market quotations—of toothpaste—of oranges—of the Sistine Chapel—

—of camels in the marketplace at Beersheba—

—of lamb kebabs sizzling over a grill—

—of the coral reefs at Eilat—

—of—of the—the—

But the pressure lifted, just then. The surging tide of his blood receded; his erection subsided. Enron caught his breath and forced himself back toward calmness.

The room was very quiet. He had to make himself look toward her. When he did, he saw that she was smiling—slyly, knowingly, perhaps? Was she aware of what had happened? Impossible to tell. She must know what effect the work had had on him. On the other hand, everyone was supposed to respond to these things differently. A purely subjective art form.

He would reveal nothing. As she said, a person's experience of her art was his own private business. "Extraordinary," he told her. "Unforgettable." His voice, hoarse and breathy, sounded almost unrecognizable in his own ears.

"I'm so glad you liked it. And shall we do the *Agamemnon* now?" she asked cheerily.

"In a little while, maybe. I would like to—savor what I have already been shown. To think about it, if I may." Enron was sweating as though he had just done a ten-kilometer race. "Is that all right? That we wait until later for the third one?"

"It *can* be overwhelming, sometimes," she said.

"And perhaps if there is something to drink—"

"Yes. Of course. How stupid of me, to haul you right in here so fast, without even offering you a drink!"

She got the electrodes off him and found a bottle of wine. White wine, warm, sweet. Americans! What did they know of anything that mattered? Gently Enron asked if there might be red, and she found some of that too, even worse, dusty-tasting stuff, full no doubt of baneful pollutants and ghastly insecticide residues. They left the studio and settled on a sort of divan before a long low window in one of her front rooms, and sat looking out at a sunset of stunning photochemical complexity, an astounding apocalyptic Wagnerian thing: enormous bold jagged streaks of scarlet and gold and green and violet and turquoise warring frantically with each other for possession of the sky above San Francisco. Now and then Jolanda sighed heavily and shook her shoulders in a little shiver of aesthetic joy. Ah, yes, such beauty, God's own heaven dazzlingly illuminated by God's own industrial contaminants.

We will go for dinner soon, Enron thought, and there I will ask her the things I must ask her, and then we will return here and I will have her right on the floor of this room, on the thick Persian carpet, and then I will go back to the city and I will never see her again; and in a pig's eye will I let her put those electrodes back on me, not tonight or any other night.

The investigation, first, though. How to bring the subject of discourse around to the area of his main interest here? A little maneuvering would be necessary. And with all this romantic business going on in the sky—

But as it happened he was able to get down to his inquiries much sooner than he had expected. She gave him the opening he needed even as they sat watching the sunset.

"The night we all had dinner, Marty, Isabelle said you were a spy. Do you remember that?"

Enron chuckled. "Of course. A spy for Kyocera-Merck, she said."

"Are you?"

"You are so very direct. It is charmingly American of you."

"I was just thinking. I've never slept with a spy, not that I know of. Unless you are. It would be interesting to know."

"Naturally I am," he said. "All Israelis are spies. It is a widely known fact."

Jolanda laughed and poured more of the abominable wine for them both.

"No. No, it is true. In our country we lived so long in a condition of dire peril, surrounded by enemies on every side, just a stone's throw away: how could we not develop ingrained habits of watchfulness? A nation of spies, yes. Wherever we go, we look, we prowl, we lift up coverlets to find out what might be beneath. But a spy for Kyocera-Merck? No. That I am not. I do my spying for my country. It is a matter of patriotism, not of economic greed, do you see?"

"You really are serious," she said, in wonder.

"A journalist, a spy—it is the same thing, is it not?"

"And you came here to talk to Nick Rhodes because your country wants to steal the adapto technology that he's working on."

She was, Enron realized, getting drunk very quickly. This conversation had veered from the merely playful into something rather different.

"Steal? I would not do that. We never steal. We license, we copy if necessary, we reinvent. Steal, no. It is forbidden by the laws of Moses. Thou shalt not steal, we are told. Imitate, yes. There is nothing in the commandments about that. And I do confess to you, freely without hesitation, that we wish to learn more about this project of your friend Dr. Rhodes, this scheme for the genetic transformation of mankind." Enron eyed her closely. She was flushed and at least half-aroused: the heat of the evening, the wine, his no doubt apparent response to *Tower of the Heart*, all had been working on her. Leaning close, letting his hand rest on hers, he said in an insinuating, confidential way, "Now that I have admitted that I am a spy, you will not mind that I must do some spying now. Yes? Good." She seemed to think he was playing a game. Very well. He was happy to amuse her. "Answer this for me," he said. "What do you think about Rhodes, truly? Is he on to something? Are they going to produce some new kind of human being over at that laboratory of his?"

"Oh, you aren't joking! You really *are* a spy!"

"Did I ever deny it? Come on." Enron stroked her arm. Her skin was amazingly smooth, the smoothest he had ever touched. He wondered if she had had herself covered in something synthetic. There were women who did that. "What about him? What do you know about his work?"

"Nothing," she said. "God's honest truth, Marty." He had told her to call him "Marty," because "Meshoram" sounded too alien for her. She giggled. Maybe the idea of being an espionage source had some appeal for her. "I'd tell you what I knew, if I knew anything, but I don't. You should have made a pass at Isabelle instead, if that's what you were after. Nick tells her things, sometimes, about his work. But she doesn't pass them along to me, not so they would be of any use to you. I just hear bits and patches."

"Such as?" He ran his hand lightly along the curve of her breast. She shivered and wriggled a little. "Come on," he said. "Such as?"

She closed her eyes for a moment and seemed to be thinking.

"Well, that they have some young guy there who's working on a big breakthrough, something to do with changing our blood so that it'll be green instead of red. And other changes beyond that. I don't know what they are. I really don't. —Here, have some more wine. It's nice, isn't it? Green blood! Better than having to drink green wine, I guess."

Enron pretended to sip the wine. Green blood, he thought. Some sort of hemoglobin adjustment? But he realized that she was telling the truth: she knew nothing. Probably it was useless to pursue the details.

Nevertheless he said, "Do you know this other scientist's name, the younger one?"

"No. Isabelle might. You ought to talk to her."

"She is a very difficult woman. I think she might not want to cooperate with me."

"Yes," Jolanda said, peering into her wine. "Most likely you're right. After all, if Israel wants to develop its own adapto technology, and you've come here to find out what Samurai has actually achieved along those lines, then by helping you, she'd be helping the cause of adapto technology. And you know how she feels about that."

"Yes."

"Me too, for that matter. I think it's tremendously scary. Frankly, it gives me the creeps."

They had been through all this before. Enron forced himself to be patient with her. "But if it is necessary, the adapto, the only step left to us for the preservation of human life on Earth—"

"Is it so important that the human race remain on Earth, if Earth is so terribly fucked up? We could all emigrate to the space habitats, after all."

He gave her some more wine. The sun had set now; the sky was swiftly turning black. Across the bay the lights of San Francisco were coming on, twinkling in the dense haze. Casually Enron's hand roamed Jolanda's generous body: breasts, belly, now her knee, now sliding up along her thigh. Such foreplay seemed to loosen her tongue, he thought. Or maybe it was loose all the time. He went on touching her regardless. She sat with her head thrown back, her eyes closed. One of the cats jumped up beside him and began to rub its head against his elbow. He knocked it away with a quick sidewise nudge.

Quietly he said, "We love our land. We fought for centuries to possess it. We would not want to leave it now, not even for some New Israel in the sky."

"The Japanese left their land. The rich ones did, anyway. They're scattered all around the world, now. They loved their country as much as you love yours. But they're gone. If they could go, why can't you?"

"They left, yes, because their islands were flooded by the rising seas. They lost all their fertile land and most of their cities, and nothing but barren mountaintops remained. They would never have gone otherwise. They would still be clinging to every rock. But they had no choice but to go. Just as we once left Israel to go into exile, long ago, two or three thousand years ago, because we were forced to by our enemies. And then one day we returned. We struggled, we suffered, we built, we fought. And now we live in the Garden of Eden. The sweet rains fall, the desert plains have turned green. We will not leave again."

"What good is staying, though, if everything is going to change so much?" Her voice had grown eerie and thin, as though it came from far away. "If we all turn ourselves into weird mutant adapto creatures, will any of us still be human? Can you still be a Jew if you have green blood and gills?"

Enron smiled. "There is nothing in the Bible, I think, about what color our blood must be. Only that we must obey the law and live honorable lives."

She considered that for a time.

Then she said, "And is it honorable to be a spy?"

"Of course. It is a very old tradition. When Joshua made ready to lead us across the Jordan, he sent two spies into the land on the other side, and they returned to tell Joshua that it was safe to go across, that the people on the other side were petrified with terror because they understood that the Lord had given their land to the Jews. The names of those two spies are not mentioned in the Bible. They were the first secret agents."

"I see."

"And even to this day we send our people forth to search out dangers," Enron said. "There is nothing dishonorable about that."

"You people see enemies everywhere, don't you?"

"We see dangers."

"If there are dangers, there have to be enemies. But the age of war between nations is in the past. There are no enemies any more. We're all allies now in the struggle to save the planet. Can it be that the enemies you people are worrying about are all in your imaginations?"

"Our history teaches us to be cautious," he said. "Three thousand years of being driven from place to place by people who disliked us or envied us or merely wanted to turn us into scapegoats. Why should it be any different today? It would be foolish of us to assume that the millennium has arrived." Enron felt himself on the defensive, suddenly. It was an unfamiliar sensation for him. He was here tonight to ask questions, not to answer them. She was very persistent, though. He took a deep gulp of the dreadful wine. "The Assyrians massacred us. The Romans burned our temple. The Crusaders blamed us for the death of Christ." The wine was going down more easily, now. "Do you know of the death camps that the Germans built for us in the middle of the twentieth century?" he asked. "Six million of us died for nothing more than being Jews. The survivors went to Israel, then. All around us were Muslims who hated us. They swore to finish the job that the Germans had begun, and several times they attempted to do it. It is not easy to live a quiet and productive life, when just on the other side of the river is an enemy who has decreed a holy war against you."

"But that was a long time ago. The Arabs are your friends now."

"It is nice to think so, isn't it? Well, their oil wealth is gone, and although our region is more fertile now than it was before the climate changed, their lands are greatly overpopulated, and so they can no longer afford the luxury of the holy war that they would probably still like to wage. So they have turned to their suddenly acceptable Israeli neighbors for technological and industrial assistance. We are all friends now, yes. We are partners. But that can always change. As things get worse and worse on Earth, those who lack our advantages may decide to turn on us. It has happened before."

"How terribly suspicious you people are!"

"Suspicious? But there is everything to suspect! And so we remain ever alert. We send our agents everywhere, sniffing out trouble. We worry about the Japanese, for example."

"The Japanese? Why?"

Enron realized that he was getting a little drunk. Which was also something that was very unusual, for him.

He said, "They are a hateful people. I mean, full of hatred. They have such great wealth and yet they are miserable exiles. Living their isolated, paranoid lives in their little super-protected enclaves here and there around the world, sealed away behind their walls, bitter about having been driven from their homes, hated by everybody else for their money and their power but hating back even harder, because their hatred is fueled by such enormous resentment and envy. And the ones they hate more than anyone are us Israelis, because we too were exiles once but we were able to go home, and it is a beautiful home, and because we are strong and enterprising and we are challenging them now for positions of power all over the world."

His hand had still been exploring the region between her thighs. Now she clamped her legs closed on his wrist, not so much to prevent him from going further as just to hold him pleasantly in place. Did she want to talk or to make love? Perhaps both at once, he thought. The two things seemed to be related, for her. She was a manic talker—the drug she uses causes that, he thought, the hyperdex—and a sexual maniac as well. I should stop all this chatter, Enron told himself, and simply pull her down with me onto that carpet. And then out to dinner. He felt as if he hadn't eaten in three days.

But he too was somehow unable to stop talking.

"The accidents of life in the greenhouse world brought Israel into world economic prominence even as they drove the Japanese from their home islands," he heard himself say. "We are moving on many fronts at once. The Israeli government has invested heavily in most of the great megacorps, do you know that? We hold significant minority interests in Samurai and Kyocera both. But the megacorps are still basically Japanese-dominated, and they are fighting to keep us out. They are eager to see us cast down from our high place. They will do anything. *Anything*. So we watch them, Jolanda. We watch everyone."

"And developing the adapto technology before Samurai does—that's going to put Israel into a stronger position in the world that's coming?"

"We believe so."

"I think you're wrong. I think we have to forget about Earth and move to space instead."

"To the habitat worlds, yes. Your great obsession."

"You think I'm silly, don't you?"

"Silly?" he cried. "Oh, no, never!"

Enron didn't even bother to try to sound sincere. He was bored and irritated by her, now. To his surprise he found himself even starting to lose sexual interest in her. She is not a she-camel but a cow, he thought, a preposterous cow with delusions of intelligence.

Even so, he kept his hand where it was.

Jolanda rocked back and forth on it, squeezing her thighs. Then she turned and opened her eyes and looked at him in an oddly flirtatious, provocative way, smiling dreamily as though she had decided to impart some immensely important secret to him. "I ought to tell you, I may not even wait around down here for the environment to decay any further. I'm seriously thinking of moving to an L-5 world quite soon now."

"Are you? And have you chosen any one in particular?"

"It's a place called Valparaiso Nuevo," she said.

"I don't know it," Enron said. They were sitting in near darkness, staring at darkness. A cat that he did not think he had seen before, very long-legged with a thin, angular head, had emerged from somewhere and was nuzzling against his shoe. The wine bottle was empty. "No—wait. I remember. It's a sanctuary world, isn't it? Where runaway criminals go to hide?" He was starting to feel light-headed from the heat, the endless talking, the wine, his own mounting hunger, the intensity of Jolanda's looming physicality, perhaps even the aftereffects of having exposed himself to her bioresponsive sculptures. Desire began to stir in him again, sluggishly at first, then with greater intensity. She was maddeningly annoying but oddly irresistible. The conversation was becoming surreal, now. "Why would you want to go there?" he asked.

Her eyes flashed at him. A stagily wicked look, a child being wicked.

"I really shouldn't be telling you this, I suppose."

"Go on. Do."

"Will you keep it entirely to yourself?"

"Keep what?" he asked. "I don't understand."

"Imagine. Swearing a spy to secrecy! But you'll be gone in a few days anyway and none of it matters to you. It doesn't concern Israel in the slightest."

"You can tell me, then."

"Yes. All right. I will." Another wicked-little-girl flash of the eyes. "But it goes no farther than you. Agreed?" *I have a secret, but I will share it with you, only you, because you are my friend and because I think you're very cute.*

"I swear it," he said.

"You've got it right that Valparaiso Nuevo is a sanctuary world, full of criminals of all sorts who pay local government to protect them from law-enforcement agencies that might be looking for them. It's run by some kind of crazy old Latin American dictator who's been in charge there since the Year One."

"I still don't follow. What does this have to do with you?"

"I have a friend in Los Angeles," Jolanda said. "Who is part of a kind of guerrilla group, in a way—they're planning to infiltrate this Valparaiso Nuevo and seize control. Take the whole place over, collect all the fugitives and turn them in for rewards. There'll be a fortune in it, selling them all. And then they'll live there like kings and queens. Fresh air, fresh water, a brand-new life." Her gaze was curiously fixed and bright, brighter even than her usual druggy glare. She seemed to be staring past or through him, into some gleaming realm of fulfilled fantasies. "My friend asked me if I wanted to join them. We'd be billionaires. We'd own a whole little planet. It's supposed to be beautiful up there in the L-5 worlds."

Enron was fully sober at once.

"When is all this supposed to happen?" he asked.

"Very soon, actually. I think they said they would—" Jolanda put her hand over her mouth. "Good God, look at what I've done! I should never have told you any of this!"

"No, it is very interesting, Jolanda."

"Listen, Marty, it's not true, none of it, not a word! It's just a story, a movie idea that they were making up, there's nothing real about it! You mustn't take it seriously. It isn't true!" She was staring at him in horror. In a low somber tone she said, "You shouldn't have let me have so much wine. Please forget everything I just said about Valparaiso Nuevo. Everything. I could get into enormous trouble if—if—" She began to cry, great lalloping sobs that shook her entire body. His hand was still caught between her legs and he feared that in her convulsive movements she would sprain his wrist.

"Shh. There's nothing to worry about, Jolanda. I'm not going to say a word to anyone about this."

Hope glistened in her eyes. But she still seemed terrified.

"You swear it? They would kill me!"

"The smart spy protects his sources, love. I am a very smart spy."

She was still trembling.

Enron said, "But you must do one thing for me. I want to meet your Los Angeles friend. I want to talk with him, with his group. To work with them."

"Seriously?"

"I am always serious, Jolanda."

"But what I just told you about has nothing to do with your—"

"Ah, but it does. There are people on Valparaiso Nuevo who would be of great interest to the state of Israel, of that I am certain," Enron said. "If these people are going to be for sale, we would like to contact the sellers very early in the proceedings. For that matter we would probably be willing to provide your friends with support of a very material kind as they undertake their project. What is your friend's name, the one in Los Angeles?"

Jolanda paused a moment before answering.

"Davidov. Mike Davidov."

Enron felt his pulse rate pick up. "Jewish?"

"I don't think so. I think it's a Russian name. He looks sort of Russian."

Enron slipped his hand free of her thighs and began to stroke her breasts again. In his most seductive imploring tone he said to her, "Take me with you to Los Angeles. Introduce me to your friend Mr. Davidov."

"I don't know, Marty—I don't think I should—"

"Tomorrow. The nine o'clock shuttle." No longer seductive. Commanding, now.

"It's no use," she said. "He's already gone to Valparaiso Nuevo. A lot of the key people are up there already, scoping the place out."

"Ah," Enron said. "I see."

He was quiet for a moment, thinking.

She leaped right into the opening he had provided for her. "Do you know what I want to do now?" she asked. "I want to stop talking about all this, all right? I'm a little bit drunk. More than a little. I've talked much too much and I don't want to talk any more."

"But if you would just—"

"No, Marty. It's too dangerous. You'll just take advantage of whatever I tell you. I want you to take advantage of me in a different way."

"Take advantage?"

"You ought to know what I mean. But here. I'll give you a hint."

She took him by the shoulders and pulled him down to the floor with her. They landed in a tangle of arms and legs, laughing, and he buried himself quickly in the billowing abundance of her. A hot mingling of aromas came upward from her, wine and desire and sweat and even, he thought, the smell of the Screen with which she protected her fantastic satiny skin. Good. Good. He lost himself in her. There had been enough talk for now, he thought. He had been holding himself back for hours, patiently playing the games of espionage with her, and now he allowed himself to put his profession aside for a little while.

"Oh, Marty," she murmured, over and over again. He gobbled the heavy globes of her breasts as though they were melons and thrust with the zeal of a prophet wielding his lance into the mysterious and apparently infinite depths of her quivering cunt. "Marty Marty Marty." She held her body tilted high, her legs far apart with her feet waving somewhere in the air behind him, and slammed her thighs steadily against the sides of his body with each of his jolting thrusts. Fucking this Jolanda was like exploring some unknown continent, Enron thought. So big, so moist, so strange, so full of wonders and novelties. It was always like that, for him, with a new woman. The Jewish Balboa, the Jewish Mungo Park, Orellana, Pizarro, plowing unceasingly onward through one uncharted hairy jungle after another in the eternal quest for the unknowable prizes at the core of their hot, throbbing hearts. But this one was a greater enigma than most. She was the mysterious kingdom of Prester John, the lost realm of El Dorado.

They lay side by side afterward, naked, sweat-shiny in the heat of the night, laughing softly.

"It's too late to go anywhere for dinner," she said. "I'll make something here. Would that be all right?"

"Whatever you prefer," said Enron.

"And then maybe you can take a look at the third sculpture, the *Agamemnon*. Would you like that?"

"Perhaps after a time," he said vaguely. "Yes. Yes, perhaps so."

She was very amusing, Enron decided. And more useful than he had suspected. This would not be their last night together after all, not if he could help it.

When they were washed and dressed and she was clanking around in the kitchen he called in to her, "What you told me, about the leaders of this plot having already gone to Valparaiso Nuevo: was it true?"

"Marty, please. I thought we weren't going to talk about—"

"Was it?"

"Marty."

"Was it, Jolanda? I have to know."

Clattering sounds, pots and pans. Then:

"Yes. They're up there already, some of them. As I said."

Enron nodded slowly. "So, then. I have a proposition. Please treat it with great seriousness. How would you like to take a little trip to Valparaiso Nuevo with me, Jolanda?"

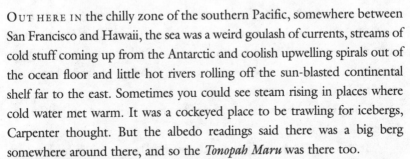

OUT HERE IN the chilly zone of the southern Pacific, somewhere between San Francisco and Hawaii, the sea was a weird goulash of currents, streams of cold stuff coming up from the Antarctic and coolish upwelling spirals out of the ocean floor and little hot rivers rolling off the sun-blasted continental shelf far to the east. Sometimes you could see steam rising in places where cold water met warm. It was a cockeyed place to be trawling for icebergs, Carpenter thought. But the albedo readings said there was a big berg somewhere around there, and so the *Tonopah Maru* was there too.

He sat in front of the scanner, massaging the numbers in the cramped, claustrophobic cell that was the ship's command center. It was midmorning. The shot of Screen he had taken at dawn still simmered like liquid gold in his arteries. He could almost feel it as it made its slow journey outward to his capillaries and went trickling cozily into his skin, where it would carry out the daily refurbishing of the body armor that shielded him against ozone crackle and the demon eye of the sun. You really had to load up on the infra/ultra drugs out here at sea, where the surface of the water reflected the light like a mirror and hurled it up into your face. Since leaving San Francisco,

Carpenter had nearly doubled his regular dose of Screen, building up his armoring, and by now his skin had turned a shimmering iridescent greenish-purple. The effect was strange, but he liked it.

The voyage had gone well enough, so far, aside from the one little problem that they hadn't yet been able to find any bergs. But it looked like that was solved, now.

"We got maybe a two-thousand-kiloton mass there," Carpenter said, looking into the readout wand's ceramic-fiber cone. "Not bad, eh?"

"Not for these goddamn days, no," Hitchcock said. The oceanographer/navigator was old enough to remember when icebergs were never seen farther north than the latitude of southern Chile, and was always glad to let you know about it. "Man, these days a berg that's still that big all the way up here must have been three counties long when it broke off the fucking polar shelf. But you sure you got your numbers right, man?"

The implied challenge brought a glare to Carpenter's eyes, and something went curling angrily through his interior, leaving a hot little trail. Hitchcock *never* thought Carpenter had done anything right the first time. The tensions had been building up, day after day, since the day they had set out from San Francisco Bay. Though he often denied it—too loudly—it was pretty clear Hitchcock felt no small degree of resentment at having been bypassed for captain in favor of an outsider, a mere salaryman from the land-based sector of the Company. Probably he thought it was racism. But he was wrong. Carpenter was managerial track; Hitchcock wasn't. That was all there was to it.

Sourly Carpenter said, "You want to check the visor yourself? Here. Here, take a look."

He offered Hitchcock the wand. But Hitchcock shook his head.

"Easy, man. Whatever the screen says, that's okay for me." Hitchcock grinned disarmingly, showing mahogany snags.

On the visor impenetrable whorls and jiggles were dancing, black on green, green on black, the occasional dazzling bloom of bright yellow. The *Tonopah Maru*'s interrogatory beam was traveling 22,500 miles straight up to Nippon Telecom's big marine scansat, which had its glassy unblinking gaze trained on the whole eastern Pacific, looking for albedo differentials. The reflectivity of an iceberg was different from the reflectivity of the ocean surface. You picked up the differential, you confirmed it with temperature readout, you scanned for mass to see if the trip was worth making. If it seemed to be, you brought your trawler in fast and made the grab before someone else did.

Back in Frisco, Carpenter knew, they were probably kneeling in the streets, praying for him to have some luck, finally. The lovely city by the bay, dusty now, sitting there under that hot soupy remorseless sky full of interesting-colored greenhouse gases, waiting for the rain that almost never came any more. There hadn't been any rain along the Pacific seaboard in something like ten, eleven months. Most likely the sea around here was full of trawlers—Seattle, San Diego, L.A. According to Nakata the Angelenos kept more ships out than anybody.

Carpenter said, "Start getting the word around. That berg's down here, SSW. We get it in the grapple tomorrow, we can be in San Francisco with it by a week from Tuesday."

"If it don't melt first. This fucking heat."

"It didn't melt between Antarctica and here, it's not gonna melt between here and Frisco. Get a move on, man. We don't want L.A. coming in and hitting it first."

By midafternoon they had it on optical detect, first an overhead view via the Samurai Weather Service spysat, then a sea-level image bounced to them by a navy relay buoy. The berg was a thing like a castle afloat, stately and serene, all pink turrets and indigo battlements and blue-white pinnacles. The drydock kind of berg, it was, two high sides with a valley between, and it was maybe two hundred meters long, sitting far up above the water. Steaming curtains of fog shrouded its edges and the ship's ear was able to pick up the sizzling sound of the melt effervescence that was generated as small chunks of ice went slipping off its sides into the sea. The whole thing was made of glacial ice, which is compacted snow, and when it melted it melted with a hiss.

Carpenter stared at the berg in wonder. It was a lot bigger than any of the ones he had seen in his training software. For the last couple of million years it had been perched snugly on top of the South Pole, and it probably hadn't ever expected to go cruising off toward Hawaii like this. But the big climate shift had changed a lot of things for everybody, the Antarctic ice pack included.

"Jesus," Hitchcock said. "Can we do it?"

"Easy," said Nakata. Nothing seemed to faze the agile little grapple technician. "It'll be a four-hook job, but so what? We got the hooks for it."

Sure. The *Tonopah Maru* had hooks to spare. And Carpenter had faith in Nakata's skill.

"You hear that?" he asked Hitchcock. "Go for it."

They were right at the mid-Pacific cold wall. The sea around them was blue, the sign of warm water. Just to the west, though, where the berg was, the water was a dark rich olive green with all the microscopic marine life that cold water fosters. The line of demarcation was plainly visible. That was one of the funny changes that the climate shift had brought: most of the world was hot as hell, now, but there was this cold current sluicing up from Antarctica into the middle of the Pacific, sending icebergs floating toward the tropics.

Carpenter was running triangulations to see if they'd be able to slip the berg under the Golden Gate Bridge when Rennett appeared at his elbow and said, "There's a ship, Cap'n."

"What'd you say?"

He had heard her clearly enough, though.

A *ship*? Carpenter stared at her, thinking *Los Angeles San Diego Seattle,* and wondered if he was going to have to fight for his berg. That happened at times, he knew. This was open territory, pretty much a lawless zone where old-fashioned piracy was making a terrific comeback.

"Ship," Rennett said, clipping it out of the side of her mouth as if doing him a favor by telling him anything at all. "Right on the other side of the berg. Caskie's just picked up a message. Some sort of SOS." She handed Carpenter a narrow strip of yellow radio tape with just a couple of lines of bright red thermoprint typing on it. The words came up at him like a hand reaching out of the deck. Carpenter read them out loud.

> CAN YOU HELP US   TROUBLE ON SHIP   MATTER
> OF LIFE AND DEATH URGENT YOU COME ABOARD
> SOONEST
>
> —KOVALCIK, ACTING CAPTAIN,
> CALAMARI MARU

"What the fuck," Carpenter said. "*Calamari Maru*? Is it a ship or a squid?"

It was a feeble joke, and he knew it. Rennett didn't crack a smile. "We ran a check on the registry. It's owned out of Vancouver by Kyocera-Merck. The listed captain is Amiel Kohlberg, a German. Nothing about any Kovalcik."

"Doesn't sound like a berg trawler."

"It's a squid ship, Cap'n," she said, voice flat with a sharp edge of contempt in it. As if he didn't know what a squid ship was. He let it pass. It always struck him as funny, the way anybody who had had two days' more experience at sea than he did treated him like a greenhorn. Though of course he was. But he could cope with that. When they handed out the bonuses back in Frisco he'd be getting the captain's stake and they wouldn't.

Carpenter glanced at the printout again.

Urgent, it said. *Matter of life and death.*

Shit. Shit shit shit.

The idea of dropping everything to deal with the problems of some strange ship didn't sit well with him. He wasn't paid to help other captains out, especially Kyocera-Merck captains. Of all companies, not K-M, certainly not now. There was very bad voodoo between Samurai Industries and K-M these days, worse than usual. Something about the Gobi reclamation contract, a blatant bit of industrial espionage that had gone awry, some crap like that. Besides, Carpenter had a berg to deal with. He didn't need any other distractions just now.

And then too, he felt an edgy little burst of suspicion drifting up from the basement of his soul, a tweak of wariness that might have had just the slightest taint of paranoia about it, except that Carpenter had had such a good education in the realities of the world over the past thirty-odd years that he wasn't sure there was such a thing as paranoia at all. The bastards were *always* out to get you. Going aboard another ship out here, you were about as vulnerable as you could be. What if some kind of trick was being set up for him?

But he also knew you could carry caution too far. It didn't feel good to him to turn his back on a ship that had said it was in trouble. Maybe the ancient laws of the sea, as well as every other vestige of what used to be common decency, were inoperative concepts here in this troubled, miserable, heat-plagued era, but he still wasn't completely beyond feeling things like guilt and shame. Besides, he thought, what goes around comes around. You ignore the other guy when he asks for help, you might just be setting yourself up for a little of the same later on.

They were all watching him, Rennett, Nakata, Hitchcock.

Hitchcock said, "What you gonna do, Cap'n? Gonna go across to 'em?" A gleam in his eye, a snaggly mischievous grin on his face.

What a pain in the ass, Carpenter thought.

Carpenter gave the older man a malevolent look and said, "So you think it's legit?"

Hitchcock shrugged blandly. "Not for me to say. You the cap'n, man. All I know is, they say they in trouble, they say they need our help."

"And if it's some kind of stunt?"

Hitchcock's gaze was steady, remote, noncommittal. His blocky shoulders seemed to reach from one side of the ship to the other. "They calling for help, Cap'n. Ship wants help, you give help, that's what I always believe, all my years at sea. Of course maybe people think different, upslope. And like I say, you the cap'n, not me."

Carpenter found himself wishing Hitchcock would keep his god-damned reminiscences of the good old days to himself. But—screw it. The man was right. A ship in trouble was a ship in trouble. He'd go over there and see what was what. Of course he would. He had never really had any choice about that, he realized.

To Rennett he said, "Tell Caskie to let this Kovalcik know that we're heading for the berg to get claiming hooks into it. That'll take about an hour and a half. And after that maybe I'll come over and find out what his problem is."

"Got it," Rennett said, and went below.

New berg visuals had come in while they were talking. For the first time now Carpenter could see the erosion grooves at the waterline on the berg's upwind side, the undercutting, the easily fractured overhangings that were starting to form. The undercutting didn't necessarily mean the berg was going to flip over—that rarely happened, with big drydock bergs like this—but they'd be in for some lousy oscillations, a lot of rolling and heaving, choppy seas, a general pisser all around. The day was turning very ugly very fast.

"Jesus," Carpenter said, pushing the visuals across to Nakata. "Take a look at these."

"No problem. We got to put our hooks on the lee side, that's all."

"Yeah. Sounds good." He made it seem simple. Somehow Carpenter managed a grin despite it all.

The far side of the berg was a straight sheer wall, a supreme white cliff smooth as porcelain that was easily a hundred meters high, with a wicked tongue of ice jutting out from it into the sea for about forty meters, like a breakwater. That was what the *Calamari Maru* was using it for, too. The squid ship rode at anchor just inside that tongue.

Carpenter didn't like seeing another ship nestled up against his berg like that. But the squid ship, hookless, specialized for its own kind of work, didn't look like any kind of threat to his claim on the berg.

He signaled to Nakata, who was standing way down fore, by his control console.

"Hooks away!" Carpenter called. "Sharp! Sharp!"

Nakata waved an okay and put his hands to the keyboard. An instant later there came the groaning sound of the grapple-hatch opening, and the deep rumbling of the hook gimbals. Somewhere deep in the belly of the ship immense mechanisms were swinging around, moving into position. The great berg sat motionless in the calm sea.

It was a little like deep-sea fishing: the trick didn't lie in hooking your beast, but in what you did with it afterward, when you had to play it.

The whole ship shivered as the first hook came shooting up into view. It hovered overhead, a tremendous taloned thing filling half the sky, black against the shining brightness of the air. Then Nakata hit the keys again and the hook, having reached the apex of its curve, spun downward with slashing force, heading for the breast of the berg.

It hit and dug and held. The berg recoiled, quivered, rocked. A shower of loose ice came tumbling off the upper ledges. As the impact of the hooking was transmitted to the vast hidden undersea mass of the berg, the whole thing bowed forward a little farther than Carpenter had been expecting, making a nasty sucking noise against the water, and when it pulled back again a geyser came spuming up about twenty meters.

Those poor bastards aboard the *Calamari Maru* weren't going to like that. But they had chosen to stay in their anchorage while a hooking was going on, hadn't they? What the hell did they expect, a teeny splash or two?

Down by the bow, Nakata was making his I-got-you gesture at the berg, the middle finger rising high.

A cold wind was blowing from the berg now. It was like the exhalation of some huge wounded beast, an aroma of ancient times, a fossil-breath wind.

They moved on a little farther along the berg's flank.

"Hook two," Carpenter told him.

The berg was almost stable again now. Plainly there was more undercutting than they had thought, but they would manage. Carpenter, watching from his viewing tower by the aft rail, waited for the rush of pleasure and relief that everybody had said would come from a successful claiming, but it wasn't there. All he felt was impatience, an eagerness to get all four hooks in and start chugging on back to the Golden Gate.

The second hook flew aloft, hovered, plunged, struck, bit.

A second time the berg slammed the water, and a second time the sea jumped and shook. Carpenter had just a moment to catch a glimpse of the other ship popping around like a floating cork, and wondered if that ice tongue they found so cozy was going to break off and sink them. It would have been a lot smarter of them to drop anchor somewhere else. But to hell with them. They'd been warned.

The third hook was easier.

One more, now.

"Four," Carpenter called. A four-hook berg was something special. Plenty of opportunity to snag your lines, tangle your cables. But Nakata knew what he was doing. One last time the grappling iron flew through the air, whipping off at a steep angle to catch the far side of the berg over the top, and then they had it, the whole monstrous floating island of ice snaffled and trussed. Now all they had to do was spray it with mirror-dust, wrap a plastic skirt around it at the waterline to slow down wave erosion, and start towing it toward San Francisco.

All right, Carpenter thought.

Now at last he could take a little time to think about the goddamned squid ship and its problems.

▼   ▼   ▼

THE ANNUNCIATOR SAID, "Dr. Van Vliet is calling on Line Three, Dr. Rhodes."

Quarter to nine in the morning. It was never too early for Van Vliet to start in on the day's toil and trouble. A lot too soon, though, for Rhodes to start in on the day's drinking. "Later," he said. "I don't want to take any calls just now."

Rhodes had been in the office since just after eight, early for him. At the end of yesterday's workday his desk had still been littered with unfinished items, and both virtual extensions had been loaded as well; and, as usual, things had come pouring in all night long for his urgent attention in the morning. The weather had taken a turn for the worse too: sweltering heat, well beyond the norms even of modern times, and scary Diablo winds blasting down out of the east, bringing once again the threat, now practically a weekly event, of stirring up devastating fires along the bone-dry grassy ridges of Oakland and Berkeley. The winds were carrying with them, also, an oppressive shitload of toxic fumes out of the valley stagnation pool, potent enough to cut acnelike pockmarks into the facades of stone buildings.

Aside from that, Rhodes had had a lousy night with Isabelle the night before, and maybe three hours of sleep. It was an all-around wonderful morning. He was restless, irritable, swept by bursts of rage and confusion and occasionally something close to panic. For almost an hour now he had been spinning his wheels, accomplishing nothing.

Time to get to work, finally.

"Open, sesame," Rhodes said stolidly, and Virtual One began to disgorge streaming ribbons of data into the air.

He watched it all come spilling out, aghast. Reports, reports, reports. Quantitative stuff about enzyme absorption from the Portland lab; a long stupid screed from one of the sub-departments dealing with a foredoomed project to provide senior citizens with lung implants instead of genetic retrofits; a formidable batch of abstracts and preprints from *Nature* and *Science* that he would never have time in this present life to deal with; a horrendous pile of crap about some employee arbitration hassle involving third-floor janitorial androids overstepping their stipulated spheres of responsibility; the minutes of a meeting at the São Paulo office of a Samurai subsidiary he had never heard of, the work of which evidently impinged in some unspecified way on his department's area of operations. And on and on and on and on.

Rhodes felt like sobbing.

Somehow his job had become all administration, very little actual doing of science any more. The science around here was done by kids like Van Vliet, while Rhodes coped with the inundation of reports, budget requests, strategic analyses, dead-end schemes like the lung-implant business, et cetera, et cetera, all the while attending an infinity of petrifyingly dull meetings and killing the occasional evening trying to fend off the troublesome curiosities of Israeli spies. For after-hours amusement he engaged in bewildering corrosive strife with the woman he supposedly loved. Somehow this was not the life he had intended for himself. Somehow he had veered off course, that was obvious.

And the unthinkable heat today—the hard, malignant, abrasive air—the hot howling wind—

Van Vliet—

Isabelle—

Isabelle—

Isabelle—

Wild unfocused sensations swept him like a sudden fever. Some kind of explosion seemed to be building up within him. He found that frightening. It was days like this, Rhodes thought, that led otherwise peaceable men to jump off bridges or commit random acts of murder. Diablo winds could do that to you. They were famous for that.

My life is in need of fundamental change, he told himself. *Fundamental* change.

What kind of change was in order, though? The work? The Isabelle relationship? Paul Carpenter had told him to break up with her and to take a job with some other megacorp. There was a lot of sense in both those suggestions.

But he simply wasn't capable of the first, he thought, and the other was tempting but terrifying. Change jobs? Where would he go? How would he break free from Santachiara and Samurai? He was immobilized, tied hand and foot—to the Company, to Isabelle, to the adapto project, to the whole bloody mess.

He put his head in his hands. He sat listening to the wind.

Isabelle—

Oh, Jesus. Isabelle.

Last night, after dinner, at Isabelle's place. Always trouble, when he stays there. He is sitting in the kitchen, by himself, sipping a Scotch. Isabelle has been very distant, cool, all evening, mysteriously so. Rhodes has never been able to understand what sends her into these periods of withdrawal, nor does she give him much help in figuring things out. Now she is busy in her little office off the living room with a memorandum she is dictating to herself about a consultation that day, one of her patients who is in deep shit.

He makes a critical mistake when she comes back in for a glass of water: trying to break through her reserve, Rhodes asks her a question about the particular problem she's dealing with, wants to know if there's some kind of special complication.

"Please, Nick." Shoots him a basilisk glance. "Can't you see I'm trying to concentrate?"

"Sorry. I thought you were taking a break."

"I am. My mind isn't."

"Sorry," he says again. "I didn't know." Smiles. Shrugs goodheartedly. Tries to make it all nice again. It seems to him that he spends at least half his time with Isabelle just trying to make it all nice again, patching things up after some misunderstanding that is mostly beyond his comprehension.

Instead of returning to the other room, she stands stiffly by the sink, hefting her water glass without drinking from it, as though measuring the specific gravity of its contents.

Says, after a bit, doom-and-gloom voice, "Yes, there is a complication. I'm starting to think that the girl is genuinely suicidal."

So she wants to talk about it after all. Or else is just talking to herself out loud.

"Who is?" Rhodes asks, gingerly.

"Angela! *Angela!* Don't you ever pay any attention?"

"Oh," he says. "Right. Angela." He had thought the patient in question was a certain Emma Louise. Isabelle can be extremely nonlinear sometimes.

He summons up what little he knows about Angela. Sixteen, seventeen years old, lives somewhere at the northern end of Berkeley, father a professor of history, or something, at the university. Under treatment by Isabelle for—what? Depression? Anxiety? No, Rhodes thinks: the girl has Greenhouse Syndrome. The new trendy thing. Total environmental paranoia. God knows why it should be setting in only now: it sounds very late-twentieth-century to him. But all the kids are getting it, it seems. A sense not just that the sky is an iron band around the planet, but that the actual walls are closing in, that the ceiling is descending, that asphyxiation is not very far away.

"Suicidal? Really?" Rhodes says.

"I'm afraid that she may be. She was wearing two face-lungs today, when she showed up for her session."

"Two?"

"Convinced that one's not enough. That the air is absolute poison, that if she takes a deep breath it'll turn her lungs to mush. She wanted me to write a prescription for Screen for her, double the usual dose. I told her I'm not allowed to write any sort of prescriptions and she went into hysterics."

"Sounds like the opposite of suicidal," Rhodes says mildly. "Hyper-concerned about protecting herself, yes, but why would that mean—"

"You don't get it. You never do, do you?"

"Isabelle—"

"She thinks that whatever precautions she takes will be entirely futile. She thinks she's *doomed*, Nick. That we are on the threshold of the final apocalyptic environmental collapse, that she is living in the last generation of the human race, and that some hideous kind of gigantic eco-disaster is about to sweep down and destroy us all in the most awful possible way. She's full of anger."

"She has a right to be, I suppose. Though I think she's a hundred years ahead of the time. But still—suicide—"

"The ultimate angry gesture. Spitting in the face of the world. Throwing her life away as a demonstration of protest."

"You really think she will?"

"I don't know. She very well might." A new expression comes into Isabelle's tense face: doubt, fear, uncertainty. Not her usual mode. She tugs unthinkingly at her hair, tangles it into knots. Pacing around the room, now. "What worries me, basically, is that this may be getting beyond my zone of professional capability. I'm a therapist, not a psychiatrist. I wonder if I should pass her along."

She is debating entirely with herself. Rhodes is convinced of that now. But there is always the possibility that she may be expecting him to offer some indication that he's listening.

"Well, certainly if you think there's any risk—"

A softer voice. The therapist voice. "It would be a betrayal of trust, though. Angela and I have a *covenant*. I'm here to guide her. She has faith in me. I'm the only human being she does have faith in." Then the tone hardens again. Instant switch: pure steel. Furious glare. Isabelle swings at the speed of light from mood to mood. "But why am I even talking to you about this? You couldn't possibly understand the depth of her insecurities. Don't you see, to send her for an outside consultation, to hand her off to some stranger at this delicate moment—"

"But if you're afraid that she'll kill herself, though—"

His mild words only heap more fuel on the fire. Isabelle is ablaze. "Look, Nick, this is for me to decide! There's a transaction here that doesn't involve you, that is utterly beyond your limited powers of comprehension, a complex personal transaction between this troubled girl and the one human being on Earth who genuinely cares for her, and you have no goddamned business sticking your uninformed opinion into—" She pauses, blinking like one who has suddenly awakened from a trance, drawing deep breaths, gulping the air in, as if even she has realized that she has gone a little too far around the bend with him.

A moment's silence. Rhodes waits.

"This is all wrong," she says.

"What is?"

"What we're doing, you and I. We shouldn't be getting into a fight over this," Isabelle says, with a welcome softness coming into her voice.

"No." In vast relief. "Absolutely right. We shouldn't be getting into fights over anything, Isabelle."

She seems genuinely to be trying to back off from her fury, her raging hostility. He can almost see the wheels shifting within her head.

He waits to see what's coming next.

And then, without warning, what comes is a manic change of subject:

"Let's talk about something else, all right? Did you know that Jolanda has been dating that Israeli? I thought that you had fixed her up with your friend Paul."

Rhodes shifts his own gears as quickly as he can, happy to be released from contemplation of the despondent Angela. "Paul was just looking for a little amiable company that one night. Anyway, he's off at sea now. —The Israeli, eh? How often has she been seeing him?"

"Every couple of nights ever since the Sausalito evening."

Rhodes considers that. He doesn't care, basically, except that Jolanda and Isabelle are good friends, and this brings up the possibility that another disagreeable evening in Enron's company may soon be forced upon him.

Isabelle says, "He's invited her to take a trip with him, you know."

"A trip? Where?"

"Some space habitat. I don't remember which one."

Rhodes smiles. "He's a shrewd one, isn't he? Jolanda's been dying to go to the L-5s for years now. I thought that guy she knows in L.A. was going to take her up there, but here's Enron making his move first. —Of course, it's never very hard for a man to get Jolanda's attention."

"What is that supposed to mean?" Isabelle asks crisply.

Oh-oh.

The voice of cold steel has abruptly returned, and the basilisk eyes. Rhodes sees that he has stepped in things again.

He hesitates. "Well—that Jolanda is a hearty, healthy girl, full of robust appetites—"

"An easy lay, is that what you're saying?"

"Look, Isabelle, I didn't intend—"

"But that's what you think she is, don't you?" She's off as fiercely as before, glaring, pacing, tugging. "That's why you set her up with your old buddy Paul. A sure thing, a night's fun for him."

Well, of course. And Isabelle knows it too. This is a group of adults; Jolanda is no nun, and neither is Isabelle. It's a lot too late to start praising Jolanda for her chastity. Isabelle, in defending her friend, is only looking for a fight. But Rhodes doesn't dare say any of that.

He doesn't dare say a thing.

Isabelle says it for him. "She'll sleep with anybody, that's what you told Paul. Right?"

"Not in so many words. But—for Christ's sake!—listen, Isabelle, you know as well as I do that Jolanda gets around a lot. A *lot*."

"Has she slept with you?"

"Isabelle!"

"Well, has she?"

In fact, she has. Rhodes isn't sure whether Isabelle knows that. Jolanda tells Isabelle all sorts of things, but perhaps has not told her that. He wonders what to say, not wanting events to escalate into real wildness tonight, but not wanting to get caught in a lie, either. He decides to temporize.

"What has that got to do with anything?" he asks.

"Has she or hasn't she, Nick?"

A deep breath. All right, give her what she wants to know.

"Yes. Once."

"Christ!"

"You were out of town. She came over. I don't remember when this was. The day was really hot, a record breaker, and we went to the beach, and afterward—"

"All right. You don't have to play back the whole video for me." She has turned her back on him, and is standing like a marble statue by the window.

"Isabelle—"

"Go fuck yourself."

"You want me to leave?"

"What do you think?"

"Are we going to break up over this?"

"I don't know. Maybe. Maybe not."

He senses a wavering in her voice, a softening. The old approach-avoidance thing, one of her specialties. Rhodes goes to her sideboard and pours himself a drink, a stiff one. Only then does he realize that he already has an unfinished one on the table. He takes a deep pull from the new drink and sets it down beside the other one.

"You can stay if you like," she says indifferently, from very far away, no energy in her voice. "Or not, whichever you prefer."

"I'm sorry, Isabelle."

"About what?"

"Jolanda."

"Forget it. What difference does it make?" He is afraid for a moment that Isabelle now is going to confess some outside affair of her own. Intending, by telling him about it, either to punish him or to help him ease his guilt. Either way, he doesn't want to hear anything like that from her, if there is anything to hear. As for him, Jolanda had been his only lapse. Going to bed with her that time had been almost automatic, unthinking: she had seemed to regard it as no more than a nice thing to do at the end of the evening, that one time, a cheerful little social grapple, meaning nothing, leading nowhere. And he had gone tumbling right along.

"Listen, Isabelle—"

Rhodes goes across the room to her and reaches toward her, letting his fingers come lightly to rest on her shoulders. His hands are trembling. The muscles of her back are knotted. They feel like slabs of cast iron.

"I'd like to stay," he tells her.

"Whatever you want." Same distant tone.

"You knew, didn't you? About Jolanda and me?"

"Yes. Of course."

"Then why—"

"To see what you'd say."

"I get a gold star for being honest, at least."

"Yes," she says. "I guess you do. Look, I'm going inside to finish what I was doing, okay?"

She walks away from his touch. Rhodes returns to the middle of the room, to his two drinks, finishes one, then the other, and after a while pours himself a third. It is terrible rotgut: Isabelle has some perverse fondness for the worst brands. But he drinks what she has, anyway. No doubt this is one of the cheap algae-mash kinds, a real scandal that they dare to call it Scotch. Still, though: given a choice between bad liquor and no liquor, he will uncomplainingly drink bad, and plenty of it. Sometimes his own capacity amazes him, these days. He hears Isabelle getting ready for bed, eventually, and goes in to join her. It is past midnight and he is exhausted. Despite the air-conditioning the hot, stale night air from outside somehow has invaded her apartment, ghostly tendrils of smelly crud gliding right through the walls, filling every room from floor to ceiling with a heavy choking fug.

She faces away from him in the darkness. Rhodes strokes her back.

"Don't." Sepulchral voice.

"Isabelle—"

"No. It's late."

He lies there stiffly, wide-awake. He can tell that she remains awake too. Time goes by: half an hour, an hour. A siren wails somewhere along the freeway. Rhodes thinks back over the evening, wondering why it had worked out this way. She's upset about the girl, Angela. That's it. A threat to her sense of professional competence. And she's probably fond of the girl, too. Countertransference, they call that. Not surprising. But then, the whole Jolanda business—

He reaches for her, touches her again.

Iron muscles. Rigid body.

He wants her desperately. Always does, every single night. His hand curves around past her arm and comes to rest on the soft mound of her right breast. Isabelle's breasts are the only soft things about her: her body is lean, taut, athletic. She doesn't move. Gently he caresses her. Breathes on the nape of her neck. No response. She could almost be dead.

Then she says, finally, "All right, if you want it so badly. Let's get it over with!"

Rolls over, turns around. Glares at him, spreads her legs.

"Isabelle, for God's sake—"

"Come on! What are you waiting for!"

Of course he doesn't want it to be like this, not at all. Except that he is helpless with her, and when she tugs him brusquely into place on top of her, he is unable to resist. Quickly, miserably, he enters her—despite everything, she is lathered and ready—and her hips begin to move, driving him remorselessly onward toward a speedy finish. He covers her face with grateful kisses; but at the same time he is shocked, horrified, stunned by what they are doing. It is an angry, murderous fuck, the death of love. When he comes he bursts into tears.

She embraces him then, cradles him against her breasts, strokes his hair, whispers soft words. Making it all good again. My God, he thinks, my God, my God.

Rhodes hears Paul Carpenter's voice, suddenly, in his mind.

—*She's a disturbed woman, Nick.*

—*No, she's simply deeply committed to—*

—*Listen to me. She's emotionally disturbed. So is her friend Jolanda, who you were kind enough to toss into my bed the other night. These are very sexually gifted women, and we who wander around looking for the solace of a little nookie are highly vulnerable to the mysterious mojo that throbs out at us from between their legs.*

Right. Right. If he had any courage, he'd flee. He knows that. But such things have never come easily to Rhodes. He is fiercely retentive, desperately eager to hang on to anything that gives even the promise of some sort of solace.

Eventually Rhodes drifts off into troubled sleep. About five he awakens, kisses the sleeping Isabelle lightly on the tip of her nose, and goes home.

By a couple of minutes after eight he is in the office. The miasma of the night still hovers over him, but he hopes somehow to lift himself out of grim depression through a hard day's work. At least, Rhodes thinks, in all of last night's horrors they hadn't gotten into yet another brawl over his research. But that was a very small comfort at best.

He held off Van Vliet as long as he could, well into midmorning. Van Vliet gave him a headache in his gut. The authorization for upgrading of

Van Vliet's hemoglobin-research budget had gone along to New Tokyo four days ago, and in all likelihood it would sail through without any objections, given Rhodes' high standing with upper-level Company management.

Until it did, though, Van Vliet would just have to sit tight. But the kid didn't seem capable of sitting tight. Two or three times a day he was on the horn to Rhodes, wanting to tell him about this or that exciting new corollary to his preliminary theoretical statement. Rhodes didn't have much appetite for another dose of that just now, not after last night, at least not so early in the day.

He killed as much time as he could, rummaging doggedly through both his virtual desks and all the clutter on his real one, signing papers without even reading them, flipping some documents down into dead storage unsigned, working mindlessly, shamelessly. Gradually Rhodes began to feel some of the newer abrasions in his soul starting to heal a little.

A couple of drinks helped him get through the bad time. The first one tasted strangely tinny—some residue from the evening before, he thought, damage to his palate from drinking too much of Isabelle's God-knows-what brand of algae-mash Scotch—but the second drink made things better. And the third went down without any problems at all.

Finally, feeling reasonably well fortified and aware he could duck his meeting with the younger man no longer, Rhodes thumbed the annunciator and said, "I'm available to talk with Dr. Van Vliet, now."

"Does that mean you'll be taking calls again, Dr. Rhodes?"

"I suppose. Have there been any for me?"

"Just one," the android said.

Isabelle! She's sorry that everything became such a mess last night!

No. Not Isabelle. "A Mr. Nakamura called," said the android.

"Who?"

"Mr. Nakamura, of East Bay Realty Associates. About the house in Walnut Creek that you are interested in buying."

Rhodes didn't know anyone named Nakamura. He wasn't planning to buy a house in Walnut Creek or anywhere else.

"It must have been a wrong number," Rhodes said. "He's looking for some other Nicholas Rhodes."

"He said that you were likely to think so. But he said to tell you that it was no mistake, that you would understand the terms of the offer right away and would be very pleased by them if you spoke to him."

Nakamura?

Walnut Creek?

It made no sense. But all consideration of the matter would have to wait. Van Vliet was on the line again, now.

He wanted to bring some new charts to Rhodes' office, right away. Big surprise, Van Vliet coming up with yet another batch of charts.

Rhodes sighed. "Charts of what?"

"Some new atmospheric extrapolations, the projected hydrogen cyanide levels and how we plan to cope with their special implications."

"I'm terrifically stacked up here, Van. Can't this wait a little?"

"But it's tremendously exciting stuff."

"Having to breathe hydrogen cyanide is exciting?" Rhodes asked. "Yes, I guess it would be. But not for very long."

"That's not what I mean, Nick," said Van Vliet. He had suddenly begun calling Rhodes "Nick," ever since the budget requisition had gone up to New Tokyo a few days before. Rhodes didn't like it much. "You see, Nick, we've come up with a really awesome set of equations that indicate the likelihood of oceanic amino-acid formation. *New* amino acids. If I could just have five minutes to show you what I'm talking about—"

"Okay," Rhodes said. "Five minutes."

Van Vliet took fifteen. Mostly that was Rhodes' fault: he let himself get interested. What Van Vliet's projections seemed to show was that the upcoming chemical configuration of the ocean might be going to duplicate, to some small and largely unpredictable degree, certain aspects of the nutrient-soup composition of the primordial sea. After hundreds of years of cheerfully filling the whole biosphere with all manner of deadly waste, mankind apparently was about to generate still another terrific surprise for itself that had to do with life instead of death: a mixed package, unexpected biogenesis along with the expectable morbidity, a seaborne reprise of the original chemical forces that had initiated the appearance of Earth's first living things, a hodgepodge of purines and adenylates and aminos stirring around and rearranging themselves into intricate polymers, some of them self-replicating, out of which might come—

Almost anything.

A shitstorm of random genetic information brewing in the depths of the twenty-fourth century's seas.

"Do you see it?" Van Vliet cried. "The potential for new life-forms emerging, Nick? Creation starting all over again!"

Rhodes summoned a hearty chuckle from some recess of his soul. "A second chance for the trilobites, eh?"

Van Vliet didn't seem amused. He gave Rhodes a reproachful look. "I mean one-celled organisms, Nick. Bacteria. Protozoa. An unpredictable pelagic micro-biota spontaneously evolving that could raise hell with the life-forms already present on the planet. Such as us."

Right, Rhodes thought. A load of strange evolutionary garbage hauling itself up out of the waters to plague an already quite adequately plagued planet.

It was an interesting speculative jump, and Rhodes said so, in all sincerity. In all sincerity, though, he didn't understand what any of this had to do with the work of Santachiara Technologies' Survival/Modification Program, at least not right away. Carefully he said, "I admire the care with which you're working out all the implications of the situation, Van. But I'm not sure I could get budgetary approval for a study dealing with diseases caused by microorganisms that haven't evolved yet."

A cool, almost supercilious grin from Van Vliet. "On the contrary, Nick. If we can project the potential consequences of a quantum jump in natural evolutionary processes, we might be able to build in defenses against new and hostile kinds of—"

"Please, Van. One step at a time, okay? Okay?"

One step at a time, obviously, wasn't the Van Vliet method. And plainly Rhodes' failure to whoop with enthusiasm over this new angle was, for Van Vliet, one more example of the associate director's hopeless conservatism. Rhodes pacified him, though, by congratulating him heartily on the new line of work, asking to see further studies, promising to take the topic of renewed biogenesis up at the very next meeting of the directors. And smoothly showed him to the door.

When Van Vliet was gone, Rhodes had one more drink, just a small one, to ease him through the transition into the day's next problem.

Which was to ponder the Nakamura call again. Rhodes was still certain that Mr. Nakamura, whoever he might be, had called the wrong number. But how odd that Nakamura would have thrown in that business about there being no mistake, exactly as though he was anticipating Rhodes' puzzled response. Something in that nagged at him, demanding resolution.

About that house in Walnut Creek that you are interested in buying.

The thought flashed through Rhodes' mind that that might be some sort of code phrase—that it referred to some secret enterprise into which Nakamura meant to inveigle him, the sale of corporate secrets, or an intricate counterespionage ploy, something like that. Things like that went on in the megacorp world all the time, Rhodes knew. Though he had never had any firsthand experience of them.

Rhodes put through a call to Ned Svoboda in Imaging and Schematics.

Svoboda was an occasional after-hours drinking companion of his, who had the rare distinction of having worked for three different megacorps in a dozen years or so: not only Samurai Industries but also Kyocera-Merck and before that the somewhat less formidable IBM/ Toshiba bunch. Svoboda was shrewd, Svoboda was about as trustworthy as anyone Rhodes could think of, and Svoboda had been around the block a couple of times. If anybody knew about corporate codes, industrial espionage, whatever, Svoboda was the one.

"You mind if I cruise over and talk to you for a couple of minutes?" Rhodes asked. "Something odd has come up and I need a little advice." And, Rhodes did not explicitly need to add, it was something best not discussed over the Company communications net. The wires had ears. That was common knowledge.

Svoboda didn't mind. Rhodes descended eight floors to Imaging and met Svoboda on the bubble-enclosed leisure terrace outside his office. He was a short, heavyset man of about forty, with dark rumpled hair and emphatic Slavic features.

Rhodes said, "I had a peculiar phone call this morning. Fellow with a Japanese name out of Walnut Creek—a realtor, he says. Says he'd like to talk to me about the house I'm interested in buying out there."

"I didn't know you were planning to move over the hill."

"I'm not. I don't know this Jap from Adam."

"Ah so."

"But he realizes that. When he phoned, he went out of his way to tell my annunciator that regardless of what I might think, this wasn't a mistaken call, that I was the Rhodes he was trying to reach and that I would really be interested in the property he had to offer. So I began to wonder, Ned—"

Svoboda's eyes widened. "Yeah, I bet you did."

"And I thought maybe it's more complicated than it appears at first glance—something that you might be able to explain to me, some kind of cryptic message that I ought to understand but don't quite see the—"

"Shhh!"

"What's wrong?"

"Just don't say anything more, okay?" Svoboda held his left arm out and let his right hand go crawling quickly across the back of it in the funny little crab-walk gesture that universally meant, *There probably are bugs here.* The Company had its spy eyes everywhere—even on leisure terraces, it seemed. Svoboda said, "You have a pen and a piece of paper on you?"

"Sure. Here."

It was a very small piece, but it was all that Rhodes could find. Svoboda clamped his lips together and wrote with exaggerated care, running his words across and down the side of the page in his effort to get down everything he wanted to say. He kept it covered with his other hand as he wrote, to prevent any hidden camera from seeing. When he was done he folded the piece in half, and in half again, and pressed it into the palm of Rhodes' hand.

"Go for a little walk and read it," Svoboda said. "Then maybe call me at home tonight if you want to talk about it any more, okay?"

He grinned and touched two fingers to the side of his head in a quick salute, and went back inside.

Rhodes, frowning, returned to his own area of the building. He thought of going into the washroom to read Svoboda's note, but on reflection he considered that there was no place in the building more likely to have a secret scanner eye mounted in the wall than in a washroom. Instead he simply leaned against the wall outside his office and opened the folded scrap, cupping it in his hand, and held it up in front of his face, very close, as if trying to read his own palm.

It said, in heavy block letters:

THIS IS A JOB OFFER. TELLING YOU THEY WANT
TO SELL YOU A HOUSE MEANS THAT THEY WANT
TO HIRE YOU.

Instantly Rhodes felt adrenaline beginning to surge. His heart was
thumping with frightening force.

What the hell was this?

THIS IS A JOB OFFER.

From whom? Why?

He read the note again, read it two or three times, and then balled it
up and stuffed it deep into his pocket.

THEY WANT TO HIRE YOU.

They? Who were *they*?

TO HIRE YOU. THEY WANT.

There had been a pretty good earthquake in the Bay Area three years
ago, six-point-something on the Richter scale. The whole building had
swayed for two and a half minutes then. This felt like that.

Rhodes was trembling. He tried to control it, and failed.

THIS IS A JOB OFFER.

Forget it, he told himself.

You don't want to mess around with anything like this. You already
have a job. It's a good one. You have a fine department, plenty of good
people working for you, nice pay, steady upward slope. You have never
worked for anybody but Samurai Industries in your life. You have never
wanted to work for anybody but Samurai Industries.

He reached into his pocket and touched the crumpled bit of paper.

Throw it away, Nick. Throw it away.

Rhodes went back into his office. More things were blinking on all
the inputs, but he ignored them. He poured himself a drink, a pretty
significant one.

He thought about what it might be like to work for another company.

Certainly he was stymied at Samurai by his own ambivalences and
hesitations. Just as he was, also, in his relationship with Isabelle. Only a
little while ago he had been thinking about the need for change in his life,
and all that came roaring back through him now, the great surge of vague

resentments, something turbulent, almost explosive, stirring inside him. It hadn't been very long ago that he had told Paul Carpenter how deeply he feared giving Samurai Industries a monopoly over human adapto technology. And Paul had come right back at him with the solution to that. *Quit Santachiara and go over to somebody like Kyocera-Merck. Take your whole department with you. Turn your gene technology over to the competition. Let Samurai and K-M fight it out for world domination.*

Was he being handed a chance to do just that?

Then he should grab it, he thought.

At least find out what this is all about, he urged himself. *Call Nakamura. Arrange to see him.*

"Get me Mr. Nakamura, at East Bay Realty," Rhodes told the annunciator giddily.

It was like making a date, he thought, that could lead to some kind of adulterous romance.

It took quite a while to get through. You would think realty agents would be eager to talk with potential customers, but evidently returning a call to Mr. Nakamura wasn't the easiest thing in the world to do. Then finally lights began to flash and a Japanese face looked back at him from the visor. The standard inscrutability: flat inexpressive gaze, androidal smile. Somehow the face looked Japanese rather than Japanese-American, Rhodes thought, on no evidence at all. That was interesting.

"I am Mr. Kurashiki," the face said. "Mr. Nakamura is deeply grateful for your response to his call. He is available to see you at any of the following times today or tomorrow."

A menu appeared on the visor: noon, two P.M., four P.M., nine or eleven in the morning tomorrow.

Rhodes felt a faint chill. He wondered if he ever actually would meet Mr. Nakamura, whether there was a real Mr. Nakamura at all, even whether there was a real Mr. Kurashiki. Mr. Kurashiki looked and sounded more like a simulation than a person.

But then Rhodes told himself that he was being silly. Kurashiki was the appointments secretary, that was all; and he was real, all right, as real as any of these Japs ever could be. Svoboda had called it correctly: this was serious business, an actual job offer coming from an actual rival megacorp.

"Noon today," Rhodes said. He would have to leave almost at once.

But that was one way to keep his legendary unpunctuality from fouling things up. It was probably wisest to be on time for this one. "If you'll give me the driving directions—"

"You will be coming from Berkeley? The Santachiara Technologies tower?"

"Yes."

"The trip will take you fourteen minutes and thirty seconds. As you enter Highway 24, instruct your car that the route module code is H112.03/accessWR52."

Rhodes tapped for thirty seconds' worth of data recall and the number came rolling out of the annunciator's printout slot. He thanked Kurashiki and broke the contact.

"Cancel my afternoon appointments," Rhodes told the annunicator. "I'm going out."

The Diablos were still blowing when his car came up from the garage: a tangible wind, a palpable wind, hard and knife-sharp and maybe fifty miles an hour, and he would be driving right into it. You actually could *see* the wind. It was traveling visibly through the larger continuum of the atmosphere. It had the form of an eerie golden aura, a kind of urinous tint: a fast-moving organic haze, a virulent phosphorescent swirl of airborne industrial contaminants sailing westward out of the factory zone on the far side of Walnut Creek. The air was so full of the stuff that it seemed fertile, capable of impregnating anything it encountered on its way toward the ocean. Rhodes thought of Van Vliet's new theory, the floating soup of amino acids out of which wondrously virulent bacteria would be generated. Maybe this wind was the key factor that would kindle into life, this very afternoon, the jolly new chemical configuration that Van Vliet said was soon due to take form in the seas.

Rhodes hated to let his car brain do the thinking. But in this case he didn't know where the hell he was going, only that the route module code was H112.03/accessWR52, somewhere out in the vicinity of Walnut Creek.

"Take me to H112.03/accessWR52," Rhodes told the car.

The car obediently repeated the numbers.

"And, by the way, where is that, exactly?" Rhodes asked.

But all the car could do was give him the route module code all over again. For the car brain, the location of H112.03/accessWR52 was a place known as H112.03/accessWR52, period.

The vehicle held the road very nicely, considering the velocity of the oncoming wind. It took Rhodes with barely a wobble through the ancient Caldecott Tunnel and into the bleached, torched-looking countryside east of the hills, where the temperature was always twenty degrees warmer because the cool breeze off the Pacific was unable to make it that far inland, even on days when the Diablos weren't roaring. Today, with the hot east wind blowing, the temperature differential was probably much greater: true desert heat out there, Rhodes thought, hot as a furnace, fry you like an omelet in half a minute. But he was secure inside the cozy sealed bubble of his car, which was taking him swiftly down the freeway, on past the venerable high-rise towers of the old quiet suburban towns, Orinda, Lafayette, Pleasant Valley, toward the sprawling ramshackle metropolis of Walnut Creek—and then, just before the Walnut Creek interchange, a zig and a zag and a departure from the trunk road, the car swinging now up into the hills. It was absolutely empty country up there, amazingly empty, dotted with the occasional gnarly form of an oak tree standing in the midst of sun-scorched grass. The car went onward through a security gate and then another, and then past a checkpoint that made the first two gates look like barriers made of cheesecloth.

Brilliant green sky-glo letters, floating in the air about forty feet up, announced:

KYOCERA-MERCK, LTD.
WALNUT CREEK RESEARCH CENTER

So there was his answer, not that he really had any doubts left by this time.

The car, in the grasp of some invisible Kyocera-programmed highway brain, moved through the checkpoint, past a series of Babylonian-looking brick buildings, and into a reception dome.

Mr. Kurashiki was waiting for him there, no simulation at all, a real Japanese human person with a certain reptilian grace. Mr. Kurashiki bowed formally in the Japanese manner, a quick robotic click of his head. A quick robotic smile, too. Rhodes smiled back but did not return the bow. The formalities were done with; Mr. Kurashiki led Rhodes into a transport shaft that conveyed him upward and deposited him in an office that, from its ad hoc furnishings and general appearance of improvisation and barrenness, was obviously used only for just such impromptu conferences as these.

It was exactly noon.

Mr. Kurashiki vanished silently. Rhodes stepped forward. A surprisingly tall Japanese was standing at the precise center of the room, waiting for him. A different kind entirely, this one. He looked like something carved out of yellow-green obsidian: sharp features, shining skin texture, glossy wide-set jet-black eyes with a single dense unbroken eyebrow line above them. Powerful cheekbones, sharp as blades.

No bow from this one. A smile that seemed almost human, though.

"Good afternoon, Dr. Rhodes. I am so extremely glad that you were able to advantage us of your presence here today," he said. "You will forgive me, I am sure, for our little subterfuge, our pretense of real-estate business. Such things are necessary sometimes, as of course I am certain you know." His voice was deep and resonant and his accent was perceptibly alien: International Modern Japanese English, the purring accent of the exile race that in its various far-flung places of refuge had begun to develop its own new and distinctive way of speaking the world language. "But I have not introduced myself. I am Nakamura. Level Three Executive." A business card jumped into his hand as if by a conjuring trick, elegant laminated parchment with gold trim, and he handed it to Rhodes in a smooth, practiced way.

Rhodes stared at the card. Its metallic lettering glowed with talismanic inner light. There was the Kyocera-Merck monogram, and the name HIDEKI NAKAMURA in flaring three-dimensional modernistic script, and a simple numeral 3 in one corner. The mark of status: Nakamura's place on the corporate slope.

Level *Three?*

Level Three was puissant managerial material indeed, just one notch below the two practically imperial levels that were occupied almost entirely by the hereditary plenipotentiary ruling families of the great megacorps.

In his whole corporate career Rhodes had never laid eyes on, let alone spoken with, anyone higher than Level Four.

A little shaken, he slipped the card into his pocket. Nakamura was now extending his hand again, this time just for a conventional Western handshake, and Rhodes took it. It felt more or less like the hand of any ordinary mortal.

Nakamura was still smiling, too. But behind the smile Rhodes imagined he perceived the cold rage that infested these high-level Japanese: despite all their wealth and power and intelligence, driven from their homeland by the furies of the sea. Forced to take up their lives here and there around the world in the midst of the hairy, ugly, smelly, big-nosed, pallid un-Japanese barbarians. And even to have to shake their hands now and then.

Nakamura said, "If I may offer you something to drink, Dr. Rhodes—I am partial to cognac, myself, and perhaps you would like to join me—"

They've really done their research, Rhodes thought admiringly.

"Yes," he said, perhaps a little too quickly. "By all means. Please."

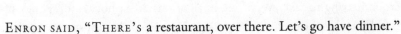

ENRON SAID, "THERE'S a restaurant, over there. Let's go have dinner."

"Restaurant?" Jolanda said. "I don't see any restaurant, Marty."

"There. *There.*" Enron lifted her arm as if it were a jointed piece of wood attached to her torso and pointed with it. "That little place with the tables out front in the courtyard, the red-and-green awnings. The restaurants up here are all out in the open like that. Because you can breathe the air here, you see."

"Oh," she said dreamily. "Oh, yes. I understand."

Did she? They had been on Valparaiso Nuevo for eight hours now and she was still moving around like a sleepwalker. Of course, this was her first time on any habitat, but still—still—

At the terminal where they came in, when all those smartass kids had come crowding around them trying to get him to hire them as tourist guides, she had seemed dazed and bewildered in the hubbub, standing by helplessly while Enron coped with them. "Who are they?" she asked, sounding like a confused child, as the insistent swarm pressed in close. And she had barely seemed to be listening as he told her: "Fucking leeches, they are. Parasites who want to charge you a fortune to help you get through customs and checked into your hotel, which any intelligent person is perfectly capable of handling for himself." He had finally hired one anyway, a big blond pudgy kid who called himself Kluge. Had hired him partly because he had begun to suspect that their services really might be necessary in a place as corrupt as this, and partly to provide himself with someone who might be able to make connections for him as he settled into the task ahead. Which was, specifically, to help them locate her conspiratorial friend from Los Angeles, Davidov, on this little world where it was not necessarily easy to locate people who were not eager to be located.

Enron had explained some of this to Jolanda also, not all, and she had nodded; but it was a dull, sleepy sort of nod. There was no light of comprehension in her eyes.

Valparaiso Nuevo seemed to be acting on Jolanda so far like a drug, some sort of narcotic. You would think that she would be hypermanic on the first day of her very first trip to the L-5 worlds after so many years of fantasizing about going to one, goggle-eyed with curiosity, running around trying to take everything in all at once. But no, no, the shock of novelty had had exactly the opposite effect. Even though she was such a heavy user of hyperdex—Enron had seen her taking the stimulant several times, now; she gobbled it like candy—she appeared numbed, stunned, up here on Valparaiso Nuevo, shuffling around dragging her feet like the slow-witted sluggish cow that she really was, beneath all her babble of the importance of art and culture and the need to protect the planet and all the rest of her asshole California politics.

Maybe it was the fresh air, Enron thought, with its relatively high proportion of oxygen and the total absence of shit like methane and toxic contaminants. She couldn't handle all that sweet pure stuff. Maybe her mind conked out if it didn't have its proper CO_2 fix. Or the light gravity, maybe. It ought to be making her giddy but instead it was somehow turning her into a zombie. Down at the terminal in the hub, they had practically been floating above the pavement, the gravitational pull was so feeble, and almost from the moment of their arrival she had been slogging around with that glassy-eyed brain-dead look on her face.

Now, after all the maddening lunatic bureaucratic customs-and-immigration routines were done with and they had checked into their hotel, it was dinnertime and they were in a town called Valdivia, a little past midway up F Spoke toward the rim. The gravity here was about .6, Enron figured. A little closer to Earth-normal than at the terminal, anyway. So far it wasn't making much difference. He hoped Jolanda would be livelier when they got back to the room after dinner.

They entered the restaurant courtyard. An oily-looking head waiter unctuously seated them. Menus blossomed out of visors set in the tabletop.

"What do you want to drink?" Enron asked.

"What?" She blinked at him.

"To drink, to drink! Wake *up*, Jolanda!"

"Oh. To drink. I'm sorry, Marty. It must be the jet lag."

"There isn't any jet lag in shuttle travel. We came right up here, bam, quicker than it would take to go from California to Tel Aviv."

"Well, it's something, anyway. I feel so strange."

"You don't like it here?"

"Oh, no, that isn't it. It's a *wonderful* place! I knew the space worlds were beautiful, fabulous, but I never really imagined—the stars, the moon—I mean, the splendor of it all, all these shining glass walls, the fantastic views you get everywhere—and the air—it's so fresh I feel drunk, Marty. I've never breathed air like this." She gave him a moony, apologetic look. "I'm so excited that I'm dazed, I guess. I feel like this is all some sort of dream. Oh, Marty, I'm so thrilled that you brought me here. —Get me a whiskey sour, will you?"

Good. At least she was coming to life a little.

Enron managed a smile. After punching the drink orders into the tabletop computer he reached across the table, took her hand, stroked it affectionately, squeezed it. Winked. Tonight in the hotel, he thought, I will lick every square millimeter of your glorious oversized body, I will drive you crazy with sex, I will fuck you sixty ways from Tuesday. And then in the morning we will go looking for your friends, your shifty Los Angeles friends who are supposed to be here somewhere, the ones who are planning to toss the old Generalissimo into the matter converter and take possession of this place. And when we find them, your Davidov and the others—

His eyes were roving randomly past Jolanda's shoulder, exploring in an automatically inquisitive sort of way the tables behind her, as he fondled her. Suddenly Enron caught sight of someone whose presence here startled him extremely.

Well, look who's here! The eyeless Kyocera Hungarian!

Enron's fingers tightened convulsively. Jolanda let out a little yelp of pain and surprise and pulled her hand away from him. She stared at him.

"Sorry," he said.

"What is it? Is anything wrong?"

"No. Not really. But something very interesting. Don't turn around, Jolanda. Just get up and walk across the courtyard. You need to pee, or something. Ask the waiter where to go. And take a good look on the way, without seeming to. The man sitting three tables behind us, facing in my direction. You'll know which one I mean."

She did exactly as she was told. Enron followed her with his eyes, watching the slow, undulating movements of her, the swaying of her hips, the ripplings of her great meaty buttocks. As she passed the Hungarian, she reacted only in the most momentary way, a quick tightening of her step and a brief sharp backward quiver of her elbows, as though a mild electrical shock had passed through her. Eyes less acute than Enron's might not have noticed the response at all. Then she moved on, her loose gown floating grandly about her, and disappeared on the far side of the courtyard.

On the way back she stole another look, flicking a glance at the side of the Hungarian's face as she went past him. She was wide-awake now, eyes bright, breathing hard, nostrils flaring. Excited, yes.

"Fascinating," she said, taking her seat. "I've never seen a face like that."

"I have."

"You know him?"

"I've had some contact with him. Long ago."

"An astounding face. I'd like to sculpt it, in clay. To run my hands over him and feel the bony structure underneath. Who is he, Marty?"

"A man named Farkas. George Farkas, Laszlo Farkas, Alexander Farkas—I forget the first name. Hungarian. They have about six first names in the whole country, Hungarians. If they aren't Georges, they're Laszlos or Alexanders. Or Zoltans. He works for Kyocera-Merck. *Victor* Farkas, that's the name. Victor. The exception that proves the rule."

"How do you know him?" Jolanda asked.

"I met him once. It was in—I don't remember, Bolivia, Venezuela, some incredibly hot place that was all jungles and vines and palm trees, a place where you would sprout green moss on your skin if you stood still for five minutes. He is in my line of work, this Farkas."

"A journalist?"

"A spy. His title with Kyocera-Merck is 'expediter.' My title with my employer is 'journalist.' We do the same sort of thing, Farkas and I, but he does it for Kyocera-Merck and I do it for the government of Israel."

"I thought you worked for *Cosmos* magazine."

He took her hand in his again. She has magnificent breasts, he thought, but she is really stupid. Perhaps there is a connection. She is a cow not just metaphorically, but a real one, a literal cow. She has been retrofitted with bovine genes to give her those splendid udders.

Quietly Enron said, "I thought I had told you all of this already and that you had understood it. The magazine work is my cover, Jolanda. I truly am a spy. That is what I do, actually, when I pretend to be a journalist. Is that clear enough? Are you willing to believe it? This was a matter that I thought was settled the night I was at your house."

"I decided the next morning that you had only been joking."

"A spy. Truly. When you told me about your friends in Los Angeles, the reason why I asked you to come up here with me and introduce me to them was that I saw a way that doing so would benefit my country. Not my magazine, but my country. I work for the state of Israel. Is that difficult for you to believe? When I left you that night, I called someone in Jerusalem on a secret scrambled line, I used code names and code words, I told them in spy language where I wanted to go and why I wanted to go there, and tickets for this trip were made available to me through special channels. And visas for us both. Do you think it is always so easy to get an entry visa to a place like this? But I did it in one night, because my government made the proper connections for me. I tell you this because I would not want you to be deceived about me in any way. I may seem sometimes like a bastard, but I am an honorable man, Jolanda."

"The other night, when I said I had never slept with a spy before, you said that you were one. You said it just like that. I believed you and then afterward I didn't. And now you're saying it again."

"If you want to believe I am a writer for a magazine, Jolanda, believe that instead. Believe whatever makes you happiest."

Enron saw that she was going to go back and forth on the issue in what passed for her mind forever. Which was fine with him. If she were ever interrogated, she would provide her questioners with a torrent of ingenuous ambivalence. Sometimes telling people the simple truth about yourself is the best way of surrounding the reality of your profession with a haze of confusion.

She said, "The man without eyes. How can he be a spy, if he can't see?"

"He can see, all right. He just doesn't do it the way we do."

"He uses extrasensory perception, you mean?"

"It is something like that, yes."

"Was he born that way?"

"Yes and no," Enron said.

"I don't understand," said Jolanda. "What's that supposed to mean?"

"A splice job was done on him while he was in the womb. I don't know who did it, or why. The time we met, it didn't seem appropriate to ask him about it." Enron allowed himself a quick glance in Farkas's direction. Farkas was busy with his dinner. He seemed calm, relaxed, concentrating entirely on his meal. If he had noticed Enron's presence, he was giving no indication of it. Enron said, "He is a very difficult man, very intelligent, very dangerous. I wonder what he is doing here. —You find his face fascinating, you say?"

"Very."

"You want to sculpt it? You want to run your hands over his bony structure?"

"Yes. I really do."

"Ah," Enron said. "Well, then. Let us find a way of arranging for that to be possible, shall we?"

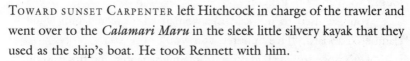

TOWARD SUNSET CARPENTER left Hitchcock in charge of the trawler and went over to the *Calamari Maru* in the sleek little silvery kayak that they used as the ship's boat. He took Rennett with him.

The stink of the other ship reached his nostrils long before he went scrambling up the gleaming woven-monofilament ladder that they threw over the side for him: a bitter, acrid reek, a miasma so dense that it was almost visible. Breathing it was something like inhaling all of Cleveland at a single snort. Carpenter wished he'd worn a face-lung. But who expected to need one out at sea, where you were supposed to be able to breathe reasonably decent air?

He wouldn't have been surprised to discover that the smell was coming from the *Calamari Maru*'s own bones and tissues, that its hull and deck and superstructure and everything else were covered with rotting loathsome pustules bubbling with decay. But in fact there seemed nothing much wrong with the ship aside from general neglect and slovenliness: black stains on the deck, gray swirls of dust everywhere, some nasty rust-colored patches of ozone attack that needed work. The reek came from the squid themselves.

The heart of the ship was a vast tank, a huge squid-peeling factory occupying the whole mid-deck. Carpenter had seen ships like this one at anchor in the Port of Oakland—Samurai Industries ran dozens of them—but he had never thought much about what it would be like actually to be aboard one.

Looking down into the tank, he saw a nightmare world of marine life, battalions of hefty many-tentacled squid swimming in herds, big-eyed pearly boneless phantoms, scores of them shifting direction suddenly and simultaneously in their squiddy way. Glittering mechanical flails moved among them, seizing and slicing, efficiently locating and cutting out the nerve tissue, flushing the edible remainder toward the meat-packing facility at the far end of the tank. The stench was astonishing. The whole thing was a tremendous processing machine. With the onetime farming heartland of North America and temperate Europe now worthless desert, and the world dependent on the thin, rocky soil of northern Canada and Siberia for so much of its food, harvesting the sea was essential. Carpenter understood that. But he hadn't expected a squid ship to *smell* so awful. He fought to keep from gagging.

"You get used to it," said the woman who greeted him when he clambered aboard. "Five minutes, you won't notice."

"Let's hope so," he said. "I'm Captain Carpenter, and this is Rennett, maintenance/ops. Where's Kovalcik?"

"I'm Kovalcik," the woman said.

Carpenter's eyes widened. She seemed to be amused by his show of surprise.

Kovalcik was rugged and sturdy looking, more than average height for a woman, strong cheekbones, eyes set very far apart, expression very cool and controlled, but significant strain evident behind the control. She was wearing a sacklike jumpsuit of some coarse gray fabric. About thirty, Carpenter guessed. Her hair was black and close-cropped and her skin was fair, strangely fair, hardly any trace of Screen showing in it. He saw signs of sun damage, signs of ozone crackle, red splotches of burn. Two members of her crew stood behind her, also women, also jumpsuited, also oddly fair-skinned. Their skins didn't look so good either.

Kovalcik said. "We are very grateful you came. There is bad trouble on this ship." Her voice was flat. She had just the trace of a European accent, hard to place, something that had originated east of Vienna but was otherwise unspecifiable.

"We'll help out if we can," Carpenter told her.

He perceived now that they had carved a chunk out of his berg and grappled it up onto the deck, where it was melting into three big aluminum runoff tanks. It couldn't have been a millionth of the total berg mass, not a ten millionth, but seeing it gave him a quick little stab of proprietary anger and he felt a muscle quiver in his cheek. That reaction didn't go unnoticed either. Kovalcik said quickly, "Yes, water is one of our problems. We have had to replenish our supply this way. There have been some equipment failures lately. You will come to the captain's cabin now? We must talk of what has happened, what must now be done."

She led him down the deck, with Rennett and the two crew women following along behind.

The *Calamari Maru* was pretty impressive. It was big and long and sleek, built somewhat along the lines of a squid itself, a jet-propulsion job that gobbled water into colossal compressors and squirted it out behind. That was one of the many low-fuel solutions to maritime transport problems that had been worked out for the sake of keeping CO_2 output down in these difficult times. Immense things like flying buttresses ran down the deck on both sides. These, Kovalcik explained, were squid lures, covered with bioluminescent photophores: you lowered them into the water and they gave off light that mimicked the glow of the squids' own bodies, and the slithery tentacular buggers came jetting in from vast distances, expecting a great jolly jamboree and getting a net instead.

"Some butchering operation you've got here," Carpenter said.

Kovalcik said, a little curtly, "Meat is not all we produce. The squid we catch here has value as food, of course, but also we strip the nerve fibers, the axons, we bring them back to the mainland, they are used in all kinds of biosensor applications. They are very large, those fibers, a hundred times as thick as ours, the largest kind of nerve fiber in the world, the most massive signal system of any animal there is. They are like single-cell computers, the squid axons. You have a thousand processors aboard your ship that use squid fiber, do you know? Follow me, please. This way."

They went down a ramp, along a narrow companionway. Carpenter heard thumpings and pingings in the walls. A bulkhead was dented and badly scratched. The lights down here were dimmer than they ought to be and the fixtures had an ominous hum. There was a new odor now, a tang of something chemical, sweet but not a pleasing kind of sweet, more a burned kind of sweet than anything else, cutting sharply across the heavy squid stench the way a piccolo might cut across the boom of drums. Rennett shot him a somber glance. This ship was a mess, all right.

"Captain's cabin is here," Kovalcik said, pushing back a door that was hanging askew on its hinges. "We have drink first, yes?"

The size of the cabin bedazzled Carpenter, after all those weeks bottled up in his little hole on the *Tonopah Maru*. It looked as big as a gymnasium. There was a table, a desk, shelving, a comfortable bunk, a sanitary unit, even an entertainment visor, everything nicely spread out with actual floor space you could move around in. The visor had been kicked in. Kovalcik took a flask of Peruvian brandy from a cabinet and Carpenter nodded, and she poured three stiff ones. They drank in silence.

The squid odor wasn't so bad in here, or else he was getting used to it, just as she had said. But the air was rank and close despite the spaciousness of the cabin, thick soupy goop that was a struggle to breathe. Something's wrong with the ventilating system too, Carpenter thought.

"You see the trouble we have," said Kovalcik.

"I see there's been trouble, yes."

"You don't see half. You should see command room too. Here, have more brandy, then I take you there."

"Never mind the brandy," Carpenter said. "How about telling me what the hell's been going on aboard this ship?"

"First come see command room," Kovalcik said.

The command room was one level down from the captain's cabin. It was an absolute wreck.

The place was all but burned out. There were laser scars on every surface and gaping wounds in the structural fabric of the ceiling. Glittering strings of program cores were hanging out of data cabinets like broken necklaces, like spilled guts. Everywhere there were signs of some terrible struggle, some monstrous insane civil war that had raged through the most delicate regions of the ship's mind centers.

"It is all ruined," Kovalcik said. "Nothing works any more except the squid-processing programs, and as you see those work magnificently, going on and on, the nets and flails and cutters and so forth. But everything else is damaged. Our water synthesizer, the ventilators, our navigational equipment, much more. We are making repairs but it is very slow."

"I can imagine it would be. You had yourselves one hell of a party here, huh?"

"There was a great struggle. From deck to deck, from cabin to cabin. It became necessary to place Captain Kohlberg under restraint and he and some of the other officers resisted."

Carpenter blinked and caught his breath up short at that.

"What the fuck are you saying? That you had a *mutiny* aboard this ship?"

For a moment the charged word hung between them like a whirling sword.

Then Kovalcik said, her voice flat as ever, "When we had been at sea for a while, the captain became like a crazy man. It was the heat that got to him, the sun, maybe the air. He began to ask impossible things. He would not listen to reason. And so he had to be removed from command for the safety of all. There was a meeting and he was put under restraint. Some of his officers objected and they had to be put under restraint too."

Son of a bitch, Carpenter thought, feeling a little sick. What have I walked into here?

"Sounds just like mutiny to me," Rennett said.

Carpenter shushed her. Kovalcik was starting to bristle and there was no telling at what point that glacial poise of hers would turn into volcanic fury. Plainly she was very dangerous if she had managed to put her captain away, and most of her officers besides. Even these days mutiny was serious business. This had to be handled delicately.

To Kovalcik he said, "They're still alive, the captain, the officers?"

"Yes. I can show them to you."

"That would be a good idea. But first maybe you ought to tell me some more about these grievances you had."

"That doesn't matter now, does it?"

"To me it does. I need to know what you think justifies removing a captain."

She began to look a little annoyed. "There were many things, some big, some small. Work schedules, crew pairings, the food allotment. Everything worse and worse for us each week. Like a tyrant, he was. A Caesar. Not at first, but gradually, the change in him. It was sun poisoning he had, the craziness that comes from too much heat on the brain. He was afraid to use very much Screen, you see, afraid that we would run out before the end of the voyage, so he rationed it very tightly, not only for us, even for himself. That was one of our biggest troubles, the Screen." Kovalcik touched her cheeks, her forearms, her wrists, where the skin was pink and raw. "You see how I look? We are all like that. Kohlberg cut us to half ration, then half that. The sun began to eat us. The ozone. It was like razors coming out of the sky. We had no protection, do you see? He was so frightened there would be no Screen later on that he let us use only a small amount every day, and we suffered, and so did he, and he got crazier as the sun worked on him, and there was less Screen all the time. He had it hidden, I think. We have not found it yet. We are still on quarter ration."

Carpenter tried to imagine what that was like, sailing around under the ferocious sky of these tropical latitudes without body armor. The daily injections withheld, the unshielded skin of these people exposed to the full fury of the greenhouse climate—the defective ozone layer, the punishing sun. Could Kohlberg really have been so stupid, or so loony? But there was no getting around the raw pink patches on Kovalcik's skin.

"You'd like us to let you have a supply of Screen, is that it?" he asked uneasily.

"No. We would not expect that of you. Sooner or later, we will find it where Kohlberg has hidden it."

"Then what is it you do want?"

"Come," Kovalcik said. "Now I show you the officers."

The mutineers had stashed their prisoners in the ship's infirmary, a stark, humid room far belowdeck with three double rows of bunks along the wall and some nonfunctioning medical mechs between them. Each of the bunks but one held a sweat-shiny man with a week's growth of beard. They were conscious, but not very. Their wrists were tied.

"It is very disagreeable for us, keeping them like this," Kovalcik said. "But what can we do? This is Captain Kohlberg." Captain Kohlberg was heavy-set, Teutonic-looking, groggy-eyed. "He is calm now, but only because we sedate him," Kovalcik explained. "We sedate all of them, fifty cc of omnipax every day. But it is a threat to their health, the constant sedation. And in any case, the drugs, we are running short. Another few days and then we will have none, and it will be harder to keep them restrained, and if they break free there will be war on this ship again."

"I'm not sure if we have any omnipax on board," Carpenter said. "Certainly not enough to do you much good for long."

"That is not what we are asking either," said Kovalcik.

"What *are* you asking, then?"

"These five men, they threaten everybody's safety. They have for-feited the right to command. This I could show, with playbacks of the time of struggle on this ship. Take them."

"What?"

Kovalcik gave him a look of sudden strange intensity, fierce, compel-ling, unsettling.

"Take them onto your ship. They must not stay here. These are crazy men. We must rid ourselves of them. We must be left to repair our ship in peace and do the work we are paid to do. It is a humanitarian thing, taking them. You are going back to San Francisco with the iceberg? Take them, these troublemakers. They will be no danger to you. They will be grateful for being rescued. But here they are like bombs that must sooner or later go off."

Carpenter looked at her as if she were a bomb that had already gone off. Rennett had simply turned away, covering what sounded like a burst of hysterical laughter by forcing a coughing fit.

That was all he needed, making himself an accomplice in this thing, obligingly picking up a bunch of officers who had been pushed off their ship by mutineers. Kyocera-Merck men at that. Aid and succor to the great corporate enemy? The head Samurai Industries agent in Frisco would really love it when he came chugging into port with five K-M men on board. He'd especially want to hear that Carpenter had done it for humanitarian reasons.

Besides, he had no room for them. Where the fuck were these men going to sleep? On deck between the spigots? Should he pitch a tent on the iceberg, maybe? What about feeding them, for Christ's sake? What about Screen? Everything was calibrated down to the last molecule.

"I don't think you understand our situation," Carpenter said care-fully. "Aside from the legalities of the thing, we've got no space for extra personnel. We barely have enough room for ourselves."

"It would be just for a short while, no? A week or two?"

"I tell you we've got every millimeter allotted. If God Himself wanted to come on board as a passenger, we'd have a tough time figuring out where to put Him. You want technical help patching your ship back together, we can try to provide that. We can even let you have some supplies. But taking five men aboard—"

Kovalcik's eyes began to look a little wild. She was breathing very hard now. "You must do this for us! You must! Otherwise—"

She didn't go on.

"Otherwise?" Carpenter prompted.

All he got from her was a bleak stare, no friendlier than the green-streaked ozone-crisp sky.

"Hilfe," Kohlberg muttered just then, stirring unexpectedly in his bunk.

"What was that?"

"It is delirium," said Kovalcik.

"Hilfe. Hilfe. In Gottes Namen, hilfe!" And then, in slow, thickly accented English, the words painfully framed: "Help. She will kill us all."

"Delirium?" Carpenter said.

Kovalcik's eyes grew even chillier. Drawing an ultrasonic syringe from a cabinet in the wall, she slapped it against Kohlberg's arm and pressed. There was a small buzzing sound. Kohlberg subsided into sleep. Snuffling snores rose from his bunk.

Kovalcik smiled. Now that the captain was unconscious again she seemed to be recovering her self-control. "He is a madman. You see what my skin is like. What his madness has done to me, has done to every one of us. If he got loose, if he put the voyage in jeopardy—yes, yes, we would kill him. We would kill them all. It would be only self-defense, you understand me? But it must not come to that." Her voice was icy. You could air-condition an entire city with that voice. "You were not here during the trouble. You do not know what we went through. We will not go through it again. Take these men from us, Captain."

She stepped back, folding her arms across her chest. The room was very quiet, suddenly, except for the pingings and thumpings from the ship's interior, and an occasional snore out of Kohlberg. Kovalcik was completely calm again, the ferocity and iciness no longer visible. As though she were merely telling him: This is the situation, you have heard the story, the ball is now in your court, Captain Carpenter.

What a stinking squalid mess, Carpenter thought.

But he was greatly surprised to find, when he looked behind the irritation he felt at having been dragged into this, a curious sadness where he would have expected anger to be.

Despite everything he found himself flooded with surprising compassion for Kovalcik, for Kohlberg, for every one of them, for the whole damned fucking poisoned heat-blighted world they had all been born into. Who had asked for any of this—the heavy green sky, the fiery air, the daily need for Screen, the million frantic improvisations that made continued life on Earth possible? Not us. Our great-great-grandparents had, maybe, but not us. Only they're not here to know what it's like, and we are. They had fucked the world in one long merry carnival of rape, and then had tossed us the battered remains. And never even had known what they were doing. And wouldn't have given a shit about it if they had.

Then the moment passed. What the hell could he do? Did Kovalcik think he was Jesus Christ? He had no room for these people. He had no extra Screen or food. And the basic thing was that this was none of his business. San Francisco was waiting for its iceberg. The berg was melting even as they dithered here. It was time to move along. Tell her anything, just get out of here.

"All right," Carpenter said. "I see your problem. I'm not entirely sure I can help out, but I'll do what I can. I'll check our supplies and let you know what we're able to do. Okay?" He looked at Rennett, who for a time seemed to have disappeared into some alternate dimension. Rennett had returned, now. She was staring at Carpenter in a coldly curious way, as though trying to see into his skull and read his mind. Her expression was challenging, truculent. She wanted to know how he was going to cope with this.

So did he, as a matter of fact.

Kovalcik said, "You will give me your answer this evening?"

"First thing in the morning," said Carpenter. "Best I can do. Too late tonight for working it all out."

"You will call me, then."

"Yes. I'll call you."

To Rennett he said, "Come on. Let's get back to the ship."

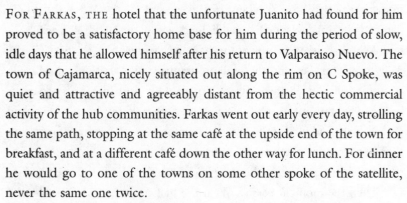

For Farkas, the hotel that the unfortunate Juanito had found for him proved to be a satisfactory home base for him during the period of slow, idle days that he allowed himself after his return to Valparaiso Nuevo. The town of Cajamarca, nicely situated out along the rim on C Spoke, was quiet and attractive and agreeably distant from the hectic commercial activity of the hub communities. Farkas went out early every day, strolling the same path, stopping at the same café at the upside end of the town for breakfast, and at a different café down the other way for lunch. For dinner he would go to one of the towns on some other spoke of the satellite, never the same one twice.

Everyone in the immediate neighborhood of the hotel quickly got used to the way he looked. The café owners, even the android waiters. His strangeness didn't bother them any more. It took only a couple of days. After that he was one of the regulars, just didn't happen to have any eyes, smooth blank space above his nose right up to the top of his forehead. Leaves good tips. Place like this, you get to see all kinds. Everyone very tolerant, very cognizant of everybody's privacy. That was the most important commodity for sale here, privacy. Privacy and courtesy. The social contract, Valparaiso Nuevo style. "Good morning, Mr. Farkas. Nice to see you again, Mr. Farkas. I hope you slept well, Mr. Farkas. A cup of coffee, Mr. Farkas?"

He enjoyed the scenery, the big sky, the dazzling stellar display, the spectacular views of the Earth and the moon. To Farkas, the Earth was a massive involuted purple box with heavy dangling green tassels, and the moon was a dainty, airy hollow ball filled with jagged orange coils, packed tight within it like little springs. Sometimes the sun would strike a neighboring L-5 world in just the right way and set off a brilliant shower of light, both reflected and refracted, spilling across the darkness like a cascade of million-faceted diamonds, a waterfall of glittering jewels. That was very pleasant to watch. This was the most enjoyable holiday Farkas had had in a long time.

Of course, he was supposed to be working as well as resting, here. But he could hardly post a sign on the town bulletin board requesting information concerning plans for coups d'état. All he could do was tiptoe around, listen, watch, try to pick things out of the air. Gradually he would make connections and find out what the Company had asked him to learn. Or, on the other hand, perhaps he wouldn't. It wasn't something that could be forced.

On the fourth day, as he was having lunch at the usual place—a garden restaurant dominated by no less than three portrait busts of El Supremo looming down out of vine-covered walls—Farkas became aware that he was the object of a conversation off at the periphery of the place. Someone who looked like an arrangement of scarlet zigzags and spirals with a big shining oval patch right in the middle—bright blue and very glossy, the way Farkas imagined an eye might look—was discussing him with the headwaiter.

They were both looking his way. There were gestures, not hard to decode: the zigzags-and-oval was requesting something; the headwaiter was refusing. And now a gratuity was changing hands. Farkas suspected that the pleasures of his solitary lunch were soon to be intruded upon.

He remembered, after a moment, who the zigzags-and-oval was: a certain courier named Kluge, one of the kids who hung out at the shuttle hub and offered to provide services for newcomers to Valparaiso Nuevo. Juanito had pointed him out to Farkas, somewhere in the early days of his visit, as one of his competitors. Juanito had spoken of Kluge with some admiration, Farkas remembered.

The headwaiter—three gleaming white rods bound with thick red twine—came over. Struck a posture of deferential attention. Cleared his throat.

"Begging your pardon for disturbing you, Mr. Farkas—a person wishes to speak to you, and he says it's extremely important—"

"I'm eating lunch," Farkas said.

"Of course, Mr. Farkas. Terribly sorry to have troubled you, Mr. Farkas."

Sure he was. He got to keep the tip, whether or not he could deliver Farkas to Kluge.

But maybe there was something useful here—an opening, a lead.

Farkas said, as the three white rods began to retreat, "Wait. What's his name?"

"Kluge, sir. He's a courier. I told him that you didn't need any couriers, but he said it wasn't that, he wasn't interested in selling you anything, but—"

"All right," Farkas said. "Tell him I'll talk to him."

Kluge approached and hovered nearby. The central eye-like structure of him turned a deeper blue, almost black, and the glossiness gave way to a matte finish. Farkas interpreted that as profound uneasiness being held under tight control. He warned himself to be careful not to underestimate this Kluge. That was one of his few weaknesses, Farkas knew: the tendency to be condescending to people who were put off by his appearance. *Everyone* was put off by his appearance at first, and had to fight to control a reaction of repugnance. But some of them were dangerous even so.

"My name is Kluge, sir," Kluge began. When Farkas offered no immediate response he added quickly, "I'm right over here, to your left."

"Yes, I know that. Sit down, Kluge. Is Kluge your first name or your second?"

"Sort of both, sir."

"Ah. Very unusual." Farkas went on eating. "And what is it you want with me, exactly? I understand you're a courier. I'm not in need of hiring one."

"I realize that, sir. Juanito is your courier."

"Was."

A little beat of silence went by before Kluge said, "Yes, sir. That's actually one of the things I would like to ask you about, if you don't mind." The big blue central eye was really black now, the look of space without stars. The scarlet zigzags and spirals were coiling and uncoiling like thrashing whips. There was real tension here, Farkas saw. Kluge said, "Juanito's a good friend of mine. We do a lot of work together. But nobody's seen him around for a while, now, and I wondered—"

He didn't finish the sentence. Farkas gave him some time to do it, but he didn't.

"Wondered what, Kluge?" he said finally. "If I know where he is? I'm afraid I don't. As I indicated, Juanito doesn't work for me any more."

"And you don't have any idea—"

"None," Farkas said. "I employed your friend Juanito only for a few days. Once I had my bearings here, I had no further need of him, and so I discharged him. It became necessary for me to make a short business trip to a nearby satellite world, and when that was finished I came back here for a brief holiday, but there was no reason for me to hire a courier this time and I didn't do so. I think I saw you at the terminal when I arrived the second time, and perhaps you noticed then that I chose to go through the entry procedures unaided."

"Yes, actually, I did," said Kluge.

"Well, then. I assume Juanito has taken himself off on a vacation somewhere. I paid him very well for his services. When you do see him again, please give him my thanks for the fine work he did on my behalf."

Farkas smiled, the kind of smile that offers an amiable termination to a conversation. He looked toward his plate and with great precision he cut a neatly triangular slice of meat and conveyed it to his mouth. He poured a little wine from his carafe into his glass, and put the glass to his lips. He took a slice of bread from the breadbasket and covered it with a thin, meticulously applied coating of butter. Kluge watched the entire performance in silence. Farkas smiled at him again, a different sort of smile, this time as though to say, *I see quite well for a blind man, don't you think?* and Kluge's coloration registered perplexity and dismay.

Kluge said, "He isn't much of a traveler, Juanito. He just likes to stay right here on Valparaiso Nuevo."

"Then I'm sure that that's where he is," said Farkas. He cut another triangular slice of meat. Smiled another smile of dismissal. "I appreciate your concern for your friend and I'm sorry I can't be more helpful than this. And now, unless there's anything else you'd like to discuss—"

"Yes, actually, there is. The real reason why I came up here to Cajamarca today to see you. You had dinner in Valdivia last night, didn't you, sir?"

Farkas nodded.

"This is a little unusual. The woman I'm working for right now happened to have dinner at the same restaurant last night. She's from Earth, from California, traveling through the L-5 worlds. She saw you at the restaurant and asked me later if I could arrange it for her to meet you."

"For what reason?"

"Your guess would be as good as mine, sir. But I think—you know—it might be something social."

Interesting, Farkas thought. A woman.

He had indeed noticed a woman in the restaurant last night, a very impressive woman, substantial and conspicuous. She had walked past his table at one point, giving off a distinctive carnal emanation, a great ambient cloud of hot female force—bright waves of heat, violet shot through with deep azure streaks—that had immediately caught his attention, automatically drawing from him an instant though brief surge of hormonal flux. He had caught her attention, too—he had not failed to take in the little quiver of surprise in her aura, the tiny flinch of surprise, as the fact of his eyelessness had registered on her—and then she had moved along.

It would be a cheery coincidence if this one turned out to be the same one. Farkas had been feeling a little horny for several days, now. His sexual drive was a thing of distinct periodicity, long stretches of eunuchlike indifference punctuated by piercing episodes of wild lustfulness. One of those episodes might be coming upon him, he was beginning to suspect. If Juanito had still been around, the kid could probably have arranged something for him. Of course, Juanito wasn't around. How providential for this Kluge to turn up, then.

"What's her name?" Farkas asked.

"Bermudez. Jolanda Bermudez."

The name meant nothing. And asking Kluge to describe her to him would serve no useful purpose.

"Well," Farkas said. "I suppose I can spare a little time for her. Where can I find her?"

"She's waiting in a café called the Santa Margarita, a short way up-spoke from here. I could tell her to come down here in half an hour, say, when you're finished with your lunch."

"I'm just about finished," said Farkas. "Let me settle up and you can take me to her right now."

"And about Juanito, sir—you know, we're all pretty worried about him. So if you should happen to hear from him—"

"There's no reason why I should," Farkas said. "But I'm sure he's fine. He's very resourceful, your friend Juanito." Farkas keyed in his lunch bill. "All right. Let's go."

The café where Jolanda Bermudez was waiting was no more than a five-minute walk from the place where Farkas had been eating lunch. He felt vaguely suspicious. It was all too neat, Kluge tracking him down like this, the woman stashing herself so close at hand. It had some of the earmarks of a setup. And yet this would not be the first time that some strange woman traveling in a remote place had become enamored of the smooth eyeless dome of his forehead. What Farkas thought of as his deformity had a distinct and potent appeal for a certain type of female personality. And he was indeed feeling horny.

This was worth checking out, whatever slight risk there would be. He was armed, after all. He was carrying the spike that he had taken from Juanito.

"There she is," Kluge said. "The big woman at the front table."

"I see her," Farkas said.

She was the one he had seen last night, all right. Those waves of violet heat were still radiating from her. She looked to Farkas like three rippling curves of silvery metal emanating from a blocky central core that was of notable size but tender and vulnerable in texture, a custardy mass of taut cream-hued flesh marked down its center by a row of unblinking eye-like scarlet spots. It was an opulent body, an extravagant body. Hot, very hot.

Farkas went to her table. When she saw him she reacted as she had the night before, with that equivocal mixture of titillation and fright that he had observed so many women display at the sight of him: her whole color scheme shot up the spectrum a discernible number of angstroms and there was a quick wild fluctuation in the heat intensity of her emanation, up-down-up-down-up. And then up and up.

"Jolanda Bermudez?"

"Oh. Yes. Hello! Hello! What a pleasure this is!" A nervous giggle, almost a whinny. "Please. Won't you join me, Mr.—?"

"Farkas. Victor Farkas," he said, sitting down opposite her. The warmth that was coming from her was strong and insistent, now, almost dizzying, erotically aggressive. Farkas was rarely wrong about such things. That was one of Dr. Wu's little gifts, his ability to read a woman's erotic temperature. But nevertheless this seemed just a little too good to be true.

Farkas watched her shifting position like a skittish girl, fluttering this way and that. "Your courier Kluge said you wanted to meet me."

"Indeed I do. I hope you don't think this is terribly presumptuous of me, Mr. Farkas—I'm a sculptor, you see—"

"Yes?"

"My work is usually done in abstract modes. Mainly I do bioresponsive pieces—you know what bioresponsive sculpture is, of course?"

"Yes. Yes, of course." He had no idea at all.

"But sometimes I like to get back to basic technique, to classical representational sculpture. And—I hope you'll forgive me if I'm putting this too crudely, Mr. Farkas—when I saw you last night, your face, your very unusual face, I said to myself that I absolutely had to sculpt that face, I had to render its underlying structure at least in clay and perhaps in marble. I don't know if you have any artistic leanings yourself, Mr. Farkas, but perhaps you are capable of understanding the intensity of such a feeling—the almost compulsive nature of it—"

"Oh, quite. Quite, Ms. Bermudez." Farkas beamed pleasantly, leaned forward, let his whole sensorium drink her in.

She went gushing on, a torrent of words coming from her. Would he consider posing for her? He would? Oh, wonderful, wonderful. She understood how unusual this must be for him. But his face was *so* distinctive. She would never be able to rest until she had transmuted it into a work of art. Of course she needed to obtain sculpting materials—she hadn't brought any of her tools with her—but she was sure that that would be possible somewhere on Valparaiso Nuevo, it would probably take her no more than an hour or two, and then perhaps he could come to her hotel room, which would have to serve as an improvised studio— she would need to take measurements, to study the contours of his face with great care—

The level of the heat radiation that was coming from her went on steadily rising all the while she spoke. This talk about sculpting him seemed to be genuine—Farkas was willing to believe that she dabbled in the arts in some fashion—but the real transaction that was shaping up here was a sexual one. He had no doubt about that.

"Perhaps tomorrow morning—or any other time, whatever would be convenient for you, Mr. Farkas—this evening, maybe—" Hopeful, eager. Pushy, even.

Farkas imagined himself sculpting *her*. He was no kind of artist at all, had never given such things any thought. How would he go about it? It would be necessary for him to learn the curves of her body, first, with his hands. Discovering by touch the true shape of all that he was incapable of seeing directly: translating the distorted geometric abstractions that he perceived into the actual rounded forms of breasts, thighs, buttocks.

"The sooner the better," Farkas said. "I'm free this afternoon, as it happens. Possibly the thing to do would be for you to make your preliminary measurements of my face today, even before you've purchased the materials you need, and then—"

"Oh, yes! Yes, that would be splendid, Mr. Farkas!"

She reached across the table, gathering his hands into hers and clasping them tightly. Farkas hadn't expected her to abandon the pretense that this was solely an artistic venture quite so quickly; but despite all his innate caution he was caught up now in her fervid sensual impatience. He had his needs, too. And it had long ago ceased to bother him that for some women it was his very weirdness of appearance that was the chief focus of attraction.

But then came an interruption. A man's voice, a ripe booming basso, crying, "There you are, Jolanda! I've been looking all over for you! But I see you've made a new friend!"

Farkas turned. From the left, a figure approaching, shorter than average, dark. To Farkas he had the form of a single rigid column of glistening black glass, tapering from a narrow base to a broad summit. An unmarred surface, slippery-looking, perfect. Farkas knew instantly that he had seen this man before, somewhere, long ago, and he went tense at once, aware now that all of this must have been staged.

Or had it been? He heard Jolanda Bermudez gasp in consternation. She had drawn her hands back from Farkas's, quickly, guiltily, at the first sound of the voice. Obviously she wasn't expecting this intrusion and was upset by it. Farkas saw her emanations fluctuating wildly. She was making small brushing motions, as if telling the man to go away.

These two must be traveling together. Farkas remembered now that the woman had had a companion with her at her table the night before;

but Farkas had seen no reason to give him any regard. Had the woman sought Farkas out on her own, though, or had the two of them carefully set him up?

"I know you," Farkas told the man calmly, with his left hand resting on the spike in his pocket. The weapon was tuned to stun intensity, just one level down from lethal. That ought to be enough, he thought. "You are—" Farkas reached deep into his memory. "Israeli?"

"Right. Right! Very good! Meshoram Enron. We met in South America, years ago. Bolivia, I think."

"Caracas, actually." It was coming back, now. The little man was a spy, of course. "The conference on seawater mineral extraction. —Victor Farkas."

"Yes. I know. You are not easy to forget. Are you still with Kyocera?"

Farkas nodded. "And you? A news magazine, am I right?"

"*Cosmos*, yes. I am working on a feature now about the L-5 worlds."

"What about you?" Farkas asked benignly, looking toward Jolanda. "You are assisting Mr. Enron with his magazine article, is that it?"

"Oh, no, I don't have anything at all to do with magazines. Marty and I met just yesterday, on the shuttle coming up from Earth."

"Ms. Bermudez makes friends very quickly," Enron explained.

"So I have been discovering," said Farkas.

Enron laughed. It was a precise, measured sort of laugh, Farkas decided, very carefully rehearsed for use on such occasions as this.

"Well," said Enron. "I won't disturb you two any further, then. But we must get together for a drink, eh, Farkas? How much longer are you likely to be staying up here?"

"I'm not sure. Several more days, at the least."

"A holiday, is it?"

"A holiday, yes."

"Wonderful place, isn't it? Such a contrast to poor old sad Earth." Enron began to move away. "Listen, you will give Jolanda the name of your hotel, yes? And then I'll call you and we can set up a date." To Jolanda he said, softly, proprietarily, "See you later, all right?"

So they *are* traveling together, Farkas thought. The sculptress and the spy. That was worth thinking about. None of this had been any accident. Obviously Enron had seen him in the restaurant last night. This meeting today had been deliberately engineered by him. Using the woman as a cat's-paw, though? Farkas wasn't sure. They are traveling together, yes, but are they working together? And if so, on what?

Enron was gone. Farkas reached for Jolanda's hand again, and she gave it.

"Now," he said. "About this afternoon—about your taking the measurements you need for this sculpture, this portrait of me that you tell me you want to do—"

▼   ▼   ▼

NAKAMURA MADE A small but imperious gesture with two fingers of his hand and the brightly glinting image of what looked more or less like a gigantic steel-jacketed hornet without wings sprang into being in the air of the vast barren room where he and Rhodes were having their little talk. It nearly filled the entire space.

"This, Dr. Rhodes, is the prototype of our starship. I show it to you not because your work for us, if you were to cast your fortunes in with us, would pertain in any way to our starship program, but simply because I am eager to demonstrate to you the extent of our far-flung scientific endeavor. May I have the pleasure to offer you one more glass of cognac?"

"Well—" Rhodes said. But Nakamura was pouring already.

Rhodes suspected that he was getting a little tipsy. Nakamura dispensed the cognac with a free hand.

It seemed safe to be drinking this much, though. Rhodes had recognized from the beginning that he was out of his depth with a Level Three man; he expected to be outflanked and overwhelmed at every step, and that provided him with a certain armor. He had already resolved that he would agree to nothing at this first meeting, regardless of the acuity of Nakamura's manipulative techniques. He was an experienced enough drinker to know that a little cognac, or even a great deal, wasn't going to alter that resolution; and it did help him fend off the anxieties that arose in this challenging situation, here on this alien turf, in the presence of so formidable a corporate figure.

The conversation had been altogether one-sided. Rhodes knew that he was here to listen, not to try to make an impression. The impression had already been made. Kyocera-Merck probably knew more about him than he did himself.

At the beginning, Nakamura had asked a few bland, nonspecific questions about Rhodes' current research projects. It was purely a courtesy: plainly Nakamura wasn't trying to elicit corporate secrets from him. Rhodes told him what was already public knowledge about Samurai's gene-splicing program, and Nakamura listened politely, prompting him now and then, guiding him through an account of the familiar and the obvious.

Then the focus shifted to Kyocera-Merck. "We too are deeply concerned about the fate of our species on this troubled planet, Dr. Rhodes," Nakamura said, as gravely as any undergraduate about to launch into some environmental harangue. "Like you, we feel that some biological modification of the race will be necessary to equip us for the coming changes; but we have not, I think, made as much progress along that road as your great company has. As you surely are already well aware, that is why I have asked you to come here today: to explore with you the possibility that you might choose to transfer your extraordinary skills to our laboratories." With a smile and a minute bowing gesture and a flick of his hand, Nakamura indicated that there was no need for Rhodes to reply just yet to this first explicit statement of the purpose of the meeting. "We have, however, made some remarkable strides toward an entirely different kind of solution. I speak of our attempts, of which you have probably heard rumors, to develop a faster-than-light spaceship that will be capable of conducting human colonists to suitable planets outside the solar system."

It was then that Nakamura brought the model of the starship prototype to vivid life in front of them.

Rhodes took an involuntary step backward, as though fearing the thing would fall on him. But all it was, he knew, was a holographic image.

Nakamura said, "You have heard reports of our starship program?"

"Only the sketchiest outlines of it," Rhodes said truthfully. "Essentially all I know is that there *is* such a program. And has been for several years."

"Yes. As there is, also, at Samurai Industries. Were you aware of that, Dr. Rhodes?"

"To about the same degree. What we hear, though, is that Kyocera is much farther along the track than we are."

"That is correct. We have made successful ground tests and are now almost on the verge of making our first experimental flight." Nakamura's eyes took on a brilliant sheen. He was offering Rhodes classified information, now: a small quid as down payment for the soon-to-be-requested quo. "A problem has developed, however, involving the nature of human perception under the extreme conditions of faster-than-light travel. And here is where our starship program and your own gene-splicing specialty overlap."

Rhodes was taken off balance by that. Was Kyocera trying to hire him to do some kind of starship work for them?

"The difficulty," Nakamura said smoothly, "is that the faster-than-light stardrive creates a variety of apparently unavoidable relativistic distortions. The occupants of the ship will travel in an altered space, in which, among other things, the visual signals reaching their optical nerves will be completely unfamiliar to them. Our eyes, of course, are designed to receive light in a particular segment of the spectrum and to decode the patterns formed by that light according to our expectations of the shape of things. Within the starship, under the influence of a drive field that is literally deforming the surrounding continuum in order to push the ship through the space-time fabric at nonrelativistic speeds, light waves will be subjected to extreme stress. The information received by the optic nerves of anyone on board will be incomprehensible. The crew will, in effect, be blind."

It was hard for Rhodes to imagine a Level Eight or Nine executive making such a speech. In the managerial ranks science was generally considered something that could safely be left to the lower echelons. But Nakamura seemed actually to understand what he was saying: his phrasing, though stilted in the megacorp-Japanese style, did not have the rigidity of a memorization.

Rhodes wondered if he was going to be asked to deal somehow with this blindness problem. That appeared to be where Nakamura was heading, anyway.

Unexpectedly, the Kyocera man said, "Do you know of a certain Dr. Wu Fang-shui?"

Rhodes was astonished. He hadn't heard that name in years.

"A legendary figure in the history of genetic surgery," he said. "The most brilliant member of his generation. A worker of miracles."

"Yes. Indeed so. And do you have any idea where he is now?"

"He's been dead a long time. His career ended in a terrible scandal. The story I heard was that he had committed suicide."

"Oh, no, my dear Dr. Rhodes. That is not true."

"Not a suicide?"

"Not dead. Dr. Wu was a fugitive for many years, yes, after the lamentable scandal to which you refer. But he has been found, and is in fact currently in our employ."

Nakamura's bland statement amazed Rhodes so much that his hand shook violently and some of his cognac spilled. Nakamura replaced it in a smooth, almost instantaneous motion.

"That's hard for me to believe," Rhodes said. "I don't mean to doubt your word, of course. But it's very much like an astronomer hearing that Galileo has turned up alive and is designing a new telescope. Like telling a biologist that a new paper by Gregor Mendel is about to be published. Or a mathematician hearing that Edgar Madison is—"

Nakamura smiled crisply. "Yes, I quite understand," he said. His tone left no doubt that he was cutting in to prevent Rhodes from running through the entire scientific pantheon in his boozy verbosity. "But the celebrated Dr. Wu chose to disappear, not to die, after the exposure of his illicit experiments in the Free State of Kazakhstan, which is, I think, the scandal to which you were referring. He underwent significant alterations of his appearance and took refuge on one of the L-5 worlds. It happens, Dr. Rhodes, that his Kazakhstan experiments included research into alternative modes of vision. He is at this very moment engaged in retrofitting the crew of our experimental starship so that they will be able to cope with the visual problems posed by faster-than-light travel."

Rhodes shakily conveyed his glass to his lips.

The sinister old bastard still alive! Performing his magic at this very moment in some K-M laboratory! Who could have imagined it?

"And if I were to join the Kyocera staff," Rhodes said, "I would be put to work under Dr. Wu in this starship project, is that it?"

"Not at all. From what we know of Dr. Wu's Kazakhstan research, he ought to be able to deal with the problem of visual perception under faster-than-light conditions in very short order, with no need for the assistance of even so distinguished a scientist as yourself, Dr. Rhodes. Aside from which, it would be foolish of us to divert you from your own present research path."

"You mean you would want me to go right on with what I've been doing at Santachiara, but under Kyocera-Merck auspices?"

"Exactly. Even though we have high hopes for our starship program, we recognize that colonization of other solar systems is only one possible solution to our problem. It would be foolhardy of us to ignore the avenue of adapto research. And we at Kyocera-Merck are greatly concerned by your company's apparent superiority in that field."

So it had occurred to them, then, that Samurai was positioning itself for nothing less than world domination.

"I see," Rhodes said.

"Therefore we are prepared to duplicate your present research facility, or to go as far beyond its capabilities as you desire. We'll provide you with whatever equipment you would need, at whatever budgetary level you deem appropriate."

Dry-throated now, Rhodes said hoarsely, "You make this sound very appealing."

"We intend to. We would hope, naturally, that you would bring most or all of your current research group over to us with you."

"That might expose me to some problems of legal liability, wouldn't it?"

"It might expose *us* to some legal liability," Nakamura said. "The corporation, not you as an individual, doctor. And we are prepared to shoulder that risk." He extended the cognac bottle. "Another?"

Rhodes quickly put his hand over his glass.

"Thank you, no."

"I believe I will," said Nakamura. He filled his glass and lifted it in a toast. He seemed gracious, relaxed, charming, now: a true pal. "It would be premature, I would think, to discuss such details as salary, now. But I'm sure you understand that we are prepared to be extremely generous, both in terms of direct compensation and in terms of advanced grade levels for you and your most important colleagues."

Rhodes' mind was whirling.

"Now, as to the connection of Dr. Wu Fang-shui to what we have been discussing," Nakamura said.

Yes. Wu was involved in this somewhere, Rhodes remembered.

"When he is finished with the starship project—a matter of just a few months, we estimate—it would be quite possible for us to transfer him to your group. As a research consultant, let us say. A senior adviser, neither superior to you nor inferior, but simply affiliated with your enterprise as a reservoir of available technical skill of a highly advanced nature. For example, we have it on good report that a member of your group has made an extremely bold, even radical, proposal for a new line of research that could be unusually fruitful, but which at this point is hedged around by potentially insuperable technical stumbling blocks. It might be the case that a scientist of Dr. Wu's stature, approaching these obstacles with a fresh vision, so to speak, might be able to offer suggestions which—"

Rhodes was stunned.

They knew about Van Vliet already? Apparently so. And were dangling no less a figure than Wu Fang-shui to help him bring Van Vliet's proposals to completion?

Incredible. Incredible.

"I will have that drink after all, I think, Mr. Nakamura."

"Certainly." Nakamura poured him a double, perhaps a triple.

From some previously untapped depth of his soul Rhodes managed to say, "You realize that I'm not able to give you any definite answer to any of this today."

"Of course. This is a serious step, virtually the restructuring of your whole life. I am aware of the strong commitment you feel to Samurai Industries, or—to put it more precisely—to Santachiara Technologies. You are not a man who makes great decisions lightly or swiftly. We know that—we have watched you very closely, Dr. Rhodes, surely you are not surprised to hear that—and we value that trait in you. Take your time.

Think things over. Discuss what I have said with your most trusted friends."

"Yes."

"I hardly need stress the importance of discretion in these discussions, of course."

"Hardly."

Nakamura rose.

"We will be in touch, Dr. Rhodes."

"Yes. Certainly."

"It has been a rewarding first meeting for me, and, I trust, for you as well."

"Yes. Very much so."

As Rhodes was leaving, Nakamura actually offered him a formal bow of the most punctilious sort. Rhodes did his awkward bearish best to imitate it.

A Level Three, bowing to *me,* he thought. Incredible.

Mr. Kurashiki was waiting to lead him back to his car. Rhodes sat in it for a long moment, feeling dazed, wondering where to tell the car to take him. It was still fairly early in the afternoon. Return to the lab? No, not now. Not in the shape he was in. He was as close to drunk as made no difference, he was soaked in sour high-tension sweat, he was altogether exhausted. He felt close to tears. An interview with an actual Level Three; an offer to design a new lab for himself, expenses be damned; and, of all flabbergasting things, Wu Fang-shui himself thrown in as office help. Rhodes was dazed.

He needed to talk to someone about this. But who? Isabelle? Jesus, no! Ned Svoboda? Not really.

Paul Carpenter, that was who. The only person in the universe he completely trusted. But Carpenter was somewhere out at sea jockeying icebergs around. For the moment, Rhodes knew, he was on his own, struggling to contain a secret that was so big it felt like a lump of molten brass in his throat.

"Take me home," Rhodes told the car.

He didn't feel at all like a Level Eight departmental head, or like an internationally respected scientist. What he felt like was a small boy who had gone swimming out too far from shore, and had no idea now of how to get back to land.

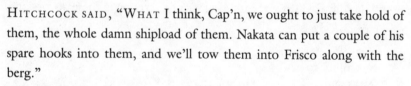

HITCHCOCK SAID, "WHAT I think, Cap'n, we ought to just take hold of them, the whole damn shipload of them. Nakata can put a couple of his spare hooks into them, and we'll tow them into Frisco along with the berg."

"Hold on," Carpenter said. "Are you out of your mind? I'm no fucking pirate."

"Who's talking about piracy? It's our obligation. We got to turn them in, man, is how I see it. They're mutineers."

"I'm not a policeman, either," Carpenter retorted. "They want to have a mutiny, let them goddamn go and mutiny. What business is that of mine? I've got a job to do. I just want to get that berg moving east. Without hauling a shipload of crazies along."

Hitchcock said nothing. His broad dark face turned grim.

In rising anger Carpenter said, "Look, don't even think I'm going to make some kind of civil arrest of them. Don't even consider it for an instant, Hitchcock. It's out of the question and you goddamned well know it."

Mildly Hitchcock said, "You know, we used to take this sort of thing seriously, once upon a time. You know what I mean, man? We wouldn't just look the other way."

"You don't understand," Carpenter said. Hitchcock gave him a sharp scornful look. "No. Listen to me, and listen good," Carpenter snapped. "That ship's nothing but trouble. The woman that runs it, she's something you don't want to be very close to. We'd have to put her in chains if we tried to take her in, and taking her in's not as easy as you seem to think, either. There's five of us and I don't know how many of them. And that's a Kyocera-Merck ship there. Samurai isn't paying us to pull K-M's chestnuts out of the fire."

It was late morning now. Kovalcik had already called twice to find out what Carpenter was planning to do. He hadn't taken either call. The sun was getting close to noon height, and the sky was brighter than ever, fiercely hot, with some swirls of lavender and green far overhead, vagrant wisps of greenhouse garbage that must have drifted west from the noxious high-pressure air mass that sat perpetually over the midsection of the United States. Carpenter imagined he could detect a whiff of methane in the breeze.

Just across the way from the ship was the berg, shining like polished marble, shedding water hour by hour as the mounting warmth worked it over. Back in San Francisco they probably were brushing the dust out of the empty reservoirs by now. Time to be moving along, yes. Kovalcik and Kohlberg would have to work out their problems without his help. Carpenter didn't feel good about that, but there were a lot of things in the world that he didn't feel good about, and he wasn't able to fix those either.

"You said she's going to kill those five guys," Caskie said. The little communications operator ran her hands edgily over her shaven scalp. "Does she mean it?"

Carpenter shrugged. "A bluff, most likely. She looks tough, but I'm not sure she's that tough."

"I don't agree," Rennett said. "She wants to get rid of those men in the worst way. Probably was just about to do it when we turned up."

"You think?"

"She can't keep them on board. They're running out of sedatives, is what she told us. Once those men are awake, they'll figure out a way to get loose. So they have to go. I think that what Kovalcik was doing anchored by the berg was getting ready to maroon them on it. Only we came along, and we're going to tow the berg away, and that screwed up the plan. Well, now she wants to give them to us instead. We don't take them, she'll just dump them over the side soon as we're gone."

"Even though we know the score?"

"She'll say they broke loose and jumped into the ship's boat and escaped, and she doesn't know where the hell they went. Who's to say otherwise?"

Carpenter stared gloomily. Yes, he thought, who's to say otherwise.

"The berg's melting while we screw around," Hitchcock said. "What'll it be, Cap'n? We sit here and discuss some more? Or we pull up and head for Frisco?"

"My vote's for taking them on board," said Nakata, who had been silent until this moment.

"I don't remember calling for a vote," Carpenter said. "We've got no room for five more hands. Not for anybody. We're packed as tight as we can possibly get. Living on this ship is like living in a rowboat, as it is. Come on, Nakata, where would we put five more?" Carpenter was starting to feel rage beginning to rise in him. This business was getting too tangled: legal issues, humanitarian issues, a lot of messy stuff. The trouble was, there were no rules any more. If he took the five on board, was he saving five lives or just becoming a co-conspirator in a mutiny that he ought to be trying to suppress?

And the simple reality underneath it all was that intervening in this squabble was impossible for him to do. He couldn't take on passengers, no matter what the reason.

Hitchcock was right that there was no more time for discussing it. The berg was losing water every minute. Even from here, bare eyes alone, Carpenter could see erosion going on, the dripping, the calving. And the oscillations were picking up, the big icy thing rocking gently back and forth as its stability at waterline got nibbled away. Later on the oscillations wouldn't be so gentle. They had to get that berg sprayed with mirror-dust and skirted, and start moving. San Francisco was paying him to bring home an iceberg, not a handful of slush.

"Cap'n," Rennett called. She had wandered up into the observation rack above them and was shading her eyes, looking across the water. "They've put out a boat, Cap'n."

"No," Carpenter said. "Son of a bitch!"

He grabbed for his 6×30 spyglass. A boat, sure enough, a hydrofoil dinghy. It looked full up: three people, four—no, five, it seemed. He hit the switch for biosensor boost and the squid fiber in the spyglass went to work for him. The image blossomed, high resolution. Five men, yes. Carpenter recognized ex-Captain Kohlberg sitting slumped in front.

"Shit," Carpenter said. "She's sending them over to us. Just dumping them on us."

"If we doubled up somehow—" Nakata began, smiling hopefully.

"One more word out of you and I'll double *you* up," said Carpenter. He turned to Hitchcock, who had one hand clamped meditatively over the lower half of his face, pushing his nose back and forth and scratching around in his thick white stubble. "Break out some lasers," Carpenter said.

"Defensive use only. Just in case. Hitchcock, you and Rennett get out there in the kayak and escort those men back to the squid ship. If they aren't conscious, tow them over to it. If they are, and they don't want to go back, invite them very firmly to go back, and if they don't like the invitation, put a couple of holes through the side of their boat and get the hell back here fast. You understand me?"

Hitchcock nodded stonily. "Sure, man. Sure."

Carpenter watched the whole thing from the blister dome at the stern, wondering whether he was going to have a mutiny of his own on his hands now too. But no. No. Hitchcock and Rennett kayaked out along the edge of the berg until they came up beside the dinghy from the *Calamari Maru,* and there was a brief discussion, very brief, Hitchcock doing the talking and Rennett holding a laser rifle in a casual but businesslike way. The five castoffs from the squid ship seemed more or less awake. They pointed and gestured and threw up their arms in despair. But Hitchcock kept talking and Rennett kept stroking the laser, casual but businesslike, and the men in the dinghy looked more and more dejected by the moment. Then the discussion broke up and the kayak headed back toward the *Tonopah Maru,* and the men in the dinghy sat where they were, no doubt trying to figure out their next move.

Hitchcock said, coming on board, "This is bad business, man. That captain, he says the woman just took the ship away from him, on account of she wanted him to let them all have extra shots of Screen and he didn't give it. There wasn't enough to let her have so much, is what he said. I feel real bad, man."

"So do I," said Carpenter. "Believe me."

"I learn a long time ago," Hitchcock said, "when a man say 'believe me,' that's the one thing I shouldn't do."

"Fuck you," Carpenter said. "You think I *wanted* to strand them? But we have no choice about it. Let them go back to their own ship. She won't kill them. All they have to do is let her do what she wants to do and they'll come out of it okay. She can put them off on some island somewhere, Hawaii, maybe. But if they come with us, we'll be in deep shit all the way back to Frisco." And worse when we get there, he added silently.

Hitchcock nodded. "Yeah. We may be in deep shit already."

"What are you saying?"

"Look at the berg," Hitchcock said. "At waterline. It's getting real carved up."

Carpenter scooped up his glass and kicked in the biosensor boost. He scanned the berg. It didn't look good, no. The heat was working it over very diligently.

This was the hottest day since they had entered these waters. It was almost like the mainland out here today, the swirls of garbage gas in the sky, the steady torrid downpour of solar energy, a river of devastating infrared pouring through the murk up there and slamming earthward without mercy. The heat was building, accumulating. The sun seemed to be getting bigger every minute. There was a nasty magnetic crackling coming out of the sky, as if the atmosphere itself was getting ionized as it baked.

And the berg was starting to wobble, all right. Carpenter saw the oscillations plainly, those horizontal grooves filling with water, the sea not so calm now as sky/ocean temperature differentials began to build up and conflicting currents came sluicing in.

"Son of a bitch," Carpenter said. "That settles it. We got to get moving right now."

There was still plenty to do. Pro forma, Caskie radioed over to the squid ship to warn them that they were going to begin spraying mirror-dust. No reply came. Maybe they didn't care, or didn't know what was involved. The squid ship was still sitting at anchor next to the ice tongue, and it looked like some kind of negotiation might be going on between the men in the dinghy and the women on board.

Carpenter gave the word and the mirror-dust spigots went into operation, cannoning shining clouds of powdered metal over the exposed surface of the berg, and probably all over the squid ship and the dinghy too. It took half an hour to do the job. The sea was still roughening and the berg was lalloping around in a mean way. But Carpenter knew there was a gigantic base down there out of sight—enough, he hoped, to hold the berg steady until they could get under way.

"Let's get the skirt on it now," he said.

A tricky procedure, nozzles at the ship's waterline extruding a thermoplastic spray that would coat the berg just where it was most vulnerable to wave erosion. The hard part came in managing the extensions of the cables linking the hooks to the ship the right way, so that they could maneuver around the berg. But Nakata was an ace at that. They pulled up anchor and started around the far side. The mirror-dusted berg was dazzling, a tremendous mountain of white light.

"I don't like that wobble," Hitchcock kept saying.

"Won't matter a damn once we're under way," said Carpenter.

The heat was like a hammer, now, savagely pounding the dark cool surface of the water, mixing up the thermal layers, stirring up the currents, getting everything churned around. They had waited just a little too long to get started. The berg, badly undercut, was doing a big sway to windward, bowing way down like one of those round-bottomed Japanese dolls, then swaying back again. God only knew what kind of sea action the squid ship was getting, but Carpenter couldn't see them from this side of the berg. He kept on moving, circling the berg to the full extension of the hook cables, then circling back the way he had come.

When they got around to leeward again, he saw what kind of sea action the squid ship had been getting. It was swamped. The ice tongue they had been anchored next to had come rising up out of the sea and kicked them like a giant foot.

"Jesus Christ," Hitchcock murmured, standing beside him. "Will you look at that. The damn fools just sat right there all the time."

The *Calamari Maru* was shipping water like crazy and starting to go down. The sea was boiling with an armada of newly liberated squid, swiftly propelling themselves in all directions, heading anywhere else at top speed. Three dinghies were bobbing around in the water in the shadow of the berg.

"Will you look at that," Hitchcock said again.

"Start the engines," Carpenter told him. "Let's get the fuck out of here."

Hitchcock peered at him disbelievingly.

"You mean that, Cap'n? You really mean that?"

"I goddamn well do."

"Shit," said Hitchcock. "This fucking lousy world."

"Go on. Get 'em started."

"You actually going to leave three boats from a sinking ship sitting out there in the water full of people?"

"Yeah. You got it." Carpenter's head felt as if it was stuffed with wool. Don't stop to think, he told himself. Don't think about any of this. Just *do*. "Now start the engines, will you?"

"That's too much," Hitchcock said softly, shaking his head in a big slow swing. "Too goddamn much."

He made a sound like a wounded buffalo and took two or three shambling steps toward Carpenter, his arms dangling loosely, his hands half-cupped. Hitchcock's eyes were slitted and his face looked oddly puffy. He loomed above Carpenter, wheezing and muttering, a dark massive slab of a man. Half as big as the iceberg out there was how he looked just then.

Oh, shit, Carpenter thought. Here it comes. My very own mutiny, right now.

Hitchcock rumbled and muttered and began to close his hands into fists. Exasperation tinged with fear swept through Carpenter and he brought his arm up without even stopping to think, hitting Hitchcock hard, a short fast jab in the mouth that rocked the older man's head back sharply and sent him reeling against the rail. Hitchcock slammed into it and bounced. For a moment it looked as if he would fall, but he managed to steady himself. A kind of sobbing sound, but not quite a sob, more of a grunt, came from him. A bright dribble of blood sprouted on his white-stubbled chin.

For a moment Hitchcock seemed dazed. Then his eyes came back into focus and he looked at Carpenter in amazement.

"I wasn't going to hit you, Cap'n," he said, blinking hard. There was a soft stunned quality to his voice. "Nobody ever hits a cap'n, not ever. Not *ever*. You know that, Cap'n."

"I told you to start the engines."

"You hit me, Cap'n. What the hell you hit me for?"

"You started to come at me, didn't you?" Carpenter said.

Hitchcock's shining bloodshot eyes were immense in his Screen-blackened face. "You think I was *coming* at you? Oh, Cap'n! Oh, Jesus, Cap'n. Jesus!" He shook his head and wiped at the blood. Carpenter saw that he was bleeding too, at the knuckle, where he'd hit a tooth. Hitchcock continued to stare at him, the way you might stare at a tyrannosaurus that had just stepped out of the forest. Then his look of astonishment softened into something else, sadness, maybe. Or was it pity? Pity would be even worse, Carpenter thought. A whole lot worse.

"Cap'n—" Hitchcock began, his voice hoarse and thick.

"Don't say it. Just go and get the engines started."

"Yeah," he said. "Yeah, man."

He went slouching off, rubbing at his lip.

"Caskie's picking up an autobuoy SOS," Rennett called from somewhere updeck.

"Nix," Carpenter yelled back angrily. "We can't do it."

"What?"

"There's no fucking room for them," Carpenter said. His voice was as sharp as an icicle. "No way. Nix."

He lifted his spyglass again and took another look toward the oncoming dinghies. Chugging along hard, they were, but having heavy weather of it in the turbulent water. He looked quickly away, before he could make out faces. The berg, shining like fire, was still oscillating. Carpenter thought of the hot winds sweeping across the continent over there to the east of them, sweeping all around the belly of the world, the dry, rainless winds that forever sucked up what little moisture could still be found. It was almost a shame to have to go back there. Like returning to hell after a little holiday at sea, is how it felt. But that was where they were going. And, like it or not, he was going to leave these people behind in the sea.

Sometimes you had to make lousy choices, just to cope with the circumstances. That was all there was to it, Carpenter thought. Life was tough, sometimes downright rotten. And sometimes you had to make lousy choices.

He turned. They were staring at him, Nakata, Rennett, Caskie, everybody but Hitchcock, who was on the bridge setting up the engine combinations.

"This never happened," Carpenter told them. He felt numb. He tried to push what had occurred out of his mind. "None of this did. We never saw anybody else out here. Not anybody. You got that? *This never happened*."

They nodded, one by one.

There was a quick shiver down below as the tiny sun in the engine room, the little fusion sphere, came to full power. With a groan the engine kicked in at high. The ship started to move away, out of the zone of dark water, toward the bluer sea just ahead. Off they went, pulling eastward as fast as they could, trying to make time ahead of the melt rate. It was afternoon, now. Behind them the other sun, the real one, lit up the sky with screaming fury as it headed off past them into the west. That was good, to have the sun going one way as you were going the other.

Carpenter didn't look back. What for? So you can beat yourself up about something you couldn't help?

Home, now.

Back to the wonderful world of North America in the greenhouse age.

This fucking lousy world, Hitchcock had said. Yeah. This berg here, this oversized ice cube, how many days' water supply would that be for San Francisco? Ten? Fifteen? And then what? Go and get another one? And every berg you took was water that somebody else wasn't going to be able to have.

His knuckle was stinging where he had split it punching Hitchcock. He rubbed it in a distant detached way, as if it were someone else's hand. Think east, he told himself. You're towing two thousand kilotons of million-year-old frozen water to thirsty San Francisco. Think good thoughts. Think about your bonus. Think about your next promotion. No sense looking back. You look back, all you do is hurt your eyes.

By the time Enron returned to the hotel, late in Valparaiso Nuevo afternoon, everything was tidy, the bed tightly made, not the slightest hint in the air of the smell of lust or sweat. You would think that no one other than Jolanda had been in the room since morning. Enron had met with Kluge, who had had no luck so far finding Davidov or any of the other Los

Angeles people, and then had gone off rambling restlessly around the habitat world for hours, killing time, sitting in cafés, randomly poking his nose in here and there, waiting until it was safe for him to go back.

"Well?" he asked Jolanda. She had changed her clothing since lunchtime: she was wearing a brightly colored kaftan now, bedecked with iridescent lateral sworls of green and pink and yellow that defiantly accentuated the amplitude of her body. Fatigue was evident in her face: coming down off her most recent hyperdex high, Enron figured. "What was it like, fucking a man who has no eyes?"

"Marty—"

"Please. We are not children, you and I. You brought him here; the room has a bed and a door that locks; I understand what must have taken place. That was the idea, was it not? For you to bring him here under the pretense of measuring him for a sculpture, and to go to bed with him?"

"It wasn't a pretense," Jolanda said, with some heat in her tone. She was sitting by the window with her back to the awesome view, the black backdrop and the blazing panoply of stars and planets and swiftly moving L-5 worlds. "I actually did measure him. I quite legitimately intend to do a portrait of him. Look—look here—" Jolanda indicated a little stack of data-cubes. "All the measurements are here."

"Did he tell you what you look like to him? You know, everything is just geometry to him. A very strange geometry."

"He said I was beautiful."

"Yes. So you are. He told me, once, how a certain woman looked to him, and I have never forgotten it. This was the other time when we met, when we were at that conference in Caracas, the one about taking molybdenum and beryllium out of seawater. The woman was from Peru, Chile, one of those countries, and she looked something like you, as a matter of fact, big like a cow up here, a very big woman all over, not fat, exactly, but well furnished and extremely—"

"Marty, I don't care."

"We were sitting by the pool, Farkas and I, and she came up out of the water like Aphrodite, do you know? A very generous Aphrodite, done by Rubens. With the breasts out to here, and the arms that were as thick as thighs, and the thighs even bigger, but everything very finely shaped and in perfect proportion, just *big*. Rather like you. And I said something to Farkas, a comment about her body, forgetting for the moment that he has no eyes, and he just laughed, and he said, 'For me she is somewhat different.' I think he said that the way she looked to him was like three barrels set on their sides and tied with a flaming cord. Or maybe five barrels. But that was very beautiful to him, he said. Each person looks entirely different to him, you know, an altogether individual shape. The information he gets with his senses, it is not like the information we take in." Enron smiled. "I'm glad he thought you were beautiful. You are, you know. Much like that woman in Caracas. And you are wonderful in bed. As I am sure he discovered."

"Do you know what you look like to me right now?" Jolanda asked. "A wolf. A little lean wolf with green eyes and dripping fangs."

"Would you like to make a sculpture of me? Here: take my measurements too. Right now!" He began to undo his belt.

"This is lousy, Marty. I can't stand a jealous man. If you didn't want me to go to bed with him, why did you throw me at him like that?"

"Because I wanted to get certain information. And that seemed like the most efficient way of getting it. Surely you understood that?"

"I suppose I did, yes," she said. "Now that I think about it a little." She shot him a fiery look. "But do *you* understand that I never would have considered doing it except that I found him attractive? I'm not a toy to be passed around, Marty. Or a piece of bait. I *wanted* to sleep with him. And I did. And I'm glad that I did! I enjoyed it tremendously."

"Of course you did," Enron said, changing his tone from one of harsh banter to a softer, more placating one. "He's an unusual man. It must have been an unusual experience." He crossed the room to her and rested his hands alongside her neck, gently kneading the soft flesh and the firm muscles beneath. "Do you really think I'm being jealous, Jolanda?"

"Yes. Damned right I do. You needed this to happen, but you didn't like it. I could see that when you showed up in the restaurant. You felt you had to hover around us, you had to keep control of the situation even as you were pushing me toward him."

Enron was a little taken aback by that accusation. Was it so? He had believed that the purpose of his breaking in on Jolanda and Farkas at the restaurant had been merely to send a signal to Farkas that they needed to talk, once Farkas's dalliance with Jolanda was out of the way. But perhaps there had been more going on than that. He could have waited until tomorrow to make contact with Farkas, after all. But perhaps he had actually needed to let Farkas know that he had some kind of prior claim on Jolanda, some degree of ownership, *before* they had gone to bed together.

He shrugged. "At any rate, did you learn anything useful from him?"

"That depends. What do you mean by useful?"

"For example, did he say anything about why he's up here?"

"He told you in the restaurant what he's doing up here. He said he was on a holiday."

"Of course. A holiday. —You really are stupid, aren't you?"

"Thank you very much."

"He's here spying for Kyocera. You knew that."

"So he's spying for Kyocera, then. We didn't talk about anything having to do with Kyocera. I took some measurements of his face and skull, and then he asked me if I would go to bed with him, and then—"

"Yes. All right."

"He doesn't seem like a blind man in bed, Marty. Or somebody who looks at a beautiful woman and sees an arrangement of barrels. He knew where everything was supposed to be."

"I'm sure he did," said Enron. He drew a long, slow breath. "Okay, listen to me, now. What I think, Jolanda, is that Kyocera-Merck has a finger in this little plot that your friends from Los Angeles have cooked up, and that the Hungarian is here as the K-M point man, here to meet with the conspirators and help them set things up."

Jolanda turned in her seat and looked up at him. "What makes you think that? Nobody ever mentioned a word about Kyocera when they were telling me about the plan."

"Why should they? But an adventure of such a kind takes money. Someone has to buy the weapons, someone has to pay for transporting them here. People have to be trained. And then there are the customs fees, the bribes, all the expenses of buying your way into a well-protected place like this with a small army. Who is their backer, do you think?"

"I don't have any idea. They never said."

"My entire purpose in coming here—do you remember?—is to meet with your friends and let them know that my country is willing to offer them whatever financial support they may need. But the possibility arises that they may already have found a very powerful partner in their enterprise."

"Kyocera-Merck, you mean?"

"So it begins to seem."

"Why would Kyocera-Merck want to overthrow the dictator of Valparaiso Nuevo?"

"For reasons of pure imperialism, perhaps," Enron said. "Kyocera is said to be in a strongly expansionist mode these days, and they may just want to add a few more L-5 worlds to their collection. Or maybe it is only that there are some people living here in sanctuary who are wanted by them. I don't know, Jolanda. But if Farkas is here, and a coup is being engineered, it gives me reason to suspect that he's mixed up in this plan somehow on K-M's behalf."

"And if he is?"

"Then I need to cut myself in on the deal. A partnership arrangement: split the costs, share the payoff. Kyocera can have this place, if it wants it. But some of the people who have been living in hiding here—those are people that *we* want. And will get, one way or another."

Enron was enjoying a long, extravagant shower just before dinnertime when Jolanda put her head into the cubicle and said, "The courier is on the phone. He thinks he's found Davidov. Do you want to talk to him?"

"Tell him to wait," Enron said.

He stepped under the water again, letting it roll down luxuriously over the dense, matted black hair of his chest, which was still covered with soap. In Israel, of course, there was plenty of water to squander on showers. But Enron had been in California just before coming here, living under the enforced Spartan restrictions of the West Coast's perpetual drought, and now he was reveling in the availability once more of unlimited water up here on Valparaiso Nuevo, where everything was recycled with maximum efficiency and nothing was rationed.

After a long while he emerged, toweling himself dry, and went into the bedroom. Kluge's fleshy, earnest face was peering out of the visor.

Enron casually wrapped his towel around his middle and moved into scanner range.

"Well?"

"Spoke C," Kluge said. "The Hotel Santa Eulalia, in the town of Remedios. Four men with California addresses on their passports checked in last week. This was one of them. He's using the name of Dudley Reynolds, but I think he's the one you wanted to find. I'll pump his picture across to you."

The visor image went blurry with download interference for a moment. Kluge was jacking his flex terminal into the output. Then the picture was clear again, and Enron found himself looking at the solido of a square-headed, thick-necked man with austere blue eyes and blond hair, almost colorlessly so, cropped very short. His skin, which must originally have been of a Slavic pallor, was a blackish purple, heavily mottled and blotched from too much Screen. It was a frightening face, big-chinned and almost lipless, a bestial Cossack face.

Enron said to Jolanda, "What do you think?"

"That's Davidov, yes. It's him, all right."

"He looks like a beast."

"He's really quite gentle," Jolanda said.

"No doubt," said Enron. He told Kluge to come back on camera. "All right, you've found them. Well done. Where are they now?"

"I don't know."

"What?"

"They checked out about twelve hours ago. They may have gone back to Earth."

"Name of a pig," Enron muttered. "We've missed them?"

"I'm not entirely certain of that. My contacts in Emigration haven't come up with any record of their leaving Valparaiso Nuevo yet. However, the fact remains that they *have* left their original hotel. I'm going to continue looking."

"You do that."

"I could use an advance on my fee," Kluge said. "My expenses on all this have been running high."

"How much do you want?" Enron asked.

"A thousand callaghanos?"

"I'll give you two thousand," Enron said. "It'll save me the trouble of having you come around with your hand out again in another day or two."

Kluge seemed very surprised indeed. Jolanda was looking at Enron in puzzlement also.

Enron took his terminal from the drawer, tapped out Kluge's account number, and pumped the money across to him. Kluge blurted his gratitude and disappeared from the visor.

Jolanda said, "Why'd you give him so much?"

"What does it matter? There's plenty of money. I was ready to let him have five."

"They don't respect you, if you're too easy with money."

"They'll respect me, all right. Kluge has dealt with Israelis before."

"How do you know that?" Jolanda asked.

"We keep records," said Enron. "Don't you think I checked on him before I hired him?" He wadded his towel into a ball, threw it across the room, and began to select clothes for the evening. "Are you ready to go out for dinner?"

"Just about."

"Good. While I'm getting dressed, call Farkas at his hotel. Tell him we're about to eat and ask him if he'd like to join us."

"Why do you want to do that?"

"To find out if he knows anything about the plan to overthrow the Generalissimo. And if he can tell me where Davidov is."

"Shouldn't you talk with Davidov before you ask Farkas about any of that?" Jolanda asked. "You're only guessing that Farkas is involved. If he isn't, and you tip him off to what's going on, you may wind up letting Kyocera know things that you'd be better off not having them know."

Enron stared at her admiringly. He let a smile slowly emerge and broaden.

"You have a good point there."

"You see? I'm not really all that stupid, am I?"

"I may have misjudged you, it would seem."

"You simply can't believe that a woman who's as good in bed as I am can also think straight."

"On the contrary," Enron said. "I have always thought that intelligent women make the best bed partners. But sometimes if a woman is too beautiful I fail to notice how intelligent she also is."

Jolanda glowed with pleasure. It was as if he had canceled out all the cruel things he had said to her with a single oblique compliment.

Indeed she is extremely stupid, Enron thought. But she was right that he would have to be careful with Farkas.

"The thing is," he said, "that time is moving along, and we haven't yet been able to locate your friends. I might as well begin sounding Farkas out. There is the risk that you mention: but there's also the possibility that I'll learn something from *him*. Call him. Invite him to have dinner with us tonight, or else lunch tomorrow."

The phone light came on again as Jolanda moved toward the desk. She looked at Enron uncertainly.

"Answer it," Enron said.

Kluge, again. "I've got your Davidov for you. He changed hotels, but he's still here. All four of them are. Spoke B, the Residencia San Tomás, in the town of Santiago."

"Are all the hotels in this place named for saints?" Enron asked.

"Many of them. The Generalissimo is a very religious person."

"Yes. I suppose he would be. What name is our man using now?"

"Dudley Reynolds, still. The other three are named James Clark, Phil Cruz, Tom Barrett on their passports."

Enron glanced at Jolanda. She shrugged and shook her head.

"They're probably the ones we want," Enron said to Kluge. "All right. Keep an eye on them. Stay in touch. If I don't answer, put the call on seek. Call me anywhere, anytime there's news. Let me know where they go, who they see."

Jolanda said, when Enron had broken the contact, "Do we try to see them tonight?"

"Are you good friends with these people?"

"I know Mike Davidov very well. The other names are ones I've never heard of at all. But of course they're all fakes."

"*How* well do you know Davidov? You ever sleep with him?"

"What does that have to do with—"

"Please," Enron said. "I don't give a damn about your chastity or the lack thereof. I need to know what kind of a relationship you had with this Davidov."

Jolanda's face colored. Her eyes flamed with anger.

"I've slept with him, yes. I've slept with a lot of people."

"I realize that. Davidov is what I'm asking about, right now. You and he were lovers, and now you turn up here with me, a visiting Israeli. How will he react? Will it bother him?"

"We were just friends. When I was in L.A. I stayed with him, that's all. It was always a very casual thing."

"He won't be bothered, you say?"

"Not in the least."

"All right," Enron said. "Call him. The Residencia San Tomás, in the town of Santiago. Ask for Dudley Reynolds. Tell him you're here with a newsman from Israel that you met in San Francisco, and that I'd like very much to talk with him as soon as possible."

"Do I say what it is you'd like to discuss?"

"No. He can figure it out. Call him."

"Right," Jolanda said. She programmed the phone. Almost at once a synthetic voice said, "Mr. Reynolds is not in his room. Is there a message for him?"

"Leave your name and our room number at this hotel," Enron told Jolanda. "Ask him to call back, any hour, whenever he comes in."

"What now?" she asked, when she was done.

"Now call Farkas, and invite him to have dinner with us."

"But shouldn't you wait until—"

"There are times when I get tired of waiting," said Enron. "A calculated risk. I need to get things moving. Call Farkas."

They agreed to meet in the town of Cajamarca, at a café right against the rim, not far from Farkas's hotel. Getting together on what was essentially Farkas's turf struck Enron as being a good idea. He wanted Farkas to feel safe, relaxed, congenial. *We are beginning to create a splendid friendship, you and I, linked by our memories of Caracas long ago and now by our confraternal acquaintance with the splendid body of Jolanda*

Bermudez: that was the idea. We trust each other. We can share significant secrets with each other for our mutual benefit. Indeed.

Farkas arrived late at the café. Enron found that bothersome. But he kept himself under tight control while he waited, ordering a nonalcoholic drink, and then another. Jolanda had a couple of cocktails, long greenish-blue drinks of a species unknown to Enron, probably sweet and sticky. And at last, nearly half an hour after the rendezvous time, the eyeless man came swaggering in.

Watching Farkas's grand, almost regal entry, Enron suddenly found himself not so sure that it was going to be all that easy to strike up a chummy and profitably manipulative relationship with him. He had forgotten, or perhaps had never bothered to notice, what a commanding figure Farkas was: extraordinarily tall, almost a giant, really, with an athlete's wide shoulders and easy grace. It hadn't been just a fascination for the bizarre that had drawn Jolanda to him. Farkas moved with wonderful self-assurance, never making a misstep as he walked between the tables, nodding and waving to the bartender, the waiters, the busboy, even some of the other customers.

And he was so damned *strange*. Enron saw Farkas as if for the first time, staring in wonder and distaste at that lofty white half dome of a head set like a chunk of marble atop the long muscular neck, the shining forehead curving up and up without interruption from the bridge of his nose to the high, receding hairline. Farkas seemed scarcely human. Some kind of weird mutant creature, a monstrous head on a human body. But of course that was what he was: a weird mutant creature.

This will take some careful managing, Enron thought.

But he was fundamentally confident that it would all work out. He always was. And so far it always had.

Effortlessly Farkas slipped into the vacant seat between Enron and Jolanda. He smiled and nodded to Jolanda with just the right mixture of friendliness and tact, and in almost the same gesture offered his hand warmly to Enron. Enron admired that. What had taken place between Farkas and Jolanda earlier that day was being tacitly acknowledged, but not rubbed in his face.

"Sorry to have been so late," Farkas said. "Some urgent calls came in just as I was getting ready to go out. Have you been waiting long?"

"Five or ten minutes," said Enron. "We've already had a drink. You need to catch up with us."

"Right," Farkas said. Instead of using the keyboard at the table he simply beckoned to a waiter, who brought him, without even having to be told, a huge snifter containing a pool of some dark liqueur.

His regular tipple, no doubt, Enron thought. They must know him very well here.

"Pisco," said Farkas. "Peruvian brandy. You would like it, I think. Shall I get you one?"

He signaled the waiter again.

"I'm not much of a drinker, thanks," Enron said quickly.

"I'll have one," Jolanda said, leaning eagerly toward Farkas and giving him a luminous smile that roiled Enron's insides with anger. She still had her last drink in front of her, only half-finished.

"You must come here often," Enron said to Farkas.

"Practically every day. A very cheerful place, very friendly, and very pretty, too. If you don't mind all the statues and holo portraits of El Supremo that they've decorated it with."

"One gets used to that," said Enron.

"Indeed." Farkas sipped his brandy. "You have to hand it to the old tyrant, don't you? The veritable reincarnation of some nineteenth-century banana-republic dictator, grabbing possession somehow of an entire satellite world and hanging on to it for all these decades. His own private empire. Assuming that he's still alive, of course."

"What do you mean by that?"

"Nobody ever sees him, you know. No one but his most intimate intimates. The governmental realm on Valparaiso Nuevo is absolutely secretive. For all anybody knows, Don Eduardo could have died ten years ago, and the news was hushed up. It would make no difference whatsoever in the way things operated here. It's like in the old days of the Roman Empire, when sometimes the emperor would have been dead for weeks or even months, and the court officials kept everything going on their own without letting anybody know."

Enron laughed, kicking the heartiness up about as high as was likely to seem plausible. "That's a funny notion, all right. But there's truth in it, isn't there? As in any properly organized autocracy, the high officials of the court do all the interfacing with grubby reality, and the emperor stays hidden away out of sight."

"And of course it's all so much easier to do that now, when Don Eduardo can be called up electronically on any public occasion without the need to disturb the real Generalissimo in his lair."

Enron laughed again, a lesser output of energy this time. He gave Farkas a cheery, slightly addled look, his best shot at appearing to be a little of a simpleton. "Tell me this, though, Victor—do you mind, my calling you Victor?—you don't *really* think that Callaghan could be dead, do you?"

"I have no idea, actually. I was merely speculating, you understand. But in truth I suspect he's still very much alive."

Watching Farkas carefully, Enron said, "It's remarkable that he's been able to hold on so long, if in truth he has. I would imagine there are many who would covet a lucrative little world like Valparaiso Nuevo, filled as it is with such highly desirable fugitives. That Don Eduardo has managed to avoid a coup d'état up till now seems like a miracle to me, considering—"

Enron was looking for a reaction, and he saw one.

It was only the merest shadowy tremor, a quick involuntary twitch of the left side of Farkas's face. It was there and then it wasn't, and Farkas was smiling serenely, a polite show of interest and nothing more. He is very very good, Enron thought. But he knows something. He must.

Farkas said, "As I pointed out, he's entirely inaccessible. That must be the secret of his survival."

"No doubt," said Enron. Very cautiously he said, "Do you think the Generalissimo *could* be overthrown, given the proper degree of planning?"

"With the proper degree of planning the devil could push God Himself off the throne of heaven."

"Yes. But that isn't very probable. Whereas Don Eduardo—"

"Is mortal, and vulnerable," said Farkas. "Yes, I think it could be done. I'm sure that there are those who are thinking about such a thing, too."

Ah.

Enron nodded eagerly. "I agree. That surely is so. In fact," he said, "I've actually heard rumors to that effect. Fairly trustworthy rumors."

"Have you?" Still no more than an amiable show of interest. But, again, the telltale twitch of the lip.

"Yes, actually." It was time to put some cards on the table. "An American group. Californians, I think."

A distinct response from Farkas, one more twitch and a significant wrinkling of the eerie forehead. He inclined his head just a bit in Enron's direction. It seemed clear that he understood now that a negotiation was taking place.

"Interesting," Farkas said. "You know, I've heard some stories of the same sort."

"Indeed."

"Just rumors, of course. A takeover of the satellite, organized from—yes, California, I'm sure that was what they were saying." Farkas seemed to be reaching into a dim, misty memory of something that he had heard that was not very important to him.

"The story is getting around, then."

"As such stories will do."

"Could one of the big companies be behind it, possibly, would you think?" Enron asked.

"Behind the story, do you mean, or the coup?"

"The coup. Or the story, I suppose. Either one."

Farkas shrugged. He still was trying to make it seem as though all of this were merely hypothetical discussion, Enron thought. "Impossible for me to say. They would need backing, wouldn't they, these conspirators?"

"Naturally. A coup d'état is an expensive pastime."

"Something that only one of the megacorps would be able to bring off, yes," Farkas said. "Or one of the wealthier countries. Your own, for example." A little more emphasis, suddenly, on that last sentence. The voice deepening: a verbal nudge in the ribs.

Enron chuckled. "Yes, I suppose we could put up the money for something like that. If we had any reason to, that is."

"Don't you?"

"Not really. No more than Kyocera-Merck does, I'd say, or Samurai. There are people here who are wanted for serious crimes against the state of Israel, certainly. Foreign spies, a few of our own more corrupt officials, and so forth. But there are plenty of retired experts in industrial espionage, also, and embezzlers, and peddlers of company secrets—people who have profited greatly at the expense of this megacorp or that and whose return to Earth for trial would be advantageous to the companies. I could almost see a joint effort being launched to extract the fugitives from this place: some big company and some prosperous country, let us say, putting up the funds together on a fifty-fifty basis. But of course all this is sheer fantasy, is it not?" Enron flicked his fingertips outward, a dismissive gesture. "There will be no coups d'état here. This is a lovely little planet, and no one on Earth would want to harm it. Besides, I understand that Generalissimo Callaghan has quite an efficient secret police. Everyone is watched here, I am told."

"Very closely, yes," Farkas said. "It would be hard to mount any sort of uprising here, except perhaps one that came from within: one that involved the court officials themselves."

Enron raised an eyebrow.

Was Farkas dropping some kind of hint? Were Kyocera's plans for taking this place over already advanced far beyond the notions of Mr. Davidov and his associates? No, no, Enron decided: Farkas is merely playing with speculative possibilities, now. If any such inner-echelon conspiracy of the Generalissimo's close subordinates existed and Farkas were part of it, he would never risk talking about it in a public restaurant, certainly not with an Israeli agent but probably not even with someone he knew. He would try to keep the secret even from himself. That was what Enron would have done, at any rate, and he did not think that Farkas was any more rash than he was in matters of this sort.

But there was no chance to follow it up just now. Jolanda, who had watched the entire duel in silence, tapped Enron's wrist and said, "The waiter is signaling you, Marty. There's a telephone call for you, I think."

"It can wait."

"What if it's our friend Dudley? You know how badly you want to hear from him."

"Good point," said Enron grudgingly. "All right. If you'll excuse me, Victor. I'll be right back."

He took the call in a shielded cubicle to the rear of the restaurant. But the face that came onto the visor was not the brutal, massive one of Mike

Davidov. Enron found himself looking once again at the softer, fleshier features of the courier Kluge. He seemed agitated.

"Well?"

"He's gone. Your Los Angeles person."

"You mean Dudley Reynolds? Gone where?"

"Back to Earth," Kluge said. His voice was hoarse with shame. "They fucked us up. He never was in that hotel in Santiago. They checked in there, and then they left and went straight to the terminal and caught the shuttle to Earth under four entirely new names. Those bastards must have a suitcase full of passports."

"Mother of Mohammed," Enron said. "Here and gone. Just like that."

"Very slippery people."

"Yes," Enron said. "Very slippery." His respect for Davidov had gone up a couple of notches. Davidov must be no ordinary freebooting thug, if he could dance his way through Valparaiso Nuevo so artfully, eluding even a clever boy like Kluge—doing his business here, concluding the preliminaries of his little insurrection, and getting out of here right under Kluge's nose.

Enron wondered whether Davidov had had a meeting with Victor Farkas while he was here. But he saw no immediate way of finding that out from Farkas without divulging information to him that he was not yet ready to share. There might be other ways, though.

"Is there anything else you want me to do?" Kluge asked.

"Not right now. No. Yes: one thing. Can you put together Davidov's path through Valparaiso Nuevo in any more detail than you've given it to me? All I know is that he was in this hotel for a while and then he supposedly went to another one under a different name and now he's on his way back to Earth. Can you discover how long he was here and who he saw? Particularly I want to know if he had any contact with the man without eyes. You know. Farkas."

"I'll get right on it," Kluge said. "I can try to run a reverse trace, all his moves backward from today."

"Good. Good. You get right on it, yes."

Enron was flaming with annoyance and frustration as he returned to the table. To have come all the way up here for nothing—well, not entirely nothing, at least he had encountered Farkas and through him had begun to link Kyocera with the uprising against the Generalissimo. That was still mostly conjecture, though. And now, assuming he cared to pursue any of this, he would have to try to hunt Davidov down in Los Angeles. Damn. Damn.

It took all his considerable self-discipline to get himself calm. Then, as he approached the table, Enron saw from the exchange of body language that was going on between Jolanda and Farkas that something flirtatious had been taking place in his absence, and he was furious all over again.

Farkas, who had been leaning toward Jolanda in an obviously affectionate manner, returned quickly and smoothly to his upright position while Enron was still twenty paces to the rear of the table. Interesting, Enron thought. Eyes in the back of his head. Jolanda had picked up some sort of signal from Farkas's withdrawal that Enron was returning, and she too had straightened up, but she had no way of swiftly repairing the way she looked: her face was flushed, her eyes were glowing. The good old hot blast of arousal was coming out of every pore of her. That irritated Enron, but also it excited his competitive lust. Let Farkas make time with her behind my back, he thought. But he will never touch her again. Whereas when we get back to the hotel this evening, I will fuck her as she has never been fucked before.

"You look upset," Jolanda said. "Bad news?"

"Of a sort, yes. It was a message from Dudley. His father is very ill and he's returning to Earth at once. So we won't be able to have lunch with him tomorrow."

"That's too bad."

"It certainly is. Such a sweet person—I feel very sad for him. We'll have to call him as soon as we get back to Earth ourselves, won't we?"

"Absolutely," Jolanda said.

As Enron took his seat, Farkas rose, smiling. "Pardon me, please. I will be back very soon."

Enron watched him cross the room, wondering if Farkas had somehow deciphered the inner meaning of what he had just said and was on his way to make some telephone call of his own. But no, no, the eyeless man was simply going to the bathroom.

Turning to Jolanda, Enron said, "He's up to his neck in this thing, I'm certain of it. He's here to set things up for Kyocera as the behind-the-scenes muscle for your friend's operation. There's no doubt about that."

"He thinks you're here to do the same thing for Israel," Jolanda said.

What a wild notion that was! Enron's eyes widened. The woman was extraordinary. Her mind constantly went darting off with hummingbird velocity into the strangest places.

The unsettling thought that she might just be right came to him, though.

"Did he tell you that while I was on the phone?" Enron asked uneasily.

"No, of course not. But I could see him thinking it. He's as convinced that Israel is the secret backer as you are that Kyocera is."

He felt immense relief. It was all just her muddleheaded speculation, then.

"Well, he's wrong," Enron said.

"What if you both are? What if there *is* no secret backer?"

"You know nothing about these things," said Enron, irritated now by this.

"Right," Jolanda said. "I am a stupid cow and that's all. You admire me only for my tits."

"Please, Jolanda."

"I have very fine tits, I agree. Many men have told me that and I wouldn't dream of disagreeing with them. But there's more to me than that, believe me, Marty. If you're lucky you may find that out."

"You misunderstand me. I have the highest respect for—"

"Yes. I'm sure you do."

Jolanda glanced past Enron's shoulder. Farkas had reappeared, now, and loomed above him.

"About dinner," Farkas said genially, as he resumed his place at the table. "As I said, I have eaten here very often. If you will permit me to recommend one or two things—"

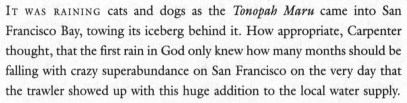

It was raining cats and dogs as the *Tonopah Maru* came into San Francisco Bay, towing its iceberg behind it. How appropriate, Carpenter thought, that the first rain in God only knew how many months should be falling with crazy superabundance on San Francisco on the very day that the trawler showed up with this huge addition to the local water supply.

The weather had been cruelly cloudless the entire second half of the voyage home, no sign of the usual, even ubiquitous, masses of water vapor that congested and whitened the sky nearly all of the time in most parts of the world. That was one of the greenhouse effects, the increase in atmospheric water vapor, which helpfully served to amplify the relatively small basic warming impulse that the CO_2 and other greenhouse gases caused. But, for some inexplicable reason, day after day out at sea the sky above the *Tonopah Maru* had been immaculate and the sun had beaten with unrestrained fury against the berg. Which had, mirror-dusted though it was, given up much of its substance to the sea under the daily solar barrage.

Still, there was plenty of it left for San Francisco. And here they were at journey's end, chugging under the venerable Golden Gate Bridge with something like seventeen or eighteen hundred kilotons of the Antarctic ice cap in tow, heading into a dark squally afternoon, torrents and torrents of H_2O dropping with lunatic irascibility upon the city by the bay.

"Will you look at that," Hitchcock said, standing on deck next to Carpenter in the drenching downpour. "Actual fucking rain."

"Beautiful," Carpenter said. "Gorgeous."

It wasn't, not really. The rain was raising clouds of ambient filth from the city streets, lifting the accretions of dust that had been building up for months or perhaps years and hurling them upward, so that the downpour became ever grayer as the airborne crud came drifting copiously down again. Streams of garbage were falling from the sky. Yes, Carpenter thought, very lovely, very pretty to behold.

There were places, he knew from his stint in the Samurai Weather Service, where a sweet, cleansing, fertility-giving rain fell practically every day: the eastern end of the Mediterranean, say, or the grain belt of Saskatchewan, or the Siberian plains. But this was not one of those places. Rain along the West Coast was such a rarity that it was more of a nuisance than anything else when it did finally arrive, generally in some kind of absurd excessiveness like this. It came with insufficient frequency to maintain any kind of water supply, serving mainly to liberate the accumulated chemical gunk on the streets and roads and turn them into funhouse slideways, to cut ghastly gullies in the withered and defoliated hills east of the bay, and to churn up the loose particulate grime that lay everywhere in the city, redistributing the mess but not removing it.

What the hell. He was safely home, and with his cargo. So the voyage had been a success, except for the one little blemish of the squid-ship event. And Carpenter tried not to think about that.

He went under cover, into the blister dome at the stern. Caskie was there, doing something to a control panel. Carpenter said to her, "Get me the Samurai facility at the Port of Oakland, will you? I need to know which pier I'm supposed to deliver this thing to. I'll take the call in my cabin."

"Yes, sir. Right away, sir!"

"Sir?" Carpenter asked her. Nobody had been sirring him aboard the *Tonopah Maru* up till now, and there was something unreal and oddly insolent about the way Caskie did it now. But the lithe little radio operator had already gone sprinting away to her communications nest to set up the call for him.

He headed below. In his cabin he found the Port of Oakland operator already waiting for him on the tiny visor of his wall-mounted communicator.

"Captain Carpenter here," he said. "Reporting safe arrival of *Tonopah Maru* with iceberg of approximate seventeen-hundred-plus kiloton mass. Requesting docking instructions."

The Port of Oakland operator gave him the number of the pier to which he was to bring his berg. Then the android said, "You are instructed to report to Administration Shed Fourteen immediately upon transferring command to pierside personnel, Captain."

"Transferring command?"

"That is correct. You will be relieved by Captain Swenson and will go immediately to Administration Shed Fourteen for preliminary 442 hearings."

"I don't understand."

"You will be relieved by Captain Swenson and will go—"

"Yes, I heard that part. You said '442'?"

"That is correct. There is to be a 442, Captain."

Carpenter was baffled. What the hell was a 442? But the android on his visor would give him only circularities instead of answers. He turned the communicator off after another moment and went upstairs.

"Hitchcock?"

The navigator's grizzled ebony face peered out of the blister dome.

"You want me, sir?"

Sir again. Something was really wrong.

"Hitchcock, what's a 442?"

Hitchcock's expression was impassive, almost smug, but there was a strange glint in the older man's exophthalmic, vividly white, bloodstreaked eyes. "Impropriety charge, sir."

"Impropriety?"

"Violation of regs, yes, that's an impropriety. Sir."

"You turned me in? On the *Calamari Maru* thing?"

"Sir, the 442 hearing will determine—"

"Answer me!" Carpenter wanted to grab Hitchcock by the front of his shirt and bash him against the railing. But he knew better than that. "Did you turn me in?"

Hitchcock's gaze was serene. "We all did, sir."

"All?"

"Rennie. Nakata. Caskie set up the call for us."

"When was this?"

"Four days ago. We told them you had abandoned a group of sailors in distress."

"I don't believe this. You told them I had aband—"

"Was a terrible thing, sir. Was a violation of all common decency, sir." Hitchcock was terribly calm. He seemed to have swollen to six times his normal size: a monster of rectitude and moral justice. "Was our duty to inform authorities, sir, of this breach of maritime custom."

"You fucking treacherous bastard," Carpenter said. "You know as well as I do that we had no room for any of those people aboard this ship!"

"Yes, sir." Hitchcock spoke as though from several galaxies away. "I understand that, sir. Nevertheless, the impropriety was committed and it behooved us to report it."

Impropriety! Behooved us! Suddenly Hitchcock had the vocabulary of a schoolmaster. Carpenter made an inarticulate sound deep in his throat. He longed to hurl Hitchcock overboard. Rennie and Nakata had appeared, and were watching from a distance, heedless of the quickening rain. Carpenter wondered what number impropriety it was to throw your navigator into San Francisco Bay in front of witnesses.

He saw now that it had been a crazy thing to do, ordering them to forget his abandonment of the *Calamari Maru*'s people. They would obey, but they wouldn't forget. And the only way they could get themselves out from under the responsibility for what he had done out there in the South Pacific had been to turn him in.

Carpenter's mind went back to that moment in the open sea, when they had seen the three dinghies from the foundering *Calamari Maru* heading their way. His callousness, Hitchcock's incredulity.

Playing the scene back now in memory, Carpenter could hardly believe the thing that he had done. He had left those people out there to die, had turned his back on them and sailed away, and that had been that. An impropriety, yes.

But still—

There had been no choice, Carpenter thought. His ship was too small. The iceberg was beginning to melt. They didn't have enough food for all those extras, or sufficient Screen, or any room for passengers, not even one or two—

He would tell the 442 hearing those things. It had been a matter of situational ethics, he would explain. *This fucking lousy world,* Hitchcock had said, back there when Carpenter had given him the order to ignore the dinghies. Yes. Sometimes this fucking lousy world compelled you to do fucking lousy things. Carpenter, understood that his behavior had seemed callous. But they might all have died, the rescuers and the rescued alike. He would have risked losing his berg, maybe even his ship, if he had attempted to—

They were all looking at him. Smiling.

"Fuck you," he told them. "You don't understand a goddamned thing."

Carpenter moved past them, scowling into their faces, and went back down to his cabin.

Administration Shed Fourteen wasn't a shed at all; it was a kind of tubelike room, a long narrow ribbon of dull gray steel attached almost haphazardly to one of the upper levels of the intricate webwork of buildings and catwalks that was the Port of Oakland's operational heart.

Nor was the hearing a hearing, really. Certainly not in the literal sense of the word, for Carpenter's voice was not heard at all except for a couple of brief sentences. It was more like a formal notification that some sort of proceeding against him was under way: an arraignment, really. An official of the Port presided over it, a doughy-faced, bored man named O'Reilly or O'Brien or O'Leary—something Irish, at any rate, but Carpenter heard the name only at the outset and forgot it, except in its broad outline, almost at once. During most of the session the man had his nose in his visor almost constantly, rarely looking up at Carpenter. Carpenter had the impression that O'Reilly or O'Brien was presiding over two or three cases at once, taking information in from several computer outputs while listening with half an ear to the droning of the bailiffs in front of him.

There was a Level Seven Samurai man on hand as Carpenter's representative, a squinty-eyed, sallow-faced fellow named Tedesco, pockmarked along his cheeks and forehead by some kind of allergic reaction to Screen. That the case should involve a Level Seven, that a Level Seven should have been waiting here all morning for Carpenter while he docked his ship and turned over his command, indicated to Carpenter that this was a serious business, that he might be in considerable trouble. But he was sure that once the investigating authorities understood the realities of the dilemma he had faced out there, everything would work out.

"Don't say a thing until you're asked to," Tedesco told him, right at the outset. "And when you answer, be sure to answer straight to the point, no discursiveness. They hate discursiveness in a place like this."

"Do I need a lawyer?" Carpenter asked.

"This isn't a legal matter," said Tedesco. "Not today. And if it becomes one, whatever counsel may be necessary will be provided for you by the Company. Meanwhile take your cues from me."

"What kind of penalties am I facing here?"

"Disqualification from the Maritime Service. You would lose your sea ticket." Tedesco's voice was chilly. Everything about him radiated disdain for this whole affair, the sordid event at sea, the troublesome filing of charges against a captain by his crew, the deplorable need for a man of his august grade to be putting in time down here on the Oakland waterfront dealing with such a nasty squabble.

"What about my grade level in the Company?"

"That's an internal Company matter. What's going on here is a Port of Oakland matter. First things first; but I don't think I need to tell you that it isn't going to do much good for your slope to have been brought up on charges here like this. However, that remains to be—"

"442 docket 100–939399," said O'Reilly or O'Brien suddenly, down at the remote other end of the tube, and banged a gavel. "Paul Carpenter, captain, suspended, stand forth and acknowledge."

"Get up," Tedesco murmured, but Carpenter was already on his feet.

It was very strange, being the focus of a disciplinary action like this. Carpenter felt like a schoolboy being reprimanded for some childish offense. Turning his ship over to Swenson, the relief captain, had been embarrassing enough, especially with Hitchcock and Rennett smirking triumphantly at him from the blister dome as he surrendered his software access; but there had at least been a sort of Conradian drama to that which made it tolerable, a theatrical solemnity. To stand here in this grotesque drafty spaghetti strand of a room, though, listening to the rain beat down on the metal roof and staring at a fat, bleary-eyed bureaucrat who didn't seem even to be looking at him, but who nevertheless held the power to injure and perhaps cripple his career—it was humiliating, it was ridiculous, it was absurd.

One of the bailiffs—a woman who looked like an android, but apparently wasn't—rose and ran through a thick skein of legalisms in a dull monotone. The charges—improper behavior, dereliction of duty, violation of regulation such-and-such and such-and-such. The accusers, named. His own crew. Some yatter about the temporary withdrawal of his maritime license pending examination of the incident. And on and on, five or ten minutes of dense technicalities that Carpenter soon found himself unable to follow.

"Entered," O'Reilly or O'Brien said. "Remanded for evidential." Bang of gavel. "Application for a 376.5 noted and denied. Application for a 793-sub one granted. Hearing date to be set and notification made." Bang of gavel. Bang again. "Continued." One last bang.

"That's it," Tedesco said. "You're free to do as you wish, now. But don't go outside the San Francisco area until this has been resolved."

Tedesco began to leave the room.

"Wait a second," Carpenter said. "Please. What was all that stuff he denied and approved? A 376-point-something, a 793-sub-something."

"376.5 is a request for a dismissal of all charges. Routinely entered and just as routinely thrown out. 793-sub one is application for release on your own recognizance without bail. You got that because your record has been clean up till now."

"Bail? I'm up on a *criminal* charge?"

"Purely an administrative investigation," Tedesco said. "But there's always the possibility of follow-ups, a criminal action, perhaps a civil action by the legal representatives of the castaways. The Port is responsible to the civil authorities for your continued presence until this has been resolved. We have made ourselves responsible to the Port, which is why no bail has been required, and therefore you are responsible to us to see to it that no breaches are incurred. We believe that we can count on your cooperation."

"Of course. But if there are going to be further charges, other court proceedings beyond this one—"

"We don't know that there will be. One thing at a time, all right, Carpenter? And if you don't mind—"

"Please. I need to know something else."

"Go on."

"I still have Level Eleven privileges, right? Housing, living expenses?"

"Of course," Tedesco said. "You haven't been found guilty of anything, Carpenter. The Port is only trying to determine the truth of the charges that have been lodged against you. And the Company is behind you. Keep that in mind. The Company is behind you." It was said without any warmth whatever, but it was the most reassuring thing Carpenter had heard since reaching port. *The Company is behind you.* His sullen and resentful crew, lacking any intelligent comprehension of the complexities he had faced out there in the Pacific, had landed him in this mess; but the Company, vast and mighty, would not allow a useful Level Eleven to be thrown to the wolves over an issue of class warfare. Carpenter was confident of that now. At the eventual hearing, he would demonstrate that a rescue had been entirely impossible, that it had been necessary for him to perform an act of what was essentially triage, weighing the survival of his own ship and people against the demands of those incompetent and mutinous strangers, and rather than sending everyone in both ships to destruction by overloading his little vessel he had reluctantly—oh, so reluctantly and painfully!—left the personnel of the *Calamari Maru* to fend for themselves in the sea. This was a difficult era, he would tell them, a time of hard choices. With the best will in the world he couldn't have saved those people. He had *had* the best will in the world. It stood to reason that a man of his intelligence and good record would not lightheartedly have left shipwrecked sailors to die, if he had had any options otherwise. Surely Tedesco must see that. O'Brien, O'Leary, whatever his name was, he would be made to see it too. The charges would be dismissed.

When all of this was over, Carpenter thought, it probably would be incumbent upon Samurai to transfer him out of the Maritime Service, considering the way this sort of thing tended to attach itself to someone's reputation, and he might lose a year or two's slope, too; but they would find a post for him in some other division, and in the fullness of time everything would be all right.

Yes. In the fullness of time.

Meanwhile it was still raining torrentially. The air outside had a sweet, yeasty smell, almost pleasant, except that Carpenter felt sure that the fragrance was the result of the stirring into the atmosphere of some disagreeable and probably hazardous toxic crap that ordinarily would be lying dormant on the bosom of San Francisco Bay.

What now?

A place to stay, first.

When he had come down from Spokane to San Francisco to take this job, the Company had assigned him to the Company's block of rooms at the Marriott Hilton, over on the Frisco waterfront. Since he was still a

Level Eleven, presumably it was still all right for him to take a room there.

But when Carpenter called up Accommodations on his flex terminal and requested the Marriott, he was told that a booking had already been made for him at a hotel called the Dunsmuir, on the Oakland side of the bay. Something about that troubled him. Why not San Francisco? Why not the Marriott? He requested a transfer. No, he was told, he must go to the Dunsmuir.

And when he got there, he understood why. The Dunsmuir was a dump like the Manito in Spokane, where Carpenter had lived while he was a weatherman, only even worse—a dreary commercial hotel that seemed to be at least a century old, in a desolate one-time industrial zone, now largely abandoned, between Oakland Airport and the freeway. It had none of the flash of the Marriott, and none of the comfort, either. It was the sort of place that catered to medium-grade business travelers who might have one night to spend in Oakland before going on to San Diego or Seattle.

The Company is behind you. Yes. But the Company was already beginning to reduce its overhead insofar as he was concerned, and he had not yet been found guilty of anything. Perhaps there was more to worry about here than he thought.

It was late afternoon by the time Carpenter was settled in the small, drab, dank room that apparently was going to be his home for a while. He put through a call to Nick Rhodes at Santachiara, and, to his surprise, it went through on the first try.

"Hey, now!" Rhodes cried. "Home is the sailor, home from the sea!"

"So it would seem," Carpenter said, in a dull, flat tone. "As I remember the poem, that's a line to be engraved on somebody's tombstone."

Instantly Rhodes looked alarmed. "Paul? What the hell's the matter, Paul?"

"I don't know yet. Possibly plenty. They've got me up on some kind of fucking court-martial."

"For Christ's sake. What did you do?"

Wearily Carpenter said, "There was this ship we met when we were out in the Pacific. There had been a mutiny on board, and—well, it's a long story. I don't feel like running through it all just now. Look, are you free tonight? You want to get together and do some serious drinking, Nick?"

"Of course. Where are you?"

"Dive called the Dunsmuir, near the airport."

"Down by SFO, you mean?"

"No. Oakland Airport, not San Francisco. That's the best the Company thinks I'm worthy of, right now. More convenient for you, anyway." Then, belatedly: "How the hell are you, Nick?"

"I'm—fine."

"And Isabelle?"

"She's fine too. I'm still seeing her, you know."

"Of course you are. I never expected otherwise. How's her goofy friend with the lavish equipment?"

"Jolanda? She's up in the habitats right now. Should be getting back in another couple of days. She's been traveling with Enron."

"The Israeli? I thought he was back in Tel Aviv."

"Decided to stick around in San Francisco. Captivated by Jolanda's lavish equipment, I gather. And then they suddenly went up to the satellites together. Don't ask me any more, because I don't know. Where do you want to meet tonight?"

"That restaurant we went to on the Berkeley waterfront?"

"Antonio's, you mean? Sure. What time?"

"Any time. The sooner the better. I have to tell you, I feel pretty miserable, Nick. Especially in this rain. I could use some good company."

"What about right now?" Rhodes asked. "I'm just about through for the day anyway. And I could use some good company too, if the truth be known."

"Something wrong?"

"I'm not sure. A complication, anyway."

"Involving Isabelle?"

"Nothing to do with women at all. I'll tell you when I see you."

"Isabelle won't be coming with you tonight, will she?"

"God, no," Rhodes said. "Antonio's, in half an hour. All right? Be seeing you. Welcome back, you old sea-dog!"

"Yeah," Carpenter said. "Home is the sailor. For better or for worse."

*　*　*

The rain clattered against the Perspex domes of the shoreside restaurant like pebbles tossed by an angry giant. The bay was almost invisible, lost in the gray of twilight and the turbulent swirlings of the storm. There was practically no one in the restaurant but the two of them.

Nick Rhodes seemed stunned by Carpenter's account of what had happened at sea. He listened to the entire story in a kind of numbed incredulity, barely saying a word, staring fixedly at Carpenter throughout the long recitation and breaking his rigid concentration only to bring his glass to his lips. Then when Carpenter was done Rhodes began to ask questions, peripheral ones at first, then more directly attacking the issue of whether there might really have been room for the warring factions of Captain Kovalcik and Captain Kohlberg aboard the *Tonopah Maru,* so that in effect Carpenter found himself telling the story all over again, piecemeal this time.

With each telling, Carpenter had more difficulty in accepting his own version of the events. It was beginning to seem to him as though it would not in any way have been a serious problem to take the castaways on board. Put five of them here, six over here, stick them in closets and heads and any other bit of available space, cut everybody's Screen ration down so that there would have been enough to go around—

Or maybe just to have towed them in their three dinghies all the way to San Francisco—

No. No.

"It wasn't doable, Nick. You just have to take my word for it. There were fifteen or twenty of them, and we had just barely enough living space on board for the five of us. Let alone supplies of food and Screen. Jesus Christ, do you think I *wanted* to maroon a bunch of people in the middle of the Pacific? Don't you think I suffered like a son of a bitch over the decision?"

Rhodes nodded. Then he looked at Carpenter strangely and said, "Did you report to anybody that you had encountered a ship in distress?"

"It wasn't necessary. They had a radio of their own," Carpenter said sullenly.

"You didn't say a word to the maritime authorities, then? You just turned away and left them there?"

"Yes. I just turned away and left them there."

"Jesus, Paul," Rhodes said quietly. He signaled for one more round of drinks. "Jesus. I don't think that was a good idea at all."

"No. It really wasn't. It was like running away from the scene of an accident, wasn't it?" Carpenter had trouble meeting Rhodes' eyes. "But you weren't there, Nick. You don't know the pressures I was under. Our ship was tiny. I had this huge berg in tow and I wanted to clear out before it melted. The people on the squid ship had been at each other's throats for weeks and seemed absolutely crazy and dangerous. And they were Kyocera people, besides, not that that was a deciding factor, but it was on my mind. Taking them on board was simply impossible. So I bolted and ran. I don't expect any applause for that, but it's what I did. As for calling for help for them, I figured that they had sent out their own SOS and there was no need for me to do it for them. As for filing an official report on the incident, I didn't do that because—because—"

He fumbled a moment for words without finding any.

Then he said, into Rhodes' suddenly unsparing gaze, "I suppose I figured that it would reflect badly on me if I told the authorities that I had encountered a ship in distress and hadn't done anything about it. So I just tried to hush the whole thing up. Jesus, Nick, it was my first command."

"You told your crew not to say anything about it."

"Yes. But they did, anyway."

"The survivors of the other ship probably reported you too, right?"

"What survivors? There couldn't have been any survivors."

"Oh, Paul—Paul—"

"It was my first command, Nick. I never asked to be a fucking sea captain."

"You let them make you one, though."

"Right. I let them. And so for the first time in my life I did something really shitheaded. Well, I'm sorry about that. But I couldn't help myself, Nick. Do you see that?"

"Have another drink."

"What good will that do?"

"It usually does me some good. Maybe it will for you, too." Rhodes smiled. "I think it'll work out all right for you in the end, Paul. The hearing, and all."

"You do?"

"The Company will cover for you. As you say, there was no way you could have brought those people onto your ship. The only thing you did wrong was to fail to make a proper report of the incident, and that's probably going to cost you some slope, but Samurai isn't going to want it to come out in public that one of its ships left a bunch of castaways to die—it looks bad even if it was justifiable—and so they'll square the court in some way and get the charges dismissed, and shove the whole story out of sight, and quietly transfer you back to the Weather Service, or something. After all, throwing you to the wolves isn't going to bring those Kyocera people back to life, and any kind of finding of guilt would become a matter of public record that wouldn't do Samurai's image any good. They're going to bury the whole event and make it seem as though nothing ever took place out there between your ship and that Kyocera one. I'm sure of it, Paul."

"Maybe you're right," Carpenter said. He could hear an odd mixture of pessimism and desperate hope in his tone.

Up till now, he had regarded everything that happened, including the 442 hearing, as relatively minor, a tough judgment call that he had handled as well as he could, all things considered, and which now because of the innate class hostilities of Hitchcock and the rest was entangling him in an administrative hassle that would at worst give him a black mark on his record. But somehow in the course of half an hour's conversation with his oldest and closest friend it had all come to seem much worse to him, the act of a criminally panicky man who had funked the only really critical decision of his life. He was starting to feel as though he had murdered the people in those three dinghies with his own hands.

No. No. No. No.

There was nothing I could do to save them. Nothing. Nothing. Nothing.

Time to talk about something else. Carpenter said, "You mentioned on the phone that some sort of complication had come up for you while I was away, that you would tell me about it tonight."

"Yes."

"And so—?"

"I had a job offer," Rhodes said. "Right after you sailed. Kyocera-Merck called me out to their Walnut Creek headquarters and I had an interview with a Level Three of theirs named Nakamura, the most ice-cold human being you could possibly imagine, who invited me to jump to K-M with my whole adapto team. They would give me a blank check, essentially, to set up whatever I wanted in the way of a lab facility."

"We talked about this, just before I sailed. You were worried about Samurai getting too powerful, having too much control over the genetic destiny of the human race. This is precisely what I told you to do: jump over to Kyocera—I think I mentioned them specifically—and set them up as a competitor to Samurai in adapto technology. Thereby forestalling the Samurai genetic monopoly that you feared so much. Well? Are you going to do it?"

"You haven't heard the whole story, Paul. There's a man named Wu Fang-shui tangled up in this. Until about twenty years ago he was the ranking genius of genetic research. The Einstein of the profession, the Isaac Newton, you might say. The trouble with him was that he got his ends mixed up with his means and carried out a truly hideous program of unethical gene-splitting experiments off in one of the Central Asian republics. Using human subjects. Involuntary subjects. Real nightmare stuff: mad-scientist stuff, you might almost say. Except that he was completely sane, just had no moral sense built into him anywhere. Eventually the word of what Wu had been up to got out, and supposedly he committed suicide. But actually what he did was to disguise himself as a very convincing woman and go into sanctuary in space—he disappeared up to one of the L-5 habitats and was never heard from again."

"And you're beginning to see yourself as some kind of moral monster equivalent to this Wu Fang person, is that it?"

"That's not it at all," Rhodes said. "What has happened is that Kyocera has peeled Dr. Wu Fang-shui out of his sanctuary habitat, don't ask me how, and has him working on the faster-than-light-starship program for them. Evidently the ship's crew is going to need some kind of genetic retrofitting, and Wu is doing it for them. After he's finished with that, Nakamura said, he'll be made available to my research group as a consultant."

"This twisted but utterly formidable geneticist."

"The Einstein of my profession, yes. Working with me."

"But you abhor him so much that you wouldn't dream of—"

"You're still missing the point, Paul," Rhodes said. "Right now we're a long way from solutions to some of the biggest adapto puzzles. The big ambitious total-transformation scheme that my kid Van Vliet laid out is full of obvious holes, and even he is coming to recognize that. A mind on the order of Wu Fang-shui's will be able to deal with those problems and solve them. Put him on the team and we'd be likely to have full adapto technology ready in no time at all. Which would mean that Kyocera would have the genetic monopoly that I've been afraid of giving to Samurai."

"And therefore you're not going to accept the offer," Carpenter said.

"I'm not sure about that."

"No?"

"I still wonder: Do I have any real right to stand in the way of a technology that will enable the human race to deal with the changes that are coming down the pike at it?"

Carpenter knew that a hole in Rhodes' logic would turn up sooner or later. And here it was. "You can't have it both ways, Nick. You say you don't want to impede progress, but you've just finished telling me that you're worried about giving one company a monopoly over—"

"I am. I repeat my question, though. My team plus Wu Fang-shui can probably produce the answers we need for survival. But my team belongs to Samurai and Wu belongs to Kyocera. If we put them together, we get things worked out within two or three years. If we don't, who knows if anybody will ever come up with the solutions to the problems? Do I want to be the key player that makes total-transform a reality? Or do I want to be the key player who prevents or seriously delays total-transform? It's all up to me, isn't it? And I'm not at all sure what I should do. In fact I'm completely mixed up, Paul." Rhodes grinned. "Not for the first time."

"No," Carpenter said. The familiar air of moral confusion rising from Rhodes almost took his mind off his own troubles. "Not for the first time."

The actual 442 hearing took place three days later, once more at the Port of Oakland's Administration Shed Fourteen. The rain had not halted for a moment during those three days: a steady maddening downpour, a drumbeat of great filthy drops pelting the entire Bay Area in a demented reversal of the long-standing weather pattern. No one could say how much longer it would go on before the iron band of drought clamped once again over the West Coast. Meanwhile, though, highways were flooding, houses were tumbling down cliffs, whole hillsides were slashed by deep gullies, rivers of mud flowed in the streets.

When Carpenter presented himself for the hearing there were only two other human beings in the room: the hearing officer with the Irish name and the androidal-looking woman bailiff. Carpenter wondered where Tedesco, who was supposed to be representing him on behalf of Samurai Industries, was. Taking the day off because of the rain?

O'Brien, O'Reilly, O'Leary, gaveled the hearing into session. This time Carpenter took the trouble of noticing and remembering his name. O'Reilly, it was. O'Reilly.

"Objection," Carpenter said immediately. "My counsel isn't here."

"Counsel? We don't have counsel here."

"Mr. Tedesco of Samurai. My representative. He was supposed to be present today."

O'Reilly looked at the bailiff.

"Mr. Tedesco has filed a stipulation of posteriori," she said.

"A what?" Carpenter asked.

"A request to be absent today and to receive a transcript of today's proceedings at a later time. He will file appropriate responses if he deems it necessary to do so," O'Reilly said.

"What? I'm on my own today?" Carpenter said.

Impassively the hearing officer said, "Let us proceed. We enter into evidence the following exhibits—"

"Hold it a second! I demand the right to a proper representative!"

O'Reilly gave Carpenter a long cool glance. "You have a proper representative, Captain Carpenter, and he will be given an opportunity to file an appropriate response in due course. I'd like no further outbursts, if you please. We enter into evidence the following exhibits—"

Leadenly Carpenter watched as Exhibit A appeared on a visor mounted at one end of the long tubular room. Exhibit A was the testimony of Maintenance/Operations Officer Rennett, describing her visit to the *Calamari Maru* in the company of Captain Carpenter. Crisply and efficiently Rennett outlined the conditions she had observed aboard the squid ship, the deposed and sedated officers, the statements of the mutinous Kovalcik. It all seemed accurate enough to Carpenter, and not in any way damaging to him. Then came Exhibit B, the statement of Navigator Hitchcock, telling how the movements of the hooked iceberg in the roughening sea had accidentally swamped the squid ship, and describing the way the three dinghies had come toward the *Tonopah Maru* seeking help, and how Captain Carpenter had ordered the crew of the *Tonopah Maru* to ignore the castaways and begin the return voyage to San Francisco. That part sounded pretty horrendous even to Carpenter; but he couldn't say that Hitchcock had distorted anything, particularly. It was merely what had happened.

He assumed that the statements of Cassie and Nakata would now be played. And then, presumably, he would be given a chance to speak in his own defense—to explain the difficulty of the situation, the limited capacity of his ship and the inadequate supplies of provisions and Screen, and to show how in that instant of decision he had chosen to value the lives of his own crew over those of the strangers. Carpenter had already decided to declare that he felt contrite for having had to abandon the castaways, that he deeply regretted the necessity of it, that he hoped he would be forgiven for having made the choice he had and for having been too flustered afterward to file a proper report. Would Tedesco approve of his taking a repentant stance? Maybe not; maybe it was a weak legal position. Fuck Tedesco, though. Tedesco should have been here to advise him, and he wasn't.

Carpenter allowed himself to feel a shred of confidence, even so. Rhodes' words kept running through his mind.

—*The Company will cover for you. Samurai isn't going to want it to come out in public that one of its ships left a bunch of castaways to die—and so they'll square the court in some way and get the charges dismissed, and shove the whole story out of sight, and transfer you back to the Weather Service, or something.*

—*They're going to bury the whole event and make it seem as though nothing ever took place out there between your ship and that Kyocera one.*

—*I'm sure of it, Paul.*

—*I'm sure of it, Paul.*

—*I'm sure of it, Paul.*

"Exhibit C," O'Reilly announced. "The statement of Captain Kovalcik."

What?

Yes, there she was on screen, stony-faced, icy-eyed, definitely Kovalcik in the flesh. She hadn't perished out there in her open boat after all. No, no, there she was, alive and staring grimly out of the visor, telling a terrible tale of survival at sea, of privation and torment, of eventual rescue by a patrol ship. Half of her people had died. All because the Samurai iceberg trawler's captain had been unwilling to lift a finger to save them.

Even Carpenter had to admit it was a frightful indictment. Kovalcik said nothing about the mutiny she had led; she went completely around the fact that *Calamari Maru* had been swamped as a direct result of her own incompetent decision to remain in the vicinity of the huge captive iceberg; she utterly left out of the reckoning Carpenter's own protests that his ship was incapable of taking on so big a load of passengers. She concentrated entirely on her request for succor and Carpenter's heartless refusal to provide it. When Kovalcik had finished speaking her terrible image still glared out at him from the visor as though it had burned itself into the fabric of the visor.

"Captain Carpenter?" O'Reilly said.

So at last he was to have his day in court. He rose and spoke, running through the whole grimy tale one more time, the summons to Kovalcik's ship, the signs of the mutiny, the sedated officers and the request to take them aboard, then the swamping of the other ship and the three dinghies bobbing in the sea. Listening to himself, Carpenter was struck by the hollowness of his own case. He *should* have taken them on board, he told himself, no matter what. Even if everyone starved on the way back to port. Even if they all ran out of Screen in a day and a half and burned right down through skin and flesh and muscle to the bone. Or else have called in for their rescue by others. But he pushed on through, limning the events, once more offering his self-justification, his arguments from efficiency and possibility, his statement of contrition and repentance for any errors committed.

Suddenly he was all out of words, standing mute before the hearing officer and the bailiff.

There was a roaring silence. What was going to happen now? A verdict? A sentence?

O'Reilly banged the gavel. Then he turned away, as though to some other case that was before him on the desk.

"Am I supposed to wait?" Carpenter asked.

"The proceedings are adjourned," the bailiff said. Picked up a sheaf of folders. Lost all interest in him, not that she had ever had much to begin with.

Nobody said a word to Carpenter as he left the building.

As soon as he reached the Dunsmuir, half an hour later, Carpenter put in a call to Tedesco at the Samurai number he had been given. He expected to get some kind of corporate runaround; but to his amazement Tedesco appeared almost at once.

"You weren't there," Carpenter said. "Why the hell not?"

"It wasn't required of me. I've seen the transcript."

"Already? That was goddamn fast. What are you going to do now?"

"Do? What's there to do? A fine has been levied for your negligence. The Port has stripped you of your sea license. Very likely Kyocera will sue us now for letting their people die out there in the Pacific, and that might be quite expensive. We just have to wait and see."

"Am I going to be demoted?" Carpenter asked.

"You? You're going to be fired."

"I—*fired?*" Carpenter felt as though he had been punched. He struggled to catch his breath. "The Company is behind me, you said at the first hearing. Fired? Is that how you're behind me?"

"Things changed, Carpenter. We didn't know then that there were survivors. Survivors alter the entire circumstance, don't you see? Kyocera wants your head on a platter, and we're going to give it to them. We would probably have kept you on if there hadn't been any survivors, if this had simply been an internal matter involving Samurai and the Port of Oakland—your word against that of your own crew, a matter of officer judgment and nothing else—but now there are accusers rising up publicly in wrath. There's going to be a stink. How can we keep you, Carpenter? We would have hushed this all up and you might have hung on with us, but now we can't, not with survivors speaking up, making us all look like shit. You think we can give you a new assignment now? Your new assignment is to look for a job, Carpenter. You have thirty days' notice, and you're damned lucky to get that. A termination counselor will advise you of your rights. Okay, Carpenter? You see the picture?"

"I wasn't expecting—"

"No. I guess you weren't. I'm sorry, Carpenter."

Dazed, his breath coming in heavy shocked gusts, Carpenter stared at the visor long after it had gone blank. His head was whirling. He had never felt such inner devastation. Suddenly there was a hole through the middle of the planet, and he was falling through it—falling, falling—

Gradually he calmed a little.

He sat quietly for a while, breathing deeply, trying not to think of anything at all. Then, automatically, he started to call Nick Rhodes.

No.

No, not now. Rhodes would be sympathetic, sure; but he had as much as already said that he thought Carpenter had brought all this on himself, hadn't he? Carpenter didn't need to hear more of that just now.

Call a friend. A friend who isn't Nick Rhodes.

Jolanda, he thought. Nice round jiggly unjudgmental Jolanda. Call her and take her out to dinner and then go back to her house somewhere in Berkeley with her and spend the night fucking her blind. It sounded good, until he remembered that Jolanda was up in the L-5s with the Israeli, Enron.

Someone else, then.

Not necessarily in the Bay Area. Someone far away. Yes, he thought. Go. Go. Far away from this place. Run. Take yourself a little trip.

To see Jeanne, for instance. Yes, sweet Jeannie Gabel, over there in Paris: always a good pal, always a sympathetic shoulder for him.

She was the one who had gotten him into this sea-captain business in the first place. She wouldn't come down on him too hard for the mess that he had made of it. And during his thirty remaining days of Level Eleven privileges, why the hell not stick the Company for air fare to Paris and a bit of fine dining at the bistros along the Seine?

He keyed into the Samurai trunk line and asked for the Paris personnel node. A quick rough calculation told Carpenter that it was probably past midnight in Paris, but that was okay. He was in a bad way; Jeanne would understand.

The trouble was that Jeanne Gabel was no longer at the Paris office. In good old Samurai Industries fashion she had been transferred to Chicago, they told him.

He ordered the phone net to follow her path. It took only a moment to trace her.

"Gabel," said the voice at the other end, and then there she was on the visor, the cheerful warm stolid face, the square jaw, the dark straightforward eyes. "Well, now! Home is the sailor, home from the—"

"Jeannie, I'm in trouble. Can I come see you?"

"What—how—" A quick recovery from her surprise. "Of course, Paul."

"I'll hop the next plane to Chicago, okay?"

"Sure. Sure, come right away. Whatever's best for you."

But his Company credit card seemed no longer good for air fare. After a couple of tries at reprogramming it, Carpenter gave up and tried car rental instead. Evidently they hadn't canceled that yet, because a reservation came through on the first shot. Driving to Chicago probably wouldn't be fun, but if he hustled he supposed he could make it in two days, at most three. He called Jeanne back and told her to expect him by midweek. She blew him a kiss.

The car delivered itself to the Dunsmuir forty minutes later. Carpenter was waiting outside the hotel with his suitcase behind him. "We're going east," he told it. "Head for Walnut Creek and keep on going." He put the car on full automatic and leaned back and closed his eyes as it started up toward the hills. There was nothing to see, anyway, but the black unrelenting curtain of rain.

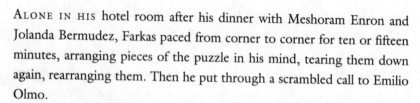

ALONE IN HIS hotel room after his dinner with Meshoram Enron and
Jolanda Bermudez, Farkas paced from corner to corner for ten or fifteen
minutes, arranging pieces of the puzzle in his mind, tearing them down
again, rearranging them. Then he put through a scrambled call to Emilio
Olmo.

"I've been sniffing around a little," Farkas told the Guardia Civil
officer. "I'm starting to pick up a little whiff of conspiracy here and there."

"Have you? So have I."

"Oh?"

"You say first. What do you know, Victor?"

"The Southern California group that you heard rumors about?
They're real. Or at least, let me say, I've picked up the rumor about them
now from an entirely new source."

"A reliable source?"

"Reasonably reliable. A friend of a friend. Someone who is very well
connected in the way of information transfer."

"Ah," said Olmo. "So the story is traveling. How very interesting.
What else can you tell me, Victor?"

"Nothing, really." Farkas saw no need just yet to provide Olmo with
details of the Israeli involvement in the plot against the Generalissimo.
That would be premature; it was clear to Farkas that Enron had some
specific proposals to make, and Farkas wanted to hear them before he
brought Olmo into the picture. If indeed he was going to bring Olmo into
the picture at all. There was always the option of cutting the Guardia Civil
man out of the scene, if the Israeli angle showed real promise. There might
be more slope to gain by letting the coup happen than by helping Olmo
snuff it out. Olmo, perhaps, could be used in some way quite other than
to function as Generalissimo Callaghan's chief policeman. The Kyocera
plan of making him Don Eduardo's successor whenever the Generalissimo
finally died would guide Olmo toward making the correct choices. But
Farkas did not know yet which side he wanted to sell out, and therefore it
was appropriate at this point to be vague with Olmo. "As I said, this was

third-party material. But I thought you would want to know that the project is being discussed in various places."

"Yes. I do," said Olmo. "Though in fact I am somewhat ahead of you. The Californians and their plans are not only real, but some of them have recently paid a visit to Valparaiso Nuevo to examine the territory."

"You know this definitely?"

"Third-party information, like yours," Olmo said. "I haven't seen them myself. But we know that they were here. We are working on tracing them, but we are having a little difficulty. Probably they have gone back to Earth already. But in that case we will be watching for them, the next time they return."

"Well, then," Farkas said. "You're ahead of me, all right. I'm sorry to have wasted your time, Emilio."

"It is always a pleasure to hear from you, Victor."

"I'll call you if I find out anything more definite."

"Please do," said Olmo.

Perhaps this was the moment to put through a call to New Kyoto and ship this thing up to higher levels. Farkas debated it inwardly and decided against it, for now. If one did not happen to be Japanese, the only way one could reach higher levels oneself was to take the initiative in situations that called for boldness and decisiveness, and then to display, when everything had taken shape properly, the excellent results that one had achieved.

Farkas slept on it. When he awoke, the patterns were clearer in his mind. Before going out for breakfast he called the number of the hotel room that Jolanda shared with Enron.

The dark, glassy column that was Meshoram Enron appeared on the visor.

"Jolanda's not here," Enron said, a little too quickly, not bothering to hide the hostility of his tone. "She's downstairs in the health club."

"Good," Farkas said. "You're the one I wanted to talk to."

"Yes?"

"We need to have another little meeting. There are some loose ends left from last night that I'd like to tie up."

Enron seemed to be considering that. But his glassy facade was unchanging: Farkas had no clear idea of the processes going on within the Israeli's mind. Enron was too well guarded. It was impossible for Farkas to read any fluctuation in Enron's emanations using only the image in a visor. He would have to be in direct contact with him to pick up nuances of that sort.

After a moment Enron said, "We're expecting to go back to Earth later today, or maybe on the first shuttle tomorrow."

"Then there's plenty of time for us to get together, isn't there?"

"This is important, you say?"

"Very."

"Anything to do with Jolanda?"

"Not in the slightest. She is a very fine woman, but you and I have more significant things to discuss than who sleeps with whom, am I not right?"

This time Farkas noticed a definite brightening of Enron's image, a distinct increase of gleam.

"Where do you want to meet?" Enron asked.

"A town called El Mirador, on Spoke D," Farkas said, picking the site randomly out of his memory. "The Café La Paloma, right on the central plaza, in forty-five minutes."

"Make it sooner."

"Half an hour, then," Farkas said.

Enron was already there when Farkas arrived, five minutes before the appointed time. The plaza, at this hour, was quiet, far emptier than it had been the day Farkas and Juanito had gone there to find Wu Fang-shui. Enron was sitting at one of the front tables, as motionless as a piece of sculpture, betraying no sign of restlessness at all. But he was tight, tight as a coiled spring: Farkas could see that from thirty paces away.

Sitting down opposite him, Farkas said at once, "There is this California project, involving a change in government. You spoke of it last night."

Enron said nothing.

Farkas continued: "A joint effort might be the best way to bring off such a project, you said. A large corporation and a prosperous country, putting up the needed funds, fifty-fifty."

"Go on," Enron said. "You don't need to remind me of what I said."

"All right, then. The point is this: Were you making an offer? Are you people willing to have the enterprise be a partnership?"

Now Enron was leaning forward, alert, intent. The rhythm of his breathing had changed. Farkas knew he had struck the right place.

"We could be," the Israeli said. "Are you?"

"It's very possible."

"What level are you, Farkas?"

"Nine."

"That's not high enough to authorize anything this big."

"High enough to initiate it, though."

"Yes. Yes, I suppose. And of course you already have the authority to go as far as you've gone."

"Of course," Farkas said, without hesitation.

"I need to go back down to Earth and talk to people," said Enron. "It isn't a question of authority, it's a question of information. I need to have some more. Then you and I can get together again and maybe we can strike a deal. I can tell you, Farkas, this is precisely why I came to Valparaiso Nuevo."

"Excellent," said Farkas. "We are traveling on converging lines. I like that. We will talk again soon."

"Very soon, yes."

The conversation was over, but neither of them moved. Enron still seemed tightly coiled: more so than before, possibly. There was just enough of a pause to allow for a change of subject.

Then Enron said, "Jolanda is really fascinated by you, you know. Does that happen often, women falling for you that way?"

"Often enough."

"I would think, with your eyes that way, and all—"

"Quite the opposite," said Farkas. "Many seem to find it attractive. You aren't annoyed, are you?"

"A little," Enron said. "I admit it to you. What the hell, I'm a normal competitive male. But no, no, it doesn't really bother me. It isn't as if I own her. And I was the one who told Jolanda to make a play for you in the first place. By way of getting your attention, of setting up contact with you."

"I'm grateful to you, then. I don't mind being fished for, with bait of that quality."

"I just didn't think she'd be so enthusiastic about it, that's all."

"She strikes me as the sort of woman who is very quick to become enthusiastic," Farkas said. This was making him uncomfortable. Perhaps that was the Israeli's intention. He stood up. "I will wait very eagerly to hear from you again," he said.

Jolanda was in the room when Enron got back to it. He had left a note for her to let her know that he had had an unexpected call from Farkas and had gone off for a meeting with him on another spoke.

"What did he want?" she asked. "Or is it all secret spy business that I'm not supposed to hear about?"

"You already know plenty," said Enron. "You may as well hear a little more. He invited me to go into partnership with Kyocera on the coup d'état."

"Invited *you?* Personally?"

"You know what I mean," he said. "Israel. He came right out and said it: asked me if we were willing to go into the deal on a fifty-fifty basis."

"And what did you tell him?"

"That we were, of course. That this was precisely what I had come to Valparaiso Nuevo to arrange. But first, I said, I had to go back to Earth and get some further information. He will assume that I mean from my government, a confirmation of interest. But in fact I meant I had to speak with your Davidov. It is important for me to know what kind of an understanding he has with Farkas, before I take any of this to Jerusalem."

"You won't need to go back to Earth for that," said Jolanda. "I had an unexpected call this morning too."

"What? Who?"

"He's still here," she said, preening for him, glowing in what struck Enron as a deeply self-congratulatory way. "Davidov. He said he saw us yesterday, having dinner with Farkas in that restaurant in Cajamarca."

"He *saw* us?" Enron repeated, in complete stupefaction. "He was *there?* No, this is impossible. He is gone, back to Earth."

"He's here, Marty. He told me so. I talked with him half an hour ago.

It was his face on the visor. It's almost as distinctive a face as Farkas's, in its way. I told him that you wanted to see him, and he said that would be fine, you could meet with him at a place on Spoke A, one of the farms. I wrote the coordinates down."

"He is gone," Enron said. "So Kluge swore to me. All those names, all those hotels, and then he and his three friends were on the shuttle back to Earth."

"Kluge may have been telling you lies," Jolanda said. "You ought to consider that possibility."

Enron struck his forehead angrily with the flat of his hand. "Yes. Yes, I should. It is Kluge who has been searching for Davidov and failing to find him, and giving us this story and that one about his comings and goings. Why was it so hard to find him? Why was Davidov always one step ahead of this supposedly clever and trustworthy courier? Either Kluge has been lying to me or Davidov is a magician who can deceive all the scanning equipment this habitat has. Let me have his number, fast!"

Reaching Davidov was the easiest thing in the world. Enron put through the call and there he was an instant later, centered in the visor: the bull neck, the colorless hair, the Screen-blemished face, the glacial eyes.

"Nice to hear from you," Davidov said to Enron. His voice was high and light and soft, a gentle Californian voice altogether out of keeping with his coarse, heavy-featured Slavic face. "Any friend of Jolanda is a friend of mine."

"I would like to speak with you in person," Enron said.

"Come right on over," said Davidov pleasantly.

With Jolanda in tow, Enron made the journey down to the hub and back up Spoke A into one of the agricultural zones, where everything was green and sparkling, a land of milk and honey. They passed farms of wheat, of melons, of rice, of corn. Enron saw banana trees heavy with yellow fruit, and coconut-palm groves, and a citrus orchard. It reminded him very much of the bountiful, ever-fruitful groves of his own country, flourishing in the twelve-month growing season and abundant rain of the eastern Mediterranean region. But all of this was built on artificial foundations, Enron reflected. The trees here grew in styrofoam, vermiculite, sand, gravel. Remarkable. Absolutely remarkable.

The coordinates Davidov had provided were those of a rabbit ranch.

Hordes of the furry little animals were skittering around in fields of alfalfa, gray rabbits and brown ones and white ones, and various combinations of colors. Davidov was standing in the midst of them, just outside the farmhouse, talking to a slender, bespectacled man in farm clothes.

Davidov was immense, a great mountain of a man who seemed as broad as he was tall. His eyes were cold and fierce but his manner, as Jolanda had indicated, was gentle, at least superficially. Enron understood, though, that with Davidov the gentleness had to be all on the surface.

He embraced Jolanda first, swallowing her impressive body into an encompassing bear hug, crushing her against him and even lifting her a little way from the ground.

Then his vast hand enfolded Enron's. His grip seemed to be a test of virility. Enron knew how to cope with that sort of thing: he let his fingers go limp while Davidov mangled his bones, then returned the squeeze with equal ferocity. It wasn't necessary to be a giant to manage a significant handshake.

Davidov introduced the bespectacled man: Avery Jones, he said. The manager of the farm. With an expansive gesture Davidov indicated the extent of the rabbit farm, swinging his beefy arm from horizon to horizon. Of course, on Valparaiso Nuevo that was no great distance. "Isn't this a fabulous place! Up to your ass in rabbits, here. A thousand ways to cook the little buggers, they have." The unyielding Bolshevik eyes focused sharply on Enron. They were as cold and hard as stone. "Come on inside and let's talk. Israeli, are you? I knew an Israeli woman, once, from Beersheba. Aviva, her name was. A real ball-buster, but smart as hell. Aviva from Beersheba. Where are you from in Israel, Marty?"

"Haifa," Enron said.

"Work for a magazine, do you?"

"Let us go inside," Enron said.

The bespectacled rabbit farmer tactfully disappeared. When they were inside the farmhouse Enron waved aside the offer of a beer and said quickly, "May we dispense with the social preliminaries? I am an official representative of the state of Israel, at quite a high level. I am aware of the plan which you propose to put into effect."

"So I gather."

"It is a plan that my country finds of great interest."

Davidov waited.

Enron said, "We are, in fact, prepared to make a financial investment in your activities. A considerable financial investment, I should add. Shall I continue, or is taking on another outside investor not of any importance to you?"

"*Another* outside investor?" Davidov said. "Who's the first one?"

Enron glanced troubledly toward Jolanda. She seemed to be smiling.

"I am aware," he said, speaking very slowly and clearly, "that the Kyocera-Merck corporation already has made a substantial contribution to your operation."

"You are? I'm not."

A little nonplussed, Enron said, "I have discussed the matter with a highly placed Kyocera representative, who assured me—"

"Yes. I saw you with him. If he assured you of anything involving his company and us, he's lying."

"Ah," Enron said. "Indeed." This was very confusing. Breathing deeply, he rocked lightly back and forth on the balls of his feet, trying to recover his poise. "So there is no Kyocera-Merck connection with—"

"None. Zero. Zilch. Kyocera isn't in it. Never has been."

"Ah," Enron said again. Jolanda's smile was unmistakable now, ear to ear.

But he was equal to the situation. In that first moment of bewilderment, recollected fragments of his conversation with Farkas earlier this morning went rushing through his mind, and though for an instant Enron felt as though he was being carried along on them like a swimmer being borne to a cataract, he very quickly succeeded in snatching order from chaos.

He saw now that he had jumped to the wrong conclusion. But so had Farkas.

They had been talking at cross purposes earlier, Enron realized. The Hungarian hadn't been offering Israel a slice of the deal at all. Obviously Farkas believed for some reason that Israel *already* controlled the deal, and had been trying this morning to cut Kyocera-Merck in for a piece. Suddenly everything was standing on its head. There were opportunities to be seized in that, Enron thought.

Calmly he said, "Tell me this, then: Are you interested in outside financial backing for your plan at all?"

"Very much so."

"Good. I am in the position of being able to provide it for you."

"Israeli money?"

"Half from Israel, half from Kyocera-Merck."

"You can bring Kyocera in?" Davidov asked.

It was like standing before a great abyss. Enron leaped blithely across it.

"Absolutely," he said.

"Sit down," said Davidov. "Let's have a beer and talk about this a little more. And then maybe we all need to go back down to Earth and do some more talking there."

▼   ▼   ▼

THE RAIN GAVE out before Carpenter was much more than fifty miles east of San Francisco. There was a sharp line of demarcation between the coastal deluge and the dry interior. Behind him lay a realm of black downpour and overflowing gutters; but when he looked ahead, facing into the swollen and bloodshot eye of the sun rising above the Sierra foothills, he could see that everything still remained in the grip of the endless drought.

He was driving into a terrain of arid slopes, rounded and tawny, with the isolated green domes of huge old oak trees standing on them like sentinels, and blue valleys shrouded by shimmering dust shadows. Above the entire scene was a vast and uncompromising sky marked only intermittently by fleecy patches of clouds. The bizarre deluge that had been pelting the Bay Area and the rest of the coastal strip for the last few days would bring no gain to San Francisco's water supply. The main reservoirs were inland, here in the mountains and foothills; and none of the rain was falling on them, no stores of snow would be locked up in the high country for use later on.

Everything was very quiet out here. Industrial pollution had strangled most of the suburban towns in this part of the Sacramento River Valley, and the depletion of the water table during the years of drought had finished off the agricultural communities beyond them. Still farther east, Carpenter knew, lay the ghost towns of the Mother Lode, and then the awesome, gigantic mountain wall of the Sierra; and on the far side of that was the grim wasteland that was Nevada. Once he crossed the mountains he would be driving through utter desert for a day and a half.

And yet—and yet—

It was beautiful here, if you could find beauty in solitude and aridity. With the death of the suburbs and the farms had come a reversion to an almost prehistoric tranquillity in the Sacramento Valley. This was how it might have looked a thousand years ago, Carpenter thought—except for the Pompeii effect of nineteenth- and twentieth-century building foundations and dry-wall boundary markers scattered all about, a multitude of intersecting shin-high grayish-white lines cutting across the dry grassy fields and hillocks like faint stains on the land, the almost imperceptible traces of the buildings that once had been there. But even those had a certain peaceful antique charm. Footprints of antiquity, clues to a vanished world. And the air out here, still and clear, seemed almost to be the air of some earlier century.

Carpenter wasn't deceived. This quiet air was as deadly as the air anywhere else. Deadlier, even, because the toxics never got blown away, here in this zone of unvarying atmospheric stagnation, they simply piled up and remained, and if you stayed around here long enough they would rot your lungs right out of your chest for you. You could see it in the trees of this pastoral region, if you took the trouble to look closely. The weird angles of the boughs, the spikiness of the twigs, the sparse and twisted leaves, all manner of genetic deformities induced by hundreds of years of ozone deficits, the buildup of aluminum and selenium traces in the soil, and other exciting forms of environmental bombardment.

The air and soil and water of our world, Carpenter thought, have become a culture medium for antilife: a zone of negative fertility, blighting whatever it touches. Perhaps some new mutant form of un-life would eventually evolve and thrive in the new medium, some fundamentally dead kind of being that would be capable of carrying on its metabolic activities on the far side of existence, reproducing beyond the grave at birth, a creature that breathed corrosive poisons and pumped hyped-up hydrocarbons through its invulnerable veins.

He sat quietly behind the wheel, letting the car do all the work, taking him up and up onto the steadily rising spine of California.

As the hours passed, even the few last traces of civilization began to drop away. He was in the foothill country, now, where people had generally built their houses from wood, and there were hardly any ruins left to see. Fire had taken care of that: the natural succession of forest blazes, sweeping across the uninhabited towns in the dry season year after year, had scoured the land of man's presence.

Peaceful. An empty world lay before him.

A total contrast to the densely populated turbulence of San Francisco, and all the other nightmare zones of urban life stretching down the coast with hardly a break all the way to the great Belial, the Beast with a Thousand Heads itself, Los Angeles. Even the thought of L.A. made Carpenter wince. That monstrous blemish on the landscape, that pullulating black hole of ineffable ugliness, where uncountable millions of harried souls huddled together in unspeakable heat and air so foul it could be cut and sliced and stacked—

Los Angeles, the city of his birth—

Carpenter could remember his grandfather's tales of growing up in an unfucked world—sentimental memories of the old Los Angeles of long ago—the late twentieth century, maybe? The early twenty-first? A lost paradise, so the old man had said, a place where the wind was fresh and clear off the ocean and days were mild and pleasant. The parks and lush gardens everywhere, the spacious homes, the sparkling sky, the snow on the mountaintops behind Pasadena and San Gabriel in the winter. Sometimes even now Carpenter would visit that vanished Los Angeles in his dreams: the beautiful unspoiled Los Angeles of the distant past, the remote and unattainable 1990s, say, before the iron sky had closed in on everything. He hoped that it hadn't all been just some senile romantic fantasy of his grandfather's invention, that it had really been like that back then. He felt sure that it had been. But it was gone now and would never return.

Onward. Eastward.

Lightning flashed in the empty sun-blasted vault of the sky, a spear-shaft of white brightness crossing the other brightness. A far-off drumroll of thunder. It meant nothing, Carpenter knew. Merely Zeus clearing his throat. The lightning was generated by heat differentials, and rain almost never came with it. All that would come was fire, cutting its scalpel path along the grasslands, them widening, widening.

The trees were different, now. Instead of oaks, there were soaring pines and slender creamy trees that might be aspens. Low gnarly clumps of chaparral—manzanita and greasewood, mainly—bordered the old highway. He saw no other cars. He was the last man alive in the world. In some places, where fire had lately been, stands of bare and blackened tree trunks stretched away in all directions for miles, rising above the charred earth.

Fire was pure. Fire was good.

Let it burn everything everywhere, Carpenter prayed. Let it sear away the sins of the world.

How strange, he thought, that the human race had survived the worst of its national rivalries and its religious wars, had put so much of the old cockeyed irrational strife behind it, had entered into an era of actual peace and global cooperation, more or less. And then this: rot and ubiquitous tropic heat and atmospheric degradation and doom. Strange, strange, strange. Nick Rhodes in his laboratory, struggling with his conscience as he strived to turn the human race into something with gills and green blood. Kovalcik out in the Pacific under that brute of a sun, filling her ship with sea monsters for the needs of hungry humanity. Poor shitheaded Paul Carpenter, so eager to haul an iceberg back to a foolish ungrateful city that he forgets what little decency had ever been programmed into him, and allows himself to abandon—

No. Don't think about that.

What you are doing right now, he reminded himself, is running away from all of that.

Fragments of some old barely remembered liturgy came to him. *Miserere. Miserere. Qui tollis peccata mundi. Agnus dei. Qui tollis. Peccata mundi.*

Dona nobis pacem. Pacem. Pacem. Pacem. Pacem.
Onward. Eastward.

The highway climbed and climbed and climbed, until it entered a comparatively straight stretch in a pass cloaked by the gathering darkness of the oncoming night. This was the high country here. Thin air, toothpick forests of slender struggling pines reaching toward timberline, above them bare rock faces like immense granite shields. All around him rose the purple-gray bulks of enormous mountains, the loftiest peaks of the Sierra.

There was actually a tiny fringe of snow on the north faces of some of the tallest ones, trapped in sheltered bowls and cirques, and Carpenter stared at those turreted patches of white as though he had been translated to some other planetary sphere, one of the moons of Jupiter, perhaps. He had seen snow maybe three times in his life before this. You had to go to the high country, two or three miles above sea level, if you wanted to see it, and then only on the north faces, and at certain times of the year.

Let it snow everywhere, Carpenter thought.

Let the land be covered from sea to sea by a shining white blanket. And let us emerge from it into a pure new springtime of sweet fresh renewed life.

Sure. Sure.

And now he was across the purple-gray mountains, on the far side of the pass, coming down by switchback upon switchback into what he assumed was Nevada. Night was descending quickly. A hard black sky, no moon, plenty of stars, the eerie silent floating lights of space habitats occasionally making their passage among them, visible to the naked eye. Time to settle down for a little while and let the car's reciprocator get a little ahead of the rate of energy consumption so that it could recharge the batteries for the next leg of the journey.

He had rarely seen such a backdrop of darkness and such an intensity of brightnesses crossing it. The sky here looked cold, cold as space itself, frigid mountain air, a terrible icy clarity to it quite different from city air, eternally swirling with muck. But Carpenter knew that it wasn't so. That was a hot sky out there, same as anywhere else. Wherever you went in this sorry world the sky was always hot, even at midnight, even at the edge of this dark and star-flecked mountain kingdom.

Carpenter pulled off the road into a turnout cut from the side of the hill he was traversing and had a bleak dinner of packaged algae cakes that he had brought with him from Oakland. He washed it down with a little sour wine from a bottle cached below the dashboard. Then he curled up and slept in the car, with the security alarms on, as though he were in the midst of some deadly city. When the sun sprang into the morning sky and came crashing against his windshield he sat up quickly, bewildered, not knowing for a moment where he was or what was happening, thinking blurrily that he might be back in Spokane, in his dismal little room on the thirtieth floor of the Manito Hotel.

There was actually a town on the valley floor just ahead of him. It even looked inhabited: a couple of dozen houses, some shops, a restaurant or two. Cars moving around, even this early in the morning.

He pulled up outside the restaurant. DESERT CREEK DINER, it said out front. It looked as if it hadn't been remodeled since about 1925. Carpenter felt as though he had been traveling in time as well as space.

Everyone inside was wearing a face-lung. That seemed wrong, wearing face-lungs in this outpost of 1925, but Carpenter put his on and went in.

A genuine human waitress. No androids, no table visors, no data pads for entering your orders. She smiled at him, eyes twinkling above the breathing-mask.

"What'll it be? Scrambled eggs? Coffee?"

"Fine," Carpenter said. "That's what I'll have."

He hadn't left California yet, he discovered shortly. The Nevada boundary was another couple of miles down the road.

His Company credit card took care of the meal. He still had that much corporate existence, apparently.

When he had eaten he set off toward the east again. The morning flowed toward him out of Utah. Everything was sandy and almost colorless here, and the landscape had the look of not having felt rain since at least the thirteenth century. There were jagged mountains here, not anything like the Sierra but big enough, pink in the early light and then golden brown. Fluffy white clouds, deep blue sky with faint yellow striations of greenhouse gases.

This was such a beautiful world, Carpenter thought, before we messed it up.

He prayed again, vaguely, incoherently. *Ave Maria, gratia plena. Ora pro nobis. Now and at the hour of our death. On us poor sinners.*

Farther to the east there were mountains of an unfamiliar kind, long chains of narrow-ridged fangs, bright red in color as if they were glowing with some interior fire. They seemed incredibly ancient. Carpenter half expected to see prehistoric animals grazing in the flatlands below them. Brontosauruses, mastodons.

No dinosaurs, though. No mastodons. Not much of anything. Pebbles, a little weedy-looking grass, some skittering lizards, that was about it. He found what looked like an old reservoir that still held some water, and stopped and stripped for a bath, which he was coming to need very badly. The water looked safe to enter. And this early in the day he could risk letting his skin have a little extra solar exposure.

The pond was dark and deep and Carpenter thought the water might be too cold to enter, but it wasn't, not especially. Tepid, in fact. But reasonably pure. There weren't any chemical stains turning the surface iridescent, hardly any pond scum here, no alligators grinning up at him out of the depths, not even a frog in sight. A real novelty for him, actual outdoor bathing in genuine unpolluted water. It felt good to be clean again. A baptism, of sorts.

A few hours' drive on the other side of those flaming gorges the countryside began to be populated again. Some pitiful scruffy farms, some miserable ramshackle houses, a few falling-down barns that looked five hundred years old. The inhabitants probably not very friendly. Carpenter went on through without stopping. Beyond the farms was a dusty town, and beyond that a city, which he bypassed. A dull gray haze lay over everything here. Even inside the sealed car, he felt a taste of interior-America heat, interior-America smog, outlying tentacles of the heavy oppressive mass of murk that pressed down everywhere on the midsection of the nation with brutal indifferent force. The air was like a fist, clamping close. He knew that if he stopped the car and stepped outside he would be struck by a blast of scorching Saharan torridity.

During the course of the morning he called Nick Rhodes, simply to tell him what had happened to him, where he was now, where he was heading. Carpenter hadn't wanted to talk to Rhodes the day before, but now it seemed wrong simply to vanish like this, without a word to him. Otherwise, when Rhodes found out that Carpenter had been terminated by Samurai he might think that he had killed himself. Carpenter didn't want that.

Rhodes' office android informed him that Dr. Rhodes was in conference. A little relieved, Carpenter said, "Tell him that Paul Carpenter called, that I've left the Company as a result of certain recent events and I'm going to Chicago for a few days to visit a friend, and that I'll be in touch with him again when I know what my plans beyond that are." He sidestepped the android's request for a number where he might be reached. For the moment this was about as far as he could go toward making contact with the life he had left behind him.

Carpenter was hoping now to reach Chicago late that night, or at the worst by dawn. The car didn't ever get tired. All he had to do was sit still and let the miles float by in their merry hundreds. He didn't have much in the way of food left now, but he didn't have much in the way of appetite, either. Sit still, yes, let the miles float by.

He passed through long stretches of terrible wasteland: slagheaps, ashes, blasted heaths. Smoke was coming from the ground in places: the remains of ancient fires burning down there, the subterranean world mysteriously consuming itself. An entire dark forest of dead trees covering a long brown strip of sharp-spined hills, with a rusting ski-lift descending out of them like a bad joke. A dry lake. A zone of dead gray earth, a tangle of blackened and twisted wires, mounds of junked cars—in the background, the skeletal traces of some abandoned city, structural girders showing, window-frames like empty eye-sockets.

Things began to flatten out. The air was brownish gray. He was getting into dust-bowl territory now, the sad dry heart of the continent, where the vast farms once had been, before the summers became furnaces and the air went bad and the rain moved elsewhere. The spacious skies and purple mountain majesties were still there, yes, right there behind him in

Utah and Wyoming, but now he was east of there, Nebraska, maybe even Iowa, and the fruited plain had gone to hell and he could find no sign of the amber waves of grain.

Yet people lived here. Through the deepening afternoon he saw the lights of towns and cities on both sides of the freeway. Why anyone would want to make his home in this place was more than Carpenter could understand, but he realized that they had probably had no choice about it, they had been born here and saw no hope of going anywhere better, or else they had been cast up by the waves of bad fortune on this beach without a sea, and here they were. Here they would stay. R.I.P.

But at least they *had* homes, he thought.

Carpenter wondered what he was going to do when this long grim odyssey from nowhere to nowhere and back again was finished, and he was ready to begin the next stage of his life. *What* next stage? Go where, do what? There was no place he could call his home. Los Angeles? He scarcely knew the place any more. San Francisco? Spokane? The Company had been his home, moving him around from Boston to St. Louis to Winnipeg to Spokane as it pleased. Wherever he might be, still he had always been in the Company.

And now he wasn't. Carpenter could hardly begin to comprehend that. No slope at all. Off the curve entirely. Level Zero.

Imagine that, he thought. What an accomplishment. The first kid in your class to attain Level Zero.

Somewhere in the middle of Illinois, an hour or two west of Chicago, traffic began to back up on the freeway and the car told him there was a roadblock ahead. No vehicular traffic was being admitted to Chicago from the west or the south except through approved quarantine stations.

"What's going on?" Carpenter asked.

But the car was only a cheap rental job, not programmed to provide anything more than basic information. The best it could do was flash him a map that showed a red cordon zone covering a vast swatch of the region from Missouri and western Illinois south all the way to New Orleans, and up the far side of the Mississippi from Louisiana to Kentucky and parts of Ohio. According to the car, the closest point of entry to the protected zone for travelers intending to reach Chicago was Indianapolis, and the vehicle proposed a detour accordingly.

"Whatever you say," Carpenter told it.

He turned on the radio and got part of the answer. They were talking about an outbreak of something called Chikungunya in New Orleans and the fear that Guanarito or Oropouche might be spreading there too. Secondary occurrences were reported in the St. Louis area, they said. Carpenter had never heard of Chikungunya or Guanarito or Oropouche, but plainly those were the names of diseases: there must be an epidemic of some sort raging down south and the health authorities were trying to keep it from reaching Chicago.

When he reached Indianapolis, around mid-morning, he was able to learn the rest of the story at the quarantine station while he was waiting to be interviewed. The diseases with the long names were tropical viruses, he was told. They were emigrants from Africa and South America and had become rampant in the new rain forests of Louisiana and Florida and Georgia—carried in nonhuman hosts, spread by ticks and other disagreeable bugs, moved along by them into the bloodstreams of the myriad gibbering monkeys and innumerable giant rodents, themselves refugees from the rain forests that once had existed in the valleys of the Amazon and the Congo, that now infested the wet, steaming jungles of the South.

Everyone who lived in the new jungled regions had to be vaccinated constantly, Carpenter knew, as one virus or another went jumping from some animal that carried it into some hapless member of the human population, setting off yet another epidemic. But this was no rain forest, up here. Why were they worrying about jungle diseases like Oropouche and Chikungunya in the drier, cooler environs of Chicago?

"Bunch of infected monkeys got on a barge full of fruit coming up the Mississippi from New Orleans," Carpenter was told at the quarantine station. "Some of them got off at Memphis and started biting people. The rest stayed aboard until Cairo. Memphis and Cairo are sealed off, now. We don't know exactly which bug it is, yet, but they're all bad. You get bitten, you puff up and turn into a bag of black blood, and then the bag breaks and what was in it runs along the floor like slime until it's empty."

"Jesus," Carpenter said.

"We think we stopped the virus before St. Louis. If this stuff ever got

to Chicago, the place would go up like a bonfire. Four million people all
packed together like this? Disease that you can spread just by *looking* at
someone the wrong way? Forget it! —Let's see your route plaque, please."

Carpenter turned the record of his journey over for inspection.

"No side trips to any part of eastern Missouri that don't show up on
the plaque? Any deviation into Tennessee or Kentucky?"

"I came in by way of the north route," Carpenter said. "You can see
what day I left California. There hasn't been time for me to go anywhere
but straight across the mountains and through Nebraska and Iowa."

"You here on business?"

"Business, yes."

A sticky moment. Carpenter was still sailing under Samurai colors: a
Level Eleven salaryman, coming to Chicago for the Company. One phone
call could spike that. But the Company still carried him on the roster. His
megacorp affiliation got him through, on into the fumigation chamber,
and on beyond it to the highway that led to Chicago.

Memphis and Cairo are sealed off, now.

Highways closed, air routes shut down, nobody goes in, nobody
comes out. Memphis and Cairo might just as well have vanished from the
face of the Earth. Monkeys come out of the jungles of Louisiana, doing
their job for the forces of chaos, and your city disappears from the world
while you wait for the Oropouche viruses, or whatever, to get into your
veins and make your body swell up and turn into a bag of black blood.
Lord, have mercy, Carpenter thought.

Christ, have mercy.

*Holy Mary, Mother of God, pray for us now and at the hour of our
death.*

In Chicago, finally, about four in the afternoon, Carpenter phoned
Jeanne Gabel at the Samurai headquarters at Wacker and Michigan, and
got her after only about half a minute of hunt-and-seek maneuvering.

"Where are you?" she asked.

"In a parking lot at—mmm—Monroe and Green."

"All right. Stay there. It'll be all right if I leave here early. I'll come
and get you."

He sat in the car, weary and bedraggled from his journey, staring in awe and dismay at the dark smoggy sky. The air in the city was a kind of oily soup that left black smears on the car's windshield. It was fantastically splotched and streaked with dense patches of mottled color, yellow and purple and green and blue all running together, the color of a bad bruise, with the sun glinting vaguely through the curtain of crud like a small, rusty brass coin. Carpenter had not been in this part of the country for a very long time; he had forgotten what kind of poisons lived in the air here. Everyone he saw was wearing a face-lung. He put his on, making sure it fit snugly over his cheekbones and jaw.

Jeanne arrived with surprising swiftness. Carpenter felt a surge of joy at the sight of her—the first familiar face since Oakland—and then, immediately, a crosscurrent of confusion. He had no idea why he had come here or what he wanted from her, this woman with whom he had maintained a kind of long-distance flirtatious friendship for nearly half a dozen years without ever once having kissed her on the lips.

He would have kissed her now, but that was hard, wearing a face-lung. He settled for a hug instead. She was a strong woman, Oriental in some fashion on her mother's side but no hint of Oriental fragility about her, and she held him tightly, a good hearty squeeze.

"Come on," she said. "You need a shower in the worst way. And then something to eat, right?"

"You bet."

"God, it's good to see you again, Paul."

"Me too."

"Things must be bad, though. I've never seen you looking this way."

"Things aren't very good," he said. "For sure."

Jeanne entered the car on the driver's side and told it where to take them. As it slid into the traffic flow she said, "I checked with Personnel and Records. You don't seem to be with the Company any more."

"I was terminated."

"I never heard of them doing that except for cause."

"There was cause, Jeannie."

She glanced across at him. "For God's sake, what happened?"

"I screwed up," Carpenter said. "I did what I thought was the right thing, and it was wrong. I'll tell you all about it, if you're interested. The main thing is, it was lots of bad publicity and it got the Company in trouble with Kyocera, and so they threw me out on my ass. It was a political thing. They had to let me go."

"Poor Paul. They really stuck it to you, didn't they? What will you do now?"

"Take a shower and have some sort of meal," he said. "That's as much of a plan as I have, right now."

She lived in a two-room flat—a sitting room with kitchen, and a bedroom—somewhere off in one of Chicago's western suburbs. The rooms were sealed so tightly that they felt practically airless and the cooling system was an ancient clanker, inefficient and noisy.

There wasn't much space for guests in the little apartment. Carpenter supposed he would have to find a hotel room for the night if he didn't want to sleep in the car again, and wondered how he was going to pay for it. Maybe Jeanne would let him sleep on the floor. He took the longest shower he dared to allow himself, perhaps six or seven minutes, and changed into fresh clothes. When he came out, she had two plates of algae cakes and soy bacon on the table, and a couple of bottles of beer.

As they ate, he told her the story, quietly and dispassionately, beginning with the distress call from Kovalcik and ending with his final conversation with Tedesco. By now it all seemed to him more like something he had seen on the evening news than anything that had actually happened to him, and he felt almost nothing as he laid out the sequence of events for her. Jeanne listened virtually without comment until the end. Then she said simply, "What a shitty deal, Paul."

"Yes."

"Have you thought about appealing?"

"To whom? The Pope? I'm out on my ass, Jeanne. You know that as well as I do."

She nodded slowly. "I suppose that's so. Oh, Paul, Paul—"

Indoors, in the hot hermetic atmosphere of the flat, they were wearing no masks. She turned toward him and he saw a look in her eyes that was bewildering in its complexity: expectable things like sorrow and compassion, and behind that what appeared to be a soft gleam of pure love, and behind that—what? Fear? Fear was what it looked like, Carpenter thought. But fear of what? Fear of him? No, he thought. Fear of *herself*.

Carefully he poured more beer into his glass.

She said, "How long do you plan to stay in Chicago?"

He shrugged. "A day or two, I guess. I don't know. I don't want to be any kind of burden for you, Jeannie. I just needed to get the hell away from California for a little while, to find some sort of safe harbor until—"

"Stay as long as you like, Paul."

"I appreciate that."

"I feel responsible, you know. Inasmuch as I was the one who got you that gig on the iceberg trawler."

"That's bullshit, Jeannie. You were the one that got me the job, sure, but I was the one who turned those people away. All by myself, I did it."

"Yes. I understand that."

"Tell me about you," he said. "What have you been up to, anyway?"

"What's there to tell? I work, I come home, I read, I sleep. It's a nice quiet life."

"The kind you've always preferred."

"Yes."

"Do you miss being in Paris?"

"What do you think?" she asked.

"Let's go there," he said. "You and me, right now. You quit your job and we'll get a little place near the river and we'll sing and dance in the Metro for money. It won't be much of a living but at least we'll be in Paris."

"Oh, Paul. What a great idea!"

"If only we could, eh?"

"If only." She took his hand in hers and gave it a quick little squeeze; and then she pulled back, as though the gesture had seemed too bold for her.

Carpenter realized that he knew nothing about this woman at all, actually. She was warm and good and kind, but she had kept herself sealed behind glass at all times: a friend, a chum, but always a boundary rising between her and the outside world. And here he was within the perimeter.

They talked for hours, as they had done in the old days in St. Louis: gossip about mutual friends, and Company rumors, and rambling discussions of world affairs. She was trying to put him at his ease, he knew; and probably herself as well. The undercurrent of tension in her was easy to detect. He was demanding a great deal of her, Carpenter realized—showing up out of nowhere like this, moving in on her, dumping the fragments of his shattered life at her feet, presenting himself without explicitly telling her what it was that he wanted from her. Which he could not do, because he didn't know.

About half past ten she said, "You must be very tired, Paul. After driving all the way from California practically nonstop."

"Yes. I'd better find myself a hotel room somewhere."

Her eyes went wide for an instant. Another enigmatic look flickered across her face, that same uneasy mixture of warmth and uneasiness.

"I don't mind if you stay here," she said.

"But there's so little room."

"We can manage. Please. I'd feel like a shit, sending you out into the night."

"Well—"

"I want you to stay," she said.

"Well," he said again, smiling. "In that case—"

She went into the bathroom and was in there a long while. Carpenter stood by the narrow bed, not knowing whether to undress. When Jeanne came out she was wearing a long robe. Carpenter went in to wash up, and when he emerged, she was in bed and the lights were out.

He dropped his clothes, all but his underwear, and lay down on the floor in the sitting room.

"No," Jeanne said, after a little while. "Silly."

Gratitude and excitement and something that might almost have been remorse flooded through him all at once. He moved through the darkness, stumbling over furniture, and got delicately into bed beside her, trying not to brush up against her. There was barely enough room for them both.

Then as his eyes adjusted he saw that her robe was open, and she was naked beneath it, and she was trembling. Carpenter slid his shorts off and kicked them aside. Gently he put his hand on her shoulder.

She shivered. "Cold," she said.

"It'll warm up."

"Yes. Yes, it will."

He moved his hand lower. Her breast was small, firm, the nipple quite hard. The beating of her heart was apparent behind it, so thunderous that it startled him.

Odd hesitations came over him. Going to bed with strange women was nothing unfamiliar for Carpenter, but Jeanne Gabel was not exactly strange to him, and yet she was. He had known her so long, and he hadn't known her at all, and they had been such good friends, and they had never in any way been intimate. And now here he was in bed with her with his hand on her breast. She was waiting. But she plainly seemed frightened. She didn't seem any more sure of what to do than he was. Carpenter feared that she might be doing this out of nothing more than pity for him, which he didn't like at all. And the wild thought struck him also that she might be a virgin: but no, no, that had to be impossible. She was at least thirty-five. Women who stayed virgin that long, if there were any such outside the convent, would probably want to stay that way forever.

She moved against him, awkwardly indicating her willingness for him to go further. Carpenter's hand slid to the juncture of her thighs.

"Paul—oh, yes, Paul—yes—"

The staginess of her words, her breathy tone, what seemed like a forced theatricality, upset him a little. But what else was she supposed to say? What else *could* she say, in this tense and strange situation, except "Paul" and "yes"?

He caressed her carefully, tenderly, still not fully believing that this was happening, that after all this time he and Jeanne were really in bed together. Nor was he entirely convinced that it ought to be happening now.

"I love you," he whispered. They were words he had said to her many times before, in an easy bantering way, and there was something of that banter in his tone now. But also there was something else—guilt, perhaps, for having crashed in on her orderly solitary life like this, in his mindless desperate panicky flight from the chaos that had enfolded him upon his return to San Francisco. And then there was that component of gratitude, also, the thankfulness he felt toward her for the surrender she was making. Banter, guilt, gratitude: not very good reasons for telling someone you loved her, Carpenter thought.

"I love you, Paul," she told him in a barely audible voice, as his hands roamed the secret places of her body. "I really do."

And then he was inside her.

Not a virgin, no, that seemed pretty certain. But it was a long time, he suspected, since she had been with a man this way. A very long time.

Her long muscular arms enfolded him tightly. Her hips were moving in what seemed like eager rhythms, though they were different rhythms from his and that made matters a little tricky. She was out of practice at this. Carpenter brought his weight to bear on her, trying to get things better synchronized. It seemed to work: she was deferring to his greater technical skill. But then, suddenly, whatever skill he had amassed over the years in these activities was swept away by a turbulent mass of dark emotion that came roaring up from the depths of him, a fierce access of desperate terror and loneliness and the awareness of the chaotic free-fall descent that his life had so unexpectedly become. There were wild windstorms in his head, howling Diablos hurling hot raging gusts through his soul as he toppled endlessly through a realm of swirling poisonous gases. He clung to her, weeping and gasping, like a small boy in his mother's arms.

"Yes, Paul, yes!" she was whispering. "I love you, I love you, I love you—"

When he came, it was like a hammer battering from within. Carpenter cried out hoarsely and burrowed against the side of Jeanne's face, and tears flowed from him as they had not done for so many years that he could not remember the last time that it had happened. For a time afterward they lay still, saying nothing, scarcely moving. Then she kissed him lightly on his shoulder and slipped out of the bed, and went into the bathroom. She was in there a long while. He heard water running; and he thought he heard what could have been a sob, though he wasn't sure, and didn't want to ask. If it is, let it at least be a sob of happiness, he thought.

When she returned, she got back into the narrow little bed and pressed herself up very close to him. Neither of them spoke. He gathered her in and she huddled against him; and after a while he realized that she was asleep. Eventually, so was he.

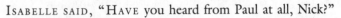

ISABELLE SAID, "HAVE you heard from Paul at all, Nick?"

"He called a few days ago," Rhodes said. "From somewhere in Nevada, I think. Told me that he'd been let go by the Company, and left a message saying he was going to Chicago, but no return number. Nothing since then."

"Why Chicago?" Isabelle asked. "Of all awful places."

"He said he had a friend there. I don't know who he was referring to."

"A woman, do you think?"

"Very likely," Rhodes said. "Paul has always tended to turn to women for comfort when he's under stress."

Isabelle laughed and rested her hands on his shoulders, digging her fingers firmly but gently into the thick, bunched muscles. "Two peas in a pod, you two are. Things get too hot for you, you want to put your heads on Mommy's bosom. Well, why not? That's one of the things it's there for, I suppose."

They were in Rhodes' hilltop flat, close to midnight, after a late dinner in Sausalito. Isabelle was staying the night. Rhodes felt calm and expansive, for a change. Tonight everything was the way he always wanted things to be: soft lights, soft subtle music floating in the air, a glass of his best brandy in his hand. And Isabelle. The relationship had been in one of its up modes for the past few days, Isabelle being relatively benign, accommodating, even tender.

He had just about made up his mind to accept the Kyocera job, despite lingering and troublesome hesitations, bouts of anguished ambivalence. Sixty-forty to take it, he thought. Seventy-thirty, some days. Some days it was seventy-thirty the other way, but those were few. Tonight it was about eighty-twenty in favor of going over to them. Isabelle wasn't even aware of the offer, yet. She knew that he had been in some sort of inner crisis for a while, but had been too tactful to probe. And with everything tranquil between them for the moment, Rhodes felt no desire to stir her to new wrath, as Kyocera's offer of greatly expanded technical facilities for adapto research was almost certain to do. Especially with Jolanda coming back from her visit to the L-5s in the morning, as Isabelle had learned earlier today: Jolanda would surely be stirring Isabelle's political fervor back to its usual degree of intensity after this brief period of quiescence.

Rhodes finished the last of his drink. "How about bed?" he asked.

"Yes," Isabelle said. But she made no move to leave the living room. Going to the window, she stood staring out at the broad view of the Berkeley hills sloping down to the bay, with San Francisco still gleaming brightly on the far side of the water. The night was clear and dry and hot, the recent heavy rains only an improbable memory now. By the light of a full moon distinct bands of greenhouse gases could be seen cutting across the sky even in the darkness, with patches of stars peeking out between them, shimmering, dancing in the night.

He came up behind her and slipped his hands under her arms, cupping her breasts.

She said, still looking outward, "I feel so sad for him. I hardly know him at all and yet it's just as though it's some dear good friend of mine that has run into terrible trouble. His whole life tumbling down in a single moment. Is there anything you could do for him, do you think?"

"Not much, I'm afraid."

"A job in your department somewhere?"

"He's been dismissed for cause. No division of Samurai could possibly hire him now."

"Under some other name?"

"I wish," Rhodes said. "You can't just make up an identity for yourself and apply for a job, Isabelle. You need to have a plausible vita to show them. There's no way he could conceal what happened from any megacorp's personnel scan."

"He can't get any sort of employment, then?"

"Nothing that suits his qualifications, no. A laborer, maybe. I don't know. For any kind of manual job he'd be competing against all those people from the underclass guilds. They've got an inside track on the junk jobs. Somebody falling down from salaryman level is going to have a hard time getting anywhere, when there are so many ahead of him in the underclass who have clean records. A high IQ isn't exactly the thing that gets you to the front of that line."

"So he's completely screwed. He's entirely out of the system, unemployable. That's hard to believe."

"I'll try to think of something," Rhodes said.

"Yes. You should."

But what? What? His soul overflowed with compassion for his old friend; but his mind was empty of solutions for Carpenter's plight. Dismissals were so rare, in the megacorp society. Recourse was so iffy.

This was very new for him, to be fretting about Paul. All their lives it had been the other way around, Rhodes in trouble or a state of bewilderment, trapped in a mess of some sort, and Carpenter coolly, carefully, explaining how he should deal with it. It was a novelty to think of Carpenter now as vulnerable, damaged, helpless. Of the two of them, Carpenter had always been the more capable one, serenely making his way through life with a sure sense of direction. Not as intelligent as Rhodes, no, not gifted in any particular way, but shrewd, self-directing, moving in an easy confident way from assignment to assignment, from city to city, from woman to woman, always knowing what his next move would be and where it would take him.

And now.

One bad moment, one faulty decision, and here was Carpenter cast loose, washed up, flung by a crazy twitch of fate onto the deadly barren shore of an unforgiving world. Suddenly the whole dynamic of their friendship had been turned upside down, Rhodes saw: Carpenter the puzzled and needy one, and he the finder of solutions for knotty problems. Except that he had no solutions.

He would have to find one, Rhodes told himself. He owed Carpenter that much. And more. Something has to be done for him, he thought. By me. There's no one else who can help him. But for the moment he was stymied.

Rhodes' mood began to decline precipitously. He found himself imagining Carpenter under Chicago's sweltering filthy skies, ambling around at loose ends in a strange city, in a toxic environment that made tonight's bands of sky gases here seem like jolly Christmas decorations.

"Bed," Rhodes said again. "How about it?"

Isabelle turned. Smiled. Nodded. Her eyes were warm, eager,

beckoning. Paul Carpenter and his problems receded from the forefront of Rhodes' mind. A burst of love for Isabelle suffused his spirit.

I will tell her about the Kyocera job tomorrow, he promised himself. Maybe not the Wu Fang-shui angle, but the rest of it, the bigger laboratory, the greater slope, the increased corporate support. She would understand that it was important for him to persevere and succeed in his work. Important not only for him, but for everybody, the whole world.

He thought of the Christmas present he had had from her last year, the holochip with the six-word mantra that defined the chief zones of his adapto project:

BONES   KIDNEYS
LUNGS   HEART
SKIN   MIND

She understood. She ultimately would not let his work come between them, of that he was convinced. For all her love of mouthing trendy antiscientific political slogans, she was aware, on some fundamental level, that it was necessary for human bodily modifications to be made before the atmospheric conditions grew much worse. And they *would* grow worse, despite all that had been done to halt further damage to the environment and undo what had already been done. BONES LUNGS SKIN. KIDNEYS HEART MIND. Five of the six would have to be radically changed; the key to the task, Rhodes knew, was seeing to it that the sixth remained more or less the same, that when his work was complete the mind within the bony housing was still recognizably a human mind.

Isabelle crossed the room, leaving a trail of clothing behind her. Rhodes followed her, watching with keen pleasure the play of muscles in her lean tapering back, the delicate knobby line of her backbone clearly visible against her taut skin, the breathtaking inward curve of her narrow waist. Her great wiry nimbus of vermilion hair stood out like a flaming crown above her long slender neck.

Just as she disappeared into the bedroom the telephone rang.

At this hour?

Rhodes flicked it on automatically and Paul Carpenter's face, red-eyed, drawn, appeared in the visor. Speak of the devil, Rhodes thought.

"I'm sorry to bother you so late, Nick—"

"Late?" Well, yes, it was. But Rhodes tried to shrug the fact away. "It isn't all that late here. But it must be the middle of the night in Chicago. Are you still in Chicago, Paul?"

"For the time being." Carpenter's voice sounded thick and slurred. He was either drunk or very, very tired. "I'm going to leave here tomorrow, I think. Coming back to California."

"That's fine, Paul," Rhodes said cautiously. "I'm glad to hear it."

There was a little pause. "It's been a good stay for me, in Chicago. I've got my head straightened out a bit, maybe. But the friend I've been visiting—well, she's got her own life, I can't just dump myself down on her for an indefinite time. And this is an awful place to live, really awful. So I thought—California—a new start—"

"Fine," Rhodes said again, hating the empty blandness of his tone. "The land of new beginnings." Rhodes wished he had something specific to offer, and felt hollow and futile because he did not.

He stared at the visor. Blurry weary eyes looked back at him. It seemed to be a struggle for Carpenter to keep them focused. Carpenter was definitely drunk: Rhodes was sure of that, now. He knew the symptoms as well as anyone.

"I called Jolanda just now," Carpenter was saying. "Thinking maybe she could put me up for a couple of days, until I had my bearings, you know, figured out what next, so on and so forth—"

"She's still up in L-5," Rhodes said. "Supposed to be coming home tomorrow."

"Ah. I thought she might be."

"She's still got that Israeli with her. He'll be coming too. And someone else, someone that they met up there. It sounded like she had a whole goddamned entourage."

"Ah," Carpenter said. "I better not figure on staying with her, then."

"No."

Another spell of silence, a sticky one.

Carpenter said, "I wonder, then, Nick, if—well, if it would be all right—"

"Yes. Of course it would," Rhodes said quickly. "With me, here? Of course, Paul. You know you're always welcome."

"I won't be in your way?"

"Don't be an asshole. Listen, call me when you get on the road, and then call me again when you're a day or so from the Bay Area. Leave messages, or whatever. Let me know when I can expect you, so I'll be sure to be here. —Are you all right, Paul?"

"Terrific. Really."

"Money?"

"I can manage."

"See you in—what, three days? Four?"

"Less," Carpenter said. "Looking forward. Say hello to Isabelle for me. You still with Isabelle?"

"Of course," said Rhodes. "Matter of fact, she's right here. If you want to talk to her yourself, I'll—"

But he was peering at a blank visor.

Isabelle, completely naked now, emerged from the bedroom, looking edgy and impatient. More like her old self: annoyed by the intrusion, by Rhodes' willingness to have allowed it to occur.

"Who was that?"

"Paul," Rhodes said. "From Chicago. He's coming back. Wants to stay with me for a little time."

Her annoyance vanished in an instant. She seemed genuinely concerned.

"How is he?" she asked.

"He looked terrible. He sounded drunk. The poor son of a bitch." Rhodes snapped off the living-room lights. "Come on," he told her. "Let's go to bed. Before the phone rings again."

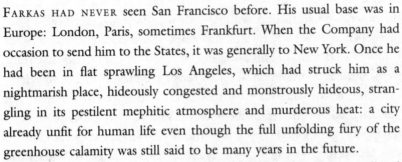

FARKAS HAD NEVER seen San Francisco before. His usual base was in Europe: London, Paris, sometimes Frankfurt. When the Company had occasion to send him to the States, it was generally to New York. Once he had been in flat sprawling Los Angeles, which had struck him as a nightmarish place, hideously congested and monstrously hideous, strangling in its pestilent mephitic atmosphere and murderous heat: a city already unfit for human life even though the full unfolding fury of the greenhouse calamity was still said to be many years in the future.

But San Francisco was very different, Farkas thought. It was small and rather pretty, situated as it was between the ocean and the bay. His special way of sight translated its hilly terrain into a pleasurable pattern of square-topped wave forms, and from the two defining bodies of water on either side of the little city came a rich and harmonious burgundy-red emanation, velvety and soothing in its texture.

Of course, the air over San Francisco was stained by its heavy burden of greenhouse gases, yes, but that was true to some extent wherever you went on Earth; and at least in San Francisco the constant wind off the sea kept the more corrosive substances from sitting in one place for very long. And though the weather was disagreeably warm, the sea breezes did at any rate hold the degree of discomfort down a little. The climate was more like that of London or Paris than of any other American city he had visited. The rest were all like ovens; San Francisco's heat was somewhat less unrelenting. But he missed the steady gentle rain of Western Europe. San Francisco baked under an unvarying blast of desert sunlight that Farkas perceived as a brilliant shower of golden daggers.

He and Jolanda and Enron had taken the high-speed underground transit capsule together from the space-shuttle terminal out in the broad, flat valley east of San Francisco. Jolanda and the Israeli had accompanied Farkas to his hotel in the central district of the city, and then had gone across the bay to Jolanda's place in Berkeley, where they were planning to stay. A few days from now, when Jolanda had finished making certain arrangements for the care of her house and pets, the three of them would go on down to Southern

California to meet with Davidov and conclude the terms of the Israeli-Kyocera partnership that was going to subsidize the conquest of Valparaiso Nuevo.

It might have been wisest, Farkas knew, for him to have proceeded straight on to Los Angeles with Davidov from the space habitat, and let the other two join them down there when Jolanda had taken care of her business here. That way he would perhaps have a chance to take a closer reading of Davidov and his associates and see how competent they really were. But Farkas was in no hurry to revisit the horrors of Los Angeles.

And, besides, he was eager to stay close to Jolanda Bermudez. His one assignation with her, in the hotel on Valparaiso Nuevo, had whetted his appetite for more. Farkas was a little abashed to admit even to himself that his decision to come to San Francisco rather than Los Angeles had been based mostly on the fact that Jolanda was going there first. After his long period of abstinence, Farkas found himself wholly captivated by the lavish generosity of her flesh, by the uncomplicated givingness of her temperament, by the easily aroused fevers of her passionate nature.

That was all very foolish, he knew, and very adolescent, and possibly risky, and probably futile as well: Enron seemed intent on keeping her out of his reach. But Farkas was sure that Enron's possessiveness was nothing more than a power game that Enron was playing out of sheer masculine reflex. He sensed that the Israeli had no real use for Jolanda except as a commodity to be employed in the service of attaining his larger goals.

Jolanda seemed to see that also. Perhaps Farkas could detach her from him while they were here. Farkas suspected, with what he was certain was good reason, that she felt as strong an attraction for him as he did for her. When this unexpected Valparaiso Nuevo adventure was behind him, he thought, it might be pleasant to spend a few weeks' holiday in and around San Francisco with Jolanda while she finished the sculpture of him that had been the pretext—a pretext, nothing more: he had no illusions about that—for their hotel-room rendezvous.

For the moment, though, he was in a different hotel room and he was alone. For the moment.

He unpacked, showered, drew a little brandy from the room's minibar. Once again Farkas contemplated calling New Kyoto to let them know what he was up to; once again, he rejected the idea. Sooner or later, he was going to have to let the Company know that he was in the process of entangling it in an international conspiracy. But there was no binding commitment yet. That would come in Los Angeles, after the final meeting with Davidov and the other plotters. Then, then, only then, would he send the details up-level to the Executive Committee. If they didn't like the scheme, or had some objection to any of its principals, whatever pledges he had seemed to give up to this point were easily enough deniable. If they did, he could probably write his own ticket upward, Level Eight for sure, possibly higher—*Victor Farkas, Level Seven,* Farkas thought, lovingly savoring the concept—Level Seven pay, Level Seven privileges, the high-rise flat in Monaco, the summer home on the coast at New Kyoto. Until the starship was ready to take off and he could put Earth behind him forever.

The telephone chimed softly.

Farkas was reluctant to let go of his fantasy of Level Seven life. But he answered anyway. There were only two people in the universe who knew where he was, and—

Yes. It was Jolanda. "Everything comfortable?" she asked.

"Very fine, yes." Then, quickly—too quickly, perhaps: "I wonder, Jolanda, do you have any plans for dinner this evening? There are Kyocera people I could call, but if you would be willing to join me—"

"I'd love to," she said. "But Marty and I are spending this evening with some people we know over here in Berkeley. Isabelle Martine, Nick Rhodes—she's a kinetic therapist, my closest friend, a fascinating wonderful woman, and he's a brilliant geneticist who's with Samurai—adapto research, I'm sorry to say, really awful stuff, but he's such a sweet man that I forgive him—"

"Tomorrow, then?" Farkas asked.

"That's why I'm calling, actually. Tomorrow night—"

He leaned forward tensely. "Perhaps we could have dinner in San Francisco, just you and I—"

"Well, that would be pleasant, wouldn't it? But what would I do with Marty? And in any case I want you to come over here, to see my sculptures—" A self-conscious giggle. "To *experience* them, I suppose I should have said. It'll be a little dinner party. You'll be able to meet Isabelle and Nick, and a friend of Nick's named Paul Carpenter, who was an iceberg-ship captain for Samurai, and got into some sort of trouble out at sea and lost his job, and now he's back in town, and we're all trying to cheer him up a little while he tries to figure out what he's going to do next—"

"Yes. Of course. How sad for him. And perhaps during the day, then, Jolanda—would it be possible to have lunch, do you think?"

Farkas felt absurd, pursuing her this way. But there was always the chance that—

No. There wasn't.

Gently Jolanda said, "I'd love to, Victor. You know I would. But we have to wait until Marty goes back to Israel, don't we? I mean, he's here now, he's staying with me, and it would all be terribly awkward—surely you see that. But later—after the thing with Valparaiso Nuevo is done with—there'll be plenty of time then, and not just for lunch. I wish it could be some other way right now, but it can't. It just can't."

"Yes," Farkas said, dry-throated. "I understand."

"Tomorrow night, then—at my house in Berkeley—"

He made a note of the transit code, blew her a kiss, broke the contact.

He was amazed at how irritated he felt: amazed, too, at his own sudden obsessiveness. It was a long time since he had behaved this way. Never, perhaps. Why did this woman matter so much? Because she was unattainable just now, maybe? There were other breasts in the world, other thighs, other lips. It seemed a little dangerous to him, his fascination with this Jolanda.

Through the hotel's guest-services menu Farkas arranged a companion for himself for dinner and three hours afterward. He had long ago learned to rely on professional companionship in times of physical needs. A good professional was almost always quick to hide her initial reaction to his appearance; and there were no troublesome involvements afterward. Farkas had never cared for emotional involvements. But the physical side of things—ah, that!—there was no escaping it indefinitely, he thought. A good thing that ways and means were available for dealing with it.

He took another brandy from the minibar, and sat back to wait for his companion to arrive.

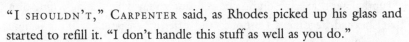

"I SHOULDN'T," CARPENTER said, as Rhodes picked up his glass and started to refill it. "I don't handle this stuff as well as you do."

"Indulge yourself," said Rhodes. "Why the fuck not?" Amber fluid splashed into the glass. Carpenter had forgotten whether they were drinking rye or bourbon. Bourbon has a sweeter taste, he told himself; but he had lost the capacity to distinguish flavors. It seemed to him that he had been drinking steadily all evening. Certainly Rhodes had, but Rhodes always did.

Have I been matching him one for one? Carpenter wondered.

Yes. Yes, I think I have.

"Indulge yourself," Rhodes said. He had said that already, hadn't he? Was he starting to repeat himself, now? Or had Carpenter simply generated a replay of Rhodes' remark of a moment earlier in his mind? He wasn't sure.

It didn't matter. "Don't mind if I do," Carpenter said. "As you so eloquently put it, Nick: Why the fuck not?"

Carpenter had reached the Bay Area earlier that day, after a wild and indistinctly remembered drive back from Chicago. The car had been on automatic the entire time, programmed to seek the shortest route between Illinois and California, stopping only when it needed to recharge itself and paying minimal attention to speed limits, and Carpenter had slept through most of the trip, curled up on the back seat like a bundle of discarded clothing. He recalled that there had been some trouble when the car bumped up against a newly extended tendril of the virus quarantine zone and had to make a wide detour to the north; he could remember seeing the sun go down over western Nebraska like a plummeting red fireball; he had a vague and untrustworthy memory of traversing a broad black inexplicable plain of heaped ashes and glossy volcanic clinkers the follow-ing dawn. That was about it for him, so far as recollections of the journey went.

His recollections of Chicago were sharper ones.

Jeanne gasping in his arms in the surprise of pleasure during a long hungry night of embracing. Jeanne breaking into convulsive sobs just as abruptly later that same night, and refusing to say why. Jeanne telling him that she had become a Catholic, and offering to pray for him. Jeanne pushing him away, finally, toward dawn, saying that she was out of practice at lovemaking and had had about all she could handle of it for now.

The two of them, masked and shot full with Screen, walking hand in hand through the Loop at midday in heat that would make Satan feel homesick, under a splotchy green sky that looked like an inverted bowl of vomit. Sensing the rotten-egg aroma of hydrogen sulfide in the air, even through the mask. Looking up at immense ancient buildings whose soaring stone facades had been carved by the virulent erosive air and acid rains into a phantasmagoria of accidental Gothic parapets and turrets and pinnacles and asymmetrical spires.

Jeanne hiding her body from him in her shapeless robe later that day, telling him she was too ugly to be seen with the lights on, and getting angry when he told her that she was crazy, that she had a truly beautiful body.

Jeanne saying at last, "It's been wonderful having you here, Paul. I mean that. To have made it real, when it was only pretend for so long. But now—if you think you can find the strength to move onward, now—"

Finishing off the last of Jeanne's meager liquor supply, then, putting it away in a steady dedicated manner that was worthy of Nick Rhodes. Trying to call Jolanda in Berkeley, hoping it wouldn't upset Jeanne too much to see him turning so swiftly to another woman, but getting only a recorded message at Jolanda's number, not even a seek-forwarding indicator. Calling Nick, then. Inviting himself to stay with him. Telling Jeanne that he was going to leave for California right this minute, and seeing the suddenly bereft look on her face, and wondering if he had really been supposed to take her words at face value when she had asked him to move along. "It's the middle of the night, Paul," she had said. And he had said, "Even so. Such a long drive: I'd better get started." The glistening of her eyes. Tears of sadness? Relief? Jeanne gave eternally mixed signals.

"Stay in touch, Paul. Come back to see me whenever you want."

"Yes. Yes."

"It was wonderful to have you here."

"Yes. Yes. Yes."

"I love you, Paul."

"I love you, Jeannie. Really."

Into the car. On the road. Eyes swollen with fatigue, tongue thickened by booze, face all stubbly. The quarantine zone. The swollen, plummeting red sun. Ashes and clinkers; and then, a thousand years later, the smoothly rounded tawny hills of the Bay Area, the tunnel into Berkeley, Nick Rhodes' apartment high up on its hillside with the fantastic view.

"Isabelle will be here soon," Rhodes said. "We'll all go out for dinner. Jolanda wants to come along too. Unless you don't want to see her, of course. She has Enron with her, you know. I told you that when you called, didn't I?"

"Yes. What the hell. The more the merrier."

A peculiar evening. Isabelle terrifically sweet, gentle, tender, several times expressing her deep concern for all that Carpenter had been through lately—the therapist Isabelle that Carpenter had not seen before, the softer woman with whom Nick Rhodes was so desperately in love. She and Rhodes were like a loving married couple in the restaurant, not in the least adversarial this time, a real team. Jolanda too told Carpenter how sorry she was for his troubles, and consoled him with a torrid hug, breasts pushing close, tongue flicking through her lips and between his, which from anyone else might have seemed an immediate invitation to bed, but which Carpenter realized was just Jolanda's standard kind of friendly greeting. Enron didn't seem to care. He scarcely looked at Jolanda, showed no sign of interest in her whatever. The Israeli was oddly remote, none of the frenetic intensity of that other dinner ages ago in Sausalito, hardly saying anything: he was physically present but his mind appeared to be elsewhere.

Dinner that night—an early one at some restaurant in Oakland unknown to Carpenter—involved a lot of wine, a lot of superficial chitchat, not much else. Jolanda, obviously hyperdexed to the max, bubbled on and on about the wonders of the L-5 habitat that she and Enron had just been visiting. "What was the occasion for the trip?" Carpenter asked her, and Enron answered for her, a little too quickly and forcefully, "A holiday. That was all it was, a holiday." Odd.

Something was bothering Nick Rhodes, too. He was quiet, moody, drinking heavily even for him. But, then, Carpenter thought, something was always bothering Nick.

"Tomorrow," Jolanda said, "we all have dinner at my house, you, Nick, Paul, Isabelle, Marty and me. We have to finish off everything I've got in the freezer." She was going away again, she and Enron, off to Los Angeles this time. Strange that they were traveling together so much, when they scarcely seemed to pay attention to each other. Jolanda said to Carpenter, "There'll be one other guest tomorrow night, a man we met on Valparaiso Nuevo. Victor Farkas is his name. It might be useful for you to talk to him, Paul. He works for Kyocera, pretty high level, and I've told him a little about your recent difficulties. Maybe he could turn up something for you with Kyocera. In any case you'll find him an interesting man. He's very unusual, very fascinating, really, in an eerie way."

"No eyes," Enron said. "A prenatal genetic experiment, one of the atrocities in Central Asia during the Second Breakup. But he's very sharp. Sees everything, even behind his head, using some kind of almost telepathic ability."

Carpenter nodded. Let them invite a man with three heads to dinner, or with none, for all he cared. He was floating now, drifting a short way above the ground, indifferent to what might be going on around him. He had never felt so tired in his life.

Jolanda and Enron disappeared right after dinner. Isabelle returned to Rhodes' house with Rhodes and Carpenter, but didn't stay. Carpenter was surprised at that, considering the warmth that had passed between the two of them at the restaurant. "She wants to give the two of us a chance to be alone," Rhodes explained. "Figures we have things to tell each other."

"Do we?" Carpenter said.

That was when the bourbon came out, or perhaps it was rye.

"Who's this Chicago woman?" Rhodes asked.

"Just a friend, from the Samurai office in St. Louis, years ago. Very dear kind woman, somewhat fucked up."

"Here's to fucked-up women," Rhodes said. "And fucked-up men, too." They clinked glasses noisily. "Why didn't you stay with her longer?"

"She didn't seem up for it. We never were lovers before, you know. Just good friends. I think sex is a very charged thing for her. She was sweet to take me in the way she did, hardly any notice at all, just told me to come right to her. A port in a storm is a welcome thing."

"Ports. Storms." Rhodes raised his glass in a toast again. Downed its contents, poured more for them both.

"Go easy," Carpenter said. "I'm not the bottomless pit that you are."

"Sure you are. You just haven't fully tested your capacity." Rhodes refilled his glass and topped off Carpenter's. Brooded for a moment, studying his shoes. Said finally, "I think I'm going to take the Kyocera job."

"Oh?"

"I'm not sure, but it's sixty-forty I will. Seventy-thirty, maybe. I'll be giving them my final decision the day after tomorrow."

"You'll take it. I know you will."

"It scares me. Working with Wu Fang-shui: we'll be achieving wonders, I know it. That's the problem. The good old fear of success."

"You may fear success, but you love it, too. Take the job, Nick. Go ahead, turn us all into sci-fi monsters. It's what the fucking world deserves."

"Right. Cheers."

"Cheers. Down the hatch."

They laughed.

Rhodes said, "If I go to Kyocera, maybe I can find a slot for you there. What do you say?"

"You've got to be kidding. You and Jolanda both. She was talking before about getting her friend Farkas to find me a job with them. Don't any of you have any common sense? I'm the guy who left a bunch of Kyocera people in the sea to die, remember?"

"They won't give a shit about that, not after a little time has gone by. I can probably get them to hire you as a favor, or else this Farkas probably could, even easier. You change your name so it doesn't look too weird, and they'll find a slot for you. Most likely some level lower than what you had, but you can work your way back up. Excellence will always out."

"Don't be crazy. Kyocera wouldn't touch me."

"I know a Level Three man there. Honestly. If I tell him he can't hire me unless he hires my friend too, who has had a little bad publicity in an unfortunate recent event, but is eager to redeem himself under another name, a fresh start—"

"Don't."

"Why not?"

"It's dumb," Carpenter said. "Dumb and impossible. Don't even try, Nick. Please."

"What will you do, then?"

"People keep asking me that question, for some reason. I don't know, is what I say. But I don't think I have a future with Kyocera, that's all."

"Well, maybe not. Here. Have another drink."

"I shouldn't," Carpenter said. "I don't handle this stuff as well as you do."

"Indulge yourself," said Rhodes. "Why the fuck not?"

Somewhere in the middle of the night Carpenter realized without any sort of anxiety about it that he was slipping into delirium. He and Rhodes were still sitting at Rhodes' living-room table, with two empty bottles in front of them, or maybe three—it was hard now to distinguish fine details—and Rhodes was still pumping the liquor into their glasses like a demented android bartender. Conversation had sputtered out long ago. The lights of San Francisco across the way were beginning to go off. It was probably two, three, four in the morning.

There were vines creeping across the windows, now. Big, snaky vines, thick as his arm, with little octopoid sucker pads on them, and heavy clusters of leaves. Everything was turning green. A green mist filled the air outside. A light, steady rain, green rain. The West Coast drought had magically ended and the San Francisco Bay Area was part of the global greenhouse now, rich and rank with tropical growth.

Carpenter looked out the window, peering between the greenery. The overnight transformation was astonishing. A green light was playing on the hillside. He saw vines everywhere, creepers, gigantic ferns, enormous unfamiliar shrubs with colossal gleaming leaves and great swollen gaudy flowers. It was a berserk garden, magical, yes, but the magic that had been at work here was a dark and evil one. Unending rain was falling, and the plants stirred and murmured beneath it, expanding moment by moment, rising and stiffening, spreading their wings.

"Let's go for a walk," he said to Rhodes, and they stepped through the sealed windows and floated easily downward into the moist green world beyond.

It was a luminous world, too. Eerie foxfire burned in it, a universal pallid flickering glow. The air was thick, wet, sickly-sweet. Everything seemed to be coated with fur. No, not fur, fungus of some kind, a dense damp growth of mold. From swollen organs burst periodic clouds of dark spores that sought and quickly found tiny crevices where they might take hold and sprout. There were no sharp edges visible anywhere, no bare surfaces: everything was overgrown. The trees, enormous and overbearing, had a lumpy, bearded look. They bulged with bewildering knobs and knurled excrescences.

The moon glimmered faintly through the mists. Lashings of wild mutant bamboo crisscrossed its pockmarked face. Green blood dripped from it across the sky.

Figures moved in the mist—trolls, strange boneless shapeless tentacular beings, alien and monstrous, that might have been natives of some other star; but as Carpenter came closer to them, he saw their faces, their eyes, and he could read the humanity that was in them. The staring stricken eyes, the gaping horrified mouths. And the scaly skins, the slithery limbs, the sagging pudding bodies, the alien forms surrounding the embedded nucleus of humanity still visible within. They too had undergone a magical transformation in the night.

Nick Rhodes seemed to know them all. He greeted them the way one would greet neighbors, friends. Introduced Carpenter to them with a cheerful wave of a tentacle.

"My friend Paul," he said. "My oldest and dearest friend."

"Pleased to meet you," they said, and passed onward through the mist, the green rain, the forest of shaggy trees, the clouds of furry spores that filled the humid air.

Dangling festoons of ropy vines covered every building. Lunatic vegetable life ran riot under a cinnamon sky. Carpenter could make out, under the whips and cords and ropes of the sprawling vines, the indistinct shapes of the ruins of the former world, lichen-stained pyramids, shattered cathedrals, marble stelae inscribed with unreadable hieroglyphs, the fallen statues of gods and emperors. At an altar drenched in green blood a sacrifice was taking place, a crowd of tentacled beings clustered solemnly about one of their own kind who was bound to a stone slab by furry ropes. A furry green knife rose and fell. Carpenter heard distant singing—it was chanting, really—all on a single note, "Oh oh oh oh," like a gentle, blurry far-off cry of inexpressible pain.

"How long has it been this way?" he asked Rhodes. But Rhodes merely shrugged, as though his question had no meaning.

Carpenter stared. The world he had known, he realized, was lost forever. The Earth of mankind was dying, or already dead, its long history over: now it was the turn of the funguses and the slime molds, the vines and the bamboos. The jungle would cover all of the works of man. And mankind itself would fade away into that jungle, a tribe of haunted, hunted creatures, hiding from the groping tendrils, seeking out pitiful niches of safety for themselves in the midst of this wild efflorescence of the new creation. But there would be no safety. Eventually the last humans would transform themselves into a vegetable species also, filling their mouths with the new spores and giving forth a generation of unimaginable new creatures.

What of us? he wondered. Those of us who have not yet changed, who still walk about in our animal forms, our rigid bones and our old human skins? Is there no place for us? Must we be swallowed up in the general disaster?

He looked past the bamboo-bound moon, toward the unreadable sparkle of the stars.

There, Carpenter thought. There: a new rebirth in the stars, that's our only hope. There. There. We shall walk up off the Earth into the sky, and we shall all be saved. Yes. While the mutilated Earth regenerates itself without us.

"Look," Rhodes said, pointing toward the bay.

Something immense was rising from it, a solid massive column of green topped with eyes, an unthinkable unknowable being. Water streamed from its shoulders and fell in sizzling clouds back into the bay. Its eyes were huge, irascible, overwhelming. Rhodes was down on his knees, and he was gesturing to Carpenter to do the same.

"What is it?" Carpenter asked. "That thing—what is it?"

"Get down and acknowledge," Rhodes whispered fiercely. "Down and acknowledge!"

"No," said Carpenter. "I don't understand."

But all the world was bowing to the thing from the waters. A great music was swelling upward and filling the heavens. A new god had come, the overlord of this altered world. Carpenter, despite himself, felt moved by the grandeur and the strangeness of the scene. His knees weakened. He began to lower himself to the moist spongy ground.

"Acknowledge," Rhodes said again. And Carpenter closed his eyes, he bowed his head, he moistened the damp earth with his tears. In wonder and incomprehension he acknowledged the world's new master; and the vision passed, and he awoke, sober and aghast, with the first gray light of morning creeping into the room. His head was pounding. There were empty bottles everywhere. Nick Rhodes lay sprawled on the floor near the couch. Carpenter pressed his hands to his throbbing temples, and rubbed and rubbed in the vain hope of pressing the pain out of them, and listened to the dull tolling sound of his own mind telling himself in bleak and utter conviction that there was no hope for the poor weary damaged old world, none, no hope whatever. All was lost. All, all, all. Lost, lost, lost. All. Lost.

All. Lost. Lost.

Lost.

An enzyme bath, a leisurely day of lounging about the apartment, an hour or two spent in Rhodes' spindizzy chamber getting all the kinks steamed out of his nervous system for the time being, and Carpenter felt almost functional again. Rhodes seemed to show no ill effects at all from his night of bingeing. About five in the evening Isabelle Martine appeared, once again very amiable and solicitous and nonirritating, and after some sherry and a little light conversation the three of them went over to Jolanda Bermudez's place north of the campus.

Carpenter was amused and pleased by the overwrought splendor of the little house—its baroque, antiquated external appearance, the multitude of small rooms within, all jammed with myriad preposterous artifacts, the drifts of incense in the air, the horde of cats, every one of them of some strange and elegant breed. It was just the sort of house, faintly ridiculous but full of eccentric vitality, that he would have expected Jolanda to have, only more so.

And Farkas, the eyeless Kyocera man that Jolanda had somehow collected along the way, up there in the L-5s—he seemed to fit right in with the rest of her things. A curio, an artifact, a one-of-a-kind.

You could not fail to be impressed by him, Carpenter thought. Enormously tall: a powerful, commanding figure, radiating self-assurance and strength, practically filling the little room where Jolanda was serving them canapés. Fine clothes, pearl-gray suit and orange foulard, boots polished to a mirror finish: high-level dandyism. Massive cheekbones, jutting chin. And above all that high smooth arching forehead, that mesmerizing expanse of blank skin where everybody else had eyebrows and eyes: a freakish monstrous thing, something out of a dream, something you never expected to see in real life. Not simply blind, but completely eyeless; and yet nothing in Farkas's movements gave any indication that his vision was at all impaired.

Carpenter cautiously sipped a drink, nibbled a canapé. Watched the changing scene.

Curious social patterns formed, held a moment or two, broke. People shifted, floated about the room.

Farkas and Enron—a huge lordly man and a small, tense, tightly coiled one—conferring in low voices in a far corner like a couple of ill-matched business partners discussing a contract that they expected soon to receive. Perhaps that was what they were.

Then Farkas went to Jolanda. They stood close to each other with Enron looking on sourly from a distance, Farkas plainly fascinated by Jolanda, every aspect of his stance telegraphing his intense interest in her. His shoulders were tipped forward and his great strange domed head was inclined toward her; he seemed to be using some extrasensory X-ray vision to see right through Jolanda's flamboyant scarlet gown to the fleshy nakedness beneath.

And she was enjoying it, flushing like a schoolgirl, wriggling about, brimming with pleasure, practically thrusting herself at him. It definitely looked as if they were setting up some kind of encounter right under Enron's nose. Certainly Enron seemed to think so. His scowl was extremely expressive. There was Isabelle intervening, now, drawing Enron off, distracting him. Loyalty to her friend, Carpenter figured. Getting the

Israeli out of the way so Jolanda could cast her net, not that Farkas appeared to require a lot of catching.

And now Enron was talking to Nick Rhodes: interviewing him again, maybe? Jolanda going over to them. An interchange of grins between Jolanda and Rhodes, oddly intimate, though only for an instant. Carpenter was reminded of things that Rhodes had said about Jolanda to him on the night of the Sausalito dinner, and realized now that Jolanda must have slept with every man in this room, and was proud of it, too.

The patterns kept shifting. At last Carpenter found himself talking with Farkas. It was Jolanda who brought him over, saying as she did, "This is our friend Paul Carpenter. You remember: I told you about him." She flashed them both warm smiles and torrid looks and went dancing away toward Enron.

"You are a Samurai man?" the eyeless man asked Carpenter right away. "Captain of an iceberg trawler, I understand."

"Was," Carpenter said bluntly, amazed at Farkas's reckless conversational style. He looked up at Farkas, several inches taller, staring at the smooth, faintly shadowy place where eyes should have been. "There was a little scandal over an incident at sea. I was terminated."

"Yes. So I was informed. It was my impression that Samurai very rarely terminates its salarymen."

"Kyocera people were involved, on the short end of things. There was an inquiry. It looked very bad for the Company's public image. So I was found to be expendable and sincere apologies were made to all concerned."

"I see," Farkas said. The phrase sounded very weird, coming from him. "And now? You have plans?"

"I thought I might rob a bank. Or kidnap the daughter of some Level One and hold her for ransom."

Farkas smiled gravely, as if those might be plausible alternatives.

"What about making a new start for yourself on one of the space habitats?" he asked.

"A definite possibility, yes," Carpenter said. The idea hadn't occurred to him. But yes, yes, space was where everybody went who had reached a dead end on Earth. The habitats! Why not? But of course he would have to find some way of getting there. He revolved the new notion dizzily in his mind.

Then he became aware that Farkas was still speaking.

"We have all just come back from Valparaiso Nuevo. The sanctuary world, you know. You might find it of some interest. Are you familiar with it?"

"I've heard about it. The last of the glorious banana republics, isn't it? Some loopy old South American generalissimo runs it as his private empire, and makes a fortune by selling protection to fugitives from the law." Carpenter shook his head. "But I'm not a fugitive. I wasn't found guilty of anything except bad management. I wasn't sentenced to anything except losing my job. And I've got no money anyway for buying my way in with."

"Oh, no," Farkas said. "You misunderstand. I don't mean that you should go there to take sanctuary. I mean you might find opportunity for yourself there."

"Opportunity? Of what sort?"

"Of many sorts." Farkas lowered the tone of his voice, making it insinuating, almost seductive. "You see, the Generalissimo Don Eduardo Callaghan is soon to be deposed by an insurrection."

Carpenter recoiled in surprise.

"He is?" This was starting to sound like lunacy.

"Indeed so," said Farkas pleasantly. "What I am telling you is all quite true. Some very capable plotters are planning to end his long reign. I am part of the group. Jolanda also, and our friend Mr. Enron. And there are others. You might wish to join us."

"What are you saying?" Carpenter asked, growing more mystified by the moment.

"It sounds quite straightforward to me. We have a few details to clarify with some people in Los Angeles, and then we will go to Valparaiso Nuevo and take possession of the place. There will be great profit in selling off the fugitives to the agencies that seek their return. You would share in the benefits, which would provide you with the funds to begin a new life for yourself in space. Since obviously there is no future for you now on Earth."

Lunacy, yes. Or perhaps some sort of sadism. This wasn't the way real conspirators talked, was it, taking complete strangers into their confidence on the spur of the moment? No, no, Farkas was spinning out these fantasies for the sake of having a little cruel fun. Or else he was crazy. Carpenter, struggling to make sense of this unexpected stream of seeming madness that was flowing so calmly from the eyeless man, began to feel anger.

"You're playing with me, aren't you? This is some sick way you have of amusing yourself."

"Not at all. I'm being entirely serious. There is a plot. You are invited to join."

"Why?"

"Why what?"

"Why ask me in? Of all people."

Farkas said calmly, "Call it a gratuitous act. A moment of spontaneous inspiration. Jolanda has told me that you are an intelligent man down on your luck. Desperate, even. Willing to take extreme chances, I would guess. And you have many skills and capabilities. All in all it seems to me as though you could be very useful to us." His voice had become a sort of a purr. "And it would give me great pleasure to be of assistance to a friend of Jolanda's."

"This is incredible," Carpenter said. "You don't know me at all. And I don't understand why you're trusting me with any of this, if there's anything to it. I could sell you all out. I could go straight to the police."

"But why would you do that?"

"For money. Why else?"

"Ah," Farkas said, "but much greater sums would be involved in the takeover of Valparaiso Nuevo than the police would ever give you. No, no, my friend, the only reason for you to betray us would be out of the abstract love of justice. Perhaps that is an emotion that you actually feel, even now, after your recent experiences. But I am highly skeptical of that. —Tell me: does what I have said interest you in any way?"

"I still think it's just a bad joke."

"Ask Mr. Enron, then. Ask Jolanda Bermudez. She says that you and she are friends. Is this not so? Then you trust her, presumably. Ask her whether I am being serious. Go, please, Mr. Carpenter: ask her. Now."

It was all unreal. A grotesque offer out of the blue, coming from someone who scarcely seemed human. But terribly tempting, if there was anything to it.

Carpenter looked across the room at Jolanda. She had said last night that Farkas might be able to turn up something for him with Kyocera, a suggestion that Carpenter had not placed the least credence in. Was this what she had meant? *This?*

No, it all had to be some joke, he told himself. A stupid little joke at his expense. Jolanda must be in on it; he would go to her and ask her to confirm what Farkas had just said, and she would, and it would go on and on, new and ever more grandiose nonsense being trotted forth all evening, until suddenly someone could no longer hide a grin, and then the laughter would begin, and—

No.

"Sorry," Carpenter said. "I'm not in the mood to be made fun of right now."

"As you wish. Forget the offer, please. I regret making it. Perhaps it was a mistake to have disclosed so much to you."

There was a sudden note of suppressed menace in Farkas's voice that Carpenter found disagreeable. But it told him also that this might not be any joke. Carpenter had already started to turn away; but then he paused and looked up into the Kyocera man's extraordinary face once again.

"You're really serious about this thing?" he asked.

"Absolutely."

"Go on, then. Tell me more."

"Come with us to Los Angeles, if you want to learn more. But there will be no turning back for you, once you do. You will be one of us; and you will not have the option of withdrawing from the group."

"You *are* serious."

"So you believe me, now?"

"If this is any kind of joke, Farkas, I'll kill you. You better believe *me*. I mean what I'm saying." Carpenter wondered if he actually did.

"There is no joke." Farkas put out his hand. After a moment, Carpenter took it.

"Dinner is served!" Jolanda called, from another room.

"We will talk further, afterward," Farkas said.

As they were walking toward the dining room, Nick Rhodes came up alongside Carpenter and said, "What was *that* all about?"

"A strange business. I think he was making me a job offer."

"With Kyocera?"

"Free-lance work," Carpenter said. "I'm not sure. It's all very fucking mysterious."

"You want to tell me about it?" Rhodes asked.

"Later," said Carpenter. They went inside.

It was two that morning before Carpenter got his chance to tell Rhodes about the conversation with Victor Farkas, after they had returned to Rhodes' apartment from the dinner party, and after Isabelle had finally gone home, explaining that she had to be in Sacramento the next day for a professional conference and couldn't stay over. After seeing her out Rhodes and Carpenter stood for a time in Rhodes' living room, in the quietness of the warm humid night, looking out at the bay.

Though they had all had plenty to drink at Jolanda's, Rhodes wanted a nightcap. He brought out a dark, odd-shaped bottle bearing a label that looked at least a hundred years old, antiquated typeface, browning paper. "Actual cognac," Rhodes said. "From France. Very rare. I feel like celebrating a little. What about you?" He looked inquiringly at Carpenter.

"What the hell. But only one, Nick. I can't manage another looper like last night."

Rhodes poured carefully. Very rare stuff, yes, no doubt of that. Carpenter drank slowly, thoughtfully. It had been a curious evening. He felt as though he had moved past some strange boundary into the realm of the completely unknown.

But Rhodes had crossed a boundary too that evening, it seemed, and wanted to talk about it.

"It was sixty-forty last night, remember? And then seventy-thirty. But all this evening the numbers kept going up, and when they got to ninety-ten I knew it was clinched."

Carpenter looked up at him wearily. "What are you talking about, Nick?"

"The Kyocera job. I'm definitely going to take it. I decided around midnight."

"Ah. Right."

"Tomorrow, I'm supposed to let Walnut Creek know which way I mean to go. Nakamura, the Level Three who head-hunted me, is waiting for a call. I'm going to tell him that it's a yes."

Carpenter lifted his brandy snifter in a formal salute.

"Congratulations. I like a man who can make up his mind."

"Thank you. Cheers."

"I'm going to take a new job too," said Carpenter.

Rhodes, who had his glass to his lips, sputtered and put it down. "What?" He looked incredulous. "Where?"

"With Farkas. Doing something illegal on a space habitat."

"Smuggling? Don't tell me that Kyocera runs drugs on the side!"

"Worse," Carpenter said. "If I tell you, I'm making you an accomplice before the fact, you know. But I will anyway, and to hell with it. They're going to knock over Valparaiso Nuevo, Nick. Some kind of joint Israeli-Kyocera venture, carried out by thugs from Los Angeles, Jolanda's wonderful friends. Seize control of the place, run it for their own private profit. Jolanda and Enron and Farkas seem to have cooked all this up last week, when they were together on Valparaiso. And now Farkas has invited me in. I'm not sure what my exact role is going to be, but I suppose it'll be something peripheral, like spreading disinformation and general fog and confusion while the coup action is taking place."

"No," Rhodes said.

"No what?"

"You aren't. This is crazy, Paul."

"Of course it is. But what other choices do I have? I'm not only unemployed but unemployable, on Earth. The place for me to go is space. But I can't even afford a ticket up."

"I could buy you a ticket."

"And if you did, what then? How would I earn a living once I was up there? Crime, I suppose. White-collar crime of some kind. This is simpler and quicker. Anything goes, out in the habitats. You know that. There's no such thing as interplanetary law, yet. We push over the Generalissimo and the place is ours, and nobody will say a word."

"I don't believe I'm hearing this."

"I don't believe I'm saying it. But I'm going to do it."

"Listen to me. I know a little about this man Farkas, Paul. He's completely cold-blooded, utterly unscrupulous. A monster, literally and figuratively."

"Fine. Just what's needed for this kind of thing."

"No. Listen. You get mixed up with him, you'll wind up on the scrap heap somewhere at the end of it all. He's dangerous, amoral, full of hate. He doesn't give a damn what he does, or who he hurts. Look what the world did to *him*. He's spending his whole life paying it back. And what does he need you for, anyway? He'll take you in for a little while and then when it's all over he'll throw you out."

"Jolanda trusts him," Carpenter said. "It was Jolanda who talked him into inviting me into this."

"*Jolanda,*" Rhodes said, scornfully. "She thinks with her tits, that one."

"And Enron? Does he think with his tits too? He's Farkas's partner. He also appears to trust him."

"Enron doesn't trust his own big toe. Besides, even if Enron and Farkas are in bed with each other, what protection does that give you? Don't go near them, Paul. Don't do it."

"May I have a little more of that cognac?" Carpenter asked.

"Sure. Sure. But promise me: stay away from this business."

"I don't have any other options, do I?"

"Your fatal flaw," Rhodes said. "Always to make a bad moral position look like something unavoidable." He refilled Carpenter's snifter. "Here. Drink. Enjoy. You cockeyed son of a bitch, are you really going to do it?"

"I really am," Carpenter said. He raised the snifter. "Here's to you and me. Our dazzling new career moves. Cheers, Nick."

▼   ▼   ▼

DAVIDOV SAID, "WE will plant one of the bombs on each spoke, seven in all, each within five hundred meters of the hub. Which is six bombs more than we really need, but redundancy is the key to the success of this enterprise. I have no doubt that the Generalissimo's counterintelligence is capable of finding two or three of the explosive caches, but finding all seven within the time allotted would probably be beyond anybody's capabilities. Besides, we *want* them to find one or two."

"Why is that?" Carpenter asked.

"To show them that we're serious," Davidov said, giving him a bland sunny smile, as though Carpenter were a child.

They were in a small, unpretentious hotel room in the town of Concepción, on B Spoke of Valparaiso Nuevo: Davidov, Carpenter, Enron, Jolanda, Farkas. The five of them had come up in installments from Los Angeles over a period of several days, first Davidov, then Farkas in a two-hop move to Kyocera's research satellite Cornucopia before coming here, then Enron and Jolanda. Carpenter had been the last to arrive, traveling by himself, an innocent research aide officially listed as a Kyocera employee through some hocus-pocus Farkas had arranged. It was about two hours since he had cleared customs at the hub terminal, using a courier named Nattathaniel, also arranged for by Farkas, to shepherd him through.

Enron, sitting on the far side of the room from the others, frowned into his drink. It had been a mistake, he had felt from the start, for Farkas to have brought this man Carpenter into the operation, and Carpenter's naive question now only confirmed Enron's opinion of him. It was hard to believe that Farkas was capable of such stupidity. Not only was Carpenter a Jonah dogged by bad luck—a loser, a bird of ill omen, dangerous to be around—but he was a fool, besides.

Only a fool would have left those marooned sailors bobbing around alive in the Pacific so that some of them could survive and tell the tale of their abandonment. And only a fool would fail to understand why it would be useful for Colonel Olmo of the Valparaiso Nuevo Guardia Civil to become aware that this was no bluff—to realize that Davidov's people really had infiltrated the space habitat with a quantity of disassembled bombs disguised as spare parts for machine tools, had assembled them successfully, and had hidden them here and there around the satellite world with the full intention of detonating one or all of them if Generalissimo Callaghan's excessively long life was not hastened immediately to its overdue finish by his trusted aides.

Of course, Enron thought in sudden surprise, the possibility exists that this Carpenter may not be the fool he seems to be. In which case he may well be something else that is even more dangerous to our interests. And Farkas has drawn him right to our bosom.

Farkas, standing by the window, facing away from the starry night, indifferent to its splendor, said to Davidov, "How soon do you want me to get in touch with Olmo?"

"Tomorrow morning, first thing. You call him, you tell him the scoop, you give him until noon to act."

"Is that enough time?"

"It'll have to be," Davidov said. "The midday shuttle will leave for Earth at quarter past twelve. If something has gone wrong and Olmo is unable to deliver, we'll want to be on it. Giving Olmo a short deadline will help to focus his attention on the task."

"It'll be focused, all right," Farkas said. "Olmo knows what's best for Olmo." He paused a moment. "He knows about this plot, by the way."

From Enron and Davidov came simultaneous expressions of surprise.

"Oh, yes," Farkas said. "Rumors of it reached him quite some time ago, I suppose through normal intelligence channels here. Long before I was ever involved in it, he approached me to see if I could help him locate the plotters. That is his job, you know, to protect the government of Don Eduardo Callaghan. But I see no problem. Don't you think he would jump at the chance to join in the conspiracy, once he realizes that its success is inevitable?"

Jolanda said, "What happens to Olmo after the coup? Do we continue to trust him? Does he really become the new generalissimo?"

"Of course," said Farkas. "He has had an understanding with Kyocera for a long time now that he would be the successor. Even though this is not entirely a Kyocera project, and we are accelerating by direct interference the end of the Callaghan reign, we think that Olmo is the best choice for the succession. We are not interested in destabilizing Valparaiso Nuevo, naturally, but simply in taking advantage of the resources that are available here. Olmo is one of those resources."

"You described him earlier as the Number Three official," Enron said. "Who's Number Two?"

"A retired bullfighter named Francisco Santiago, Callaghan's best friend from the old days in Chile. Technically he holds the office of President of the Council of State. Forget about him. He's ninety years old and senile, and has no real power whatever. Olmo will take care of him."

"Can we rely on this Olmo to take care of the Generalissimo, though?" Carpenter asked. "Olmo sounds pretty slippery to me. What if he decides to sell us to Callaghan in return for a guarantee of the succession? He could easily be playing both sides here. He stands to inherit the place either way. And that way he doesn't have to mess around with a coup."

"Well?" Davidov said to Farkas. "Olmo is your man. Can we trust him?"

"We will be giving Olmo the choice of betraying Don Eduardo and becoming the Supreme Ruler of Valparaiso Nuevo himself by the middle of tomorrow afternoon, or of dying with the Generalissimo and everybody else when we blow the place up. Which option do you think he'll go for?"

"And if he decides, after it's all over, that he'd just as soon not continue to do business with a bunch of ruthless criminals and ruffians from Los Angeles, and with the sinister megacorp and the imperialist Jewish state that are behind the criminals and ruffians?" Carpenter asked.

Enron put his hand to his forehead in despair.

Something must be done about this, he thought.

"Don't you comprehend," Enron said icily, "that the purpose of bringing Kyocera and the state of Israel into the project was to protect against precisely that? This Olmo is Kyocera's creature. He knows better than to turn against those who have placed him in power. I suspect he has no desire for trouble with the state of Israel, either."

"No doubt," Carpenter said.

"All right," said Davidov. "So be it. The bombs are being put together right now, and they'll be installed tonight. Tomorrow at 0700 hours, Farkas, you will be in touch with Olmo. By noon sharp, we are to have confirmation of the death of the Generalissimo from him, code signal IDES OF MARCH, very subtle. We will be waiting at the terminal. Our departure clearances will be ready. If the signal doesn't come by the deadline, we put ourselves on board the twelve-fifteen shuttle out and leave. Carpenter, your job is to get down to the terminal sometime during the morning and wait for us to show up. The shuttle is not to take off without us, do you understand? That is your responsibility. You will if necessary entangle yourself in some kind of dumb, noisy passport hassle with the authorities there, any kind of distraction that you see fit to create, for the purpose of delaying the departure until we arrive, or until you receive the IDES OF MARCH signal on your flex."

"What happens with the bombs if Olmo doesn't come through?" Jolanda asked. "Do they go off?"

"They'll be set to explode at half past one. That gives us a little leeway for dealing with things if Olmo runs into last-minute problems."

"And if he does run into problems? Do we just leave, then, and the whole place is destroyed?" she asked.

"All or nothing, yes," said Davidov easily.

"I don't like that, Mike. Aside from the moral issue, which is a pretty significant one, because there are thousands of innocent people here: but what profit is there in that for anybody, if we just blow the place up?"

"Olmo won't disappoint us," Davidov said. "This is his big opportunity as well as ours." He stood up. "Meeting adjourned," he said. "You know where to find me if you need me."

"Anybody interested in a drink?" Jolanda asked. "There's a bar downstairs."

"Let's go," Carpenter said.

As they left the room, Enron came up beside Farkas in the corridor.

"May I speak with you a moment?" he said.

Farkas had disliked Enron from the first; and the relationship had grown no warmer as their partnership had developed. He could forgive Enron his arrogance, his stubbornly self-serving persistence toward ends regardless of means, even his barely concealed contempt for anyone who did not happen to be Meshoram Enron. Farkas could understand such attitudes.

But Enron was *irritating*. He was like a huge bluebottle fly who perpetually droned and buzzed in your face. He never let up; and that was very tiresome. Still and all, they were partners. Farkas valued Enron's quick and mercurial intelligence, if not his character or his personality or his table manners. So Farkas listened carefully to what Enron had to say, there in the drab little corridor of the unpretentious hotel in the town of Concepción on Spoke B of Valparaiso Nuevo.

What Enron had to say was annoying and offensive: for the Israeli's whole point was that Farkas had casually and negligently introduced a spy for Samurai Industries into this extremely delicate cooperative project. It was an accusation that struck directly at the heart of Farkas's sense of his own competence and judgment.

The really maddening thing was that Farkas was more than half-convinced that Enron might be right.

"Look at it this way," Enron said. "We have here a man who committed a very serious error of judgment when he was caught in difficult and complicated circumstances, and got terminated for it, primarily as a public-relations move by Samurai because he stupidly left a bunch of marooned Kyocera people alive to tell the tale, and now has absolutely no future in the megacorp system. So he has turned to a life of crime, right? Right. But when did you ever hear of a Level Eleven salaryman being terminated, cause or no cause, and simply accepting it without appeal? *Nobody* gets fired from Level Eleven. Nobody."

"As you have said, what Carpenter did was a very serious error of judgment."

"Was it? He had a skinny little iceberg ship with no room for extra passengers, and here were God knows how many Kyocera people looking to come aboard. What would you have done?"

"I would not have become involved to that degree in the first place," Farkas said.

"Right. But suppose you had, anyway?"

"Why are we talking about this event now?"

"Because I think Carpenter, having completely and utterly destroyed his career in the corporate world but still feeling that he belongs to that world, may very well be planning to redeem himself with Samurai by selling Don Eduardo your ass and mine."

"It sounds farfetched."

"Not to me," Enron said. "Consider. Who is Carpenter's best friend since boyhood? The Samurai gene scientist Nick Rhodes. He goes running to Rhodes when he gets into trouble, and Rhodes, who is, let me tell you, a confused, cowardly, insipid man who luckily for him happens to be a genius, says to Carpenter, let us suppose, that his only way to put his life back together is to go into corporate espionage. Two wrongs will make a right. Catch Kyocera or Toshiba or someone like that doing something despicable, and bring word of it to the high-level slant-eyes of Samurai so that they can slap the villains publicly across the wrist, and you will be rewarded by restoration to the Company's good graces, Rhodes says. For example, Rhodes tells him, our dear Jolanda is having a certain Kyocera swashbuckler named Victor Farkas as a dinner guest tomorrow night. You come along, and suck up to Farkas, and maybe you can get a clue to something ugly that Farkas is involved in on Kyocera's behalf, because the odds are about ten to one that Farkas *is* involved in something ugly, and—"

"You are building something very great out of nothing at all," Farkas said.

"Let me finish, will you? Carpenter shows up at the party and eventually you and he are talking, as was intended all along. Carpenter is waiting for an opportunity to seize on something useful. And suddenly you are inspired to take him into our project, this total stranger, this refugee from a wrecked Samurai career. Why do you do this? God only knows. But you do. And for Carpenter it is a miracle. He will expose Kyocera's role in something truly evil, that makes his own abandonment of a few squid catchers at sea look like a child's tea party. We will be apprehended by Don Eduardo's Guardia, and this Carpenter will be a hero. He is given a fresh slate and a promotion of two grades."

"In my judgment there is no likelihood that this hypothesis is in any way—"

"Wait. Wait. More. Do you know that he's one of Jolanda's lovers? The night I first met all these people, Carpenter was with her. He took her back to his hotel that night."

Farkas was startled by that unexpected thrust. But he covered himself as well as he could.

"What of it? She doesn't seem to be famous for her chastity."

"Jolanda was in on this plan before you and I were," Enron said. "It was she who brought me in, do you realize that? So now she has brought her friend Carpenter in as well, because he is at loose ends and she wants to help him. Jolanda knows that Kyocera is one of the factors behind this coup, and then Jolanda finds out that her friend Carpenter's balls have just been cut off by Samurai as a favor to Kyocera, and she sees a way for him to get them back again. So she arranges the little dinner party where you meet him and very obligingly take him into your confidence and affiliate him with our project. Can it be that she has maneuvered you into doing just that, precisely in order that her dear Carpenter can sell you and me and Davidov—who also have been her lovers, of course, but what does that matter?—to the Guardia Civil, and by so doing regain his career with Samurai?"

"You make her sound like a devil," Farkas said.

"Perhaps she is," said Enron. "Or perhaps she is in love with Carpenter, and the rest of us are simply toys for her."

Farkas gave that possibility some consideration.

He felt profoundly uneasy. Enron seemed to be jumping to a whole host of conclusions. But the more Farkas thought back over this affair, the more clearly he saw that he might well have been maneuvered by Carpenter's friends into a position of doing something useful for the fallen Samurai man. What reason had he had for embroiling Carpenter in the plan, anyway, if not to win points with Jolanda? She had all but asked him directly to do something to help Carpenter get back on his feet. Well, he had, in that wild moment of spontaneity at Jolanda's party; and by so doing, he had needlessly made them all—himself, Davidov, Enron, the Company itself—terribly vulnerable.

Could it be, Farkas wondered, that this schoolboy infatuation of his with the overexuberant California woman's silken thighs and glorious breasts had led him into catastrophic foolishness?

"I think I should talk to Jolanda," he told Enron.

She and Carpenter were sitting in the bar: on opposite sides of the table, nothing very compromising about that. As Enron and Farkas appeared, Carpenter rose and excused himself, and headed off toward the washroom.

"A good idea," Enron said. "Will you order a Scotch and soda for me, Jolanda?"

Farkas slipped in beside her as Enron went in the direction that Carpenter had taken. In a low voice, as though Enron might be able to hear him even from halfway across the bar, he said, "Stay with me tonight?"

"I can't. You know that. Marty would be furious."

"Are you married to him?"

"I've been traveling with him. We're sharing a room here. I can't just go off with you like that."

"You want to," he said. "I can feel the heat coming from you."

"Of course I want to. But I *can't*, not with Marty here. Especially not tonight. He's tremendously nervous that something is going to go wrong."

"As a matter of fact, so am I," Farkas said. Her refusal angered him; but it meant he would have to try to find out what he needed to know in just the few moments that remained before Enron and Carpenter returned. He hoped that Carpenter would take his time, or that Enron would find some way to delay him. "What worries me is your friend Carpenter," he said.

"Paul? Why?"

"What do you know about him? How trustworthy is he, really?"

He could see Jolanda's emanations changing: she was growing wary now, radiating higher up in the spectrum, a jittery ultraviolet signal. She said, "I don't understand. If you didn't trust him, why did you bring him in?"

"You asked me to."

She went farther up the spectrum at that.

"I suggested that you might know of an opening for him with Kyocera," Jolanda said. "I wasn't expecting you to invite him into *this*."

"Ah. I see." Still no sign of Carpenter returning. "Do you think we're at risk, having him here?"

"Of course not. Why are you suddenly so suspicious of him?"

"Nerves, I suppose. I have nerves too."

"I never would have imagined."

"All the same, I do. Tell me, Jolanda: how well do you know Carpenter, anyway?"

"A friend of a friend, actually."

"That's all?"

"Well—"

Color rising on her face. Farkas could feel the infrared output.

"I'm not talking about bed, now. How long have you known him? A year? Three years?"

"Oh, no, nothing like that. I met him a few months back, when I was out for dinner with Nick Rhodes and Isabelle and Marty. He had just come to San Francisco from somewhere up north and Nick asked me along as a blind date for him. That's about all there's been, just that one evening."

"I see," Farkas said. "Just that one evening."

He felt a sinking sensation in the pit of his stomach. You have let this foolish woman make an even bigger fool out of you than you realized, he thought bleakly.

"But I certainly don't think," she said, "that he's any kind of risk to us at all. Everything I know about him leads me to think that he's an extremely intelligent and capable—"

"All right," Farkas said. "That's enough. He's coming back."

The plan was that they would eat in separate groups that night, Enron and Jolanda together, Farkas and Carpenter by themselves, Davidov with the others of his mysterious Los Angeles crowd. As they were splitting up Jolanda drew Carpenter aside in the hallway and said in a low voice, "Watch out for Farkas."

"What do you mean? Watch out for what?"

"He doesn't trust you."

"He got me involved in this in the first place."

"I know. He's having second thoughts. Perhaps Marty said something to him about you."

"Marty? He's got no reason to think I'm—"

"You know how Israelis are. Paranoia is their national hobby."

"What do you think is going on?" Carpenter asked.

Jolanda shook her head. "I'm not sure. Farkas was asking questions about you just now. Whether I think it's risky having you as part of the group. How well I know you. He said it was just nerves. Maybe so, but I would be careful of him, if I were you."

"Yes. I will."

"Watch him like a hawk. He has no morals at all, and he's terribly quick and strong, and he can see in every direction at once. He can be dangerous. I know what he can do," she said. "I went to bed with him once, just once, and I've never been with anyone like that. So quick, so strong." Jolanda reached into her purse and drew out three little octagonal yellow tablets. "Here. Take these and keep them with you. If you find yourself in any trouble, these may help you." She pressed them into the palm of Carpenter's hand.

"Hyperdex?" Carpenter asked.

"Yes. Have you ever used it?"

"Now and then."

"Then you know. One will be enough for ordinary circumstances. Two, if very unusual."

Carpenter said, "Are you sure Farkas is thinking bad thoughts about me? Or are you having an attack of nerves too?"

"I might be. But he *was* asking questions about you a minute ago. Do I trust you, and things like that. It didn't sound good, but it might be nothing. Just keep on guard, is all."

"Yes."

"Your nerves? They aren't bothering you?"

"No," Carpenter said. "I don't give a damn about anything, any more. I think my nervous system must have shorted out sometime back." He grinned at her and gave her a quick peck on the cheek. "Thanks for the pills," he said. "And the warning."

"Don't mention it."

An early dinner, alone, at his hotel. An evening of watching videos in his room, by himself. Then to bed. Tomorrow was the big day. Early to bed, early to rise.

I know what he can do, Jolanda had said. *I went to bed with him once, just once.*

Just once. Surprise, surprise. She got around, that girl.

Well, Carpenter thought, tomorrow would tell the tale.

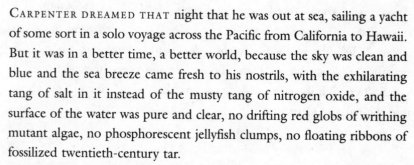

CARPENTER DREAMED THAT night that he was out at sea, sailing a yacht of some sort in a solo voyage across the Pacific from California to Hawaii. But it was in a better time, a better world, because the sky was clean and blue and the sea breeze came fresh to his nostrils, with the exhilarating tang of salt in it instead of the musty tang of nitrogen oxide, and the surface of the water was pure and clear, no drifting red globs of writhing mutant algae, no phosphorescent jellyfish clumps, no floating ribbons of fossilized twentieth-century tar.

All he wore was a pair of ragged cutoff jeans, but he went out on deck every morning in no fear of the sun, which rose unhaloed by any murk of greenhouse gases and shed a soft, gentle, almost delicate light on the sea. He listened to the wind and set his sails, and did his shipboard chores and was done with them by midmorning, and sat reading or strumming his guitar until noon. And then he tossed the safety line overboard and went overboard after it, and had himself a little swim, paddling alongside the boat through the clear, sweet, warm, unpolluted water. And in the afternoon—

In the afternoon he saw an island sitting all by itself in the sea, a small one, uncharted, three palm trees and a patch of green shrubbery and a lovely white beach. A tall voluptuous dark-haired woman was standing in the calm translucent surf waving to him. She was naked except for the merest scrap of red cloth around her loins. Lustrous bronzed skin gleamed in the bright tropical light, heavy breasts, strong thighs—

"Paul?" she was calling. "Paul, it's me, Jolanda—come ashore and play with me, Paul—"

"I'm coming," he called, putting his hand to the tiller. And went to her, and tossed down his anchor in the shallows, and swam toward her waiting arms—and—and—

And the telephone was chiming.

Wrong number. Leave me alone.

Wouldn't stop, either.

Fuck off. Can't you see I'm busy?

On and on, relentless, remorseless. Finally Carpenter reached out with his toe and activated it.

"Yeah?"

"Time to get up, Carpenter."

Victor Farkas's nightmare face was looking at him out of the visor.

"What for?" Carpenter said. "It's—what, not even six in the morning, right? I don't have to get down to the terminal for hours yet."

"I need you now."

What the hell was this? A change in the plan? Carpenter was fully awake in an instant.

"Anything wrong?" he asked.

"Everything's smooth," said Farkas. "But I need you. Get your clothes on and meet me in half an hour. The town of El Mirador, on Spoke D, at a café called La Paloma, which is in the middle of everything, right on the plaza."

I would be careful of him, if I were you. Watch him like a hawk.

"Do you mind telling me why?"

"Olmo is going to meet me there. We'll be discussing important things, as you know. I want a witness to our conversation."

"Wouldn't it make more sense to ask the Israeli to be your witn—"

"No. He's the last person I'd want to be there. You're the one I want. Hurry it up, Carpenter. El Mirador, Spoke D. Half past six at the latest. It's about halfway from the hub to the rim."

"Right," Carpenter said.

There was no way of refusing. The sudden alteration of the program was strange, yes. If Farkas wanted him along with him for his chat with Olmo, he should have told him that last night. But they were a team; this morning was the critical time; aside from Jolanda's uneasiness, Carpenter had no reason to believe that the man who had recruited him for this enterprise was summoning him now to some sort of betrayal. Farkas said he was needed; Carpenter had no option but to go.

Still—even so—

He has no morals at all, and he's terribly quick and strong, and he can see in every direction at once. He can be dangerous.

Carpenter showered and dressed quickly. He felt alert and keyed up, now, but before he left the room he swallowed one of Jolanda's hyperdexes. The stimulant would make him that much sharper: give him a little extra edge, if anything unusual began to happen. Carpenter tucked the other two pills into his shirt pocket. He had brought a light sleeveless woolen vest along on the trip, because he had heard that the air on a space habitat was kept at a temperature cooler than he was accustomed to; he pulled the vest on now, not so much because he was chilly as to keep the pills from falling out of his pocket if he leaned forward.

The only way he knew of getting to Spoke D was to go down to the hub, change spokes, and ride the elevator back up. It seemed to him that there were connectors in midspoke, but no one had told him anything about how to use them.

At this hour the Valparaiso Nuevo day was already in full swing. People were bustling around everywhere. The place was like a gigantic airline terminal, Carpenter thought, that knew neither day nor night, and functioned under artificial illumination twenty-four hours a day. Except the main source of illumination here wasn't artificial. It was supplied by the adjacent solar body, which also functioned twenty-four hours a day, hanging right up there in the sky available for use at all times.

The up-spoke elevator was marked with exits. When the one labeled EL MIRADOR came up, Carpenter stepped off and looked around for the central plaza. Signs directed him. He came in a few minutes to a curiously quaint cobblestoned expanse, with open-air cafés lining its border. It was all like fairyland, this place, an unreal world. But of course it *was* an unreal world. Or an artificial one, at least.

Carpenter caught sight of Farkas at once, across the way, standing out from the others in the plaza like an elephant in a herd of sheep. He went to him.

Farkas was alone.

"Olmo not here yet?" Carpenter asked.

"We are having our discussion with him in the outer shell of the satellite," said Farkas. "It is the only safe place to talk of such things: entirely outside the pickups of the Generalissimo's sonic detection system."

That sounded very odd to Carpenter, a conference in the outer shell. He began to worry again. Perhaps an even finer edge would be a good idea. As Farkas led him toward a doorway in the wall behind the café,

Carpenter reached under his sweater, pulled out another of the hyperdex pills, and popped it into his mouth.

He crunched it between his teeth and forced himself to swallow it. Carpenter had never taken a hyperdex that way before, straight, no water: the taste was amazingly bitter. He had never taken one hyperdex right on top of another before, either, and he felt himself lighting up almost immediately, entering into an almost manic mode. He wanted to run, to leap, to swing from treetops. That was a little frightening, that sense of becoming unhinged; but he felt, along with it, a potent sensation of heightened awareness, of quickened reflex, such as was completely new to him. Whatever surprises Farkas might be planning for him in the space satellite's outer shell, Carpenter was confident he would be ready to deal with them.

"In here," Farkas said.

He opened the door in the wall, and beckoned Carpenter to go ahead of him.

Carpenter peered through the door into a realm of darkness.

"I won't know what I'm bumping into in there," he said. "You're the one with the trick vision, Farkas. You go first."

"As you wish. Follow me, then."

They entered the shell. The bright and cheery plaza of El Mirador vanished behind them. They were in the dreary behind-the-scenes carapace of Valparaiso Nuevo now, the dark, secret skin of the satellite.

Once inside, Carpenter realized that the place wasn't entirely dark: there was a narrow catwalk just to his left, illuminated in a sparse way by a row of antique-looking incandescent bulbs set into the low ceiling, giving the merest possible glimmer of yellow light. As his hyperdex-augmented vision adjusted to the dimness, Carpenter saw piles of black slag, ballast of some sort for the satellite, he supposed, heaped here and there, and what looked like golf carts, probably for the use of maintenance people. Beyond was a zone of complete blackness, dark as space itself.

There was barely room for Carpenter to stand upright. Farkas appeared to be maintaining a half-crouching posture. Deeper in, the ceiling seemed even lower.

He and Farkas were all alone in here.

"Where's your friend Olmo?" Carpenter asked. "Late for our little appointment?"

"He is just ahead," said Farkas. "You don't see him? No. But with my trick vision, as you put it, I have no difficulty making him out, standing right over there."

There was no one in here but the two of them. Carpenter was totally certain of that.

So there was going to be trouble. He took the third hyperdex from his shirt pocket, conveyed it to his mouth, chewed it and swallowed it.

It was like a bomb going off in his head.

Farkas said, "What are you doing?"

"I don't see Olmo," said Carpenter. "Or anybody else." His words came out slurred. His voice sounded to him as though he were speaking in an echo chamber.

"No. In fact Olmo isn't here."

"I didn't think so."

"Indeed," Farkas said. "It is just you and me, here. Tell me something, now. You are still in the pay of Samurai Industries, are you not, Carpenter?"

"Are you crazy?"

"Answer me. You are spying on us for Samurai, yes or no."

"No. What kind of bullshit is this?"

"I think you are lying," Farkas said.

"If I were still working for Samurai," said Carpenter, speaking terribly slowly, sounding as slow as a robot whose charge was running down, making an effort to keep his voice intelligible as the third hyperdex unloaded its full impact on his nervous system, "would I be mixed up in a wild scheme like this one?"

Instead of replying, Farkas pivoted, knelt, came up with something from the ground in his hand—a jagged lump of slag, maybe?—and swung it in a level arc toward Carpenter's head. But the hyperdex was doing its work. Carpenter was prepared for some sort of attack; and, the moment it came, he moved back and to one side, easily outpacing Farkas's movements, so that Farkas's arm moved futilely through empty air. Carpenter heard the bigger man's grunt of surprise and displeasure.

He jumped forward, trying to get around Farkas and return to the daylight of El Mirador. But Farkas blocked the door; and when Carpenter attempted to feint past him, Farkas simply spread his enormous arms and waited for Carpenter to run into them. Carpenter backed off. He glanced quickly over his shoulder, saw nothing but stygian gloom behind him, and backpedaled into it even though he had no idea of where he was going.

Farkas came after him.

"Keep heading that way," Farkas said. "You'll fall off the edge. There's a shelf there, just before the layer of protective tailings, and then there's a drop, and you'll go right into the gravity well. It's a long floating fall, but by the time you hit bottom at the rim, it'll be Earth-one gravitation. Very messy for you."

Was he bluffing? Carpenter had no clear idea of the geography in here. He hesitated just a moment, and Farkas lunged. The man was quick, and he was huge; but once again the triple hyperdex dose made the difference. To Carpenter, Farkas's movements seemed ponderous, almost glacial. It was easy to avoid them. Carpenter stepped aside, catching no more than a glancing blow on his left shoulder. He heard Farkas, puzzled and angry, muttering to himself.

But Farkas was still standing between him and the exit from the shell. And Carpenter had no idea of what lay behind him, closer to the satellite world's skin.

Further retreat might be just as unwise as Farkas had told him it was. Ahead of him was Farkas. *He's terribly quick and strong,* Jolanda had said, *and he can see in every direction at once.* Yes. But there wasn't much choice. Carpenter pulled his head down, getting his center of gravity as low as he could, and went running straight at Farkas. As Carpenter came within reach, Farkas caught hold of him, and they grappled furiously for a couple of moments. Carpenter was altogether unable to budge him. Farkas was huge and immensely strong, and Farkas was braced. His hands had found Carpenter's throat and he was squeezing.

Carpenter went into manic overdrive, jigging about wildly, writhing, going limp and suddenly tightening up again. Somehow he twisted himself about and wriggled free of Farkas's grip and danced away. A lucky shift of his weight: it was, he knew, probably not a trick he could manage a second time.

Farkas came after him, moving unerringly as they passed into a zone of deeper darkness where Carpenter had almost no notion of what lay around him. Vaguely he saw Farkas's long arms stretching toward him, dark lines against the darkness. Carpenter probed cautiously backward with the tip of his foot, trying to find out whether he was approaching the abyss of which Farkas had spoken, or, conversely, whether Farkas was backing him into a dead end. But he was able to learn nothing. He was practically unable to see, now.

Farkas could see, though.

In front of him and behind, too. The blindsight gave him 360-degree vision, Jolanda had said.

Carpenter heard Farkas's rough breathing. He sensed but did not see the massive form approaching him. Carpenter had superhuman speed on his side, but Farkas could see, and he was bigger and stronger. Here in the dark it was an unequal match.

In one smooth rapid motion Carpenter pulled his woolen vest off and held it lightly, by the tips of two fingers. Farkas came barreling forward. Carpenter waited for him, bracing himself as solidly as he could.

Their bodies collided. Carpenter felt a tremendous blow against his chest and he thought that all the air would leave his lungs in a single gust. His whole rib cage seemed to be collapsing.

But he was able to put the pain away and stay upright. He brought the sweater up, holding it like a noose, and as Farkas leaned down toward him for the coup de grace Carpenter drew it quickly down over the dome of Farkas's head, twisting it around Farkas's neck at the bottom end, pulling its hem up and tucking it through, tangling and knotting it, fastening it like a hood over Farkas's head. He seemed to have plenty of time to do what needed to be done. Actually it took probably no more than a tenth of a second.

Farkas howled. He bellowed. He stamped his feet and uttered muffled roars of fury.

There, Carpenter thought. *Does your blindsight work through a layer of wool?*

Evidently not. Farkas raged and blundered in the dark like a blinded Cyclops, and Carpenter, a lithe, frantic Odysseus, moved quickly around him, giving Farkas a powerful shove as he went past, spinning him completely around. Farkas stumbled, regained his balance, came charging toward Carpenter with enormous velocity.

He was fast, but Carpenter was faster. Once more Carpenter stepped aside. In the blackness he could make out almost nothing, but he was aware of a breeze as Farkas, arms pinwheeling, went rushing past, growling angrily, taking huge clattering steps.

Then a sudden shriek of—astonishment? Rage? Horror?

A long outcry, dopplering off into silence.

And then what sounded like an impact, a dull sound far away.

"Farkas?" Carpenter called.

No reply.

"You fall down the hole, Farkas? You dead down there?"

All quiet. Silence. Silence.

Farkas was gone, then. Really gone. It was hard to believe, all that dark force snuffed out. That strange man. Carpenter stared into the darkness.

But he felt no sense of triumph in the moment of victory, only disorientation and fatigue. He knew that at just this moment he had reached the hyperdex high and was beginning the journey down the other side. The high had been *very* high; the descent was going to be awful.

He was assailed by a dizziness of a kind he had never known before, and an almost overwhelming nausea. The whole universe was reeling about him. He dropped to his knees and clung to the rough invisible surface below him. It was swaying, pulsating, rippling. His stomach began to heave. They were dry heaves, and they went on and on, until he thought they were going to turn him inside out like a starfish, and when they were over he crawled a short distance away and lay with his cheek against the rough scraggy ground for a long while, feeling the triple dose of hyperdex blasting through him like a trio of hurricanes. No news bulletins came out of the darkness from Farkas. Farkas was gone. Farkas was dead.

It might have been hours that Carpenter lay there. He spent a good while in a kind of hallucinatory state. Then he returned to full awareness again, or something close to it.

He quivered, he shook, he moaned, he wept, as the last of the hyperdex overdose burned its way through his overstressed nervous system.

When he tried to stand, he found that it was impossible. His legs were rubbery and his skull felt hollow and he had no physical strength at all. He lay down again, and waited, and after a time he became a little more calm. Slowly he started to crawl forward, feeling his way, making absolutely certain that no abysses were before him, and eventually Carpenter realized that he had returned to the zone where the faint light of the incandescent bulbs provided him with a little guidance.

He found the door that led back into El Mirador.

"Farkas?" he called one last time, looking behind him into the dark. Nothing. Silence.

He staggered out into the cobblestoned plaza.

He had no idea what time it was. Somewhere during the struggle in the shell, his wristwatch had been ripped away. But the morning seemed to be well along. Most of the tables at the plaza-side cafés were full, now. Carpenter found one that wasn't and slumped down into it. He sensed that people were looking at him curiously. He wondered how battered and bruised he was, and how filthy.

He felt drained, numb, dazed.

The hyperdex was still blazing in his brain. Its accelerative force had worn off somewhat, and he was able to move now at a normal pace, but his thoughts were driving in wild circles at the speed of light and then some.

Was a triple dose fatal? Should he get himself to a medic?

One will be enough for ordinary circumstances, Jolanda had said. *Two, if very unusual.* He had taken three.

He shivered and trembled. It was an effort to keep from falling face forward onto the tabletop.

An android waiter said, "Can I get you a drink, sir?"

That seemed like an incredibly funny question. Carpenter burst into wild laughter. The android stood beside the table, patiently, politely.

"Or something to eat, perhaps?"

"Nothing, thanks," Carpenter forced himself to say. "Nothing at all." His voice still sounded blurry and too fast. Thanking an android, too!

The android went away. Carpenter sat quietly. Breathe in, breathe out.

After a time, Carpenter remembered that Davidov's plan had called for Farkas to get in touch with a certain Colonel Olmo of the Guardia Civil at seven this morning and tell him that bombs had been planted all over the habitat, that Generalissimo Callaghan would have to abdicate by noon or the whole place would be blown up. Had Farkas actually delivered the 0700 ultimatum to Olmo?

No. No. At 0600 hours Farkas had been chasing Carpenter around the shell of the satellite. Farkas had wanted to dispose of the Samurai Industries spy first thing, before getting on to speaking with Olmo. So the ultimatum had never been delivered, most likely, unless Farkas had jumped the schedule and spoken to Olmo in the middle of the night.

Olmo knew nothing about the deadline, then. The coup attempt had misfired.

But the bombs were still set to blow at half past one.

"Excuse me," Carpenter said to a woman at an adjacent table. His voice was hoarse, ragged, broken, the voice of a torture victim recently released from the grasp of the Inquisition. "Can you tell me what time it is?"

"Eleven-thirty," the woman said.

Jesus. Less than thirty minutes to go to the putative deadline for the abdication. Two hours until the time the bombs were supposed to go off.

Carpenter began to see that he must have been zonked out on the floor of the shell for hours after the fight with Farkas.

He looked around for a public communicator wand at his table and found one clipped to its left side. Its keyboard was tiny and his fingers seemed as thick as tree trunks, and when he tried to remember the call code for Davidov's hotel room he came up with fifty thousand different eight-digit numbers in a fifty-thousandth of a second.

Calm. Calm. He threaded a path through the maze of numbers and found the right one, and punched it in.

No answer.

No hunt-and-seek, either.

Carpenter punched the "help" node and told the wand to go looking for Davidov anywhere on Valparaiso Nuevo. Why that hadn't been done automatically, Carpenter didn't know; but in a moment the communicator came up with a null code for the desired person.

Where was Davidov?

He tried the number of the room that Enron and Jolanda were sharing. Nothing.

Something very wrong here. Where was everybody? The bombs were ticking.

He took a deep breath and punched what he hoped was the directory code, and told the communicator wand that he wanted to talk to Colonel Olmo of the Guardia Civil. The communicator got him a line to the Guardia operations room.

"Colonel Olmo, please."

"Who is calling?"

"My name is Paul Carpenter. I'm with—" He almost said *with Samurai Industries,* and caught himself. "With Kyocera-Merck, Ltd. I'm an associate of Victor Farkas. Tell him that. Victor Farkas." It was very difficult for him to enunciate clearly.

"Wait one moment, please."

Carpenter waited. He wondered how much to tell Olmo, whether he should spill out the whole conspiracy scheme to him. It wasn't *his* responsibility to deliver the ultimatum. He was only a flunky in this thing. On the other hand, he was the one who had removed Farkas from the picture, and nobody knew that except him. Was it now his duty to take Farkas's place in the program?

A voice said, "What is the nature of your call, Mr. Carpenter?"

Jesus. Jesus.

"It's a confidential matter. The only one I can communicate it to is Colonel Olmo."

"Colonel Olmo is unavailable now. Would you like to speak to the officer on duty, Captain Lopez Aguirre?"

"Olmo. Only Olmo. Please. This is very urgent."

"Captain Lopez Aguirre will be with you in a moment."

"Olmo," Carpenter said. He felt like crying.

A new voice, brusque, bored, said, "Lopez Aguirre speaking. What is this in connection with, please?"

Carpenter stared at the wand in his hand as though it had turned into a serpent.

"I'm trying to reach Colonel Olmo. It's a matter of life and death." He struggled to make his words understandable.

"Colonel Olmo is not available."

"I've already been told that. You've got to put me through to him all the same. I'm making this request on behalf of Victor Farkas."

"Who?"

"Farkas. *Farkas.* Kyocera-Merck."

"Who am I talking to?"

Carpenter started to give his name again. Then he said, "Who I am doesn't matter." He was still fighting the hyperdex, stumbling over his own tongue. "What matters is that Mr. Farkas has very important information to give to Colonel Olmo, and—"

"Who are you? What is this all about? You are drunk, are you? You think I have time to speak with drunks?"

Christ! Lopez Aguirre sounded very annoyed. In another moment, Carpenter realized, Lopez Aguirre was likely to send someone over to the plaza to pick him up for questioning, a suspicious character, a public nuisance. Toss him in a back room somewhere, get around to him after lunch. Or maybe some time tomorrow.

He shut the communicator wand off and headed across the plaza, expecting a Guardia Civil man to step out from behind one of the palm trees and clap a set of magnetos on him before he reached the far side. But no one interfered with him. He moved jerkily, in double time, still hopped up on the hyperdex to some degree. He knew that he would be for hours more.

Into the elevator. Down-spoke to the hub, to the shuttle terminal. Most likely that was where everybody was, Enron, Jolanda, Davidov, Davidov's people. Waiting to catch the twelve-fifteen shuttle if Olmo turned out to be unable to topple Generalissimo Callaghan from his throne.

Through the glass wall of the elevator tube Carpenter caught sight of a clock. Quarter to twelve, now. Unless Davidov had had some kind of backup scheme ready, the noon deadline was going to run out without anything being communicated to Colonel Olmo. Which was not the really serious problem. The really serious problem was that when the ninety minutes of grace expired and nothing had been heard from Olmo, the bombs were going to go.

At the terminal, the outbound shuttle was all ready to take off. Carpenter saw its gleaming shaft jutting right into the rim of the docking module, and the shuttle itself stretching upward behind it. Bright confusing signs blinked everywhere. Where the hell was the embarkation lounge? he wondered.

He found himself in some kind of waiting room. Half a dozen local kids were slouching around in there. Carpenter remembered seeing them upon his arrival: couriers, they were, sharp operators who preyed on the incoming travelers. He looked for the one who had checked them through customs—Nattathaniel, that was his name—but didn't see him. But then another one, a hefty, pink-faced blond boy who was probably not as soft as he seemed to be, came over and said, "Help you, sir? I'm a licensed courier. My name is Kluge."

"I've got a ticket on the twelve-fifteen to Earth," Carpenter said.

"You go right through that door, sir. Shall I get your luggage from the locker?"

Carpenter's luggage, such as it was, was still in his hotel room. To hell with it.

"I don't have luggage," Carpenter said. "But I'm looking for some friends who are supposed to be taking the same shuttle out with me."

"They'd be in the embarkation lounge, then. Or on board the shuttle. Boarding time's come and practically gone, you know."

"Yes. I wonder, have you seen them go past?" He described Enron, Davidov, Jolanda. The courier's eyes lit up at the description of Jolanda, particularly.

"They haven't been through here," Kluge said.

"You're sure of that?"

"I know those people. Mr. Enron, of Israel, and Ms. Jolanda Bermudez. And the other one, the big one with the close-cut hair, he uses various names. I worked for Mr. Enron and Ms. Bermudez the last time they were here. I'd have seen them if they had come past here anywhere in the last hour."

Carpenter's eyes grew wide with dismay.

"You'd better go into the lounge, sir," Kluge said. "They'll be calling last call any minute now. If I see any of your friends come in, I'll tell them you've already gone on board, will that be all right?"

Where were they? What the hell had happened?

Olmo had been supposed to discover some of the bombs. That was the plan, Davidov said: to have him find *some* of the bombs. So that he would know that the threat was no bluff. Suppose this Olmo had found the bombs, then, or several of them, at any rate, and had found the ones who had planted the bombs, too, Davidov's men, and had used whatever cute little methods the Guardia Civil of this place usually used to extract information. And had rounded up the rest, Davidov, Jolanda, Enron—was holding them in interrogation cells somewhere, meaning to go around and talk to them later in the day, or maybe tomorrow—

"Final call for Flight 1133," a voice said over the terminal speakers. "Passengers for San Francisco, Earth shuttle, on board now, please—"

"You'd better go on in there, sir," Kluge said again.

"Yes. Yes. Look, when they show up, tell them I'm on board, and—listen, tell them also that Farkas didn't deliver the message this morning. Do you have that? Farkas didn't deliver the message."

"Yes, sir. 'Farkas didn't deliver the message.'"

"Good. Thank you." Carpenter rummaged in his pocket and came up with one of the local coins. Callaghanos, they called them. Not really coins: currency plaques, actually. He had no idea what this one was worth, but it was a big silvery-looking one with a *twenty* on it, and it would have to be enough. He handed it to Kluge.

"Final call for Flight 1133—"

Where were Enron and Jolanda? Where was Davidov? In custody: Carpenter was sure of that.

And Olmo had discovered the bombs, yes. But had he discovered *all* of the bombs? Did he have any idea how many had been planted? Had he thought to ask?

Carpenter entered the lounge. He half expected to be arrested the moment he showed his identity plaque, but no, they told him that everything was in order, so apparently he was in the clear, not linked in any way to the conspirators, too unimportant even to notice during his short stay on Valparaiso Nuevo.

Noon.

He was supposed to create a disturbance if the others hadn't arrived on time—cause a delay, make them hold the shuttle until the rest showed up. At the check-in counter he said, "Some friends of mine aren't here yet. You'll have to wait on the departure until they arrive."

"That's impossible, sir. Orbital schedules—"

"I saw them last night, and they were definitely intending to be here on time!"

"Perhaps they are already on board, then."

"No. A courier out there who knows them said—"

"May I have their names, sir?"

Carpenter rattled off the names. He was still speeding. The desk steward asked him to repeat them more slowly, and he did. A shake of the head, then.

"Those people are not on this flight, sir."

"They aren't?"

"Reservations canceled. All three. We have an entry here on the board that they will not be taking the flight."

Carpenter stared.

They've been arrested, he thought. No doubt of it now. Olmo has them, and with any luck they've been telling him about the plot, unless, of course, they've been stashed away for interrogation later on.

And the bombs—the bombs—had Olmo found them all? Did he know?

"If you don't mind, sir—you'll have to take your place on board, now—"

"Yes," Carpenter said mechanically. "Of course."

Moving with the leaden tread of a dying robot, he went lurching onto the shuttle. Looked about for Jolanda, Enron, Davidov. Not to be seen. Of course not.

Let himself be strapped into his gravity cradle. Waited for the shuttle to push off.

Enron. Davidov. Jolanda.

A colossal bungle. He could do nothing. Nothing at all. Make them delay the flight? They wouldn't. They would simply pull him off and stick him in restraint at the shuttle terminal. Suicide, is what that would be.

"Please sit back, enjoy the flight—"

Yes. Sure.

The shuttle was moving outward, now. Quarter past twelve, exactly. Carpenter put his hands over his eyes. He had felt a little while before that he was as tired as he had ever been, but he suspected now that he had gone beyond that, that now he was tired as he could ever possibly get. If you could die of sheer weariness, he thought, he would be dead by now.

"What time is it?" he asked a man in the opposite seat, a long while later.

"Valparaiso Nuevo time?"

"Yes."

"One twenty-eight exactly."

"Thank you," Carpenter said. He turned toward his porthole and stared fixedly out, wondering which side of the shuttle was facing toward Valparaiso Nuevo, and, if it was this one, which of the many little points of light out there was the habitat he had left a little while before.

He didn't have to wait long to find out.

The explosion, when it came, was like the sudden distant blossoming of a scarlet flower in the sky. And a second flare of red, and a third.

▼ ▼ ▼

RHODES WAS CLEARING out his desk when the annunciator light went on and the android outside said, "Mr. Paul Carpenter is here to see you, Dr. Rhodes."

It was Rhodes' final day at Santachiara Technologies, and he had a million and a half things to do. But he could hardly tell Paul Carpenter that he was too busy to see him.

"Tell him to come in," Rhodes said.

He wasn't prepared for the change in Carpenter's appearance. His old friend looked as though he had lost twenty pounds in just a matter of weeks, and aged ten years. His face was haggard, his eyes were vacant-looking and rimmed with red, his long yellow hair had lost most of its luster. Carpenter had shaved off his beard for the first time in Rhodes' recent memory, and the look of the lower half of his face, gaunt and hard and outjutting, was altogether unfamiliar.

"Paul," Rhodes said, going to him, wrapping his arms around him. "Hey, fellow. Hey, there!"

It was like embracing a sack of bones.

Carpenter smiled grimly, a ghostly burned-out smile. "A crazy time," he said softly.

"I'll bet it was. You want a drink?"

"No."

"Me neither," said Rhodes.

Carpenter flashed him that dead, practically expressionless little spectral smile again. "You didn't give it up, did you?"

"Me? Not a chance. I've got a serious habit, fellow. But I can do without it right now. Sit down, will you? Relax."

"Relax, he says." Carpenter chuckled hollowly. He gestured at the packing crates, the stacks of cubes and virtuals. "You going somewhere?"

"This is the last day. I start at Kyocera on Monday."

"Good for you."

"I'll be taking most of my people over with me. Hubbard, Van Vliet, Richter, Schiaparelli, Cohen—all the key personnel. Samurai is appalled, of course. They're talking big lawsuit. Not my problem."

"No?"

"Kyocera will indemnify."

"Nice," Carpenter said. "I'm very glad for you, Nick. Go over there and genetify the hell out of things. Fix everything the way it needs to be fixed. A new human race that can breathe methane and drink hydrochloric acid. Do it, Nick. You and Dr. Wu."

"I haven't talked with Wu yet. He's still up there on Cornucopia, retrofitting the crew for the interstellar trip."

"Cornucopia?"

"The Kyocera research satellite. Practically next door to the place that—"

"Ah," Carpenter said. "Yes."

Neither of them spoke for a time.

"What a shitty thing. Valparaiso Nuevo."

"Yes."

"Isabelle still hasn't even begun to cope with it. Jolanda was her best friend."

"I know," said Carpenter. "What vitality that woman had! I can't believe she's—"

"No. Neither can I."

"I saw it blow up. Sat there on the shuttle, watching it, thinking, Jolanda, Enron, Davidov. And all those thousands of other people. But mainly Jolanda. Jolanda. Jolanda."

"Don't talk about it, Paul. Don't even think about it."

"Sure."

"You certain you don't want a drink?" Rhodes asked.

"Listen, if you'd like to have one—"

"Not me. You."

"I don't dare touch it. I had a hyperdex overdose while I was up there. Only thing that saved my life, but it ruined my nervous system for a long time to come."

"Hyperdex? Saved your life?"

"A long story," Carpenter said. "Farkas decided he needed to kill me, and Jolanda tipped me off and gave me some of her pills, and—oh, shit. Shit, Nick. I don't feel like talking about it at all."

"You shouldn't," Rhodes said.

It was unbearable, he thought, to see Carpenter this way, this dazed, woozy shell of a man, this wreck. But Carpenter had been through so much, the iceberg thing, the firing, the trip across the country, the L-5 explosion—

They sat in silence again for a while.

The thing about a friendship that goes back this many years, Rhodes told himself, is that when a moment comes when it's more appropriate not to say something than to say something, you can just keep your mouth shut. And the other one will understand.

But after a time it was impossible for him to sustain the silence. Quietly Rhodes said, "Well, Paul? What now? Do you know?"

"Yes. I do."

Rhodes waited.

"Back to space," Carpenter said. "I've got to get out of here. Earth is fucked, Nick. At least it is for me. I have nobody here but you. And Jeanne, I guess, but I don't really have her. And I don't want to mess her up any more than she already is, so the best thing I can do is to leave her alone. I don't want to stick around and watch things continue to fall apart here."

"They won't," Rhodes said. "We're going to fix them. Or rather, we're going to fix ourselves so that we can handle what's about to come down."

"Fine. You do the best fix you can, Nick, and more power to you. But I've got to get out of here."

"Which habitat will you go to?"

"Not a habitat. Farther."

"I don't understand," Rhodes said. "Mars? Ganymede?"

"Farther, Nick."

Rhodes was baffled, at first. Then, gradually, he moved Carpenter's words around in his mind and began to extract some sense from them.

"The starship project?" Rhodes asked, incredulously.

Carpenter nodded.

"For God's sake, why? Aren't the L-5s far enough away?"

"Not nearly. I want to go as far as it's possible to go, and then go even farther than that. I want to get the hell away. Purge myself of all that's happened. Start over."

"But how can you? The starship project—"

"You can do it for me. You can get me in there. It's a Kyocera thing, Nick. And as of Monday you're a very high-level Kyocera scientist."

"Well, yes," Rhodes said, though he was taken aback by the idea. "I suppose—I will have some influence there, yes. But that's not what I mean."

"What do you mean, Nick?"

Rhodes hesitated.

"You really want to be part of the crew?"

"Yes. Isn't it clear that that's what I'm saying?"

"Well, then," Rhodes said. "Consider, Paul. The eyes—"

"Yes. The eyes."

"You want to be turned into a thing like Farkas?" Rhodes asked.

"I want to get away from here," Carpenter replied. "That's the essential thing. All the rest is peripheral. Okay, Nick? You've got it now? Good. Good. I want you to help me. Pull strings for me, Nick. Pull strings like you've never pulled before."

There was passion in the content of what he was saying, Rhodes thought, but none in his tone. Carpenter seemed like a man talking in his sleep: his voice was flat, affectless, eerie in its tranquillity. Rhodes was frightened by it.

"I'll see what I can do," he heard himself saying.

"Yes. Do." The ghost smile again. "It's for the best, Nick."

"If you think it is."

"It is. I know so. Everything always works out for the best, Nick. Always."

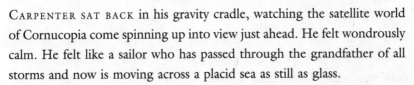

CARPENTER SAT BACK in his gravity cradle, watching the satellite world of Cornucopia come spinning up into view just ahead. He felt wondrously calm. He felt like a sailor who has passed through the grandfather of all storms and now is moving across a placid sea as still as glass.

It was all arranged. Nick Rhodes had done it all: notifying the powers that be at Kyocera that he had a nominee to fill the vacancy in the starship crew now that Farkas was dead, and making it be known that he expected his new company to take the nomination seriously. Then miraculously maneuvering the cashiered Samurai man Paul Carpenter into position for the opening despite all the difficulties that that involved, guiding him through the entry interview and everything that had followed. And now, sending him up to Cornucopia, where the members of the crew were being prepared for their strange voyage.

"Look," someone said across the aisle. "There's the habitat that blew up. The wreckage of it."

Carpenter didn't look. He knew that there was a gigantic mess scattered all over the L-5 zone, that pieces of Valparaiso Nuevo were orbiting every which way and that mop-up crews would be collecting bodies for months to come, as well as trying to get the biggest chunks of debris turned around and shoved into trajectories that would take them toward the sun before their orbits decayed and dumped them down on Earth. But he didn't want to see it.

He looked the other way, instead. Behind him and down, in his landlubber's way of seeing things: downward to the Earth.

How beautiful it was!

A perfect blue ball, gleaming brightly, mottled with bands of white. The wounds mankind had inflicted were invisible. There was no way to see, from this altitude, the squalor, the ruination, the foulness. The bleak new desert zones that had been fertile agricultural areas a few generations back, the steaming fungoid forests covering the sites of abandoned cities, the drowned shorelines, the clotted garbage in the seas, the colorful patches of poisoned air, the long dreary miles of blackened and withered wasteland that he had passed through during his feverish trip to Chicago and back. No, the view from up here beyond the stratosphere was altogether superb.

A lovely world. A jewel among planets.

Too bad we messed it up so badly, Carpenter thought. Fouled our own nest in a glorious centuries-long orgy of stupidity, transformed our wondrous and perhaps unique world into a thing of horror. Which now is continuing the transformation itself, with a power that is beyond our control, so that we have little choice now but to transform ourselves as well if we want to go on living there.

What else could you feel, looking down at that blue globe of seeming perfection and thinking of the Eden it once had been and what we had made out of it, but rage, pain, fury, anguish, despair? What else could you do but cry and howl and beat your breast?

And yet—yet—

Take the long view, Carpenter told himself.

The damage was only temporary. All would be well. Not soon, of course. There were those who said that the planet had been wounded; well, then, the planet would eventually heal. There were some who felt that it had merely been stained; if that was the case, the planet would need some time to cleanse itself. But it would. It would. Everything would be repaired. A hundred years, a thousand, a million, however long it took: but it would clean itself up. The planet had plenty of time. We don't, Carpenter thought, but it does. Life would go on. Not necessarily ours, but life of some sort. If we must be replaced on Earth by another kind of life, because we were such poor stewards of our domain, so be it. So be it. One kind fails, another kind eventually takes over. Life is persistent. Life is resilient.

"Passengers bound for Cornucopia, prepare for docking," a loudspeaker voice said.

The Kyocera research satellite's shimmering spokes came looming up. Carpenter glanced at it indifferently. He was still looking back at Earth, lost in what felt to him like some kind of mystic revelation.

A visionary glimpse came to him now of the new race that Nick Rhodes would create. Monstrous, yes, scales and goggle eyes and webbed feet and green blood. But what of it? To themselves they would look beautiful; and to themselves they would be. In the new and strangely transformed Earth of a hundred years to come they would be perfectly at home, comfortable in the different air, altogether at ease in the furnace heat.

He could see Rhodes and Isabelle down there, at peace with each other at last, a lovely couple man and wife, holding hands, growing old together. Children, even. Little monsters. A burgeoning tribe. Life goes on.

The shuttle was docking now. Three or four Cornucopia-bound passengers were getting off. Carpenter went up front when his name was called and passed through the hatch.

Cornucopia, what he could see of it, looked a lot like the Port of Oakland: no fancy carpeting or wall coverings, no landscape plants, no decoration of any kind, just miles of metal everywhere, a gridwork of bare structural members. Everything strictly functional. Utilitarian. That was all right. He hadn't come here for a vacation.

"Mr. Carpenter? This way, please."

A couple of Kyocera salarymen waiting for him. Leading him down bleak hallways, through stark corridors.

A door, finally, labeled in glowing luminous letters:

PROJECT LONG JUMP
AUTHORIZED PERSONNEL ONLY

This must be the place, Carpenter thought.

A long jump indeed. All the way to some other star.

Well, he was ready for it. He felt calm, determined, fully committed: he reached that point beyond all caring, now, and was entering this place the way, in some earlier century, he might have entered a monastery.

Of his own free choice he was leaving the world behind him, and good riddance to it.

That world had become an excessively difficult place. Breathing itself was a problem; so was dealing with ordinary sunshine, which was no longer ordinary; and so was the question of doing the right thing, Carpenter thought. He had tried to do the right thing most of his life, and had only fitfully succeeded at it. Not his fault: he had tried. Then he had involved himself in a wrong thing, with catastrophic results. And Enron? Jolanda? They too had tried to do the right thing, according to their own lights. And in the course of doing it they had sought to make their individual accommodations to life in this difficult era, and eventually they had made one accommodation too many, and they had died for it.

A tough proposition, life in this difficult era. Carpenter wanted a fresh start.

And he knew he would get it here. They would take him and change him and send him to the far reaches of the universe. Fine. Fine. He, too, could be persistent and resilient. You fail on one world, you pick yourself up and go on to another one. Rebirth, always rebirth: that was the way. As one of the Kyocera men put his hand to the door plate Carpenter allowed himself another vision. This one was brief, redemptive: a golden-green sun, a shimmering lemon sky, a forest of glistening fronds, a lake of pure pearly water. The new Eden, an untarnished paradise, waiting to be found and settled by the chastened, humbled race of man. Of whose vanguard into interstellar space he would be a member.

No, he told himself.

Allow yourself no dreams, and then there will be no disillusionments. Make the voyage; see what happens; hope for the best, but count on nothing. And perhaps this time we will do a better job of it.

Or perhaps not.

The door opened and a face peered out. For one astonished moment Carpenter thought that the ghost of Victor Farkas was standing there, waiting in the doorway to receive him.

But no—no, this wasn't Farkas. The same eerie, eyeless domed head, yes. But this was a youngish, wiry man, much shorter than Farkas had been, olive skin, narrow shoulders, wide ironic mouth, a general expression of cool youthful insolence. Not Farkas.

Carpenter said, "I'm the new starship crewman. Paul Carpenter."

The eyeless man nodded. "Come on in, and welcome to Project Long Jump," he said. He put out his hand. "My name is Juanito."